For Joyce.

As soon as a person becomes an Object of appetite for another . . . a person becomes a thing and can be treated and used as such by everyone.

- Immanuel Kant

These mammals are hell-bent on fashioning new gods
So they can go on being godless animals.

- Father John Misty

A DARK SPECULATIVE THRILLER

ASHES OF THE REPUBLIC

ASCENT OF DENNISON SERIES

JAMES CHESTERTON

Published by Broken Ledger Press

ISBN: 979-8-9951710-0-3 (eBook)
ISBN: 979-8-9951710-1-0 (Paperback)
ISBN: 979-8-9951710-2-7 (Hardcover)
ISBN: 979-8-9951710-3-4 (Audiobook)

We the People of the United States, in Order to form a more perfect Union, establish Justice, insure domestic Tranquility, provide for the common defense, promote the general Welfare, and secure the Blessings of Liberty to ourselves and our Posterity, do ordain and establish this Constitution for the United States of America.

Chapter 1

2026

This wasn't the first time Charity had journeyed through this landscape of red rocks, prickly pears, and rust-colored trailheads. She'd been here years ago—at the age of maybe four or five, back when her father had still been around—and although it'd been some time, she still remembered it clearly.

She recalled her mother looking at the iron-red buttes and mesas. "They make you feel so insignificant, don't they, kids?"

That had, of course, triggered her father.

"Don't listen to this zealot, you two," he'd said, glaring at his companion. "You should never feel insignificant. To anything. Or anyone."

Charity shook off the memory and navigated her rented Ford Mustang toward the sentinels in the distance, pulling into the driveway of a large construction site to better take them in: massive Courthouse Butte to the north dwarfing its better-known neighbor to the left, Bell Rock, each found somewhere in the background of every Jeep commercial for decades.

Charity noted the sign posted outside the gate:

Coming Soon! The Sedona Home of Taggert Ministries!
Your Direct Connection to the Lord Jesus Christ!

She got back into the Mustang and passed Bell Rock, its eponymous shape overwhelming the horizon as the curve of the road turned west to reveal the majesty of Cathedral Rock, its deep rust-colored spires piercing the cloudless blue sky. She drove into Sedona proper, stopping at an intersection that allowed art-market pedestrians to cross, then watched as a Hispanic mother held her lively daughter's hand during the crossing, the girl nearly pulling her exhausted parent to the other side. While Charity waited, she recalled the event that brought her here.

The invitation from her boss, Iwanna Dennison, had come as a surprise, and Charity still worried that it was an error, inadvertently blurted out at a time of great stress during the awkward funeral rituals of the wealthy. However, the more she thought about it as she slowly passed through West Sedona, the less odd it became. Yes, Iwanna Dennison was one of the most powerful women in the world, as much for her own accomplishments as for those of her family. But they had spent the last two years working closely together on a high-profile project that only they knew fully about. There was, she supposed, a certain intimacy about that. In doing so, they had gotten close, sharing meals and even an occasional drink after a long shift in the labs. With limited references to relationships outside the office, Charity surmised maybe they were even friends.

Despite being harsh with many in her employ, Iwanna had never treated her in that manner, though that probably had to do with Charity's background. She and Iwanna had more than a few things in common, and that had garnered Iwanna's respect. Not only did Charity hold a bachelor's in computer science from the University of Oxford—which she'd acquired at the age of nineteen—but she'd gone on, two years later, to get a master's in robotics from Johns Hopkins. She'd gotten the job as project lead from her first day on the job with Iwanna, and now she was on the cusp of releasing her—*their*—first product.

No, she thought, *this makes sense, her reaching out to me. We deserve this friendship.*

The invitation had come two weeks prior at the funeral of Iwanna's fiancé. While talking quietly among a small cadre of fellow employees who had been permitted to attend the ceremony, Charity watched as Iwanna broke apart from her own scrum and began walking toward her in a black Oscar de la Renta that, she noted, represented a departure from her typical form-highlighting dresses. Black pearl earrings accented her pale-white skin and platinum-blonde hair. Smart. Stern. Expressionless.

Iwanna took Charity by the elbow and gently extracted her from the group, then whispered, "I have a home in the desert. I'd like you to join me there."

"Sure, of course," Charity replied, knowing any hesitation would be met with scrutiny. "I'm so sorry about what's happened," she added, and watched as a flash of pain passed over Iwanna's face at the mention of the man in the closed casket. That pain was quickly replaced with her preferred stoicism.

"Thank you," Iwanna replied, expression as stiff as her words. "I feel like I'm at a crossroads, Charity. And that you're one of the few people who could possibly understand."

"Because of the similarities in our families?"

"That is unfair to our families. Because of our *fathers*." She released a flat smile, turned her head down, and started to return to her fallen captain. "I look forward to seeing you. My office will make the travel arrangements."

The instructions and arrangements for travel had been precise, and Iwanna's assistant made clear the importance of punctuality in Charity's drive north from Phoenix. This wasn't something to be taken trivially.

With Uptown Sedona in her rearview mirror, Charity continued following the directions provided by Iwanna's assistant. This was not a house found on Google Maps. She reached the last paved road and looked for the outline of a driveway she was assured would be evident and, when she made out the worn red dirt, turned the car into it. She realized she was now on the opposite side of Cathedral Rock, with Bell and Courthouse no longer in sight, obfuscated.

She understood why spaces like this brought people to spirituality; Sedona was well known as a melting pot of the full spectrum of mysticism. Her father had encouraged and financed her visits to spectacular sites all around the world. The pyramids and Taj Mahal lived up to their reputations, but it was places like the Grand Canyon and Victoria Falls that truly reached her soul. She added Sedona to that list.

Charity was not interested in the creations of man, knowing full well the costs associated with such endeavors. Her mother's reaction to standing before the red rock formations of Sedona—overwhelmed by a sense of awe and insignificance—was a common, if not ubiquitous response to such natural beauty. Charity, however, felt the same God that had created those beautiful, powerful formations had also created her. She looked at them as kin.

In less than a half mile, she was at the entrance to a narrow valley, bounded on both sides by the same glowing red rocks, with only a STOP sign as evidence of modernity. A pitch-black crow, twice as large as any she had seen before, sat on a tree branch just ahead, contrasted by the endless blue Arizona sky behind it. She waited for what she knew was next: a gentle buzz ahead of her. As if simply appearing, the source of the sound hovered outside her closed window. At first glance, it was simply a carpenter bee, larger in size than a honeybee and entirely black due to lacking the yellow fur. Charity was unsurprised and observed her new friend with great interest as it hovered in perfect stillness with grace, far too exact for an insect. This was enabled by a last-minute design change she'd ordered to make the forewing replicate that of a hummingbird, which flaps up, down, and sideways, enabling the precision it now exhibited.

"Hello, Ms. Malodor," the mechanical bee said in as sweet a tone as if it were shilling for a honey-based breakfast cereal. "Welcome to Sedona Stronghold. Please proceed for eight-tenths of a mile and park in the area to your right. Have a great day."

"Thank you," she said with the full knowledge that had she not obeyed, a swarm of those same drones would have surrounded her car and blinded her line of sight until armed guards could be dispatched.

She parked and exited the car, looking at the home. It was embedded in a wide, gently sloping hill, like a baseball pitcher's mound, with a single pathway carved in the front that was wide enough for no more than two people, leading to the hub in the middle like the spoke of a wheel. As she approached the entrance, something moved in her periphery to the left. Instinctually, she froze. Turning her head slowly, she observed a snake, about three feet in length, twenty feet away. It too decided to halt.

Is this one of ours? she asked herself. She looked closer and noted there was no rattle on the tail, and the black body with thick white stripes did not resemble the diamondbacks she had seen in photos.

"First time up close with one?" a voice asked from the entrance to the mound.

Without taking her eyes off the snake, Charity said, "Hi, Iwanna—and yes, I haven't come across one of these before. I'm guessing that's not a rattlesnake."

"Don't worry, you're completely safe. That is a friend. A king snake. They're not venomous, and they eat the rattlesnakes."

Charity looked skeptically at her hostess for the first time. "That little thing? Wouldn't the rattler just bite him and be done?"

Iwanna, as if to demonstrate her confidence, walked directly to the king snake, and when she came within five feet, it decided to pick up its head. She stared down while the serpent remained still.

"They're immune to the venom, so they first constrict it until it's exhausted, then eat it whole, starting at the head. No noise." She stepped forward. "No warning." Another step forward. "Silent consumption."

The king snake reconsidered its path and turned to the right, heading toward the brush on the perimeter.

Relieved, Charity continued toward her hostess and put out her hand, which was at first joined and then used to reel her in for a light embrace.

"I'm glad you came, Charity," Iwanna said, some hesitation in her voice. "I . . ."

Charity had never seen her boss hesitate before.

"Come," Iwanna settled on saying. "Let's go inside, where there are fewer snakes."

<hr>

"I enjoyed seeing a member of the hive in action," Charity said as the door closed behind her. "This first version performed as expected." She looked around and took in the ultramodern decor of Iwanna's home: white as an Alpine peak in every direction, the rust color coming in from the vast picture windows contrasting beautifully.

"You should be very proud of your creation. What inspired you to their design?"

Charity considered the question. "I've always loved bees. My grandfather had a couple of hives at his farm in New Hampshire, and he would suit me up to get a closer look. To me, no other creature on Earth raises such a wide range of emotions. Admiration of their brilliant abilities. Fear of their sting. Appreciation of their part in the greater natural order."

"Envy of their compliance to the needs of the hive." As the words came out of Iwanna's mouth, she almost imperceptibly shook her head, as if regretting her own statement.

"They are one of God's most inspirational creatures," Charity said, not missing the subtle flare of Iwanna's eyes at the mentioning of God. "To develop a drone capable of invoking those characteristics was an honor for me. I still remember your directive the first day I arrived at the Colorado lab: 'Make me something so breathtaking that no one will ever try twice to defeat it.' What can be more fearsome than thousands of these units working as one?"

Iwanna nodded gently while walking toward the vast great room, camouflaged in her ankle-length white dress. The room was entirely functional, the function being to provide a place to sit and stare at the collection of rust spires just outside the windows. Bare walls and floors. A couch with matching chairs directed toward the twenty-foot-high glass windows filled with beauty.

As she followed, Charity noted the simple but obvious wealth of the space. She noted a series of museum glass cases to her right against the wall.

"I know I have said it before, but I will always be in your debt for providing me the opportunity to do this work," she said.

"Well, please, you are underselling yourself. I was lucky your father reached out to me and convinced me you could be assigned to any project and deliver it. I must admit I was skeptical that a twenty-year-old could be dropped into that situation, managing a team of engineers three times her age, but he was right. To have that working prototype two years later is incredible. You should be proud. How was your drive from Phoenix?"

"Perfect. Brought back some old memories. My father brought us out here when I was young."

Iwanna sat on a couch perfectly positioned between the picture window that looked straight out to the red rocks, then gestured to the chair to her right, indicating that Charity should take a seat as well. "Interesting. I can't picture him in a place like this. He strikes me as much more of a city boy. Or, if I'm being honest . . ." She managed a grin. "Extraterrestrial."

As she sat, Charity laughed. "That would certainly be more accurate." Then she looked at Iwanna, who had redirected her attention to her lap. "I am happy you invited me here, Iwanna. With everything going on . . . everything that has happened in the last three weeks . . . I just didn't expect you to reach out to me."

Iwanna either failed, or didn't care to hide, her preoccupation with something. She kept her head down, as if in prayer, and took a moment to respond. "It was probably a mistake—asking you to come here—but you are right. It has been a very challenging few weeks." She redirected her blank gaze out to the rocks. "Growing up as you did, were you able to find people that you could trust? That weren't just your friend because of who your father was?"

Charity matched Iwanna's objective, matter-of-fact tone. "I had my mom the whole time, and we have . . . had . . . a good relationship." She paused. "A great relationship, actually, and she kept our circumstances quiet when we moved to Texas. We had access to anything we wanted but didn't flaunt it. Word got out about who my father was when I was in grade school, and yes, everything changed. The girls I was friends with either stopped speaking to me altogether or started buttering me up to get in my good graces. I was too young to understand why. I get it now, but back then, I felt very betrayed by it all. So, long answer to your simple question: No, I didn't have anybody I could trust. I stuck with my mom and my brother because everyone else had an ulterior motive."

In a sad whisper, Iwanna said, "Yes, that was my experience as well, but without my mother." She seemed to decide to wade further into self-revelation, despite clearly struggling to trust Charity, who was growing more and more curious as to why she was really there. "He was on to the next one pretty quickly after I was born."

"I was lucky in that respect," Charity conceded. "I'm sure your father was very busy, but he obviously loves you very much." Realizing she could have tripped on a land mine, she added, "At least, he seems to. Always glowing when he talks about you."

"Yes, I am his most prized possession." She looked up. "Did you ever feel like that? You're a beautiful young girl. Successful athlete, brilliant student. Do you think if you were less than all that, his opinion would change about you?"

Charity gave the question considerate thought. "I think there's evidence for that. He did love to brag about me, especially before his business took off, when he had time to consider me and the rest of us. But we were never in the spotlight like you are, so the world didn't really know us." She attempted to lighten the mood. "It's hard to say what motivates fathers like ours. They are a species unto themselves. I don't think it's a question of if they love us; I think they just don't know how to express love at all, regardless of if they feel it or not."

Iwanna seemed to accept her answer—and, for the first time, she looked Charity directly in the eyes as she said, "That's thoughtful, and probably correct. There are times I look at him and he's like a little boy with me. *Clueless.*" She nodded. "I'm guessing your father doesn't exert much influence on you these days, then?"

"He does with my brothers and sisters, but he seems to hold fire when it comes to me. I think he knows I see through him and that if he confronts me, I'll make that evident."

"Really?" Iwanna said, surprised. "Challenge him?" She seemed to contemplate this for a moment and then said, mostly to herself, "That is not what I expected." After some consideration, she continued, her voice cracking almost imperceptibly when she asked, "So you've been free the whole time? Never been given your path?"

"Yes," Charity said without hesitation. "My path has always been my decision."

Iwanna's response was barely a whisper. "I can't imagine," she said, sighing. "I'm afraid of what I will become when I make the wrong choice."

"Really?" Charity interjected, propelled by curiosity, and she could tell Iwanna realized in that moment how vulnerable she'd just been—that she was likely speaking out loud rather than consciously feeding their conversation.

Iwanna gave her a pointed look. "I've liked you since day one, Charity," she said with the tone of a seasoned diplomat. "And not just because we share similar upbringings. You have an . . . earnestness about you. A trustworthiness."

"I've had nothing but a positive experience with you as well, Iwanna," Charity said, feeling like she was stepping onto a branch of unknown fortitude.

Iwanna laughed. "Don't start bullshitting me now!" she said. "You've been nothing but fearful of me, just like everyone else."

Charity joined her in the laugh. "Both things can be true," she said. "It was . . . *is* fear . . . but it comes from a respect for you as a person. Not from your title or your family. You demand quality. Precision. So do I. When people have not demonstrated that, you've rightfully made your disappointment known. Albeit, sometimes with a great deal of . . . vigor."

She looked up again to make sure she hadn't overstepped. Iwanna's expression of actual warmth told her she had not.

There was a pause during which Iwanna looked Charity over, as if in final assessment of an expensive item before deciding to purchase it. Then she said, "I invited you here because I have a sensitive matter that cannot be known to anyone outside of this house."

Charity was shocked to see the expression on Iwanna's face. It was hope. She immediately responded with genuine affection, "Whatever you need, Iwanna."

Iwanna exhaled, then rose and walked in front of Charity, who had done the same, and gently embraced her. After a few moments, she whispered, "I'm pregnant."

Charity's pure expression of joy had her tighten her embrace and then bring them face-to-face. "Oh, Iwanna, that is such wonderful news!" she said, thinking at once of Iwanna's recently deceased fiancé, who was surely the father. This child was a gift from God. However, when Charity pulled back to look her in the face, she was met with an expression of dread.

Iwanna pulled back, slowly and sadly. "I can't keep it," she said, watching Charity go silent with contemplation.

"Why?"

Iwanna turned and walked toward the picture window, and Charity thought she caught moisture in her eye. "There are many reasons—and frankly, I'm not sure which one is the one that matters. My father and his position. My responsibilities as CEO."

Charity heard an unmistakable choke.

"My fear, Charity. My fear of so many things. Childbirth, parenting a child. *Alone.*" Iwanna's head fell. "Losing him has shattered me. I don't know what to do with the pieces." She turned in the ultimate gesture of vulnerability, exposing her tears to her guest. "How can anyone from this family raise a child properly? With love? We only know lust—for power, for wealth." She turned back to the window, staring out at the Sedona landscape, the start of the sunset's glow on the rocks appearing. "My only love is gone now, and if I go forward with this pregnancy, I will be reminded of that every day for the rest of my life, and I fear I'll never be able to move on."

Charity stood in frozen silence as Iwanna continued.

"But the more honest reason, Charity, is that my imagined freedom at this moment is just that—*imagined*. I must continue my role in all this as expected. As it was programmed into me. And the child would just be a distraction from my mission." She turned her back to Cathedral Rock and met Charity's eyes, seeking absolution.

"But you don't have that choice," Charity said flatly and immediately, with the conviction of the zealots her father had always warned her about.

Iwanna flinched, visibly taken aback by the rebuke. She stayed frozen in place, and Charity watched her expression slowly shift from fear, pain, and sadness and devolve rapidly into anger.

"Excuse me?" she snapped.

"Iwanna," Charity said, backpedaling in tone only, "you have options beyond that. Give the child up for adoption. You can cover that. But surely you have enough respect for God and the Constitution to avoid the path of murder. This is an opportunity, a gift, to keep your fiancé alive!"

Iwanna raised her head and, with resignation, said, "I didn't realize you were that religious. I know your father isn't, and you never mentioned it at work. Where did it come from?"

"My mom. Her family. It was the reason my father gave for leaving her. He felt being with someone in a cult was beneath him. But it helped me to realize my place in the world."

Iwanna darted a look at her guest and snipped, "Oh really? You had an *epiphany*, did you? And what was that?"

Charity hesitated at the change in tone but knew she had no choice but to finish the thought. "Well, just that I had a gift that came from the Lord, and if my father chose to use his only to enrich himself, I had to use it to benefit my family." She thought on it a second more and decided to add, "And my country."

Now Iwanna exhaled loudly and laughed sardonically. "Wow. Someone this intelligent and they got to you as well: thinking you're special in the eyes of God. You gave up your actual father and replaced him with an imaginary one that lives in the sky! Fascinating. You sound like a good soldier, Charity," she said tersely.

Each word hit Charity with the force of a hammer striking an anvil. No one had ever challenged her faith before, and it was something she had never had time to question, being fast-tracked in school to keep pace with her prodigious capabilities and ultimately landing her first job at Dennison Robotics in their nascent robotics division. She was simply using the materials provided to her by God to deliver products and capabilities the Earth had never seen before. But for the challenge to come from *this* person, of all people—the daughter of the sitting president of the United States and de facto leader of the American Christian right—doubled the impact. To have all of this delivered with the very same gentle ferocity her father had employed in his verbal strikes against her mother felt even more disorienting. She was breathless and didn't know what to address first.

"My Lord, of course, how much can you be expected to take? Your fiancé killed in the Mexican War, and now this? Of course you are upset. This type of thing could cloud anyone's judgment, and it's obviously done that to you," Charity reasoned. "Please, take some time to think about it and allow the Holy Spirit to reenter your soul!"

Iwanna prowled toward Charity—and in her posture alone, she made it clear that her guest's campaign was officially over. She stopped only once they were nose to nose. In a barely audible voice, she growled, "I'm having the abortion, you condescending church mouse. Here. *Today.*" She laughed as she took in the horror on her employee's face, as if feeding off it, letting it breathe into her simmering embers. Embracing her decision, she added, "Oh come on, Charity! What did you think—I would be one of those trashy single moms?"

"Single moms? Like *mine*, you mean?" Charity barked back. "What about the Bible? What about the Constitution? Your father is the man who brought this nation back to them!" Her anger was transforming into sorrow, then confusion.

Hissing, Iwanna said, "It's still all black and white to you, isn't it, little girl? I allow you into my home, into my . . ." She trailed off, face pale with rage. "And you *dare* to castigate me with your moral convictions!" She took Charity's hand and began to lead her back to the front door. "You had your head in those books too early and too long," she said as the door opened automatically. "Perhaps you should focus that intelligence on the world you've been missing. Those laws don't apply to *us*. They are just a means of controlling the hive! You *do* see that, don't you?"

Like a revelation in an Escher painting, it appeared to Charity instantly, and permanently. Trying to recover, she said, "You can't do this to people—*lie* to people like this, manipulate them like this! The rules *have* to apply to everyone, especially you." Seeing the smirk on Iwanna's face, she escalated her retort. "You're a fucking hypocrite! People need to know about this!"

Iwanna let go of Charity's hand and stepped in front of her. "You've seen what happens to people who threaten my family, haven't you? Your estranged daddy can't help you here."

Every landslide began with a single stone kicked out of place, and Charity felt the dangerous shift of it deep in her bones. Everything she'd come to believe was shivering under the threat of a full-blown collapse.

"You are no longer my employee," Iwanna declared, "and I promise that once I'm through with you, only your father will be willing to hire you again."

She walked toward one of the display cases at the entrance and lifted the glass, removing a colonial-era revolver and aiming it at Charity's head.

"You've misjudged me once today. Now you need to make another assessment: Would I keep this slaveholder's gun loaded in the display? Black and white enough for you?"

Charity felt her legs quake in anticipation of the shot.

Iwanna continued, speaking in a whisper, "If I learn you've been talking out of line, you'll have your answer. Wherever you are." As Charity turned in tears toward the house's exit, Iwanna referred to her head of security and barked, "Jonathan, get her out of here!"

Jonathan entered and positioned himself behind Charity, pinning her arm behind her back forcefully, making it clear she should not resist. He then began leading her out through the door—which Charity felt was overkill, seeing as she was willingly leaving anyway.

Iwanna stood beside the doorway and said, "And by the way, we're making your bees lethal to make sure the vermin who killed my fiancé don't ever cross that border again. What would your *God* have to say about that?"

Charity, still escorted roughly by Jonathan, was forced to quicken her pace. As they crossed a flower bed on their way to her Mustang, he shoved her face first into the wet soil. She turned to see his pistol aimed at her head, at which point she burst into hysterics.

"I'd wait a second if I were you," she heard Jonathan say. "Hold still."

And then she heard the rattle and looked up to see the diamondback's head emanating from its coiled body, poised to strike.

Resigned that she wouldn't leave this place, that Iwanna or the snake would end her, she just stared at it. They held each other's gaze in stillness, both unsure of their situation and what to do next.

Then she thought about her mother and what she had had to endure to get her to this point, how her father treated her, the shame he used to destroy her, and Charity decided she wasn't going to give up so easily.

She gently retreated from the snake, which maintained its frozen stare and slowed the expression of fear in its tail. As she brought herself to her knees, Jonathan said, "That was impressive. Exactly the way to deal with it. Now get in the car and do it all over again."

When she stood up, some dirt and a flower fell from her hair to the ground, and she saw it was a lily. She picked it up and held it in her hand as she walked around the rattler and got into the Mustang. When she looked back, she watched it begin its journey toward the main entrance. The same place she'd encountered the king snake.

◆••————————••◆

After she watched Charity drive off, Iwanna returned to the great room and sat before Cathedral Rock. She prayed, asking it to help her destroy the sorrow.

And it obliged.

Chapter 2

Driving too fast, Charity returned to town and saw a sign for the airport and turned right. A half mile up the road, there was a parking area occupied by only one car. Perfect. She drove into a space, got out, and blindly followed the signs to something called a vortex, assuming it was one of the many hiking trails in the area.

It was late in the day. The sun's oppressive presence in the sky had retreated to a warm and more docile position just beneath the horizon. Charity found herself alone in the mystical presence of one of Sedona's vortexes, peering out over the open space of flat red rocks, waiting for their energy to guide her. She inhaled a deep breath of air.

Several minutes later, she found a comfortable sitting place and was able to bring herself to a semblance of calm. She began ruminating on everything Iwanna had said and how that inevitably capsized everything Charity had come to believe in.

All the people she'd met in her life—those associated with both power and religion, the preachers and politicians—were lying. It was the only explanation, and her source was one of the most powerful women in the world. One who had to know the truth.

Charity had accepted the offerings from her father—the education, the journeys, the connections—because she'd believed he actually cared about her. She never forgave him for the abandonment of her mother, so the relationship remained distant and, particularly after he helped her get her first job with Iwanna, professional.

She also knew her father had to be complicit in this. It was just not possible he could not be aware of this grand deception, and she knew full well he would maximize this awareness to his greatest profit. There was little evidence of any political support of the Dennison administration from him over the last several years, but there were several key military contracts with his companies. She knew where there was a quid, there had to be the undisclosed quo.

But now she was in real trouble, and knowing full well Iwanna didn't make idle threats, her father was the only solution to her situation. She took out her iPhone and called him.

"Well, hello, dear. To what do I owe the honor?"

Charity tried and failed to hide her condition in her first syllable. "I'm in a bit of trouble with Iwanna."

"How could that happen? You were doing so well there. I've heard nothing but good things."

As she rewound the events in her mind, her voice began to shake. "She wanted to get closer to me, reveal herself to me, and I didn't accept what I was shown. I think . . . I *know* she's going to hurt me."

"Oh, I'm sure it's not all that bad," he said mechanically and condescendingly—his default setting.

Giving up, she just let her emotions go. "You must know they are hypocrites, using lies to get what they want from people. All of them!" His gentle, knowing laugh enraged her further. "Don't you fucking condescend to me!"

"Careful with the language. That will be three Hail Marys, daughter."

She was close to going over the edge but managed to step outside herself for a moment and calm down. "You never believed, so why did you let my mother bring me in? The church? Indoctrinate me?"

"Because when I left, I knew she needed that support. To take that from her would have put you at risk. When you ask people to do very hard things, like raise a prodigy alone, you need to give them some form of hope that makes it all worth it."

Charity thought over these new variables and began forming new hypotheses that her brain turned into new conclusions. "You didn't have to do that to her," she said.

"I knew I'd never win custody, and she made it clear she didn't want me around. But really, Charity, your lives weren't all that bad." He waited a moment before asking, "What happened today?"

"Iwanna invited me to visit her at her Sedona house. She's clearly dealing with something with her father and wants to break away from him but doesn't know how."

Her father laughed. "Well, her instinct to go to you was spot-on there!"

Charity scoffed. "She's killing her unborn child."

Her father was quiet, digesting that for a moment. "Deep down inside, you know that unborn child is dodging a bigger bullet."

"I didn't react well when she confided this in me."

"How so?"

"I threatened to reveal her," she said, her sentence punctuated by his loud huff on the other end of the call. "She said she would ruin my life, and if I did say anything, she'd kill me."

"Hmm," her father said. "That is a problem. She'd do it too—kill you, that is—without hesitation."

Charity had already come to the only solution available to her. "I need to ask you for one more thing, and then I will be out of your life forever."

"So dramatic. This is unlike you."

"I will never forgive you for what you did to my mother—but helping me now, in the absence of being a part of my life, is the least you can do. I know you have access to everything I need to disappear and come back as someone else. Face, fingerprint, and iris alteration. New government documents. I have nothing to tie me to this life. Before, it was education, and up until today, it was this job. I'll figure the rest out, and I've got the money I made for the last two years. Make this happen and I can start all over, and she can't threaten me."

He thought for a moment. "Under one condition," he began, and she fought the urge to scream. "You make contact with me once a year on your birthday to let me know how you are. That's all I ask—a ten-minute conversation. Agree to that, and I'll make the arrangements."

Charity reviewed the events of her day, the decision she was about to make, and she realized it was all too easy. There was nothing appealing enough in her current life to make her fight to keep it.

"That's fair. Okay."

Her father sighed with resignation. "Last thing, daughter: What do you want your new name to be?"

Chapter 3

May 3, 2046

Fifty thousand feet above the Washington Park neighborhood of Denver, a Delta Boeing 939 propelled at a speed of Mach 1.13 toward its San Francisco destination.

Thirty-eight thousand feet lower, storm clouds began to gather and build strength. They would release their payload of hail upon Aurora, Colorado, which was 7.57 miles east of where Lily lived. In seventeen minutes and twenty-five seconds, that hail would fall, eventually resulting in property damage amounting to $43.76 million US.

Seeing the storm clouds, Lily shortened her run and came straight home, just in time to avoid being pelted by the initial onslaught picking up steam on its journey to her neighbors. As the door closed behind her, her phone rang, and she saw it was once again her father, and once again, she denied the call. *Not my birthday,* she thought.

The call prompted her to look at her watch and note the time: 6:43 a.m. She'd make some coffee and try to find a job again, hoping that it would signal to him, wherever he was, that it had been twenty years and she could make it on her own. She didn't need his help.

At the same time, Jeff Maslow slept unsoundly in his studio apartment in nearby Westwood. A framed picture of Jesus Christ hung on the wall opposite Jeff's bed, four feet, two inches above his sleeping head.

And at 6:59 a.m., he rolled over on his mattress, knocking an empty bottle of Coors Premium IPA to the floor, fortunately only two inches below. It rolled to the corner of the room, stopping at the base of his half-packed suitcase.

On the floor above him, Cheryl Daniels, aged forty-eight years and four months, was completing her session with the latest release of the SKYN line of personal AI massage devices, which learned the most pleasurable ways to bring the user to a full and sustained release, measuring the input from her Apple Watch, home sensors, and X feed. Based on her current heart rate, the humidity, and two new likes, it estimated Cheryl's climax would occur in thirteen minutes thirty-seven seconds.

Startled by the bottle, he immediately looked at his watch, and his naked thirty-nine-year-old chiseled, athletic frame popped up, facing Jesus. He thought he heard something drop onto the floor above him as he tripped to the kitchen table.

He ran the Colorado WorkingPlace app on his tablet and placed his finger on the scanner, confirming his presence via the implanted microscopic chip that held his unique cryptographically secured identity. In an instant, the system took his personal history, education, work experience, skills, salary requirements, and personality profile and matched them against the thousands of contract jobs available. If it required in-person presence, the system also noted Jeff's location and ensured he was within a sixty-minute commute.

Despite his Loyola University undergrad with honors, the bidding closed, and the system indicated no opportunities. Jeff assumed it was because it noted his sign-in of 07:03:12, an obvious red flag indicating someone who did not take his job search seriously, as job auctions throughout the state started promptly at 7:00 a.m.

And then a window popped up.

MIGHT WE SUGGEST THESE GREAT JOBS YOU
APPEAR QUALIFIED FOR:

Slaughter technician, Globeville
Pew polish and wax technician, Colorado Springs

He rejected the proposed jobs and received a text from the Colorado unemployment office ten seconds later noting his failure to obtain work and the subsequent application of unemployment benefits to start at 8:00 a.m. The text also provided his remaining annual balance: twenty-five hours, thirty-four minutes, and forty-five seconds, counting down for good measure.

It was May, he knew. Something like the third. Or fifth. That wasn't a lot left. He brought up his bank account balance, which appeared as a hologram emanating from his watch, and performed a back-of-the-napkin estimate that told him he had about two more weeks before he would be out of funds. It was either send out an SOS to his sister for cash or just give up and move back east. His father in Connecticut would have loved the opportunity to help him, but after learning about the source of *his* wealth sixteen years ago, Jeff had disconnected from him entirely, wanting no part of it. He was going to overcome the career-limiting decision to get a degree in English—most school districts were outsourcing the jobs to lower-cost teachers from countries like Ireland and Scotland, which enabled a cost-effective model at market rates and terms without unions getting in the way. The state-mandated core curriculum of American Math, American Science, American History, American Christianity, and football received utilized full-time, in-person American teachers. The non-core classes of language and the arts went to the visa holders. After all, did a teacher need to be an American to talk about Shakespeare's sonnets or other such things that didn't matter in the real world?

The humor of the situation was lost on him—and had been since about five years ago, when he was removed from an adjunct job at a community college in Boulder, which had sustained him for his first years in Colorado. The money wasn't great, but it was regular and appropriate to his background and expertise. This made it an outlier, providing a sense of normalcy he could not replicate. As much as Boulder tried to hang in there, the state-controlled educational system was left with very few options when overtaken by waves of elections that went only one way.

Jeff was unceremoniously dismissed when a copy of Walt Whitman's *Leaves of Grass* was confiscated during a routine body-and-bag scan while he was entering the campus. The best his dean could do to help was keep it off his public record, stating the book was part of research into rampant liberalism in the mid 1800s, not curriculum. Sioban O'Reardon from Ireland was hired to teach Contemporary American Literature.

He texted the owners upstairs who were riding the wave of income generated from their trust accounts, benefitting from the massive government-driven gentrification of the historically working-class neighborhood that allowed them to purchase multiple lots of property at mandated discounts. This was all part of the state ROC (Reclaim Our Cities) project in the early 2030s. He told them he could be available for household work today if they would have him and that he could do twenty hours this week. This would enable him to be classified as a part-time employee, minimizing the damage to his unemployment benefits. If he could get just enough hours from this and an extended contract sometime before the end of the year, he might accumulate enough credits to qualify for his voter certificate—which was the result of an amendment to the Constitution that took place sixteen years ago, requiring sustained and documented employment to vote. It was part of the same congressional session that eliminated term limits for the president.

He decided a nap was in order, and as he lifted out of the chair, he looked at the base of the fence outside through the tattered shade, then dropped onto the mattress he had lying on the floor. He realized he would soon turn forty and would likely still be living in this basement after aimlessly hopping around for years in the state. About a month ago, he decided it was time to tuck his tail between his legs and get out. Two weeks later, he'd met Lily, and that plan had been put on hold. For now.

At 9:13:31 a.m., he jolted up from a dream (or was it a nightmare?) that featured him on the line at a hog farm, but he couldn't recall in what capacity. A bell had woken him before he could find out.

His response had arrived from upstairs, assigning six hours for today and the promise of more to come "with hard work." Six seconds later, the unemployment office told him they had stopped his benefits for the rest of the day and clawed back the hour and fourteen minutes' worth he had received that morning. For the second time, he rolled out of bed, drank the puddle of beer left in the bottle, and put on shorts and a T-shirt to face the shrub-related challenges of his day.

◆•∙————————∙•◆

Back in Washington Park, Lily's job search too came up empty. Colorado's addiction to robo-therapy continued, and the demand from the wealthy for a human psychologist remained flat. Their lives were perfect—and to seek help implied otherwise.

MIGHT WE SUGGEST THESE GREAT JOBS YOU
APPEAR QUALIFIED FOR:

Roller-skating waitress, Vicksburg
Stewardess, Colorado Springs

She did not receive a text from the unemployment office: She never applied. She went back to the site. *Stewardess.* No one even tried to mask the misogyny and homophobia anymore. They could just leave it all in plain sight in an ad like this one, saying *No men need apply*. She read the job description for a corporate flight attendant in the Springs, a fifteen-minute commute by Amazon Air. She needed to break the monotony that had started when she'd left her last job waiting tables four months ago. If she couldn't get a job as a therapist, maybe it was time to expand her horizons. She clicked Apply.

Chapter 4

May 6

Reverend Brady Taggert knew he had them in his grasp. They were always attentive and respectful, but that was only because of the cross hanging behind him. In times like these, with the lights down but for the spotlight on his face, with his last words still bouncing off the back of the former hockey arena that he now called a church, it was all about *him*.

The silence allowed him to insert his wisdom directly into their souls, getting past their conscious and unconscious defenses. This was why he loved this work so much, did all he could to expand his audience—his *flock*. Every consciousness in the auditorium was hanging on every word that came out of his mouth.

But of course, every now and then, it was a good move to mention the guy who died on that cross behind him.

"'Every kingdom divided against itself will be ruined, and every city or household divided against itself will not stand,'" Taggert said into the microphone. He paused for effect. "You think I'm quoting that great Republican Abraham Lincoln right now, but I'm not. Those are the words of our Lord in the Gospel of Matthew."

Meanwhile, at the border, a family slowly and carefully crossed the river headed north, rowing their small boat as quietly as possible toward the faint light ahead. As soon as they reached the shore at latitude North 44 degrees, 32'60", longitude West 75 degrees, 42'0", they scrambled out, pulled the boat up behind them, and collapsed from their labor.

The father pulled his two young children, aged six and nine years, into his lap. He hugged them, knowing the soil beneath them would bring the prosperity he could not find in his homeland on the distant banks behind them. He cried, and his wife joined the embrace and the weeping because they knew things would be better now.

◆•·——————··◆

The congregation sat in silence, which Taggert attributed to their awe of his delivery. In fact, they were largely confused. And many hungover.

Taggert continued. "In Matthew chapter thirteen, Jesus said . . ." He read from the Good Book:

> *"'The kingdom of heaven is like a man who sowed good seed in his field. But while everyone was sleeping, his enemy came and sowed weeds among the wheat and went away. The servants asked him, "Do you want us to go and pull them up?" "No," he answered, "Let both grow together until the harvest. At that time, I will tell the harvesters to first collect the weeds and tie them in bundles to be burned.'"*

"There are those in this country who thought, some time ago, that there would be civil war, and yet there was not. For those of you who were here at that time, we know it was a precarious period in our country's history. People were literally dying in the streets. They blamed guns, but we knew better. They blamed abortion laws, but we knew better. They blamed pronouns. Their skin color. Religion. Jesus Christ. But *we knew better*."

A steady murmur of agreement filled the silence like cream through coffee, dropping and spreading.

"This mighty nation was at the precipice of collapse, and we turned it around. We saved those poor souls who said they didn't know their gender. How horrible it must have been for them, to be born with such sickness. There is no ambiguity any longer, documented in our Constitution. Now we provide them therapies and medicines to cure them of their delusion. There was once a pope, a leader of millions, who claimed to be Christ on Earth, enforcing medieval beliefs and superstitions about how God wanted people to behave, devised by supposedly chaste men. But yet again, I say, *we knew better*."

The audience felt charged, and that charge was strengthening.

The reverend looked out over his flock, eyes gleaming. "But it hasn't been all victory for our cause," he continued. "We still have much to fight for. Medicine has provided us with a world free of sexual disease and long-term birth control, which many have used as permission for promiscuity, having sex in alleyways at a moment's notice with the wink of an eye from across a bar, like feral cats."

◆••————————••◆

Back at the border, the family sat up after several minutes of peace. As the father stood, he was struck by a needle of pain in his neck, after which he thought he heard a faint, persistent buzzing.

"Careful, guys. We may have hit a bee's nest somewhere. I just got stung."

"Ow!" the son said. "Me too."

They all then heard the cries of the daughter.

"It's night," the wife said. "Bees don't fly at night. How can—ow!"

◆••————————••◆

"Thanks to the discovery on the Argyre Plain on the planet Mars of the perfectly formed Protestant cross, humanity no longer has any doubt of the existence of God in the universe. They didn't find a Catholic cross, now did they?"

The crowd mumbled in agreement.

"Since then, our Fourth Great Awakening has brought us a world community that has unified Christians under a single banner, allowing our government to finally settle these long-standing divisions in our country. Our *Christian* country."

The "amens" were no longer a murmur, with many closing their eyes and babbling "in tongues," their volume increasing in competition with one another.

"Do enemies still exist in this country, planting weeds in our fields?" Taggert continued, his flock now fully captured by the moment, feeling his power—*their* power, their superiority over the rest of humanity, secured by their faith in the Lord Jesus Christ. They nodded in agreement. *Of course these enemies still existed,* they thought. Right outside those doors, they worked their evil every day.

"Oh yes, they are out there. This is why we must ensure our influence on those who lead us as our representatives in government. Some think they are entitled to serve simply because of what family they come from—but I believe this is still America, where people earn the trust of those who ask them to govern. Trust in not only the ability of the candidate, but also in their values." He paused to let his purpose sink in. "You know, we've been paying close attention to my opposition over the last few weeks. Particularly on Sundays. Would you believe there is no evidence she has attended *any* church services in those weeks?"

His audience was visibly shocked.

"Now, please understand that I, of course, support her father. Always have. The Lord gave him to us to lead the nation, and he has done that admirably. But when it comes to who should lead this state . . . well, let's just say I think it should be someone *from* this state, whose values are consistent with its citizens."

And for his punch line, he closed his eyes as the murmur of agreement spread throughout the arena, rising to a crescendo that signaled his return. He opened his eyes.

"Which is why it is imperative I be made governor of the great state of Colorado!"

And as intended, they exploded with rapture. Rapture at their power in this space, away from their homes and workplaces where they were just another person. Here, with this man in front of them, explaining who they really were.

They were superheroes.

Back at the side of the river, they revealed themselves with a gentle glow, like fireflies that didn't blink. A fifty-strong swarm formed a perfect wall in front of the family, half an inch off the ground to thirteen feet high and twenty feet across. Their combined buzzing was not loud enough to drown out the cries of the daughter and, increasingly, the son and mother, who could not explain what was happening.

A hologram appeared in the middle, just in front of the wall. It was a man's head wearing a beige, broad-brimmed hat with a thick black band. He was white and smiling like a maître d' in a five-star restaurant.

"I'm sorry about that, folks, but I'm afraid I'm going to have to ask you to get back in your boat and go back to your own country. We have rules and laws, and you must follow them."

"But we are seeking asylum," the father said, eyes wide and desperate.

"Then do it at our consulate, eh?" the hologram replied. "We have had enough of your country's trash. Now, please get back into the boat and head on out. Otherwise, the BuzzKills will be switched to attack mode."

Without hesitation, the family complied, rowing themselves to near exhaustion back to the southern banks of the St. Lawrence River—back into New York.

Chapter 5

Jeff finished trimming the hedges on the perimeter of the backyard just as the sun dipped below the Rockies, his energy spent by the ninety-five-degree heat throughout the day. He submitted his digital time slip, which had been tracking his location, activity, and movement since he punched in at 10:00 a.m., the metrics assuring payment only for the period of active labor, separating that from bathroom breaks and the little rest time he required. As he descended to the basement for a shower, he was hit by a wave of loneliness and thought of his house on the hill back in Connecticut, where he'd enjoyed a fulfilled childhood raised with his sister by loving parents in an upper-middle-class household. The world had changed quite a bit since then, and his generation was still figuring out how to navigate the career challenges brought on by changes in the economy, law, society, and technology.

He emerged from the shower and texted Lily that he was heading to get a burger at the Heaven's Gate Bar and Grille. Not long after getting dressed, he read her reply:

Already ahead of you. Better get over here before the bartender sweeps me off my feet.

Through his digi-lens, he received an iSpy request from Lily, which would send the video coming through her contact lenses and stream it directly to his, triggered by a focused thought owners were able to customize. He focused on the word *accept* and was instantly looking at the vision of dissonance that was the man behind the bar, angry eyes trying to hide behind a plastic smile, hair slicked back into a ponytail, nose flaring with each consonant.

"No, I'm not new here," he said from a distance that felt too close to Jeff. "This is actually *my* place. My regular bartender called out and I didn't have a backup, so I drove up from the Springs to cover. I'm assuming you're not a regular. I'm sure he would have told me to look out for someone as hot as you. I'm Koy Taggert," he said, turning the smile up with the expectation of recognition—which Jeff was pleased to see Lily refuse to provide.

"What was that?" she asked with a deadpan delivery. "Did you say 'yogurt'?"

The man's smile flattened. "*Tag-gert.*"

The letters *OMG* appeared under Jeff's view, the product of Lily's thought-text.

Jeff smiled and appreciated her sense of humor. Even though their relationship was still developing, he enjoyed every moment together. They'd met at a job fair in Pueblo and struck a connection on their awareness that they wouldn't get a callback from any of their applications.

"Siri," Jeff said out loud, "tell Lily I'm on my way."

The words appeared under her last message, and he watched her head go up and down. It could have been her acknowledgment of his message or, less likely, her agreement with something Koy had to say. He thought, *Disconnect,* and the video ended.

Fifteen minutes later, he entered the bar, greeted by a herd of beheaded deer on the wall and a lone beaver that snarled at him while sitting on its hind legs. Seeing the conversation was still underway—Koy leaning in, elbows on the bar—Jeff decided to hang back and watch for a bit, admiring Lily's beauty and ability to appear interested, chin on hands, her long red hair draped over her shoulders. When her smile turned flat, however, he moved in, pulling up the stool next to her, deciding against putting his arms on the bar that was covered by sticky, round relics of drink glasses past.

"Hey there," he said, interrupting something about Koy's house in the Springs. He kissed Lily, and Koy stood up, looking as if he'd just fumbled the football that led to a pick six.

"What can I get you?" he asked Jeff, voice wooden.

"Whatever she's having," he said.

"Maker's Mark old-fashioned," Koy said as he departed down the long bar.

"'Bout time," she said. "Leaving little ol' me alone. I thought he was going to make a move."

"You're not alone," Jeff said, pointing to the blond young man in the small kitchen to the side of the bar, cleaning dishes.

"Subtle entrance," Lily commented, changing the subject.

"You were holding your own, but it was fun to see his expression."

"And how was your day?"

Jeff knew Lily was still looking for a job. Interestingly, she never expressed concern about her job-seeking failures—at least, not the way he did. She was being selective and seemed in no rush to land something. Meanwhile, prior to meeting her, he'd been planning to abandon ship and return to the East Coast, where he could at least rely on family for more support. He'd decided it was best to downplay his situation a few dates ago, doubting his ability to get anything full time. She was clearly in a different league intellectually, adding to the mystery of her unemployment.

"Rejected by the market once again," he said. "I'm starting to explore opportunities outside of my field. No one seems to want an American to teach English . . . in America." He sighed and shook his head. "How about you?"

She sipped her drink while listening to the end of the commercial from the holovid behind the bar.

"I'm Iwanna Dennison, and with God as my witness, I approve this message."

"I've got an interview to be on a flight cabin crew," Lily said. "Exactly what I was aiming for when I got that degree in psychology."

"See Mick Jagger like you've never seen him before! Rolling Stones Tour '46, live onstage at Dennison Field!"

"Where was that degree from again?" he asked.

"I went to school abroad," she said, clearing her throat.

"When's the interview?" Jeff asked, taking the hint.

"Tomorrow at 3:13."

"So precise."

She smiled. "Yes, our world of precision has made everything so—"

"Swiss."

"Well, at least we have the mountains for it."

"We'll be losing some of them soon," Jeff noted.

"Oh really?" Lily said skeptically. "How?"

"The landlord's wife was just telling me her husband is working on a project that removed some in a valley about two hours south of here."

"Probably knocking down some old buildings or something."

"Nope. She said they're taking out the mountains."

Lily laughed with a note of condescension. "Well, you must have misunderstood her. You can't take out a *whole mountain*." She looked at him like he was the most gullible man on the planet.

"*Mountains,*" Jeff corrected. "Plural."

"Why would anyone want to remove a mountain—or *mountains?*"

"I have no idea. She likes having her little secrets."

"Do you know what it would take to get rid of a mountain?"

"I'm not arguing with you—I'm just telling you what she said, and I'm pretty sure I heard her correctly."

With a grin, she said, "Your ears weren't muffled in any way?"

Jeff was thrown off by both the candor and accuracy of the statement. He had only shared his discomfort about the landlady with Lily yesterday, and it'd immediately become an inside joke, a punch line, between them.

"Don't laugh. I think she's making a move. Invited me in to cool off this afternoon. Want to come back to my place? Maybe she'll take the hint if she hears us."

"You assume she's listening in?"

"Yep."

Lily checked her watch and thought for a moment. "Okay, but how much have you had to drink? It can't be too long."

"This'll be my first."

"Siri," she said, "authorize Jeff Maslow for intercourse until 11:30 tonight."

He nodded his acceptance.

Siri replied, "Jeff Maslow is authorized for a roll in the hay until 11:30 p.m."

Apple had loosened the reins on Siri's content, allowing her to match the diction she observed from her owner. The app, Consent, came into standard usage in the late '20s to document approval for sexual encounters.

Jeff's watch confirmed with a buzz. Then he said, grinning, "You know, if you fucked me twice, it would really send her a message."

"What did you just say?" Koy asked as he arrived with Jeff's drink. "Did you not see the declarations at the door? That language isn't permitted here."

To ensure businesses were able to avoid the discomfort of serving customers whose morals did not meet their exemplary high standards, states permitted the use of "declarations." These were to be clearly posted outside their place of business, detailing a litany of phrases and behaviors that would lead to refused service. These included, in the case of the Colorado version, "sexual deviance," which permitted them to throw out anyone they suspected of being anything other than heterosexual.

Enforcing such declarations wasn't always easy, however, as the criteria to identify suspects varied for each location, with some using an "effeminate lisp" as reason enough to assume a patron was homosexual. These were enabled by the 2027 US Supreme Court decision *Chick-fil-A v. Massachusetts*, where the fast-food chain received the support of fourteen of the nineteen justices for a victory that allowed it, as a private corporation, to refuse service to the full spectrum of LGBTQ+ membership. When, in Charleston, Senator Lindsey Graham was denied a spicy chicken sandwich and a side of nuggets by a particularly homophobic server, the corporate policy was changed to require a manager's approval before denying the protein.

To minimize the lost revenue to companies that enforced this, the party developed the St. Paul Fund to support any business that could evidence the practice negatively impacted their sales. The Provincetown, Massachusetts, location of Chick-fil-A was often empty but solvent, subsidized as a monument to the company's victory.

Lily and Jeff, still under scrutiny from the bartender, paused to ensure no punch line was forthcoming. When they realized he was serious, Jeff went straight-faced and said, "I'm sorry, we were just jerking around. We meant no disrespect."

Koy thought for a moment, looked at Lily, and said, "Well, okay, then." He placed Jeff's drink on the bar.

They looked at each other for a few seconds as he slipped out of hearing range, and Jeff caught Lily darting her eye behind him. He turned around to what he thought was an empty bar and found a well-dressed young man looking right past him at her, leering.

"Did you just get a hookup request?" Jeff asked.

Lily glared at the block ice cube in what was supposed to be a straight-up drink and dipped her finger in to stir it. "So much for neat," she said. "You're very observant, Mr. Maslow."

"Seen the move, yes. Actually once had a woman accept the request and go straight to the guy that was hitting on her." He turned again and found the man acknowledging he was busted with a slightly guilty grin and faint wave in his direction. "Well, you must be flattered. He's a baby. Whatever happened to basic civility?"

Lily kept her eyes on Jeff, respectful to not even glance at her digital suiter. "All of you guys became like lions on the Serengeti once Dennison hit those back-to-back home runs."

President Dennison, in the spring of 2026, put the full weight of the National Institutes of Health behind the development of a birth control pill that held a twenty-year effective duration, paired with another medication that opened a twenty-four-hour window of fertility, should the woman wish to get pregnant. The former became known on the right, over time, as "mags," for the whore Mary Magdalene, and the latter as "ferts," for "fertility." A year later, the president announced that the government had cured all known sexually transmitted diseases and that Dennison Pharma would be manufacturing vaccines for each under a contract from the FDA. The orgy was on. For some reason, this failed to distract the world from his invasion of Chihuahua, Mexico.

"Gotta give him credit. Getting rid of the STDs was a big win," Lily said.

"Definitely a higher priority than childhood cancer," Jeff said. "Still doesn't excuse that asshole back there hitting on you when you're obviously with me. Is it safe to assume you turned him down?"

Lily coyly cradled her chin in her folded hands. "Turned him down?" she echoed, blue eyes narrowing. "Don't you mean *them*? And did I miss the conversation where we committed to each other?"

Jeff caught her eye darting again to someplace—or some*one*—behind him, and she nodded, admitting she had received another request.

Suddenly, a piercing klaxon rang out through the bar. Jeff's vision instantly tinted as the system painted his head with a crimson light to make him easily identifiable as the threat. The barrels of five handguns and one shotgun emerged in the hands of dishwashers, line chefs, and even a janitor—all cocked and pointing at Jeff.

"Anger detected!" said an unseen monitor.

Jeff raised his hands over his head and rolled his eyes. "Unarmed."

After three seconds, the monitor declared, "No arms detected. Stand down."

One of a group of twentysomethings gathered at a table yelled, "Where's your gun, you fag?"

Jeff replied with a middle finger as they holstered their arms. One said, "Fuck, I'm empty." Jeff watched him go to the ammunition vending machine, select .38 Revolver, and collect the dropped box of one hundred rounds, which he promptly opened to fill eight empty chambers.

Lily, ignoring them entirely, returned to their original discussion. "Why would that make you angry? We just met a little while ago."

The corners of his mouth turned down, but then he caught himself and straightened out. "I recognize we haven't had *the conversation*, so you would be well within your rights to see other people. It was about *him*, not you. And I just thought . . . I don't know, I guess I thought this was going well."

Lily grinned. "I like you, Jeff, but I've got to be honest: The job thing matters to me. Not because I care about how much money you make, but because it just looks like, well . . . like you've given up."

That hit him like a brick. He avoided her eyes for the first time since he could remember, embarrassed at the implications and truth of the observation.

"You're right," he said to the floor. If she was going to be brutally honest with him, then it was time he matched that energy. "But honestly, you're the only reason I'm not back east."

He looked up for her reaction. As usual, she was impossible to read.

He cleared his throat. "I haven't committed to you—*exclusively*, at least—but I'm looking to give us a chance to see if there's something here."

He knew he was probably getting too emotional and might be actively scaring her off, but if her concern was his lack of a job, he needed to nip that in the bud now. If it was a deal-breaker, then they had a solid reason to go their separate ways, and he'd hightail it back to the East Coast—maybe even book a flight that night.

"When I was a kid, my dad's company had one of those bring-your-kid-to-work days, and he drove us in real early to beat the traffic. We wound up on Fifth Avenue, right by the park, Fifty-Ninth Street, and there's this slope down so you can see everything coming up. The light in front of us turned green. Then the next one, and the next one, just in time to let us through, and I knew then that it was going to be okay—that despite all the chaos and silliness, we'd get to his office."

Lily kept her eyes locked on him, a subtle tug at her brows that suggested more confusion than curiosity. He wondered if she'd ever been to New York but figured he'd ask later.

"Anyway, my point is: That's the way I used to feel when I first got out of college. Nothing but green lights ahead. And then, one day, I looked around and they were all red, and I was going nowhere." He forced himself not to look away from her as he added, "I was just hoping you might be one green light in all of this."

She didn't look turned off—probably more surprised than anything to find a man in this day and age willing to expose himself like this.

Then, to cap off the argument, he said, "I know it's early, and you're totally right to keep your options open. I get it, really. I'm working harder to get a job that will allow me to stay."

"I just think, at this point, you need to broaden your options if you decide to do that," Lily said. "It's what I've had to do. Look, twenty years ago, this would have all been perfectly normal, so I get the frustration. We'd both have jobs in our chosen careers and would probably be settled down with kids and a picket fence. The reality is we're the tossed generation, so we've got to find a way to deal with it." She watched him nod in agreement. "But, like I said, this is fun, so you figure things out."

"You're going to fuck the young man behind me, aren't you?" he asked, half joke, half question.

"What is it with you two?" Koy had returned—interrupting the answer Jeff desperately wanted, causing him to finally lose his patience.

"Jealous much?" Jeff said.

"Out!" Koy barked. "Now! Or I'll call the GA."

"Do you want us to pay our tab first?" Jeff asked.

The conflict between commerce and Christ was quickly resolved. "Siri, collect payment," Koy said curtly. In the area between them, the tab appeared in a hologram.

"Siri," Jeff said, "pay the tab and add sixty-nine cents for the tip." Then he came closer to his host. "What's it like in that silly little head of yours? To have all these urges and then be sanctimonious? Lamely try to wash it away with those stupid declarations?"

"Those declarations document my beliefs, which are sacred!"

Jeff took a full swallow of his drink, then placed the glass gently on the bar. "They document nothing but your *hypocrisy*." He pulled closer to Koy's chest to accentuate his point. "You're a fucking bartender, not a crusader for God. This happens outside the bar, you're picking your teeth up off the ground."

He walked out as Lily finished her drink and followed him. On the other side of the door, she asked, "Christ, the GA? Guardian Angels? They exist around here?"

Somberly, Jeff said, "Unfortunately, yes."

As they exited, Koy made a call.

Chapter 6

May 7

The next morning, Lily pulled into the Meadow Lake Airport terminal dressed to the nines for the interview with Liberation Air. She announced herself to the bot at the front desk and was asked to join the others in the waiting room. She turned and entered to find eleven women seated placidly, not a single skirt above the knee. Lily panicked, instantly remembering her internal debate about where to leave the hem. She'd opted for at the knee—not below it. Her fellow invitees apparently had better intel on the company.

I should have known better—down here, so close to Colorado Springs. What was I thinking, dressing like their cartoon version of a slut?

She debated turning around and withdrawing from the interview altogether when the only other door opened. A man in his late thirties walked out and called, "Ms. Osbourne?"

The others broke their station and looked around at one another, missing the one person of interest at the entrance doorway. "Um, sure, that's me," Lily said, feeling the heat emanating from the angry eyes of the others before her, presumably with earlier appointments. With no one leaving the office she was about to enter, Lily correctly assumed she was the first to be interviewed.

"Please, come in," the man said with a welcoming gesture. He sat, pointed to the chair, and said, "Have a seat. I'm Zeke."

Short for Ezekiel, Lily told herself. *He's a local.*

"Thank you, Mr. Proctor," she said, showing off that she'd done at least some basic research before the interview.

"Welcome. So, tell me, what brings you here today?"

Lily was attuned to the latest trends in interviewing etiquette and looked early on for clues into the weaknesses of the interviewer based on the questions they asked, which generally exposed them as either someone more interested in talking about themselves to show off their power or someone interested in ensuring the position was filled with the best candidate. She had been hit on, laughed at, and cried to in any number of interviews. This opener was a new one, but she fielded it confidently.

"Well, I read the job description, which clearly emphasized the emotional intelligence required for the role: someone who can read a situation well and respond appropriately. I love to travel, get along great with people, and am currently unemployed, so it seemed like a good match."

Zeke picked up his tablet, swiped to an app, looked at it momentarily, and placed it back on the desk. He was a handsome man, presenting a mix of pilot confidence and small-business owner, but with an edge of— was it *gentility*? The way he focused on her, his fluid motion as he dealt with the tablet that she knew was telling him the results of her body scan for lie detection. The aviator sunglasses sat on top of his full dark hair, and the latest styles in athletic clothing highlighted his biceps nicely. Just beyond the right one, she caught a picture frame, and while he verified her truthfulness, she picked up on a photo of an older man in full captain's uniform, in his sixties, a Boeing wide-body 878 behind him, arm around a younger, beaming Zeke. She could make out the pattern on a small pin on Zeke's collar. It was the old gay pride rainbow flag, since banned by the 2034 legislation that prohibited all graphic representations of the spectrum. Pink Floyd's *Dark Side of the Moon* was now contraband.

That was it for the gallery. *No family, no coworkers. No wife.* It was harder to tell these days—especially out west, with everyone back in the closet—but Lily felt confident drawing the conclusion she just had.

"Your undergrad and master's were in psychology from Arizona State. Good school, not great, and your preinterview reveals much greater intelligence than the typical ASU grad."

Damn, she thought. The tech was getting better.

He continued. "Why are you dumbing yourself down just to serve drinks to rich guys on a private aircraft?"

Despite the provocation, Lily didn't react negatively. Instead, she smiled. "My minor was in economics, and my bank account is running low. So I'm applying those skills to the situation." Reading his approval as he chuckled, she continued. "I'll be honest: I didn't intend to stay in Colorado this long, but it is such a beautiful part of the country, and I know what a dogfight it is to get a job as a psychologist, with such little demand for mental health in the region." She hesitated for the first time, concerned that it may have come out as an insult. "The rest of the country is overwhelmed with applicants for psychologist positions. I had enough in my account to last for a while, but the well is starting to run dry."

"People don't like to expose their weaknesses to strangers," Zeke said.

She stayed quiet.

"Especially to educated elites."

Still quiet.

"No one to send money from back home, to keep you afloat? Dad? Brother?" he asked, very intentionally seeing how far he could push her.

Lily *was* getting aggravated, which she could see was showing up on her scan. She watched him take a peek at the tablet and then return his eyes at her.

"If I told you I was an orphan, you'd know I was lying," she replied, "so how about this: My father would be happy to help, but I don't want to depend on him."

"Any guy in the picture?" he asked, not letting up.

Guess he's straight, she thought. *Here comes the move.* But then she paused momentarily, realizing she was being baited.

"Dating someone, but nothing serious," she said, deciding to play along.

He picked up the tablet again, and her awareness of what he was doing must have appeared on her face as he caught her eyes. "This bugging you?"

"No," she said. "I'm sure it's telling you I'm telling the truth. Have to admit, I didn't spot the detector when I came in."

"Thermoscans don't lie. And you're right. You're very confident."

No response.

"Is that why you wore that dress?" he asked.

Ready for this question, Lily said, "Well, on the one hand, I could have just blended in with all your other candidates. On the other hand, with the role, I know what many of your clients are looking for, so I wanted to exhibit that I had all the criteria—documented and *undocumented.*" She resisted the urge to smile at him for fear of appearing flirtatious. "It's a fine line between culture and commerce. This morning, I estimated it to be three-quarters up the patella."

Zeke responded with a loud "Hah! And I assume you know who my leading corporate client is?"

Dammit, she thought. Unprepared again. "Well, to be honest, no."

"My fleet spends a good deal of time flying executives from Dennison Enterprises."

"Ah," Lily said as Zeke glanced down at the tablet. She tried to compose herself, knowing there had to be an alarm going off on the screen. "Is it safe to assume you're referring to the same family as the president? And candidate for governor?"

He held her gaze. "Yep, that's the one. This area has been a hub for them for many years—at least, since Iwanna settled here. Is that a problem for you, Ms. Osbourne? Many of your flights will transport executives from the firm to locations throughout the country. Sometimes to other parts of the world."

She wondered if she had finally blown what had seemed like a pretty good string of wins, but then realized it wasn't disappointment on his face, but curiosity. "I've been here long enough, so I wouldn't have applied if working around them was an issue. The family is everywhere."

Zeke maintained his gaze, giving no indication of the decision he had already made. Then he smiled faintly, walked to the door, and opened it.

"Thank you, ladies," he said to the room. "We've identified our candidate, and we don't want to waste your time. Have a good day."

As he closed the door behind him, Lily heard an unhappy interviewee say, "Fuck! You've *already* wasted my time!"

Zeke returned to his seat and said, "Make sure when you go to the company dressing room to have the uniform printer produce a skirt *exactly* that length." He extended his hand over the desk, and she rose to accept it. "Welcome to Liberation."

A familiar alarm rang out, followed by, *"Anger detected. Multiple threats. Triple G alerted."*

Zeke opened the door to the lobby again. This time, instead of seeing an area populated by eleven calm interviewees, Lily saw eleven stewardess rejects, each raising a gun at the other—and then, seeing her peer through the open door, shifting to aim at *her*.

She immediately backstepped out of view.

"Damn, I probably should have seen this coming. I'll be right back," Zeke told Lily as he drew his .45 revolver from its holster.

Lily sat calmly as he sprinted to the emergency of his own creation.

Unable to keep up with the increase in gun-related incidents caused by expanding access to all weapons to all citizens, many states had instituted local chapters of the Triple G organization Good Guys with Guns.

Some called them a fast-reaction citizens brigade akin to a volunteer fire department—the key difference being they brought fire, not water. Others called them government-sanctioned posses.

All public spaces and many private had installed Lyssa—the leading Dennison product for detecting anger—and when an incident broke out, the system alerted all members in the immediate area in an attempt to subdue the subject with an overwhelming response. Unfortunately, the definition of *subdue* was never made clear, and each response tended to be a special snowflake, with zero prosecutions nationwide for the sometimes excessive behavior of their membership. After all, these were the *good* guys. Not the bad guys. One needed to set aside the fact that the application to join Triple G was online and one's acceptance was largely immediate, but for the simplest of background checks and confirmation of political party affiliation.

Lily peeked again into the waiting room, where Zeke found a circle of seven women pointing their pistols at another circle of four, presumably the ones who had lost it at learning they couldn't even get an interview for a stewardess job. As hiring preferences tilted back toward men over the last decades, the help wanted ads for women began to look like the 1960s. Flying the friendly skies had become an appealing, albeit low-paying, way to pay the rent.

Zeke watched as Triple G members busted into the lobby and joined the armed clusterfuck, each randomly picking a target—some the ladies who had lost their temper, ready for armed vengeance against Zeke, some the ladies aiming their guns at the ladies who had lost their temper. Zeke froze upon realizing at least one gun was aimed right at him.

Lily, unable to sit through this, placidly stood in the doorway. This was, unfortunately, not her first clusterfuck.

"Okay, everyone, listen!" Zeke yelled. "I'm a captain in the Triple G and outrank everyone here."

"Fuck that!" said one of the late entrants. "I'm a major!"

"Anger detected," Lyssa announced.

"I'm *not* angry," the major said.

"Lyssa, stand down!" ordered Zeke, only for her to then accuse *him* of anger detected.

Lily continued to stand back, torn between scoffing and laughing.

"Lyssa, I'm not angry. Stand down for thirty minutes," Zeke said, turning to address the people crammed into the small lobby. "Everyone, listen to me. This is my place. I own it. Some folks were not happy about not getting a job today—"

"A fucking *interview*, not a job!" said one.

"Okay, okay, that's fair," Zeke said. "An interview. And I'm sorry about that, but the candidate was prescreened and did extraordinarily well on the interview."

"Did she put out?" asked another applicant, darting a glance at Lily.

"I have a recording of the whole interview that I'm happy to share," Zeke replied firmly. "This was a fair process."

"I never got into the room! How is that fair?" asked another. "How can you be sure she's the best fit for the role and not any of us?"

Zeke hesitated momentarily, sweat sparkling on his upper lip. "You were all prescreened. I'm sorry it didn't work out. I will take this valuable feedback and change the hiring procedures here at Liberation."

"I think *valuable feedback* should include a round in your head," said the angriest lady.

"Did you just *threaten* him?" the major asked.

"She did," replied one of the major's companions.

All five of the Triple G members raised their firearms on her, and she began to shake and cry, lowering her .22 at once.

"Okay, look, everyone, *please* just holster your guns," Zeke said. "Ain't no one shooting no one today. I understand your frustration and know this is a tough economy, but I'm sorry, I only have one job for now. Hopefully, things will get better, so I invite you all to reapply and promise I will only give fair interviews to screened candidates."

Like a wilting flower, the center of the circle lowered their arms and holstered their guns, followed by the outer circle, followed by the Triple G, followed by Zeke.

The major walked over to Zeke as the ladies exited the room. "Hey, look, sorry," he began, nodding at Zeke's badge. "Didn't see who you were. I head the custodial staff over at the main terminal, and we're all in the service."

"No problem. These things can get a little crazy. Appreciate the help." Zeke looked down to find two puddles of urine. "Hey, you think you can get someone over here to take care of that?"

Zeke returned to his office, closed the door behind him, and sat back down as if nothing had happened.

"So, you're a Good Guy with a Gun?" Lily asked somberly, abandoning her vigil beside the now-closed door and returning to her seat.

"Yes."

"And in that scenario, what exactly gave you the high ground to apply the label 'good'?"

"Not angry, I guess."

"So good guys don't get angry?" Lily asked without amusement.

Zeke sat there silently, taking her in—his newest employee. "If it makes you feel any better, I don't believe in the organization. I get your position: It results in more violence than if we just made sure only responsible people had guns, but this is the reality. I need to be a part of that. Especially with the business I'm in."

"Why is that? So you can fit in?" Lily asked with immediate regret.

Zeke flushed, though she could not tell if it was with anger or because he was being outed. It took him a minute to respond. "All of this is my own doing. I get it. I want someone smart in the flight attendant position, someone I can trust and work well with. I suppose I can't have my cake and eat it too, with your smart comment—but smarter still would be to get to know me first before making insinuations."

Lily, properly berated, said, "You're entirely right, and I'm sorry. It's just . . . the *you* I met in the interview was different from the one I saw five minutes ago, and it surprised me. I understand if you want to change your mind about offering me this position." She began to get up for dismissal.

Zeke laughed. "You think I'm ever posting a job again after this? I started with you for a reason. I knew you'd be perfect for the role but invited other interviewees, just in case."

Lily sighed through her nose.

"See you tomorrow?" Zeke asked.

"Sure, and thanks. I'm sorry, I was out of line," she said as she left his office.

Chapter 7

Cheryl swiveled a snifter in her right hand, eyeing Jeff coquettishly. "Were you trying to make me jealous when you brought your little friend over the other night?"

"What?" he asked, taken off guard. He'd been summoned by her first thing that morning to discuss "work opportunities" at the house. "Isn't it a little too early for—"

"Answer the question, Jeff."

"No, honestly, I had no idea you'd be interested in someone in my, uh . . . position," he said, even though it was a blatant lie. He *definitely* knew Cheryl was interested, but he'd brought Lily over not to make her jealous as much as to ward her away.

"She's cute," Cheryl said. "A little . . . tan, but cute."

This wasn't new to him. He spent his high school and early college years fending off the many female suitors interested in a handsome, intelligent, and sensitive young man who could also throw back beers with the best of them. He kept in shape with a simple running routine, the only remnant of a high school baseball career as a catcher that otherwise disappeared when he went to college. In those first two years, he'd observed how easy it was to have sex on demand, with campus-specific Tinder groups removing almost all the friction in the process. Though he wasn't complaining, it got old once he entered his junior year. He immersed himself in internships and studies, graduating magna cum laude and a born-again virgin, then committed to making his postgraduate relationships meaningful.

She slapped his ass. "I'm always looking out for you guys. It's a shame you have to do all these lousy jobs. Just not enough beaners anymore. Where did you say you went to school again?"

"Loyola."

"Never heard of it. But, I mean, did it matter? Why do you even need a degree to teach a language we already know, silly?"

It required all of Jeff's self-control to not respond to her statement. Cheryl was stunning, blonde, and fit like the cheerleader she likely was in her youth. Her level of self-assuredness was consistent with that of a reigning beauty queen, common for American women at the time who equated beauty with power.

"You put yourself in this position. The Lord gives us opportunities all the time, with the skills He gives us, the situations He puts us in, all to ensure the cream rises to the top. We are all part of the plan, and the sooner you see that, the sooner you'll take advantage of those opportunities. You know what I mean, Jeff?"

"Sure, Cheryl."

"You're a smart kid. I'm sure you get it. Take, for example, the position you're in now." She sat down at the kitchen table, her head at the same level as Jeff's crotch—about six feet away—and looked straight ahead. "Living in my basement, dating someone of questionable integrity, out of work, and practically begging for anything to earn some money. That's gotta be tough for you."

Jeff was seething at the suggestion that Lily was of questionable integrity but maintained a stoic look to hide it.

"But maybe," she continued, "you can seize an opportunity that may be right in front of you. One that can help you in the short and long term." She lifted her skirt above the socially acceptable knee length that Jeff assumed was typical in her church fellowship. As the hem settled above her mid-thigh, she spread her knees apart. "What do you think, smart guy? I bet there are great rewards if you seize opportunities like this."

Jeff forced his gaze back to her face. "Well, Cheryl, this is all very flattering, really. I had no idea this was what you had in mind. Lily's the first woman I've dated in years, honestly, and it's early and all, but it's going well."

"I don't believe that, honey. Look at you!" She tsked, eyes gliding over his body from head to toe. "No way you were a vol-cel."

Voluntarily celibate.

Jeff began to realize he wasn't being given a choice in this matter—and that a refusal, in fact, would more than likely put him on the street. This, combined with the understandable hesitance for Lily to commit, had him put up a cursory last line of defense. "Shouldn't we worry about Jake getting back?"

"Oh, well, now you're jumping to conclusions, honey," she said, closing her legs. He couldn't tell if she was feigning offense or genuinely offended. "Nothing's going to happen *now*, anyway. I don't have time to set up the apparatus."

Jeff decided there could be no positive definition of the word *apparatus*.

"I just wanted to see if I could get you to agree, which I clearly have. We'll pick this up another time. And now you need to scoot." She got up, shooing him away with a flick of her hand. "Jake will be home pretty soon from that site I was telling you about."

"Yeah, about that . . ." Jeff pretended to laugh, happy for the change in conversation. "I must have misunderstood you when you told me about it because, of course, you can't just *remove* a mountain."

"Not a mountain. *Mountains.*"

"Well, either way, you can't just remove them."

Without blinking, she said, "Of course you can, stupid."

He paused, searching her expression for signs of jest. There were none. "How?"

"Sorry, that part I can't tell you, but don't you worry, it will be good for all of us. Hey, you know, you'd probably do great out there. They're looking for guys like you. Strong and smart and handsome. Jake keeps talking about mind and body and all that crap. You want me to put in a word for you?"

"With Jake?"

"Yeah, sure, he likes you and how you've been working around here. We'll get someone else to take that shithole downstairs."

"Well, sure. I mean, if you're okay with that, I'd love to get something a little more stable."

"I'll do that for you. You're a nice guy." Slapping him on the ass once again, she said, "Now, scoot. Go dream about our next meeting."

Chapter 8

May 8

The air traffic control supervisor looked down from the tower at Meadow Lake Airport and watched the XTI TriFan 2000 gently land on the general aviation tarmac. It was the latest edition of the successful line of large private aircraft with vertical takeoff and landing capabilities, making it a combination of jet and helicopter. This one was owned and operated by Liberation Air.

The virtual ground controller behind him reported the event visually and audibly, the strip of data containing the plane's flight plan changing to green and its status to *Landed*.

"Liberation Seventeen on the ground at terminal two."

It was lonely for him, surrounded by stations operated by AI controllers when just seven years ago they had all been occupied by actual human beings. Still, the alternative of being laid off was much worse, and not even he could deny that the virtual controllers methodically guided traffic through the airspace with ease and unwavering accuracy.

This was especially the case at Meadow Lake, which was densely populated by both civil aircraft and the significant military presence in the area. Virtual controllers would communicate with their "peers" at other airports and those controlling the airspace surrounding and above, each supervised by no more than two human controllers, to whom the virtual ones escalated the more complex decisions.

"Niiice," he said as he applied the magnification to his augmented reality goggles and zoomed in on the new girl's ass and chest. "That Zeke sure knows how to hire them."

The VC rudely disrupted his leering. "Amazon eight-eight-two-seven, winds three-one-seven at two-one, runway three-three cleared to land."

"Cleared to land three-three, Amazon eight-eight-two-seven."

◆••————••◆

Glistening from the ninety-degree heat, walking from the terminal to the first flight of her new job, Lily thought about the situation, trying to positively spin it in her head with little effect. She had studied to help people with their mental illnesses, and here she was, ready to take her newly found waitressing skills to great heights—around forty thousand feet, specifically—serving cocktails and glimpses of her inner thigh. Like Jeff, she had a way out that she was not leveraging. Unlike Jeff, there was enough in her bank account to last for a bit. As with all things, supply and demand kept her out of her chosen field. When the federal government began passing laws that permitted insurance companies to label mental health treatments as "luxuries," the push for online AI therapists began. This led to the majority of Americans resorting to the cost-effective use of digital nonhuman therapists over a biological health-care worker.

After spending three years trying to break into that industry, Lily gave up. Rather than be even further in his debt by asking her father for help opening her own private practice, she went to the service industry. Americans still preferred their food to come from living, breathing biological servers so they had someone to look down upon. The early robots had not yet been programmed to display inferiority.

She climbed the stairs to the beautiful aircraft. A disproportionately small rotor was built into each wing, and there was one under the tail, aiming down for the eventual helicopter-like takeoff. Zeke, who had just supervised the landing from the one-person cockpit, met her at the top.

"So . . . are you excited for your first trip?"

She smiled and said, "Sure, can't wait."

"Oh come on, you can't be burned out yet. You just got here. Have you ever been in one of these babies?"

"Just the large commercial ones," she lied. Glancing inside the cabin, she added, "Wow, pretty lavish. Is the toilet gold?"

He laughed. "I thought about it. This was a big investment. I need these guys to fly however they feel most comfortable."

With a smirk, she said, "You mean guys and *gals*, right?"

He matched her sarcasm. "Sure, *sometimes* they bring along a girl-friend." Seeing her reaction, he continued. "Look, I'm just a service provider and don't control who comes to me to pay. But you know as well as I do, once the government stopped prosecuting human resource malpractice and all those manly civil court justices started throwing out bias suits in batches, a lot of these companies went back to forming their boys' clubs at the top of the org charts. Sure, there are plenty of women in middle management. But the guys taking these aircraft, they're entrenched at the top. And they like their toys."

"Is that what I am?"

He seemed to notice the topic was affecting her. "I'm not going to lie: They're going to ogle and love that skirt you're wearing—especially if you hike it up when we're off the ground. Not saying you must, just that it has happened. The simple fact is that this is one of the few places they get to see someone as beautiful as you unmonitored. They may even speak inappropriately. But I won't allow them to go further, and they will not touch you."

She looked at him incredulously. "Right. You're going to tell some executive, 'Hands off the waitress,' and risk losing their business over it."

She watched him turn very serious. "I can do little about *what* they say, but every passenger is required to sign a contract that specifically states that physically touching staff is a red line for this company. I have too many women in my life to let that happen."

Lily nodded gently, satisfied with his response, and walked into the cabin, where she sat in a plush third-row seat. "So where are we off to, Captain?"

"We will transport the CFO and his staff to Little Rock."

"Arkansas?"

"You'd be amazed at what the infusion of federal funds into the Southern states has created."

"I can take a guess: *loyal conservative voters.*"

Zeke's silent smile told her all she needed to know, but it quickly disappeared as he eyed his first passenger coming through the door. "Mr. Corey, good to see you again," he said as he walked to greet him. Lily popped up.

"Hi," Corey replied flatly, then walked to a seat in the back corner toward Lily. "And what have we here?" he asked, perking up.

She matched Zeke's enthusiasm. "I'll be your hostess for the trip out to Little Rock, Mr. Corey."

He unabashedly looked her over from head to toe. "Well, that's nice to hear, Miss . . . ?"

"Lily," Zeke said. "She's our most recent hire, and I'm sure she will be with us for some time."

Done with his inspection, Corey continued to the back of the plane. "Good to know. Scotch and soda, honey." As he sat, he asked, "Will you be joining us, Zeke?"

"Actually, yes, sir. With so many flights, I'm looking to hire an assistant in Little Rock, so I've lined up some interviews."

"Good for you. Make sure you apply the same criteria you did to land Miss Lily here."

"You bet," Zeke said as he walked toward the cockpit. "Lily, when you're all set, just join me up front, and I'll show you where everything is." He closed the door behind him.

Lily poured the drink and brought it to Corey as he reviewed his tablet. He opted not to look at her as he said, "Appreciate it. The others should be here in a bit, and they know to leave me alone. I'll let you know when I need something."

"Understood," she said as she went to join Zeke in the cockpit.

As she entered, she was struck by the bare space. There was only one seat for a pilot, and aside from the physical controls like the yoke and throttles, multiple screens provided the instruments she presumed were necessary to fly.

Zeke began the tour. "We could do this whole flight remotely, but some clients prefer the comfort of having an actual pilot on board. It'll take a few years to catch on, but the glut of unemployed pilots I have access to makes it cheap to have someone here."

"Would it fly itself, or does someone fly it from the ground?"

"A little bit of both," he said. "For the cargo flights or the ones where the client doesn't care, I can have one guy in the office handle five flights at a time. They manage the takeoffs and landings and let the autopilot do the rest. The plane takes commands digitally from the air traffic controllers and does what it's told. Since it can land on any surface, we cut out much of the commute time that is usually part of the travel."

"It can land anywhere?"

"Pretty much, depending on the size. This one seats eight, so it's a little bigger, but it still easily fits in most companies' parking lots."

"Cool," she said.

"So . . . that wasn't too bad, right?" Zeke gave her a hopeful look. "He took in an eyeful, but that was it. He's one of our busier customers, so he probably won't have the time for any naughtiness. Can't speak for the kids he'll have with him, but even so, they tend to follow his lead, so this should go smoothly."

"Sounds good to me. I'll be able to take care of myself, don't worry. So, the other day, you said something about wanting someone intelligent on these flights. You regretting that yet?"

Coming back to the topic sooner than he wanted, Zeke said, "No, I'm not. I spend most of my time trying to run this business, and with all the AI, I don't need much human help. For *this* job, however, I do. But let's face it, you saw the applicants I get. You were a rare find."

Lily nodded, offering him a warm smile. Were they . . . allies, potentially? If so, she felt compelled to come clean—and, perhaps, invite him to do the same. "I'm sorry about what I said," she confessed, the roar of the aircraft's engine muffling her words. "I know very well how hard it is—"

"Let me stop you there, Lily," he said firmly. "I'm not sure what exactly you were insinuating yesterday, or even where you're going now, but I'd caution you against drawing conclusions about someone who you've only just met—who also happens to be paying you." He paused, giving her a meaningful look that she struggled to decrypt. "Maybe we'll get to a point where we have that level of trust," he added more softly, "but we're not there yet."

Lily raised her hands. "I'm sorry I keep doing that. It's a habit: skipping to the chase. I grew up in a straightforward house, and I can't shake the habit. It's lonely for a lot of us."

"I understand—really. Let's just let it run its normal course."

The service bell rang—which, despite all the change in the industry, was still the traditional ding that had been heard in commercial airplanes since the dawn of time—and a blue light turned on in the cockpit area opposite the pilot seat.

"I'm being summoned," she said with a bright smile as she opened the door.

As it closed, Zeke could hear one of the junior employees exclaim, "Wow, she's smoking!"

He turned on the cabin camera to make sure she had it under control and could hear her say, "Now, now, boys. Nice of you to say, but there's no poles on this plane."

"Hey!" Corey barked. "Knock it off. Brandon, you're being disrespectful."

They immediately sat down in their seats and looked anywhere but at Lily, who walked toward Corey after he gestured for her to lean in.

"I know Zeke has rules and I respect them, but you let me know if you want to break any. I'll make it worth your while."

Lily didn't miss a beat. "Understood," she said with a coy smile and walked toward the front to take orders from the suddenly well-behaved young men.

Chapter 9

May 9

Here Jeff was again, in his apartment, being turned down for jobs he was more than qualified for, only to then receive a text from Cheryl confirming household labor—three hours' worth—starting in thirty minutes.

And he didn't request it this time.

Still hoping to parlay this (whatever *this* was) to the job she'd mentioned, he showed up at her door on time. She opened it wearing a mischievous grin ear to ear. "Hey there, Jeffy. C'mon in."

She was in a long T-shirt—his worst fear realized. He appreciated that she wasn't even trying to dress the whole routine up at this point. Those in power rarely need plausible deniability.

"I've got good news and better news. Which do you want first?" she asked, leading him inside.

He followed, tentatively closing the door behind him. There was still time to run away, he thought—only to hear the dead bolt lock. Cheryl continued into the living room.

"Let's work our way up and start with just the good," he said.

"Well, Jake spoke to the guy in charge of that town I was telling you about, and he's going to give you an interview for a teaching job. No guarantees, but a recommendation from someone like Jake will go a long way."

He was at first happy and thankful, then skeptical and leery. There was still better news to come.

"Wow, that's awesome, Cheryl. I didn't realize the project was a whole town. I really appreciate it."

"No problem, sugar. It's in the mountains outside of the Springs, so I assume you know you'll have to live there."

"That makes sense. I'm sure it's beautiful."

"It is, which brings me to the better news." She paused, staring back at him. "Jake and I are moving out there too!"

Jeff's brain was working overtime to unwrap the implications of her pair of announcements.

"They just got the okay to open up to buyers. Renters will come later. Isn't that great?"

He knew he had no choice but to match her excitement, which, to her credit, was legitimate. "Excellent news for you guys!"

Cheryl sat on the couch, and her face went serious, then sad, as she looked out the window onto her neighborhood. "Hope I'll be able to make some nice friends out there," she said more to herself, nibbling on a cuticle. "It's not that far, but I'm leaving behind my family here, and my friends too."

This was taking an unexpected turn.

"We have fun, behind closed doors . . . I hear they're so tight-assed down there." As if remembering she was not alone, she looked at Jeff and continued. "You excited, Jeffy?"

He hesitated just enough to see her smile turn upside down and realized he had to fix it. "Sure . . . I mean, it sounds like a great opportunity."

Exactly what she wanted to hear. "I'm glad you think so because I was hoping you'd show your appreciation this morning. You familiar with the Wholly Ghost?"

Assuming she was referring to the third member of the Holy Trinity, Jeff, fully accustomed to masquerading as a believer, said, "Sure, Cheryl, of course. I seek guidance from Him." He coughed on his lie. "All the time."

"Not *Him*, silly. Follow me."

She led him to one of the guest bedrooms: for all intents and purposes, a perfectly normal twin-bed setup with furnishings that could easily be from the 1930s. "You've really never done this before?"

"Cheryl, I'm not a virgin," he said, still confused.

She laughed at his ignorance. "You're adorable, Jeffy. So, I'm going to go in my bedroom. In the meantime, you should take your pants off. Your shirt too—if you want; that's up to you." She slowly leaned in as if to steal a kiss, put her hand behind his head, and, just before the moment of impact, yanked a hair from his head.

"Ow!"

As she pulled back from her would-be kiss, she said, "Sorry about that, honey. Just a souvenir."

Still confused, he said, "Sure, Cheryl, if that's what you want."

"In a little while, I'm going to appear on the bed, but I'll be in the other room."

And then, it hit him. He realized what was going on. He recalled reading an article about the products and their similarity to devices developed to help devout Jews meet their Sabbath-day laws, such as the one where they may not turn things on or off. In 2000, GE had developed Sabbath Mode for their refrigerators that, on Saturdays only, disconnected all lights and digital displays when the door was opened. Nothing was technically turned on or off, allowing the user to simply grab a snack without invoking the wrath of God.

Then, in 2035, Amazon developed the Wholly Ghost as a similar innovation, but with the goal of circumventing the rules surrounding marital infidelity. Its cameras scanned the form of each body and created a virtual replica in another room using sonic waves and lasers, the result being a frighteningly accurate rendition of a human body that moved and, most importantly, *felt* real.

"You'll know what to do, Jeffy," she told him while closing the door.

He went for the shirt-only option and, for a few minutes, stood awkwardly at the foot of the bed. Then he heard a light buzzing as she slowly appeared, first as nebulous light, then as a naked rendition of herself, head on a pillow, legs demurely crossed, her eyes radiating excitement as she scanned his image.

"Mmmm," she said. "That's what I thought. Time to earn that interview I gotcha, Jeffy."

He got on the bed and hesitated, not knowing how to approach the act. He reached out and touched her virtual knee, feeling the focused pressure returned by the sonic waves. It wasn't the texture of skin, but it had the detailed shape and solid feel of the real thing, even if it didn't exactly feel like a knee.

"Good start there, Jeffy. I'm sure you'll be a natural at this once you get used to it. I wouldn't worry too much about foreplay. If I were you, I'd find the objective and just attack it . . . aggressively."

Resigned to the bizarre fact that he would soon be fucking air, he did as he was told, moving in closer as she opened her legs to receive him, then lined up the target. As he completed his first thrust, he heard, both from the virtual Cheryl and clearly from her bedroom, "Ow! Fuck, my eye! Goddamn it, it's in reverse again!"

Chapter 10

Not long ago, this mountain was capable of ending civilization, Iwanna thought as she looked through the west-facing window of her home just outside of Colorado Springs. If it were still an active military facility, her father would have the launch codes. Now Disney was looking to fill those missile tubes with water for their latest park, which she assumed would have a name that was suitably thematic, such as Armageddon Valley. But first, they needed to convince her to sell it, and she wasn't ready.

A pair of moose grazed in the foreground of her view, a funnel of smoke from a brush fire climbing up and disappearing into the clouds behind them.

The meeting scheduled to start in six minutes and twenty-eight seconds was the one she'd just so happened to have been avoiding for the better part of her adult life. Her family had spent the last couple of decades in power muddying the waters of commerce with their political missteps—the repercussions from things like invasions and the use of nukes for public works projects diminishing foreign interest in dealing with American companies. *Clear out one little Rocky Mountain valley with a contained*

1.7-kiloton explosion 899 feet underground, and suddenly, no one wants to buy your automated housekeepers.

Now she hoped she could clear up the logjam and reach the potential of her business endeavors. And those of her peers. She left New York around twenty years ago and came here at her father's request to run the newly minted Dennison Robotics. The Springs had few private clubs and zero Michelin-Starred restaurants. Barely even a decent spa.

There were moose.

She turned her back on her view of the mountain and walked toward her desk in the vast space of her sparsely furnished office. It wasn't lost on her that the room had been designed for warmth and delivered none of it. There was a bookcase built into the wood-paneled wall and two well-lit exhibit tables covered by glass, evenly spaced between her desk and the door. A thin tablet floated on its magnetic pedestal over her desk.

There was a knock at the lone entry, and she said, "Come."

The door opened, and Patrick, the head of her household staff, walked in briskly. "Hal is outside, Ms. Dennison, and Reverend Taggert is running three-and-a-quarter minutes late."

"Thank you, Patrick. Please send Hal in now, and Taggert when he arrives."

"Okay, Ms. Dennison. Just a quick reminder: I will be out this afternoon, but Rebecca has everything under control until my return."

"Remind me why."

"My mother is being released."

Iwanna took the tablet while she said, "Oh yeah. Are they taking good care of her?"

There was a pause, and she looked up, unaccustomed to pauses.

Patrick said, "It is a hospice situation at this point, Ms. Dennison. She doesn't have the med-credits for the surgery."

"That's unfortunate, Patrick." And then: "I assume you'll make up the hours."

"Of course, Ms. Dennison."

"Oh, and Patrick, there were two moose on the property again. Can you take care of them?"

"Of course, Ms. Dennison."

He exited, leaving the door ajar for Hal, who walked in, marched stiffly toward his target, arrived in front of her desk, and folded his hands in a perfect at-ease stance.

She looked up and presented him a genuine smile. "Hi, Hal. Good to see you."

"Ms. Dennison, good to be here." Then, approximately three seconds later, he added, "Is everything okay with Patrick? He seemed ever so slightly distracted. He's never distracted."

"I believe his mother is ill."

"Ah, that would explain it." He took a seat in the leather chair in front of her. "What would you like to discuss first, Ms. Dennison?"

Two flashes of light in succession from the picture window, followed by faint explosions, announced the demise of the moose.

"How big is his church?" Iwanna asked.

In a monotone, he said, "He's got about four million members globally and an impressive following for his self-help books. Has a ghostwriter pump out two a year, propaganda for the Lord in the guise of spiritual healing. Since the discovery of the Argyre Cross on Mars—and all the conversions to Christianity it created—he has been working hard to create a central Protestant church under his authority, specifically appealing to converted Muslims and Jews. And it's been working. When he moves into an area, he buys out old houses of worship and local Christian denominations and offers them a franchise. He's created in-home crash courses in Christianity, and just the revenue for the resulting baptisms is making him a pretty penny."

"There's a lot of charlatans out there perverting the teachings of Christ," Iwanna noted, resting a hip against her desk. She pinched her brows. "What makes him any different?"

"He has included a lot of material about how to live a good Christian life in modern times and co-opted Eastern meditation techniques that became popular in the '20s to better strengthen his . . . let's call it *bond* with them." He looked at her for a reaction.

"So he's brainwashing them."

"More or less. Where the Buddhist approach is to allow the practitioner to open their mind and tamp down their egos in search of greater meaning for their lives in harmony with others and nature, he redirects that calm to Jesus and himself, making sure to point out that only his way of meditating is God's way and that if they follow anyone else's practice, they welcome the devil to occupy their soul."

"That's one way to protect his brand."

Their conversation was punctuated by the gentle whoosh of nuclear-powered engines. Two minutes later, there was a knock at the door, and Patrick entered once again. "Reverend Taggert, Ms. Dennison."

"Thank you, Patrick."

As Taggert shuffled inside, her smile disappeared, and she asked Hal under her breath, "You think this will work?"

Without hesitation, he whispered, "Assuming he continues his typical behavior patterns, yes, he should take the offer. If not, you have other options. Oh, I should mention, his congregations also have incredible birth rates. Statistical aberrations from the rest of the population."

The brim of Taggert's cowboy hat had entered the room a second before he did, followed by his towering frame and pit-bull chest. He'd been a linebacker at the University of Alabama before his calling, where he had become best known for imposing a thundering hit on an exposed wide receiver leaping for a ball over the middle. The receiver had been paralyzed for the better part of his adult life, and when fetal stem-cell surgery for his type of injury became available in Europe, he was forced to leave the country to walk again, the procedures having been long banned in the United States.

As Taggert sauntered in, his head turned to take in the lit tables, settling on the one about six feet off his path to the right. He stopped, and

Iwanna could tell he was debating, as many before him, whether to stray from the direct path to take a closer look. He stopped about twenty feet from where she and Hal were waiting.

"Well, Ms. Dennison, I have to say, I don't know anyone lucky enough to visit Wyatt Ranch. I am truly honored." He behaved as if he were meeting a rock star for the first time. "If I do say so myself, Ms. Dennison, you're a vision."

Iwanna couldn't help but glance at herself in the mirror. She *was* a vision, especially for someone at sixty-four. She'd once read a front-page article in the *Newspaper Times* refer to her as a "1970s Barbie, but whiter, with a figure untarnished by childbearing," and she hadn't quite known how to take that.

"Thank you, Reverend," she replied smoothly.

"And I might add," he went on, eyes twinkling, "that you don't look at all like the monster they say you are."

Iwanna pressed her lips together, feigning a smile. Then, she nodded at the table. "Go over and take a look, Brady," she said, addressing him by his first name. "It's somewhat relevant to our meeting."

He smiled, unashamed that he had been caught, and turned toward the table, the bright morning light reflecting off the glass and into his eyes, thwarting his view. He adjusted his position, and the item that first caught his eye was the distinctive semicircular shackle used to restrain African slaves, rusted but intact. Above it was a matching collar and, to the right, a banjo that he assumed came from the same period, which the placard indicated to be the 1820s. He considered the situation and turned back toward the path, head down, deciding how to appear to react.

She rose to greet him, extending her hand.

As he shook it, he said, "Those are some interesting artifacts, ma'am. I wonder if I should be concerned." He smiled coyly to indicate this was a half-hearted attempt to generate controversy. "Some of my flock are Black."

"Nine percent," Hal said, stone-faced, from his place in the leather chair.

Taggert looked at Hal and said, "Impressive." He peered over Iwanna's head for the first time, where an artistic rendition of the 2028 electoral map was centered perfectly behind her. It was all red. Below that, a wooden placard read:

"I Cannot Afford the Luxury of Sentiment,
Mine Must Be Cold Logic."
—*General George Marshall*

"Are you suggesting that my ownership of these historical artifacts makes me a racist, Brady?" Iwanna asked. "And here I thought you were a serious candidate for the conservative team."

Taggert looked up in shock at the suggestion.

"These are simply a reminder to me, and to anyone I welcome here, of the horrors of that terrible institution. No person should be enslaved."

Recovering, Taggert said, "Of course, I never meant—"

"That includes us, as well. It is a universal truth that no man or woman should be unduly controlled by another, made to perform acts that violate their humanity. Unless, of course, they have proven themselves inhuman."

"Amen," Taggert said, still visibly unnerved by the conversation and on the defensive. He removed his hat and held it in his hand.

Sitting back in her chair, Iwanna continued. "Back then, it was easy to identify the African and put chains on him. Then, it was based on skin color. But before that, it was based on tribe. Do you know where the word *slave* comes from?"

"No."

"*Slav.* The Baltics. The Slavs were slaves to the Russians. And Arabs. Sold by Jews. They were White, so the idea that only Black people were treated harshly throughout history is false. It has happened before, and it could happen again if we're not careful."

Hal interceded, "Ms. Dennison believes this is where you share common ground."

Taggert sat in the chair before her. As he did so, Iwanna asked, "Do you think your Savior will return before such a thing could happen? Minorities taking their revenge?" She conjured a smile to lighten the tension.

He returned it, hesitantly, and said, "He is not on a timeline, Ms. Dennison. I could never claim to know God's plans."

"But it sure helps business if people *think* He's coming back any day now, doesn't it?" she replied quickly. Hal placed his hand on her shoulder, and she laughed softly. "I'm just teasing, Brady. Don't mind me. How do you feel the race is going?"

He looked at her, confused.

"The political race," she clarified. "Not the *human* race. We already know the answer to that."

Taggert laughed. "I don't have your money, but I have a spirited following spreading my message."

"And what message is that, exactly?"

He considered the question. "One of hope. A vision of the state as a vessel to further the cause of Jesus Christ in this country."

"And how will you do that, exactly?"

"By leading through His example, making decisions as He would have."

"Like which, exactly?"

Irritated, he said, "You keep saying that. Are you trying to provoke me?"

Hal interceded. "I think what Ms. Dennison is trying to point out is that, though you are obviously an inspired leader in the Christian community and very adept at running your church, it doesn't neatly translate when you consider the flock in the state isn't all Christian. There are atheists, for example, that might take issue with your statements just now."

"Yeah, well, that's fine. There's not enough of them to stop me from winning. And who knows? Maybe I can win some over."

"In the primary, yes, that is true," Hal said. "If you win it, you can do whatever you like. But before that, there's the decision on the best vision that keeps those forces at bay once the candidate takes office."

"I agree," Iwanna picked up, "that the spirit of your church needs to be in the center of what we are trying to accomplish here. And make no mistake: I see these as two parts of the same whole. Politically, to the outsider, everything looks easy now that the old system has been replaced by the ascendancy of the Make America Dominate party, but there are still fundamentals, many constitutional, that we cannot skip. Knowing how much to ignore the enforcement of local laws. Knowing when you have the plausible deniability to get away with a thorny action. Knowing when you've gone too far. These rules are all unwritten, tested for decades, many by my father. And this state is not quite yet—"

"*Compliant,*" Hal enjoined. "We think there might be a way to show the face of everyone's best interests here, through commerce, while furthering our mutual cause."

"Team up, you're saying?" Taggert replied.

"Yes," Iwanna said. "I'm sure you can beat me in the primary. You've proven yourself on the air and have taken some good swings at me while I sit here, spend money, and remain disengaged. It's gotten me a lead, but it's slim. My concern is that if we keep taking shots at each other, we destroy any opportunity to join forces in the future, regardless of who wins, and that helps neither of our causes."

Taggert grinned. "You didn't like my commercial about you not goin' to church?"

"Ms. Dennison has always been a conscientious Christian," Hal intervened, tone just stern enough to ensure the punch landed. "Just because she doesn't do it in your thirty-thousand-seat arena does not change that fact, and I think suggestions like that are an excellent example of how you might burn the bridge here to Wyatt."

Taggert's grin disappeared, message received. "Okay, well, maybe that was a cheap shot on my part. So what are you two thinkin'?"

Hal placed himself in the chair at the side of Iwanna's desk and leaned toward Taggert.

"Aside from Ms. Dennison's political aspirations, she is developing a special community in a place not far from here. It will be entirely new, from the ground up, and with her as governor of this state, she can enact laws that would greatly advance its purpose: one as a place where our shared American experience can be furthered, nurtured, unmolested by many of the outside influences we find in our society today. We've called them Residences Affordable for Naturalized Dennizens. RANDs, for short."

"Interesting," Taggert said.

Right on cue, a hologram video appeared above the desk: a vision of the newly cleared valley in an old ghost town called Vicksburg not far from where they sat. He invited Taggert to stand and look at the live images of the location, with many buildings and apartments in their final stages of construction, the 3D printers passing over the site and leaving behind synthetic walls stronger than concrete in their wake.

Taggert stood up and walked around the hologram, impressed with the size and extensive activity underway.

"In fact," Iwanna joined in, "we have quite a few of these opening throughout the country. We were hoping Colorado would be the inaugural location. The goal is to slowly expand its borders to meet the anticipated demand for quality housing at a reasonable price, designed especially with our constituency in mind."

"Tell me more," Taggert said.

"We're going to need a church in our new town," she said. "And then in the rest of them around the country. Who knows—maybe one day, the world."

Hal pulled up to his right and pointed at a clearing on the top of a hill north of the town. "And that's where we'd put in your new church. We've left plenty of space, and over time, once the town starts to grow, we'll design it so it can be expanded to whatever we need."

Taggert's eyes widened. Now, at last, he saw the offer.

"Let Ms. Dennison deal with the sinners in the capital," Hal said. "You will be her exclusive partner against the sinners in the rest of the state, and eventually beyond, starting with Vicksburg Gulch. Most importantly, we've researched your specific religious doctrine, Reverend, and we very much agree with your beliefs and practices, particularly those that emphasize the importance of procreation. We think that aligns perfectly with the RAND objectives, ensuring the long-term labor we need without reliance on . . . imports."

"The filth from the south," Iwanna said bluntly, wanting to ensure there was no ambiguity.

Hal continued. "There were many churches to choose from. This element distinguished yours from that of your contemporaries. Of course, this comes with all the perquisites of such a relationship."

Taggert paused, studying Iwanna and Hal carefully. "I think it's important, since you brought it up, to make clear distinctions between my principles in this space and your father's. I don't know yours, so I'm just going to assume they're the same as his."

"They're not," Iwanna said, "but for ease of conversation, go ahead."

Taggert stood up and took a further look around, starting with the bookshelves, scanning one section. "Amazing how Machiavelli's philosophies apply today as much as they did for him back then."

"We are a predictable species," Iwanna said with a hint of dismissiveness. "But I do think there is a path to breaking these constant swings of the pendulum, left to right, to bring peace. You would call that paradise, no?"

"Despite what your man here may have indicated, I'm not that simplistic, Ms. Dennison. So you might be shocked to hear that I don't necessarily trust anything that you would describe as paradise or the means by which you would lead us there. Because unless you've put the brains of your robotic products into all of humanity, there is no breaking those natural instincts."

Iwanna looked up from the tablet report she was reviewing to find Taggert looking straight at her, catching her red-handed in her inattentiveness. He suddenly became more interesting.

"That's fair," she said, returning his gaze. "Maybe we're both allowing our prejudices to color this discussion: mine of the clergy, yours of Dennisons."

"Your father takes things too far when it comes to sexual behavior," Taggert began, as Iwanna had expected he would. "I know what he did to enable it, and his motivation, but that is not what we preach at my church. We know that God created our bodies to give us pleasure and that it would be foolish not to take advantage of that in our time on Earth. We have always sought to take the stigma *away* from sex that many churches have put on their disciples for centuries. That said . . ." Taggert pulled a thick volume from an eye-level shelf, examining it. "Sex must always be within the confines of marriage." He opened to a random page toward the back of the book. *"Always."*

"I know," Iwanna said, returning his tone. "And although my father has always been careful to say all the right things, in the right order—overall, I agree. He implies otherwise." Taggert's brows raised in a way that dared her to look directly at her father's implications, calling them out for exactly what they were, and she thus had no choice but to rise to the task. "He *implied* that the whole world should be one big orgy."

"Yes," he said, raising his index finger. "And that's hard for me to get past."

"You must understand that when he got rid of the STDs and pushed the mags, he was still concerned with winning over voters. He felt he had to give them what they wanted," she explained, "which was to fuck like rabbits. But I promise, you and I are in complete agreement on this issue."

"Yes, he is well known for projecting his own desires, but this is a critical discrepancy between his leadership and mine."

"Well, Brady, he does outrank you by just a bit—"

"Those pills should be outlawed!" Taggert regained his composure. "In this state, at the very least. Will you put *that* in your platform?"

"She'll consider it, Reverend," Hal chimed in diplomatically. "To do so would be an implicit contradiction with her father, and you know how he tends to react to perceived insults."

"Yes, I've seen. Is this why you moved to Colorado?" Taggert asked as he turned to look at her again, waving the book he still held in his hand. *"Atlas Shrugged?"*

She smiled and leaned back in her chair. "It'd be very dramatic to say yes, but no. My father asked me to come here when he bought out a failing tech company."

Taggert said, "Hah!" and bowed his head with a continued chuckle. "Sure, Ms. Dennison. We don't need to go into *how* it failed."

The tech company had gone bankrupt after being attacked by the government—influenced directly by the Dennison administration—devaluing it to the point where it was a steal. Iwanna felt her stoicism shiver. How had Taggert learned about that?

She faced him. "Is there something you want to share on that front?"

"Let's just say I don't plan to run into the same business troubles they did." He slid the book he'd pulled a while ago back onto its shelf and gave Iwanna a pointed look. "With that settled, let's get to it. Where the hell is Vicksburg Gulch?"

"You'll find Vicksburg Gulch on a map soon enough," she said. "As long as I can be assured I'll be the governor come January."

The offer, now fully on the table, seemed to visibly empower the reverend. He and Iwanna had spent the better part of the year jabbing lamely at each other, deliberately refusing to land a blow significant enough to sabotage any future collaboration—and now, here that collaboration was. Iwanna wished she could dive into his mind. *Was he aware that he was in a position of rare power?*

Initially, nobody had believed Taggert would stand a chance in the race, but early polling showed that the reclusive nature of the local branch of the Dennison family was working to his advantage. The family was a national institution, but Iwanna was a mystery, with very few public statements and even fewer appearances, so the conservative electorate was split, which gave him a chance.

"Tell me more about your project, *Iwanna*," Taggert said, incorrectly pronouncing the *w* as a *w* and not a *v*.

Hal stepped in. "Over time, after demonstrating a sustainable and mutually beneficial relationship built on trust, you may refer to Ms. Dennison by her first name. That time is not now."

"It's okay, Hal," she said.

"My concern, Ms. Dennison, is that our guest is already misunderstanding this, so I'd like to clarify your relationship," Hal said.

She said nothing, effectively allowing him to proceed.

"Reverend Taggert, we are all looking for the best outcome in the long term for all our interests, many of which overlap, but not all. We've withheld resources so far, and changing that policy would not be in your best interest."

"Are you threatening me?"

"Of course not," Hal said. "These are facts that should be obvious. We've done nothing but spread a few dollars in some admittedly basic commercials and are leading you by five points. You didn't think that's all we had in the arsenal, did you? You've seen what her father does to people, haven't you? You see this meeting as one of strength and who has it. We see it from a purely strategic perspective. Though working together could provide nonzero sum returns for both of us, we're happy to end this now and refer to a more tactical approach."

Hal paused, seemingly to let that sink in. All the while, Iwanna continued to watch Taggert—those ruddy cheeks of his growing even redder as if permanently wind-burned. He pushed out his chest, barrel-like rib cage straining against his flannel. He looked the part of bumbling rural conservative, but something told her he was just another wolf in sheep's clothing.

"After demonstrating your commitment," Hal proceeded, "we will share the details of our endeavor in Vicksburg and the rest of the country. For now, let's say it is a development venture that will reflect the

Dennison family's long-held beliefs in the markets and the role of government in them."

Taggert processed his new understanding momentarily before walking back to the glass case near the doorway. "So you really think someone wants to put these on you?"

"Metaphorically, yes," she said. "With the government as the holder of the keys. And in some cases, the links that bind them together."

Taggert returned to the desk but did not sit, instead opting to gaze at Hal, who returned it without expression. "Your man here is pretty good. Can you at least tell me how many new members of my flock I'll be receiving?"

"Phase one is scheduled to include six thousand new citizens," Hal replied. "If all goes as planned, we will be expanding rapidly."

"I asked how many of my flock."

"More or less, six thousand."

Taggert blinked. "All of them Christians? And how exactly do you expect to be able to pull that off?"

Hal repeated, "Demonstration of commitment, Reverend."

Taggert sat, exasperated, and returned to peering back at Iwanna. "I assume you are looking for my full-throated support?"

"Of course. After all, you wouldn't hesitate to bolster a future business partner, would you? As I benefit, so do you," she said.

Hal included, "You know, rising tide and all that."

Taggert chuckled. "Are we using that line of bullshit on each other now?"

Hal let a flat smile appear. "Fair point. But in this case, I think it applies."

Taggert again rose, walked a few paces from the desk, and replaced the hat on his head. "I assume you've documented this agreement for my lawyers?"

"Yes," Hal said, "along with the necessary nondisclosures."

"Of course. Well, Ms. Dennison, I do hope you meet expectations and that this will be as beneficial as you say it is. I still think I have a shot in November, but I guess I'll take the bird in hand, in this case. Maybe I'll revisit in six years."

Rising to meet him, Iwanna said, "Well, it is a democracy, I guess, so that certainly is your right." She extended her hand. "Hopefully by then, I've convinced you it's not in your best interest."

"Yes, I hope so as well." He tipped his hat to Hal as he walked toward the door.

"Patrick will escort you, Reverend," she said. "I look forward to working together."

"Sure," Taggert said while exiting. Then, as an afterthought, he stopped and turned. "Now I'm interested in what's in the other case."

"I'm afraid that's personal, Reverend," Iwanna said.

As the door closed behind Taggert, she turned to Hal. "How badly could we hurt him?"

"Well, let's just say I almost burst out with laughter at his use of the phrase 'full-throated.'"

"Hal!" she said and then looked at him with a coy smile.

"Apologies. He's had several indiscretions with some of the lambs in his flock."

"Oh my. How young?"

"Too young." When he saw the expression on her face, he said, "Don't worry, Iwanna, this is entirely tactical. He'll be dealt with when the time is right."

She got up, walked toward the glass case closest to her desk, and looked it over.

"Once he signs the papers," she said, "move ahead with the opening and schedule the other locations for the rest of the year."

"Understood." Hal exited.

She returned to the ten-foot-high glass window, pulling out her inhaler and pressing the button that would give her exactly thirty minutes of opiate relief. Then she pushed it again.

Who knows? she thought. *Maybe that old mountain can still end the world we live in.*

She decided to tell Disney to go fuck themselves.

Chapter 11

Jeff returned to his apartment in a near-catatonic state of bewilderment, unsure of where to start in trying to sort it all out. He'd spent years applying for jobs the right way, and yet it hadn't been until he'd resorted to the unsavory measure of cuckolding his landlord that he'd finally secured real employment.

But *was* it cuckolding? He'd never touched her!

He read a text from Lily asking if she could come over, an offer he enthusiastically accepted, and only a few minutes later, there was a knock on his door. Jeff froze, skeptical. No way was she already there on his doorstep.

A terrifying thought possessed him: *Did Cheryl tell Jake? Did he figure it out?*

Jeff motivated himself to peel open the door and was met at once by the imposing figure of the bearded Jake Daniels in front of him. His smile, which was definitely oblivious, instantly permitted Jeff's heart to start beating again. *Either he doesn't know, or he knows and doesn't care.*

"Jeff, how are you?" Jake asked cheerfully. He had a scar above his left eye, about an inch long, perfectly straight, which Jeff was only noticing now for the first time.

"G-good, Jake. You? Come on in."

As he entered, Jake asked, "You drained from all the work she made you do?"

Jeff froze before collecting himself. "I appreciated it. Always good to get work."

"No doubt, but it's been a big help around here," Jake said, clapping him on the shoulder, "and I'd rather give the work to you than some beaner."

Jeff's laugh came out lame and half-hearted, but Jake didn't seem to notice. "As it turns out, me and Cheryl are going to be moving out of here," he said.

"Oh really? Wow. Uh, so just selling the place?"

"Yeah, you in the market?" Jake asked with a laugh. "Kidding. But look, I remember you telling me that you wanted to be a teacher, and I may have an opportunity if you're interested."

"Sure, that would be great. Appreciate you thinking of me."

"If Cheryl trusts you, I trust you. It's sort of a start-up I've been working on for the last few years—a gated community outside of Colorado Springs—but not fancy and by invitation only."

"Interesting," Jeff said.

"Yeah, word will get out soon enough, but for now, those of us working on the project are building it up on people we know. I mentioned you to the woman running the school and said you're a hard worker and a good tenant, so she's gonna give you a call. No guarantees, but do good on the interview and you should get an invite. Ain't the good old days where I could just find a homeless guy to do the yard work, but I'll figure it out. You always did a good job."

Jeff was suddenly ripped inside from witnessing an act of legitimate kindness unlike any he had seen in his time out west, from a man who referred to Mexicans as "beaners," whose wife not fifteen minutes ago had taken a hit to her eye from his virtual penis. His nervous system was overloading.

"I-I-I don't know what to say," he stuttered. "I appreciate this so much. Hopefully, I won't screw it up for you."

"Hey, you ain't screwing anything," he said, and Jeff had to choke back a laugh. "Just be straight with her and assume she's done a background check. She's at Dennison, so she's got the resources. If you get it, you'll need to move into the town. If you don't, I'll let you know if the new owner here wants you in the basement."

"Can't thank you enough, Jake."

"No problem. Good luck, and maybe we'll see you out there. I'm headed back down tomorrow."

Jake left, and Jeff closed the door behind him, his hands trembling—from what, he had no idea. There were so many potential sources.

He decided to take a shower. As he was toweling himself off, he heard his phone ring with a RealTime request from an unknown number. He answered with audio-only and was met with, "Mr. Maslow, sorry to call you without notice, but my name is Brianne MacMahon. Your name was given to me by Jake Daniels. I was hoping to talk to you about an opportunity here in Vicksburg."

Jesus, that was fast, he thought. He composed himself a second, then said, "Yes, of course, thank you. Sorry, I didn't expect to hear from you so quickly."

"We're very efficient here, Mr. Maslow."

"Of course you are. If you give me a minute, I'll be ready for you."

"No problem at all."

Jeff scrambled to find his suit and threw it on without underwear. He turned on the video, and a crisp hologram of Brianne appeared in front of him—just her head, and at the same height, as if she were standing right there. Her blonde hair was in a bouffant, Jeff estimating at least three inches above her scalp, and though the holovids generally deducted twenty years, he suspected she was in her fifties. Her smile was friendly but formal.

"Hi, Brianne. Nice to meet you," he said.

"Again, sorry for the sudden intrusion."

"Not a problem at all."

"We rely heavily on the references of our trusted members, and Jake tells me you're a really smart guy living in his basement. How did that happen?"

With a smile, Jeff said, "Well, I made the mistake of trying to become an English teacher. Maybe not so smart after all."

Brianne nodded knowingly. "Well, who could have forecasted the profession's challenges when you entered your degree? Nonetheless, you are very well suited for what we are doing here. We are looking for capable men of mind and body. I'm assuming the standards at Loyola are still impressive, even if they were starting to stray a bit to the left at the start of the 2000s. Did you experience much of that?"

Jeff had been out west long enough to see the play. "Well, I was also in the English department, so it was even worse there. But let's face it: It was like that in most universities then. If you look into my background, you'll see I worked in finance, my dad worked for CFK Bank, and I moved out here for a reason."

"I see you were let go from your first teaching job in Baltimore. Unfortunately, there is no detail regarding why, as the school system is since defunct. What was that all about?"

Jeff knew this would come up at some point and was ready for it. His approach was to hover close enough to the truth, should something else appear about what had happened. "I'm glad you brought that up because it's another good example of why I'd work out well at your school. I was hired by the city right out of college, actually at the same school I did my student teaching. I started with freshman and sophomore English, so pretty much the standard curriculum for that time."

"Woke garbage," Brianne said.

He nodded in agreement. "Easy enough to deliver, but then my department chair came in a couple of times to observe and complained I wasn't giving the literature enough modern-day focus on things like slavery and multiculturalism, so she suggested for my next lesson that I cast *Macbeth* in that context."

"My Lord," she said, laughing. "What did you do?"

"I looked at her and said that it wasn't *Othello* and there were no Black people in Scotland at the time, so I couldn't do it, and also that it was inappropriate for her to pressure me to do that. I probably got a little hot about it because I couldn't believe it was happening."

"For good reason."

"I was still in my probation period, and because I didn't fall in line, she just let me go. That's when I decided to come out west."

Jeff was always impressed with this version of the story, especially as it was entirely the *opposite* of what had happened. His new department chair had been, in fact, a Dennison supporter hell-bent on removing the "liberal scourge" from education and had hired Jeff because he had thought, based on the interview, that Jeff was of like mind. When he came in to observe Jeff's lesson on the language of fascism, with a compare and contrast of Nazi propaganda to some of the modern-day essays pulled from *The Wall Street Journal*, he demanded a retraction and an apology for lying to his students, yelling at Jeff from across his desk, calling him a "fucking libtard" in the process. When Jeff jumped behind the desk and came up in his face, holding him by the collar, the department chair realized the error of his ways. Jeff was dismissed and knew he wouldn't get work in education anytime soon, so he went west. He took a job teaching on a reservation in Arizona and used that to justify a little too much time "finding himself" with various substances. Ten years of not finding himself brought him back to Denver, where he was able to get a job in banking operations. When detailed records were archived in the underfunded Baltimore Department of Education, he started looking for work in teaching, eventually landing in Boulder.

Brianne liked the answer. Very much. As her virtual face gleamed, Lily bounced through the door in her flight attendant uniform. She turned to find Jeff in his interview, saw Brianne's floating head, and quickly picked up on the scenario.

"Hi there," Lily said. "Sorry, didn't mean to interrupt."

"No problem at all, Miss . . . ?"

"I'm Lily."

"Lily and I are soon to be engaged," Jeff hopped in. "Just waiting to make sure I can provide before getting down on one knee."

"How lovely," Brianne said, still focused on Lily. "She's quite fetching. Well, Lily, you're just in time to hear me offer Jeffrey a job at our site in Vicksburg Gul—well, Vicksburg for now. Once we're done with our . . . renovations, we'll be rebranding the town." She returned her attention to Jeff. "Our approach to this project is somewhat unique, Jeffrey. We are looking for well-rounded individuals, men and women of strong moral fiber, capable of physical and intellectual labor. When we are done, it will be a thriving community engaged in some of the most important innovations of our lifetime. I hope I'm not selling this too strong."

Jeff nodded and said, "No, not at all. It sounds exciting."

"It is, very. We are inviting key individuals to help us fill the foundational roles necessary to sustain a modern, robust community. This will, of course, include teachers, and needless to say, we like your credentials and personal references. Don't seem to be any skeletons in your closet, either."

"Inviting?" Lily said.

"Ah, you picked up on that," Brianne said. "Yes, as a privately held operation, we will be able to apply certain . . . eligibility criteria to those who will make up our little community. Well, Mr. Maslow, it was excellent speaking with you. Let me know your decision as soon as you can."

Jeff thought for a moment and said, "Look, I won't play this game with you. You know what I'm doing now and where I'm living, and though everything's been great here at Mr. Daniels's place—"

Lily coughed.

"—I'm thankful he thought enough of me for the job, which I'd love to accept right now, if that's okay."

What Jeff was really thankful for was the money his father had spent on his going-away gift when he had left: a very expensive but thorough scrubbing of his online presence, after which he'd deleted all of his social media accounts.

Brianne's smile grew bigger. "Excellent news. I'm looking forward to you educating our children in a manner consistent with the values of this community."

"Can't wait," Jeff said as the hologram disappeared.

"How was your day, fiancé of mine? I was unaware I was lucky enough to be dating a man of *strong moral fiber*," Lily said.

He pulled her toward him in an embrace and said, "Thanks for that. Again, I'm not trying to push this. As I'm sure you've figured out, these people are very family-oriented, and I need this job. I figured you'd be okay with the line."

"Yes, I am aware. I've picked up the last three tabs."

"Wow, didn't think you were counting. As much as I have a shit-ton of misgivings about this thing they're describing, I'm just about at the point where I'll take anything. And, as you have rightly pointed out, I need to be able to take better care of you."

She gave him a peck on the cheek and said, "I'm starting to believe that line of bullshit. Take better care of yourself. I've got me under control."

Jeff looked down and performed a quick calculus before getting serious, holding her closer, and looking her in the eyes. "Point taken. So, I need to tell you something in that spirit."

"Uh-oh," she said.

"That job interview came at a cost."

It didn't take long for Lily to figure it out. "Landlady?"

"Yep. She got me upstairs this morning and threatened me if I didn't . . . take care of her."

She laughed. "Really? And did you?"

Looking down again, he said, "Have you heard of the Wholly Ghost?"

Lily went from scoffing in disbelief to hysterically laughing in an instant, needing to sit down on the couch, tears in her eyes while looking up at him for confirmation that he was serious. As she settled, she asked, "You didn't really?" Seeing he did, she added, "Oh my! Well, I have so many questions . . ."

Joining her in the humor of the situation, he said, "Well, I don't have many answers. It was brief."

She seemed to hold in another outburst. "That good, huh?"

"It was on the fritz. Backward. I jabbed her in the eye."

And with that, Lily lost it, falling off the couch and onto her knees with laughter.

In a moment of calm, Jeff asked, "Well, I guess I don't have to worry about you being angry?"

"Angry? This is the highlight of my week, though I wish you had the whole session. I'm dying to know what that silly device is like—and you're telling me a bug cut you short? Though it sounds like she paid the price."

Jeff nodded with mixed emotions. "It's been a crazy morning, Lil. Her, the job, Jake came down here. I'm a fucking mess right now."

"Good. Let me tell you about the naughty Dennison guys who talked dirty to me at fifty thousand feet on our way to Arkansas."

Jeff's eyes opened a little farther. "So this thing I just interviewed for? It's for Dennison too."

"They practically own the state at this point, so not a shock. It was a good day. My boss assures me he's got my back. We'll see if that holds true, but he did today. It was a plane full of frat boys."

Jeff, relieved of the guilt and tension and activities of the day, collected his thoughts for the first time and leveled out. The people upstairs and their connections. The state of everything around him. His unconscious reticence about this new endeavor that he almost had to take.

He lifted and carried her to the bed, happy he didn't drop her on a beer bottle. "Let's just pay attention for now, see what's going on, and take it from there."

"Oooh, I feel like a detective already," she said.

"Would you mind if I pick up where I left off before I was interrupted earlier?"

"Okay, but let me go get my glasses first so I don't get retinal damage!"

They both laughed and proceeded.

Chapter 12

May 26

After the European Union condemned his invasion of Mexico, President Dennison and his loyal Congress retaliated by banning their food in the United States. Restaurants could no longer brand themselves as Spanish, French, or even Italian, and an entire cottage industry of lawyers rose up, specializing in working around these restrictions so the whole sector could stay afloat. There was, after all, only so much barbecue the country could eat. All of them, as part of their title, legally added the word *American* to their cuisine. American Roadhouse. American Grill. American Diner. *Café*, however, was out.

To celebrate his new job, Jeff decided to take Lily out on a proper date at none other than Giovanni's American Flatbread Tavern, which featured everyone's favorite dish: wood-fired flatbread featuring several different toppings with cheese melted over them and a wide variety of red-gravy-covered noodles.

The host, formerly maître d', sat them at a table toward the back, his low expectations for a tip evident on his face and demeanor.

As they sat, Jeff said, "Well, at least he didn't spit on us."

Lily laughed as she joined him at the table. "It's amazing what passes for high-end these days."

"As long as they serve us. I'm starving. Actually took a run this morning." He looked around at the only semi-fancy restaurant that would fit his budget and wondered what Lily might be comparing it to, if she was comparing it to anything at all. "Eat at a lot of fancy restaurants growing up?"

"Yes, Jeffrey, on occasion, we would eat at a nice restaurant," she said with a knowing smile.

"We?" he said, returning the smile.

"My father and I, yes. Should I go dig up my autobiography?"

"Yes, why not?" Jeff tried to play his response off as an intentionally not-so-subtle request to learn more about her, but her expression only soured. He sighed, sitting back in his chair. "Look, I get it. You don't like talking about yourself—"

"Not about myself. About my past."

"Okay, fine, but don't look at me like I'm being nosy," he replied, and she only peered back at him without so much as blinking. "I almost feel the need to pry it out of you."

"We'll get there, Jeff. Just not yet."

"Okay. One last thing: Is there a body involved?"

She contemplated the question seriously before responding. "Dead or wounded?"

"Either."

"We'll get there, Jeff," she repeated, following it with a laugh to ensure he understood there was, indeed, no body.

The waiter arrived with the same attitude as the host. Without bothering to look up from his tablet, he said, "Drinks?"

"I'll have a cosmopolitan," Lily said.

"Manhattan," Jeff added, only for the waiter's eyes to shoot abruptly to his.

"I can serve you a whiskey with vermouth," the waiter said pointedly. All too quickly, Jeff recalled that the names of liberal enclaves—much like *Italian*, *spaghetti*, and *pizza*—were also verboten.

"Sure, bring me that. Sounds better than what I asked for."

The waiter departed.

"Finally decided to take me on a real date," Lily commented. "What do you have planned after this? A movie?"

"I hadn't thought about it, but sure, what would you like to see? The variety is endless."

Lily laughed at the sarcasm. With Disney forced to fire all known homosexuals, production had come to a screeching halt, and their under-staffed theme parks could not handle the volume. When their stock prices dropped to abysmal lows, Fox Corporation swept in and bought the whole company, changing the creative direction of their productions.

Playing along, she said, "I hear the new *Dead Liberal Poets* is up for an Oscar."

"How about the remake of *Beauty and the Beast*? Thank God they finally made LeFou go through conversion therapy! He was just too flamboyant."

Lily's expression darkened immediately.

"Hey, sorry," Jeff said.

"No, it's fine," she said as she pulled it together. "If it was a joke, it'd be different. The fact that it's real is what makes me sad." She sighed, then nodded at the menus before them. "You know what you're having? We want to make sure we have our order ready for when Mr. Happy arrives."

Jeff scanned the menu. "I'm thinking the noodle-tubes with Russian vodka sauce. You?" *Russian* was okay.

"I haven't had"—she looked both ways conspiratorially—"*pizza* in a while. So of course, I'm going to order the *American flatbread*."

"Good choice, madam. I mean, *miss*. You good?"

"Yeah. Guess I can't hide my past entirely, huh? I keep hoping everything will make a turn, but there's too much momentum, and it's all going one way."

The waiter arrived with their drinks, which he placed dismissively in front of them, then took their orders and left.

"Don't take this personally, Jeff," Lily went on. "We have this in common, at least. I haven't dated for a while, and I'm trying as much as possible to live in the present. But I have to admit that I have mixed feelings about your new job."

"Why is that?" he asked, though he could already guess.

"It's aligned with the Dennisons," she said, shrugging. "Which is to say, with everything wrong with the country."

"There's something to all this, right?" he said. "This Vicksburg community?"

She nodded in agreement. "Yep, and none of it good. We are in the belly of the beast. What are we going to do about it?"

"If I thought it would be any easier back home, I'd just move there, but it's not. If I'm honest, I want to see what's going on firsthand. I've only witnessed the consequences of all these bad decisions they keep shoving down our throats. Denver still seems somewhat normal, but this new thing . . . this sounds different. I want to know what they're up to, and I've got a rare chance to see it on the inside."

Lily considered his comments. "It worked out well, then, with me working in the Springs. I agree: We need to know. I'm tired of sitting on the sideline too. Let's investigate together and see what's going on down there."

Chapter 13

June 1

The following Sunday, Taggert sat on his throne next to his queen/wife, Mary—she on a slightly smaller, slightly lower, somewhat less shiny pseudo-throne. He listened to the hymns from the choir, "He's My Rock, My Sword, My Shield" ringing in his ears.

It was time for him to deliver the sermon. The congregation were returning to their seats, knowing another affirmation of their superiority was next on the menu. Just as he solemnly started to lean forward, there was a rustle of movement to his right. He froze, astonished, and fell back into the seat as the angelic smile of Iwanna Dennison blew kisses to the audience, her right hand waving as she approached the podium.

Just before she climbed the ten steps to the top—one for each commandment—she turned to Taggert, upped the smile, and blew one final kiss, putting her hands together in a praying gesture that warmly thanked him for the support.

His look that darted at the director quite clearly said, *What the fuck?*

Into the communications system, the director said, "Her security paved the way, and she just walked on!"

With all the vigor he could muster, Taggert waved a wholehearted "You're welcome!" to Iwanna as he sat back and gripped the lion-shaped ends of the armrests. It was only a small comfort that the applause for Iwanna was considerably loud, but not nearly what it would have been for Mary. Iwanna was not feeding the same rations they were.

Years of elite education, ballet, culture, and business acumen beamed from Iwanna as she thanked everyone and beckoned them to sit.

"Thank you so much!" she said. "I'm sure this is a surprise for all of you." She turned and nodded to her host. "But though it may have seemed unlikely, I'm not surprised that the reverend invited me here today to meet his beloved congregation. In fact, he *demanded* I come here in person to thank you!"

Polite but hesitant applause ensued, along with a smattering of "Amen!"

"First and foremost, I spoke to my father the other day to share the good news with him, and the first thing he said to me was, 'Please, tell everyone there I love them and thank them for their support.'"

There was a polite return.

"Okay, so enough of the teasing." Iwanna give them all a thin, flirty smile. "Me and the good reverend have been going at it for a while now because we both want to lead this state. I know I'm not from here, but when my daddy asked me to set up my life and business in the Springs, it was for a reason, and I did it obediently a little over twenty years ago. No, I am not from here, but at this time, I consider myself *of* here, and I couldn't be prouder."

Taggert heard it first: the start of a crescendo. His grip on the lions tightened.

"Reverend Taggert asked me to sit down with him earlier a couple of weeks ago, and we met at Wyatt Ranch to discuss our visions for the state and how we thought we could work together to achieve them. And you know what we found?" She looked back again and asked Taggert, "Do you want to take it from here, Reverend, or do you want me to continue?"

He nodded humbly and waved for her to proceed.

"We found," she said, "that our visions were the same! His through a lens of the Lord Jesus, mine through a lens of the country. After about an hour of discussion, we devised a plan. As it just so happens, Dennison Enterprises was preparing the grand opening of our newest, exclusive community not far from here in the mountains outside Colorado Springs. The reverend shared his desire to continue to spread the Lord's word, and I heard him. I shared my desire to use all the resources at my disposal to govern with the guidance of someone who best represents the Lord's interests here on Earth and in the great state of Colorado."

The crescendo began to grow.

"And it was obvious! Even though I'm sure he could have whooped me good in the primary, he suggested that he become the lead pastor for all the Dennison communities in the country and help me as the chief religious liaison in my administration, and I accepted his offer. We have sheathed our swords and will now work together, hand in glove, to ensure the ongoing prosperity of the body and soul of this state!"

Taggert wondered if the glove was rubber and who was wearing it.

The crescendo hit twelve, and Taggert, crying on the inside, stood up to join the throng.

Iwanna waited for the cheering to die down before saying, "Thank you all for your support, not of me but for the reverend and my father. I am just their vessel, and I humbly accept their support and guidance as I look forward to joining the family of conservative governors throughout this great land. We continue solidifying our hold at the state and federal levels. We are ensuring our destiny on Earth, making it ready for Jesus's return in the Rapture."

As the noise went to fifteen, Iwanna exited the stage and walked to the wings—and with her back to the crowd, she mouthed, "You're welcome," to the reverend and his bride. She stopped before the director, and through his earpiece, Taggert heard her curtly say, "Cue the ascension."

He glanced nervously at Taggert, who met his gaze with wide eyes, and heard her bark, "Don't fucking ask him! You heard me. I am *telling* you, run that shit you run at the end of every service!"

The director looked across the way at the special effects coordinator and nodded his approval. Outside, they heard the roar as a holographic Jesus—radiant, smiling, arms open and welcoming from the podium from which she had just come—slowly rose above the crowd, now waving, occasionally pointing as if he recognized someone, winking, rising higher as an additional hologram appeared of the sky at the top of the ceiling in the arena. Just before "exiting," he made a shooting gesture with both hands playfully into the crowd, blew the smoke out of each finger, holstered the invisible revolvers, then shot up into an imaginary sun as the sky closed behind him, leaving only the rafters and lighting equipment in his wake.

Fuck, thought Taggert. *That's a twenty.*

Chapter 14

June 3

For the first time in a while, Lily was excited about work. Today's flight was once again for Dennison Enterprises, and while she wasn't a big fan of the childish behavior and missed the old days when such displays were frowned upon, knowing she had the protection she needed made it easier. The pay was good for this market, she got to travel a bit, and if she was lucky, she'd get to go abroad.

She missed traveling. With the tariffs from the European Union and the general hostility toward Americans of all stripes, being able to do it within the confines of work at least minimized the risk of being harassed by locals. For today, though, she had the privilege of visiting the great state of South Dakota—Rapid City, specifically—well known as the Venice of the American West-Midwest.

Lily walked into the terminal at Meadow Lake Airport and stopped, very suddenly feeling nauseous.

"Hey, Job, how's it going?" she asked as she approached the TSA guard desk at the only gate. He wore a polished badge with a less polished expression, solemn, mechanical motions, eyes darting. He stood at

5 feet 6.5 inches in height and had a 48.25-inch waist, stretching the outer limits of standard government uniforms. She would have assumed he was a Dennison product but was pretty sure they weren't building bots at 280 pounds. He was actually 292.6.

"Good, Ms. Osbourne. Everything okay?" he asked. "You seem a little pale."

"I thought I was about to puke all over your nice clean floor, but other than that, I'm good."

She proceeded through the gate, passing through unseen scanners. The light at the stand turned red.

"Please wait a minute, Ms. Osbourne," Job said.

Lily stood there, confused. Surely there had to be some kind of a mistake. Why would she be setting off alarm bells?

He tapped the screen in front of him several times, read for another moment, and asked, "Can you please join me in the interview room, Ms. Osbourne?"

Zeke, who had walked through the gate moments after she had, joined them. "What's up?"

"Sorry, I need to discuss something with Ms. Osbourne privately before I can let her through. This should only take a few minutes," Job said, reassuring them both.

Zeke looked around and asked, "Lily, do you mind if he does it here?" Then to Job: "Is it a problem? The terminal is empty."

Lily, thoroughly confused, said, "I don't mind. You can tell me here."

Job debated for a moment before saying, "Okay, well, huddle up, at least." He gestured for them to come closer. He cleared his throat, fixing his eyes on Zeke instead of Lily as if afraid of addressing her directly. "It appears the young lady is with child—an unregistered child."

Lily burst out laughing. "Not possible, Job. I'm on the mag."

Job asked, "Are you claiming, then, that you are not sexually active?"

She was no longer laughing. "That is none of your fucking business, Job, but I'm telling you the mags are one hundred percent effective, and I'm not pregnant!"

Job stared at her and, after a moment, tapped his handheld tablet three times. They now heard emanating from the device a low, distant thump-thump: 123 beats per minute, 23.4 decibels loud, 43.5 hertz pitch.

"That is your child's heartbeat, Ms. Osbourne. Appears to be about six weeks. Are you claiming this is a virgin birth?"

And now Zeke was enraged. "You are way the fuck out of line here! Get me your supervisor, now!"

With the grin of the weak but empowered, Job said, "I'm sorry, Mr. Proctor, but he's unavailable right now. You are free to file a report at the airport site if you like. In the meantime, I'll be registering Ms. Osbourne's child for a Social Security number. You can wait over there."

Lily stood in silent disbelief, weighing the likelihood of the scan being an error, knowing it was certainly not. The technology had been around for too long. She had somehow taken a fert. It was the only way, and since she didn't own any ferts . . .

Could Jeff have done this in a desperate attempt to keep her in his life? She concluded that no, the idea of such a thing was sociopathic, and she was pretty sure Jeff wasn't a sociopath. But she had to remain open to the possibility.

As if delivering her a parking ticket, Job said, "I've registered the fetus in the system, which will notify your doctor." He approached with a hand-held device. "Please place your finger here so I can upload the baby's Social Security number."

Mind still racing, Lily complied without the reality of what she was doing setting in. Job's device let out a baby's giggle when it completed its task.

"You need to check in with your doc within the next ten days, and the system will take care of it from there. But don't miss it, or you'll be flagged in the statehouse." He tapped on his screen, and then the gate lights lit green. "Have a nice day," he said without sarcasm.

Lily went straight to Zeke's office, where he followed, closing the door behind him.

She said, "I've heard about this but can't believe it's real. Informed I'm pregnant by a TSA guard. Insanity!"

"If you'd waited around, he would have offered to do a pelvic exam," Zeke said, trying and failing to lighten the mood. "Sorry," he added, noticing her reaction. "With abortion a federal crime, they can use federal facilities to enforce it. You know your pregnancies need to be registered and synced up with your menstrual reports. If you're passing through an airport and they identify an unregistered pregnancy, they assume you're flying off for an abortion."

With simmering anger, Lily said, "But it's only six weeks."

"There's a heartbeat—"

"There is no heart!"

"True, no chambers and nothing that *looks* like a heart, but there is a tube that will become the heart, and it generates electrical pulses they have a sensor for." He gave her a once-over. "You still able to do the flight?"

It took her a moment to snap out of her deliberations. "Huh? Oh yeah . . . sure, I'm in. Just got to figure out what I'm going to do here."

Zeke looked at her as he sat at his desk, then turned to look at the photo behind him. "You do that," he said. "But before you make any final decisions, come see me first."

She looked up. "Why?"

His lips parted, about to provide her the answer, but he closed them with a grimace. "You decide your next steps. Then come see me. That's all I can say."

Two hours later, as they started their approach to Rapid City, Zeke asked, "Have you seen the monument since he changed it?"

"No, why would I bother?"

"Don't be shy about your politics, Lily," he said, smiling.

Catching herself, she said, "I know, you're right. I guess I just feel comfortable with you. But no, I haven't seen Dennison's addition. Why?"

"Go check on our guests and let them know we're on our approach. Then come back and sit right where you are."

She went out and returned after serving another round, still clearly distracted. "These guys just don't take a break, do they?"

"The medical advances for cirrhosis have made things easier for them." He looked outside to check their location. They dropped vertically out of a cloud layer just over Grizzly Bear Falls and hovered north at a reduced speed. He motioned her over to the window, and she saw it for the first time since the modification seven years ago in 2039.

"They put an office right here?" she asked Zeke.

"Yep. Great place to hold press conferences, don't you think—with your face in granite on the side of a mountain?"

She looked and laughed.

Leftmost was Washington, looking vaguely south and toward the Earth. He once said:

> *"However political parties may now and then answer popular ends, they are likely in the course of time and things, to become potent engines, by which cunning, ambitious, and unprincipled men will be enabled to subvert the power of the people and to usurp for themselves the reins of government . . ."*

Then Jefferson, looking southeast to the heavens, who once said,

> *"Bigotry is the disease of ignorance, of morbid minds; enthusiasm of the free and buoyant, education and free discussion are the antidotes of both."*

Roosevelt, harshly toward the forest of the east.

"I ask that high ideals be demanded in those that represent you; that you insist upon honesty and courage and uprightness and fair dealing in public life . . ."

Lincoln, tired, toward the southwest.

"There is no grievance that is a fit object of redress by mob law."

And Dennison, farthest to the right, almost behind Lincoln. A profile shot of him facing east, but with a little of his chest.

"Some guys tell me they prefer women of substance, not beautiful models. That just means they can't get beautiful models."

Lily laughed and said out loud, "Of course, the fucker is looking over his shoulder."

Chapter 15

June 4

Iwanna sat in her office, which, as an add-on to the original house at Cheyenne Mountain, was equipped with hover mobility. So, to be more precise, she was in her Cheyenne Mountain office parked in the middle of what would soon become the town square of Vicksburg Gulch, the first of the many RANDs opening nationwide.

While the physical locations were being prepared, emphasis was placed on the Vicksburg branch, both to ride the coattails of Iwanna's presumed nomination to be governor and to use it to demonstrate the Dennison vision of the future. With her in the governor's mansion, the modifications and additions to state laws and ordinances would be a much easier accomplishment.

Of course, like many things Dennison, this wasn't an original concept. The company town had existed in many iterations in the United States, most famously in Pullman, Illinois. Upon opening in 1881, it provided workers with above-average-quality housing at a reasonable price on a property that was walking distance to the factory in which they manufactured the famous Pullman railroad cars. The lesser-known project of this type was the vision of a cartoonist based in Florida who opened a theme park, which he felt qualified him to become an urban developer, although his proposal for an Experimental Prototype Community of Tomorrow in the mid-1950s was eventually shot down by the Disney board. It was to be a magical place where only employees would be allowed to live, which would have most certainly reflected the company's demographics at large. Like Celebration, but Whiter. Instead, it was later taken off the trash heap and converted to another theme park, named after its acronym: EPCOT.

Now, Iwanna's vision was coming to life in a former ghost town nestled in the Colorado Rockies, created in the gold rush in the 1800s. The first wave of renters in the community gathered just outside her doors to watch her cut the ribbon that would trigger the opening.

Iwanna's early plans for the RANDs coincided perfectly with Dennison's acquisition of a small AI security company, Tactical AI Solutions, that had developed early versions of what they now sold as the FlyingFortress line of drone/AK-47 hybrids—"for those times when face-to-face isn't an option." The manufacturing facility was eventually converted for Charity's weaponized BuzzKills, complete with a metallic stinger that, in its initial deployment, would only be used to prick the trespasser. They were programmed to fly in predetermined formations, starting at twenty-five units, that could patrol long lengths of border and detect heat, motion, and sound; alert a human agent back in the United States; and carry out whatever orders necessary for the situation. There were prototypes of a version that could inject the target with neurotoxins that would paralyze them, then permit a larger drone to lift the subjects and fly them back to the other side of the border. Versions that could kill on contact were also blackboarded at the administration's request, the resulting analysis since classified.

As things developed around the world and the "America First" vision was brought into actuality, there was no need to deploy the bees to the southern border for one simple reason: No one was trying to get in. The government then opened the sale of the bees to foreign countries with similar problems, with an extensive menu of customizations. Canada was one of the first customers.

The plan for Vicksburg—now Vicksburg Gulch, at Iwanna's direction—was not only to create a community for Dennison employees but one that leveraged the new AI robot technologies in development for the last several years. The most important and booming developments of those early years related to the manufacturing of highly realistic human robots, believable in movement and facial expression. The missing piece was the combination of the AI brains with the waiting bodies in which to place them. The critical feature was the training mechanism itself, leveraging modern surveillance technology to convert the observations of humans in their natural state into the personalities of the robots, giving them generalized behavior in everyday social settings along with specialized knowledge of whatever task they were designed to perform. They had footage of hundreds of occupations, from barista to lawyer. In the legal field, the emphasis was corporate, but civil would certainly not be far behind, with customization in all practices and jurisdictions. In other words, Dennison targeted autonomous services in the blue- *and* white-collar realms. It would take other companies years to catch up to the amount of data to which Dennison Robotics had access through government surveillance, by which time Dennison had cornered the nascent market.

Just outside her door, Iwanna's beta team was preparing the ice cream shop attendant bot to demonstrate Vicksburg's wonders to employees who had already accepted the invitation to move to the town.

She stood across from the lead project manager, Anatoly Boyko, who had been with the company since the start—a junior engineer from back when Charity ran the project. He came to the US in 2025 when he was forced to leave his home country of Ukraine, released in a prisoner exchange after being held for five months and tortured by the Russians to obtain knowledge about the militarized drone program that he ran in Kyiv, which he never revealed. The State Department, when reviewing his case, flagged him to Iwanna, who scooped him up for Dennison Robotics.

"We've got the bot perfectly synchronized with your speech, Ms. Dennison," he reported in a mild, firm tone, his accent still slightly detectable. "As you speak, it will go to next step in the demonstration, so you deliver it as written, and she will take it from there."

"Any chance of a screwup here?" she asked.

With enough pause to make her look up from the tablet she was reading during the presentation, he said, "No, ma'am. We've run dozens of rehearsals. It will be great, and there's so much more to come."

"Good to hear. Thank you."

"Yes, ma'am." He started to exit backward, caught himself, turned, and walked out.

Chapter 16

Lily sat in the living room of her spacious, single-story bungalow, the Amazon Body Scanner fired up and ready to be remotely controlled by her gynecologist, who was scheduled to call in three minutes. Her father insisted on only the best for his kids, provided he didn't need to deliver it himself, so her doctors were located in either New York or Boston, with high-speed planes commuting Lily for appointments when she had lived in Austin as a teenager.

She fidgeted with her hair that was pulled up into a bun, then put her hands on the chair's armrests, then fixed her hair, then asked herself why she gave a crap about what her gynecologist thought about her appearance and put her hands forcefully to her sides.

As she started to think about the stark reality of being a mother, the holovid rang, and she answered. A Black woman in her sixties appeared in a half-body hologram four feet in front of her.

"Hi, Dr. Spector," she said, receiving a warm, compassionate smile. "How're things in New York?"

"Hi, Ch—" Her long-time doctor corrected herself. "*Lily.* It's been a long time." She took Lily in, studying her face carefully. "Wow, they really did a great job on your surgery. Subtle, enough to change your facial scans. But they kept . . . your beauty. Your spirit."

"Thank you, Doctor. That's nice of you to say. I've adjusted well enough."

"I have to say, I was surprised by the reason for today's appointment. Is this cause for celebration?" Seeing Lily's heart firmly on her sleeve, she continued, "Oh, I see. And in Colorado."

"Yeah, and it makes no sense. I don't even own ferts."

Dr. Spector turned somber as she looked at what Lily presumed was an unseen tablet. "Well, I'm here and have no idea how things are out west, so I'm only basing this on rumor. I have known you and your family long enough to be comfortable asking this question. Is it safe to assume you're not religious anymore?"

"Yes," she said. "Safe to assume." She managed a smile.

"So you haven't been around any congregations over the last few months?"

"No. Why?"

"Well, what we hear through our channels are instances of deeply religious people slipping ferts in the drinks or food of women they suspect are on mags to punish them for being sinners. And to bring another child into the world."

"Right, as Jesus would do. How screwed up is that?" Lily said.

"Yeah, it's pretty bad—and *very* hard to prove."

"Well, I can assure you I haven't been in a pew since my father's third marriage."

"Ah, how is he these days?" Dr. Spector asked, perking up.

"No idea. We're in one of our distant phases."

"Well, that's easy to believe," Dr. Spector said with a smile. "That's the lifestyle he's pulling off."

Lily changed the subject, used to having people prying about her father. "This makes no sense. I can't think of a single person who might . . ."

She froze, looked down, and shook her head back and forth, the realization only sinking deeper with every shake. "No, no way." After more thought, she looked up and said, "Yeah, I know where I got it. Mystery solved."

"You think somebody intentionally slipped you a fert?"

"I don't think—I *know*," she said with certainty, "and I'll find a way to deal with him. But in the meantime, what are my options?"

Now it was time for her doctor to look uncomfortable. "Well, they've documented the fetus, so they'll keep treating it like a living human from this point forward." Then, in the tone of someone who thought they might be monitored, she added, "I'll be honest, there are no options that I can see, but I do want to check you out. Can you turn on the scanner?"

"All ready to go," Lily said, letting "no options" sink in. She sat back, hoping against hope that maybe, with the long-term relationship she'd established with Dr. Spector and her familial connections, there might be some wiggle room.

Dr. Spector remotely controlled the scanner, a device Amazon had put on the market ten years ago that remotely provided the equivalent of a functional MRI. Though pricey at the outset, the company worked with insurance companies to make it a household appliance available to any medical professional. They managed to fight off government attempts to break their patent—Dennison looking for one more way to profit from another firm's intellectual property.

Lily saw the change in Dr. Spector's expression. The scanner's rays focused on the top right region of her abdomen, then zoomed in to a smaller and smaller radius. Then it turned off.

"Okay. So, there's a problem, Lily . . ."

Jeff opened the door to his apartment and let in Lily, her eyes swollen and red. She went straight into his arms and limply hugged him, devoid of energy, her emotions spent on the ninety-minute walk to get there and trying to make sense of her predicament.

Enforcement of the federal abortion laws tended to vary from state to state, and particularly in the Southwest, claims of miscarriage were investigated as murders. With modern medical tech as good as it was, the presumption was almost always an intentional loss of the fetus, and prosecutions with a jury of peers were often successful.

He held her quietly as she shivered in his embrace.

"So, which do you want first," she managed to ask into his side, "the bad, the worse, or the insane?"

"I'm a big fan of insane, so let's get that one out first."

She snorted with laughter, again into his side, and said, "That bartender—Taggert's kid—put a fert in my drink."

Jeff jolted back, his hands still holding her shoulders, trying to suppress the simmering volcano of rage that was building inside him. He wanted desperately to hold it together for her but was already largely failing. "I think I can guess the second one now."

"Yep."

And then he went through the same processing she had at the airport, reaching the same conclusion she had been dealing with for the last two days. He let go of her shoulders to pace the room, looking down at his fists. "I'm going to *kill* that motherfucker," he said quietly.

"Not what I need right now, Jeff," she said.

He didn't respond immediately, as if finishing in his head the plan to kill Koy, but then looked up and saw her expression. He calmly returned in front of her. "I can't even imagine what the third is."

"It's ectopic," she said. Noticing that the implication didn't register immediately, she explained, "The embryo is in my fallopian tube."

And then it hit him.

"That's dangerous, right?"

"Yep."

"And let me guess: They don't care."

"Nope, they don't."

He thought more. "What about out east?"

"It's up to the states. With the fetus registered here, their rules apply. If I had the surgery in New York, Colorado would demand they extradite me for murder."

"What are you supposed to do?"

Exasperated, Lily said, "Let the miscarriage happen naturally."

"But—"

"Yes, it could kill me," she said bluntly.

She leaned back into him, and they held each other silently, contemplating her reality.

Chapter 17

"And so, my new fellow citizens," Iwanna began, standing before an audience of approximately six hundred people, "I welcome you to Vicksburg Gulch, a place we could only dream of a decade ago. Here, we don't need walls to keep us safe. Of course, because of my father's success, we don't need them at the border anymore, either!"

The definition of a negative net migration seemed to be an unimportant distinction to the Gulch's newest citizens. There was a smattering of polite applause regardless, which Iwanna felt was ungrateful, considering the fact that every new citizen had been handpicked.

She cleared her throat and continued. "I can't begin to tell you how excited I was when my father asked me to take over the Western region of Dennison Enterprises, not just because of the beautiful countryside and beautiful people, but because it was a part of the country that once again represented the spirit of entrepreneurship and adventure the West has always stood for. This is where people came for opportunity and made it one of the greatest states in the nation. And now, as I humbly seek your nomination for governor, I have the opportunity to lead the citizens of this state as their representative while also providing them the chance to be part of something unique, something special—something unseen on Earth. You accepted our invitation to live here because you knew it would be a chance to live side by side with your fellow Americans. *Real* Americans!"

She allowed her words to settle in with the audience before continuing.

"You may have noticed there are no gates around our community, and that's because you will all be protected by the Dennison Robotics patrol BuzzKills, which we've repurposed after our successes at the border."

A swarm of ten bee drones flew down from above in perfect formation, horizontally lined just above Iwanna's head and flashing alternately. Then they formed a cross that shone brightly, and several in the crowd fell on their knees and began rambling unintelligibly. The bees re-formed over the group in a halo and then shot straight up into the heavens.

"Don't they make you feel safe?" Iwanna said. "So, aside from the affordable and beautiful housing we've delivered here, we will also be standing up new businesses to provide you with your every need. You'll wonder if you ever have to leave Vicksburg Gulch!"

The audience cheered, making their approval clear.

"Except to go to work, of course!" she added, noting a decrease in enthusiasm. "You'll be the first to meet our debut line of service bots, who are here at your command to provide you with your needs, whatever they may be. And it just so happens I've brought one along with me!"

From the curtain behind Iwanna walked out Queenie, looking like she had just finished serving a vanilla cone in 1956. Her movement was perfectly natural. Her blue eyes and blonde hair matched well with her 32Cs, which, though well covered and without cleavage, poked prominently through the tight blouse featuring the Dennison Dessert's logo just slightly above the left breast. She beamed and waved to the crowd like a pageant winner accepting her crown.

"Hi there, Queenie," Iwanna said.

"Hi, Ms. Dennison. Thanks for having me here!" The developers clearly favored a more Southern than Western accent.

"It's great to have you here!" To the crowd, Iwanna added, "Anyone in the mood for some ice cream?"

On cue, a ten-year-old girl with pigtails waved her hands. "I am! I am!"

Iwanna motioned her up to the stage, bent onto one knee, and put out her hand. "My name's Iwanna. What's yours?"

"Stephanie."

"Hi, Stephanie. Do you like ice cream?"

Stephanie's eyes lit up immediately. "I *love* ice cream!" she said, much to the crowd's delight, though Iwanna would have preferred a reduced amplitude as she wiped the spittle from her nose. "But my mommy almost never gives me any because she says I'm a little bitch sometimes."

The crowd gave a divided reaction, half gasping in shock, the other half hooting at the precocious young lady. Iwanna was distinctly in the former category and shot a look at Anatoly that asked, *Who the hell picked this kid?* However, knowing it was scripted and that the robot was awaiting its cue, she trudged along.

"Well, I'm glad you like it because our Dennison robotic assistant here can probably help with that. Her name is Queenie. Like Dairy Queenie." While winking at the crowd, she added, "Don't worry, they won't sue us! Why don't you go ask her for some?"

Without hesitation or thanks, Stephanie walked over and barked, "Give me a double scoop of mint chocolate chip on a sugar cone!"

There was another smattering in the crowd who thought this was a darling exchange. They watched with smiles as Queenie said, "It would be my pleasure," with a perfect tone and facial expression. Queenie walked behind the freezer, grabbed a sugar cone from the counter, and scanned the options. "You sure you don't want vanilla or chocolate?" she asked. "I have what you requested but want you to know there are other options."

"I said mint chocolate chip! Whatareya, deaf?"

Iwanna watched the robot closely during this exchange and froze. What was it she saw on Queenie's face? Was it . . . a flash of annoyance?

She walked back to Anatoly and whispered, "Cute kid. That was the best you could do?"

He replied, "Unfortunately, yes. The others were worse."

"So all of Queenie's behavioral programming came from the surveillance of people in towns with similar demographics as we have here?"

"Well, Ms. Dennison, there's a baseline code we start out with, sort of a vanilla personality that can't be attributed to any one place. But then, for the bots that will be working here, we thought it would be better if the town thinks of the bot as one of their own. So yes, Queenie should fit right in. Why do you ask?"

"Give me another one!" Stephanie shouted, the remnants of the bottom scoop around her mouth, the top scoop on the floor.

Iwanna said, "Because I could have sworn . . ." She stopped to watch Queenie observing the situation, not moving, smile gone while looking sternly at Stephanie. "Are you sure they can't go south on us? Be *too much* like what they see in the surveillance?"

Queenie said, "I'd prefer if you ask nicely, missy."

"No, definitely not, Ms. Dennison," Anatoly said, albeit with less conviction.

"Look at her!" Iwanna said.

Stephanie shouted, "Screw you! They told me you were a robot. I don't have to kiss no robot's ass. Give me another cone! This one was broken!"

"Shut her down, now!" Iwanna commanded.

Anatoly started to dart behind the curtain but tripped on a raised board on the impromptu stage, falling on his face.

Queenie put the smile back on and said, "Certainly." She grabbed another cone, filled it with two scoops of chocolate, and walked around to stand over Stephanie. "You sure you don't want to ask nicely?" she asked sweetly.

"Gimme! *Now!*"

Queenie turned the cone in her hand, raising it in a daggerlike fashion, scoops in front, and shoved the cone in Stephanie's face. "Get some manners, you little trailer park bitch!" She rotated and swiped the cone up, down, and all around to ensure she covered her face thoroughly.

There was a sudden frenzy of activity. Then, a familiar alarm, followed by *"Anger detected!"*

Anatoly watched, frozen, visibly fearing what would happen to him when this was all over.

Stephanie pulled out a .22-caliber handgun from under the belt of her dress—which wasn't quite as surprising as it should be, given nine was the legal carry age in Colorado. With the other hand, she wiped the melted ice cream from her eyes, replacing them with tears as the crowd laughed and hollered. Like Jesus would.

Thirty people in the crowd drew their various weapons, one burly man unsheathing an AR-45 from under his long coat, all aiming at the nine-year-old girl. It occurred to some they were risking killing a child to protect a bot, but the scenario had played out so many times over the years that their responses were automatic.

Queenie smiled as Stephanie pulled the trigger and the round bounced off Queenie's head and ricocheted into the crowd—entering fifteen-year-old Cody Wappinger's brain.

As Iwanna's security detail tackled Stephanie to the ground, Queenie leaned over the girl with a menacing sort of smirk. "Of course they built me bulletproof, you little twat." Then she walked behind the curtain to Anatoly and said, "Goin' on a cigarette break," just as he hit the Shut Down button on the remote control tablet. All movement stopped, and her eyes closed.

The roar from the crowd drowned out Stephanie's tantrum in full progress on the stage—crying, screaming, swearing, kicking, punching—all fed from the laughter that was everywhere until it wasn't, as they found Cody bleeding out on the floor.

Chapter 18

Lily left the locker room at the airport for a quick flight to Fort Worth, this time with one of the other four pilots at Liberation Air—a hotshot former Space Force captain from California. This was the third pilot she'd met and the third one from a coastal state. Zeke, who had just walked toward her through the doors from the tarmac, was hiring like-minded staff.

Iwanna would be so amused, Lily thought, by her current circumstances, and she wondered if it was even possible that Iwanna had engineered it. She decided it was not. And though she knew that their situations were very different, Lily regretted her reaction to Iwanna's revelation so many years ago.

This is such a vulnerable state to be in: a life inside you, with the world outside enforcing its will on your mind and body. Iwanna truly had no one and was asking for help. And all I gave her was dogma, Lily thought. *False dogma, at that.*

It took Zeke a single glance to know Lily was not in her usual frame of mind, so he escorted her through the door of his open office and closed it behind them, choosing to sit next to her.

"How do you feel?" he asked.

"Mostly okay, but there's some pain on occasion." She paused, giving him a hard look. "Turns out there's a funny hitch to the whole thing."

"I suspect not so funny."

"Nope. The pregnancy is ectopic."

And unlike Jeff, Zeke instantly understood the dangerous scope of her circumstances and let out a gasp of frustrated air. "Jesus, you're kidding me."

"Nope."

"The boyfriend know?"

"Yeah, I told him, and he's just as angry as I am."

Zeke contemplated a moment before saying, "I am not prying here, but you *are* aware of how this happened, right?"

"Yes, of course. I had it under control, but someone decided to screw that plan up."

"It had better not be what I've been hearing about," he said.

"If you're hearing that monsters are going around with ferts up their sleeve, then yes."

Her words seemed to hit him like a punch. He folded forward, burying his face in the space between his knees, and started to cry.

"This used to be my community," he told her. "I believed, mostly. But more than that, these were my family, my friends. We all knew each other, marked time with each other. Sure, as I got older, my faith faded, and as I . . . learned more about who I was, some of the teachings became problematic, but I did not lose my family over them. I was still accepted."

Lily held his hand as he continued.

"Then all of this came. The hatred. Then it took power, first over our politics, then over our religion. Now over—"

"Everything," Lily said.

"Everything. I didn't think anyone in my community could do something as evil as this. But here you are." He sat up and tried to compose himself. "And now I'm crying about your situation, which isn't helping."

"It's okay. I know you've been suffering too."

"I didn't think anyone would be so observant to notice that pin in the photo. I think I left it there in defiance of what they've done to us . . . put us in hiding to serve what they think their God wants."

"It's evil to claim to speak on behalf of God."

"It only took one beating from the Triple G to make me take that pin off my lapel."

"Good Guys with Guns did that?" she asked.

"No, Good Guys with *God*. They get confused all the time."

"So they beat you on behalf of God. Does it click with any of them how ridiculous that is to anyone who has actually read, studied, and followed Jesus's teachings?"

"This is their community, just like it was mine. The leaders believe what they want for their own profit, and everyone else falls in line."

"So many good guys out here . . ." She laughed.

"Yeah, it's amazing we even need cops anymore. What made it worse was that I knew the beating came from a competitor, some local Air Force guy who was getting financing to start a private air service. I was only two years in, still struggling to get clients, and he got word about me, then used a buddy of his in that vigilante group to send the message. That Jesus sure knows how to swing a pipe."

"Unbelievable."

"It was clear which direction things were going, so it was either pack up or get in the closet."

"Iwanna was the one who gave you the big break?" she asked.

"Indirectly. Those thugs made the mistake of giving me my lesson in the airport parking lot. After they left, I just sat there bleeding, deciding if I should go to a hospital, and her right-hand man, Hal, came out of the terminal. He was shocked to find me there. I didn't tell him why it happened, but he drove me to the hospital. On the ride over, I told him about my start-up, and he convinced Iwanna to give me the contract. Dennison was just starting to expand, so they were doing a lot of traveling."

"See, those good guys got you the big gig. You should be thanking them."

As if coming out of a trance, Zeke said, "I took over the conversation. But I'm glad. I haven't told anyone outside of my family that story. Anyway, you guys decide what you're going to do?"

"I have an option that he's not aware of, one I'd prefer not to use. Of course, I will, but then again, you told me to make my decision and then talk to you first." Lily began to tear up as her temporary escape from her situation ended. She said as if pleading to a judge for mercy, "So whatya got, boss?"

He leaned toward her and took both of her hands in his. "The only option is surgery, but you know that."

"Yep."

He returned to his desk to grab his tablet, tapped a few times, and appeared to be typing a message. She watched in tense silence as he got his answer, then looked at her. "I'm going to need you to take a flight for me next week. Can you do that?"

"Sure, of course. I work for you."

"It'll be fully automated. No pilot. You just go into the cockpit, and it will take you to the chosen destination."

Her disappointment at the apparent change of topic started registering, and he took her hands again.

"You have to go meet a friend of mine," he said. "In Mexico City."

Lily smiled and nodded.

Chapter 19

Iwanna's father and brothers had hard-earned reputations for losing their tempers, but Hal knew Iwanna well enough to know that wasn't her style. He'd witnessed her raise her voice once—at her brother, Junior, the current vice president of the United States—and he'd more than deserved it. But for the whole situation with Queenie, Hal wasn't sure what to expect. Each outcome was equally terrifying. For all the bluster of her male family, Iwanna's quiet bite was often far worse.

"Do you have anything *remotely* close to a good explanation for what happened out there?" Iwanna asked Hal as soon as she stormed into his office.

He leaped out of the leather chair he'd been sitting in as if propelled by a spring. "No, ma'am, I don't. I trusted Anatoly, and he failed me."

"Sounds like you're not accepting responsibility."

"Not at all," he remarked. "I'm responsible to you, and I failed as well. I've already begun making plans to replace him. I fear that won't be easy, however, what with his exposure to all our proprietary knowledge. He's been around since—" He stopped immediately and said, "I promise he will be dealt with. We'll find someone else."

"And are you *sure* there's no way to get it out of his head?" She feigned thought, hooking a finger on her chin like a stereotypical philosopher. "To get it out of his head, *keep* it out of his head, and ensure no one can ever get to it afterward?"

Hal swallowed hard, realizing she was unapologetically implying the worst.

He watched as she approached her tablet and began scrolling through online accounts of the story. He carefully read over her shoulder. To his relief, the majority called it a minor incident at a new Dennison start-up and avoided details of what had effectively been an assault on a minor, even in some cases turning it into a positive reflection of the lengths Dennison will go to provide for their people, essentially shifting to the RANDs and how good it was for the company to provide low-cost, high-quality housing for their employees. But the few others—those not under direct influence from the party, no doubt—had a more accurate depiction of the event, complete with a photo and video clip of the moment of icy impact. And Cody being put into the ambulance.

"I thought I told you to get those photos back from *The Denver Sun*?" she asked.

"He got it to the newsroom fast."

"Find out who wrote the article and put him on the list for when I take office. For now, call them a deepfake."

"Yes, ma'am."

She tossed the tablet toward the desk, and the magnet lifted it to safety. "I try not to run things like my family. You know that, right?"

Still at attention, he said, "Yes, I do."

"What would happen to you if this happened to Junior?"

Without hesitation, he said, "VD. And an anti-bonus."

American corporations had, with the lifting of several onerous laws and regulations that made it difficult to straighten out the occasional employee who fucked up, relaxed their corporate policies to reflect a more 1960s perspective. Dennison Enterprises had more leeway than most, implementing the corporate retraining program called Virtual Discipline to remind employees of their responsibilities to the company. He had never had to do this before, his role as personal assistant to Iwanna allowing him to avoid such things. He had heard it framed as a simple company policy training regimen delivered within a virtual world that leveraged modern psychological research to reinforce the policies and consequences of failure at Dennison. He'd also heard it was like waterboarding, but without the water. The far more benign anti-bonus was just that: a clawback of a percentage of your last bonus, depending on the severity of the screwup.

"What do *you* think should happen here?" Iwanna asked icily.

"Those sound fair."

"I'm going to suspend the sentence for now."

"Entirely up to you, Ms. Dennison. I understand either way but appreciate that you are considering delaying. I would like nothing more than to demonstrate my ongoing value to you and the company."

She got up from behind her desk and stood before him, softening her voice. "Hal, you've been great. What you've done on this project cannot be matched, and this is your first mistake, so let's see how things go for the next few weeks—which are, needless to say, critical to our success. I am sure you'll make up for this incident. Just take care of that family with the brat."

"That has already been seen to, Ms. Dennison. They have been offered three months rent-free in their apartment."

Iwanna visually cringed at giving away profit, but after thinking about it for a moment, she seemed to agree it was the best option. "Okay, that sounds right. Throw in a free ice cream at the shop."

"Good thinking."

"As far as Anatoly is concerned, he will be hard to replace. Perhaps he should have a refresher?"

Hal had thought it might come to that. "I'll make it happen. A level two?"

"One. We don't want to break him, but that can't happen again."

"Understood. I'll make the arrangements."

Chapter 20

June 6

It was a beautiful day when Jeff moved into his apartment in Vicksburg Gulch, which turned out to be a perfectly reasonable and comfortable one-bedroom with a balcony looking west through the valley, which still retained some of the lush greenery that he was sure had been far more abundant a year ago. *How the hell did they clear all of this out?* he wondered as he surveyed the landscape around the complex.

Lily came out to join him, silently taking in the scenery.

After a bit, she asked, "We making a mistake with this little adventure?"

He didn't answer immediately, unsure of what he believed. "We can't drive ourselves crazy about how we got here. The reality is that what's going on is happening everywhere, and it's even harder to get our line of work out east. If anything, we're just getting a preview of what they're planning for the rest of the country. Living here, living elsewhere—honestly, I'm not sure it matters."

"I heard things didn't go well for our illustrious leader the other day. Apparently, she tried to demonstrate some new AI, and it went apeshit. Assaulted a little girl."

"What the hell does AI have to do with this town?"

"You need to do your homework. All the shops here will be manned by Dennison robots."

"Let me guess: in Dennison-owned shops," Jeff said.

"Uh-huh. They've cornered the market. So much for free enterprise. I'd hold off on ordering an ice cream until they've worked out the bugs," she said with a bit of a smirk.

"Good advice." He let some time slip by, enjoying the view. For what it was worth, this new living arrangement was quiet and private, for all he could tell. He looked at Lily. "You okay if we talk about your . . . issue?"

Once again, she hesitated, and once again, he noticed. He could only assume a part of her didn't want to involve him at all, but he had a right to know, even with the condition of the pregnancy. He couldn't help but wonder what she'd be thinking if the pregnancy was viable.

"Zeke is offering to help me," she said, "and I get the impression it's not his first time."

"How?"

"Fly me down to Mexico, where he has a connection." She was relieved to see the relief on Jeff's face.

"Well, Mexico has the best medical system in North America, so it makes perfect sense. I'm coming with you," he said.

"No, there's no need to risk the two of us. It's bad enough Zeke's involved. I don't need to worry about the both of you being brought up on murder charges."

Jeff's expression didn't change as he replied, "Accessory to murder. I checked." Then, firmly, he looked her in the eye and said, "I'm going with you. Not up for discussion. You are not alone in this, and someone should be there with you."

It was the first time Jeff had made anything close to a demand in their relationship, and he had to admit that he liked the way she was responding to it. She seemed genuinely relieved, impressed, and also maybe even a little turned on by his confidence.

"Why don't we go take a walk through your little hamlet?" she asked, taking his hand and leading him to the door.

<hr>

The fifteen-minute hike to town was teeming with people enjoying the beauty of their surroundings and the luxurious appointments of the new buildings and businesses. Jeff had assumed the Gulch would be a haven for the wealthy, but that did not seem to be the case. There was no advertising about the many residential properties going up for rent and sale. Yet the believers were coming, arriving in pickup trucks, not private jets.

As they walked past the ice cream shop's overhang, he saw what he thought was a minor flaw in the otherwise perfect woodwork: practically a dot at 9.3 feet above the ground. He took a closer look and noted that it didn't take long to get the cameras up and running.

Suddenly, a metallic bark caught his ear to his right, and they watched a robo police dog approach a couple walking on Main Street. It was the size of a typical German shepherd: 25.3 inches in height, 42.7 inches in length. It broke its canine character to ask the pedestrians in a gentle, harmless voice, "Identification, please."

The couple looked at each other, not nearly shocked enough, and touched the head of the dog so it could read their digital implant with an identity scanner. As they did, a uniformed police officer approached.

"Hey, folks, sorry about that."

"*Are* you?" the Black male asked as he took his finger off the dog's head.

"I know what this looks like, but honestly, we just got these things in, and I have no control over how they're programmed. This town is privately owned, so the chief has to take the tech they give him. I was told that they should learn over time and specialize in picking things out of the norm for their environment."

"Like Black people in this town?" the woman asked.

Maintaining his smile, but clearly caught off guard by the couple's forward response, the officer said, "Well, yes, I suppose that's right." Then, looking at the dog patiently observing this interaction, he said, "Orren, come." As the dog sidled up to his master of the moment, the officer caught sight of Jeff and Lily. With an even less welcoming smile, he asked, "Anything I can do for you . . ." He appeared to wait for input and then, after receiving it, added, "Mr. Maslow?"

Surprised by the sudden attention, Jeff stuttered, "M-m-me? No, not at all. We were taking a walk."

"Well, you're going so slow it almost looks like you're watching something that doesn't concern you."

Jeff stared at the officer, debating whether to respond. He was getting tired of being spoken to like a child, and though he wasn't quite sure of the capabilities of the metal canine, he calmed himself quickly enough to disengage, look at Lily, smile, and continue their walk without being bitten. Or worse.

"To protect and serve," he muttered as they pulled out of earshot. He looked up ahead, and his heart dropped with fear. "Oh fuck," he whispered. "It's her."

As always, not missing a beat, Lily said, "Sugar mama?"

"Not now, Lil. This is dangerous."

They were on a collision course with Cheryl and Jake that could not be avoided. Right before impact, he put on a brave face.

"Hey, guys! I was wondering when we'd run into each other." He reached out his hand to Jake. "When did you move in?" He maintained his focus on Jake, not risking a glance at Cheryl.

After the firm-gripped reply, Jake said, "Last Sunday. What'ya think?"

"It's beautiful. Perfect. Still can't thank you enough."

"No need. We demanded, you supplied. Who's the young lady?"

Jeff stuttered, realizing he had zoned out. "This is my girl . . . fiancée, Lily."

"Oh really!" Cheryl said, walking over to Lily for an embrace but keeping her eyes on Jeff. "When did you pop the question, big guy? Congratulations, dear!"

Watching the hug with horror, he said, "Um, last weekend. Seemed as good a time as any."

"Well, good for you, honey. He's quite the catch. Especially now that he has a paying job and a new place to live," Cheryl said, patting Jake's chest. "That my man got him."

"Yeah, it all seems to have worked out great," Lily said, unfazed by Cheryl's obvious little game.

"So, when do you start classes?" Jake asked.

"Middle of August. I think the roster is up to ten."

"That's great. What do they have you teaching?"

"Journalism and American English. They don't seem too strict on my credentials."

Jake looked at Cheryl with a smile. "Yeah, well, you'll find that's generally true around here. We prefer to make our own decisions. Don't need any government dorks telling us how and what to teach our kids."

"Yep," Jeff said.

Jake had enough and grabbed Cheryl's hand. "Well, hope it all goes good." With a glance at Cheryl, he said, "You know, some of these kids today can be real assholes." While her husband started forward, Cheryl snickered and, as she followed, tweaked Jeff's nipple harshly as they began their stroll.

Once they were out of range, Lily asked, "She pay you a visit yet?"

Jeff flushed and stared at the sky as his blood pressure slowly decreased. "Not funny."

"Sorry."

"She's batshit, and I'm not sure she cares if she gets caught. But if he finds out, he will disembowel me all over this street."

"Can I get the apartment if he does?"

She had succeeded in bringing him down. "No. You're not a Dennison employee. You'll be out on your ass in a heartbeat, and I'm sure they'll be very efficient about it."

Lily approached, squeezed his cheeks, and gently kissed him. "It was virtual, and all you did was poke her in the eye. You're good." And then, with a genuine smile, she added, "I'm glad you're coming with me to Mexico. Thanks."

Chapter 21

Jeff sat in the kitchen drinking a Florida coffee that tasted like a blend of a wrestler's armpit and turtle shit. Quality coffee was sacrificed the day the United States shut itself off from the world's trade and economy. Despite modern advances, developing new agricultural products on land previously dedicated to other crops didn't make for an easy transition. Florida had still not proven to be a viable substitute for Ethiopia or Costa Rica. Or New Jersey, for that matter.

He returned to the bedroom to bring Lily a glass of water as she relaxed after their walk.

"You feel okay?" Jeff asked.

Not taking her eye off the glass, she said, "Yeah." She placed it on the table and seemed to decide to address the expression on his face. "I appreciate your concern. It's just a lot to deal with. At the same time, I have to worry about what this could do to me, if we get caught, and getting my boss involved. It's a crime, and one they're not shy about prosecuting."

"Don't worry about me, and if you need anything, just ask."

"And rest assured," she added bitterly, "I'm not done with Koy."

He returned to reviewing the curriculum for his five sections of two classes that just arrived in his inbox: Investigative Journalism in Modern America (2016–today) and American English. Brianne was at least honest enough to point out that, until they found a principal and curriculum co-ordinator deserving of their trust, she was borrowing the class outlines for all courses from a school outside of Amarillo, Texas. The principal there was an old college friend of hers she'd met at Southern Methodist. Brianne promised Jeff that the materials were on their way and that he should do his best until they arrived.

Peeking over his shoulder, Lily asked, "That's a joke, right?"

Grabbing her hand from behind him and pulling her in for a kiss, he said, "Nope. Modern America began in 2016."

She continued to scan the documents on his tablet.

Discuss the role effective investigative journalism plays in reflecting
the sociopolitical foundations of a culture,
enabling its advancement.

She said, "You know the answer to that one, right, Professor? None! Journalism advances *no one's* culture! It tells you what the culture did."

Entertained by her growing anger, he said, "I'm aware, dear. They will hang it on the word 'investigative,' as opposed to regular journalism. Bucket all journalism under investigative, and you have free rein to dig into anything."

"You can't teach that shit."

"We knew what we were getting into coming here."

"Yeah, but I didn't think they were brazen enough to document it."

"They were and are. This is the curriculum at Bushland High School in Texas."

She looked at the page again and read out loud: "'Woodrow Wilson's CPI: Modern applications.' What the hell is CPI?"

"Had to look that one up. To ensure support for entering World War One, Congress formed the Committee on Public Information. They used it to quell any opinion against the war, particularly communists and social-ists. They monitored news coming into the country, filtered it before it got to the media, and bombarded them with their side of the story. Without enough resources to prove them wrong, the media just accepted it as truth and printed it."

Her anger increasing, she asked, "And this is being considered for *today*?"

"Funny you should ask. I dug a little deeper, being the good educa-tor that I am. The committee was reinstituted by Congress very quietly last October."

Pulling up a chair to join him with her own cup of swamp water, Lily said, "They're not going to be happy until this country is literally at each other's throats. This needs to stop. Somebody needs to step up and do something about this."

Jeff sat back and watched her seethe. "Relax. The reality is that even today, you can't have a civil war. There's no territory to be claimed. Even the reddest states have a high percentage of liberals. We're all cohabitating. What are they going to do, fence us in?"

Chapter 22

June 7

The following day, Lily's father sat in her living room, waiting for her to return from a run. When she entered, she reacted as if he wasn't there, sitting across from him and taking off her sneakers.

"Should you be running in your condition?" he asked blandly. When it was clear she wasn't going to answer, he added, "How could you keep this from me?"

She turned to go into the kitchen to make a cup of tea. "You want one?" she asked.

"No, I had some on the way down. Charity, c'mon, be reasonable. I understand you'd prefer to stay away from me—"

"To be *independent* from you is more accurate. I'll remind you this was not our agreement. It isn't my birthday." She didn't want to push him too far because she realized, much to her dismay, it gave her a little comfort to know he was still engaged.

Resigned, he said, "Sure, fine, whatever. But not with this. Let me help you. We can bring you up to the ship, and you won't be breaking any laws."

"How'd you find out?" she asked, returning and sitting back on the sofa.

"That doesn't matter. There were many ways I could have found out. It only takes one of them to work."

She still had not laid an eye on him, staring instead at her cup of tea. "I can't prove it, but you're indirectly responsible for this."

"Are you suggesting *I* gave you a fert?"

"No, for the way things are, which enabled some asshole to give me a fert without consequence. Without the *fear* of consequence. But you are also responsible for the fact that what I need to do to stay alive is a crime."

Now she was looking at him, and he actually appeared to be genuinely concerned: eyebrows in a knot, face slightly pale. There was a rare glimpse of humanity evident on his face—a face better known as the global avatar of avarice and greed.

"I'm not a politician. You know that. I stay away from all this nonsense. It's bad for business."

"And the last job you got me? Coincidence?"

"She's a businesswoman, Charity. That was a great opportunity."

"She's broadening her scope."

"I had no idea she would get involved in politics when I got you the job. My opinion is that she was pushed in by her father. All my intelligence told me she wanted nothing to do with it. But look, put all of that aside—you can't go ahead with this silly plan of yours when you have a safer option."

"I can do whatever I want. I understand your concern, but I can no longer rely on you. I just can't. I've been sitting back, trying to live my life under the assumption that I am powerless to fight these people that you enable, but I just can't do it anymore. I see what's going on down here on the ground, and it's pretty obvious no one else will help. I don't have enough hypocrisy in me to remain associated with you at the same time. I'll be fine."

His gaze never left her face: part adoration, part exasperation. "I'm sorry to burst your bubble, but your first instinct on this is probably the correct one."

"Well," Lily snapped back, "the last two times you got involved in my life, a man killed himself and I worked for a sociopath. So with all due respect, I'll take my chances."

Resigned, he got up from the couch and looked around. "This is . . . quaint. Do you get many homeless squatting in the backyard?"

"What homeless?"

"See, there's something you haven't given them credit for, the Dennisons. They solved that years ago, and now we don't get assaulted for money anymore. See the problem, fix the problem."

"Still don't buy it," Lily said.

Realizing there wasn't going to be any real conversation, he said, "I love you, Charity, no matter how much you want to push me away. And deep down inside, you know I only want the best for you. That is my only motivation. I hope someday you'll see that and let me help you, but in the meantime, I'll respect your wishes and step aside. Please know, the door is always open. And that if this goes south, I will insert myself into the situation."

She had her back to him, but she felt the heat of his gaze.

"Okay," she said.

He opened the door and stopped. "I have to say, this is unlike you, and I fear the further you get away from the discipline you once had, the more you put yourself at risk."

The door closed behind him. A second later, Lily heard a slight hum. And he was gone.

Chapter 23

June 8

Job was on duty and by Lily's estimate, even more arrogant than before he had discovered her secret. She and Jeff walked through the empty line.

"Good to see you as always, Ms. Osbourne."

Lily walked through the security scanners without a response, and the green light went on. Job checked the monitor as a formality and said, "Glad everything is going well with the pregnancy."

Jeff immediately got in Job's face but worked to keep his voice and emotions down so as not to trigger the anger systems. "Your job here is to make sure the passengers aren't carrying explosives," he reminded Job, knowing full well that firearms had been permitted on aircraft since 2031. Somehow, Congress decided to draw the line at explosives, even though a bullet hole piercing the skin of a plane at fifty thousand feet was a likely death sentence for all involved. "There is nothing else that is your business, so I suggest you shut the fuck up when addressing her from now on."

Job didn't so much as flinch. While maintaining eye contact with Jeff, he went over to his tablet, tapped, and said, "Well, Mr. Maslow, I'll certainly keep your advice in mind, but for now, how about you move on and let me do my job? Why are you here, anyway? Is it Take Your Baby-daddy to Work Day?"

Jeff didn't move, and for a moment, Lily looked like she might be debating whether to come back and intervene. But Jeff went through the security scanner and, on the other end, turned to ask, "Am I pregnant, fuck face?"

"No, sir, I'm sorry to say you are not. That would have made my quota for the month."

Lily couldn't conceal her annoyance. "Now a good time to be calling attention to yourself, Jeff? To *us*?"

"I'm sorry, you're right, but that smug asshole needs a beating."

"Sure, why don't you do that once we get back from our trip. Add assault of a federal officer to our growing litany of charges!" she grumbled, and this seemed to bring him back to center, the reminder achieving the desired effect.

"Okay, I'm good. Promise," he told her, calming down. "No issues going forward."

They walked into Zeke's office, and Jeff went to meet him. "Hey, I'm Jeff. I really appreciate what you're doing here."

Zeke joined in the handshake. "You're welcome, but you should know I help people whenever I encounter these situations. I don't advertise because I'll certainly get caught. Still, if something appears, whether it's this or a teenager trying to avoid mandated conversion therapy, I look for ways to help. I'm lucky; I've managed to build a business here, and this one can help people. It's why I was in the Air Force and volunteered in the city. I may have shed the church and the community, but these are the values I was raised on, not the perversions they're preaching now."

Lily said, "All true, but you're being humble. This is riskier because I will still be around when it's over. Unless you're planning on firing me."

Zeke laughed. "Why would I let go of my best hostess? The Dennison folks love you!"

"How ironic," she said.

"Let me show you guys the flight plan I've programmed . . ."

He touched his tablet, and a hologram of a 3D map projected between them. They could see a smaller version of the plane Lily had been flying in—the TriFan 1500—lift off vertically from the airport and start heading south toward New Mexico.

"This needs to look like a normal flight for my company. As much as the air traffic controllers have a view of the entire country and its border areas, they are still very regionalized and almost all AI-driven, so keeping to normal patterns typically keeps anything from getting flagged for human review. We don't go there often, but on occasion I fly someone from Dennison down to Los Alamos in New Mexico."

"I really don't want to know why anyone from that company would be going there, but I can take a guess," Lily said.

"I don't even bother to ask. Interestingly, it is usually Hal, and he is typically alone." Seeing Jeff's face, he added, "He's assistant to Iwanna Dennison."

"Yeah, that sounds ominous," Jeff said.

"The thing that works to our advantage here is that Denver Center—the air traffic control sector we are in—ends, for the most part, at the border with New Mexico, which is covered by Albuquerque Center." As the hologram showed them the flight path, he continued. "You'll fly into Los Alamos and land, but you'll stay on the plane, and then the flight will change to visual flight rules, which means you're not asking for any tracking by air-traffic control. You'll still be on their radar, but they won't do anything for you, and since they are bots, they'll just ignore you. From there, it will be straight down over the border, then southeast toward Mexico City."

"Won't the Mexicans have a problem with us crossing over?" Jeff asked.

Zeke gave a slight grin while he answered, "Well, it goes without saying they are paying a lot of attention to military aircraft, making sure Dennison doesn't try to invade the rest of the country. But I filed a flight plan with them that will kick in once you cross over. As long as you stick to that, they don't have a problem with private aircraft. My friend Anna will pick you up at the airport and take you to the clinic, then back once you're all set. They've come pretty far with this procedure, so you can move an hour after the surgery and just take it light for a week. You're just going to work from the headquarters for a few days to recuperate. No need to show you out on sick leave. You arrange for the miscarriage report in the system?"

"Yes. My doc is willing to register it in two days."

"How did you manage that?" Jeff asked.

"Well," she said, "let's just say she has a bit of a crush on my father and is always looking for a way to meet him again. He brought me to an appointment when I was sixteen, and she hasn't stopped asking about him since. I may have pointed out how grateful he will be if she helps us out."

Zeke said, "Fortunately, the government hasn't been able to break into patient files yet, so that should be the end of it. But don't worry, they're trying."

Jeff's expression had changed. "Your *father* knows? And why is your doc obsessed with him?"

His fearful reaction reminded Lily of her whole life, with everyone around her deferential to her every need, kissing her ass and seeking access in fear of displeasing her father. Then she reminded herself Jeff had no idea that this was a father's instinctual fear for his pregnant daughter.

"No," she reassured him, lying. "Don't worry, he doesn't know, but my doctor certainly didn't need to know that. She just has a crush. Having him help me was plan B, but I'm happier with how this is going." She smiled at Jeff to put him at ease and then turned to Zeke, angling for the change in topic. "It looks like your plan should work great."

"It has so far. I've done this to Mexico and Canada about a dozen times. Just need to continue to be careful. If there's a problem and I feel like they've picked up on what's going on during the flight home, I have a contingency. It's a little complicated, but it should work."

"What does it involve?" she asked.

Zeke tapped his tablet a couple of times and brought up a map of the border area between Colorado and New Mexico to the south. They shared a corner border in the west that ran almost the entire northern border of New Mexico, a perfect line that then continued on past New Mexico into neighboring Oklahoma. He zoomed into the bottom right corner where northeast New Mexico met with southeast Colorado.

"I don't want to get into too much detail. The less you know, the better, but there's a small glitch in this area between the physical ground borders of the states and the airspace that sits above it. Even though this area is part of Colorado, the airspace above it is enforced by New Mexico, and police in Colorado can't fly into it." He added a smile. "Let's just say I can take advantage of that if I need to."

"I like a man who thinks ahead," Lily said.

"The plane is programmed to go, so whenever you're ready, just hop in and the doors will close behind you. When you land the second time, you'll be in Mexico City."

"Or prison," Lily said.

Jeff was like a kid in a candy store during the trip. As much as he tried to just sit and be there for Lily, she could tell he was enjoying the ride and wanted to explore.

"You want to see the cockpit?" she asked, grinning.

"Sure, why not. You good?"

"Yeah, I am," she said, kissing him. "I appreciate you doing this. It's easier with someone here."

"Like I said, whatever you need. I'm not trying to be a white knight here, and I know you don't need one. But I'm partially responsible, so I should be here. You shouldn't have to be alone for this."

She led him into the cockpit, and his eyes lit up. "Where's all the equipment? Wow, they have really stripped these down to the basics."

"I know very little about all of this. But Zeke told me they're designed to fly on autopilot with the presence of a pilot; autonomously, without anybody here at all, like right now; or even remotely, controlled by a pilot on the ground. There are basic controls that pop out of the floor if someone needs to fly manually, but it's pretty much these screens to let us know what's going on."

Jeff completed his brief tour and then looked ahead toward the New Mexico desert. "My dad kept trying to get me to go into flying. He always had his license but then really started going up a lot once he started teaching and had the time to travel."

Lily opened the cabin door, and they walked back to sit for the remainder of the flight. "I didn't know he was a teacher. You said he worked in finance."

"Most of my life, he did. Like a machine. Then he just quit, started teaching at a college nearby, and enjoyed his life for the first time. The irony is that he instantly became a better father," Jeff added with a bitter laugh, pausing to shake his head. "But then he made the mistake of revealing to me how he was able to quit everything and start over like that."

"How?"

Jeff seemed to debate sharing further. "I really can't get into it, but let's just say he helped himself to some money that wasn't his. It was a huge disappointment for me, and I think it affected my ability to trust anyone."

"Of course."

"Look, it's been a long time since I dated someone this long—and that was intentional. I willfully avoided getting involved with anyone because I wasn't ready, in my head and in my life. I'm not saying I'm there now, but I'm at least on the path for the first time in a while. Now that I actually care about the opinion of the woman I'm dating, yes, I am taking it carefully."

Lily appreciated Jeff's sincerity and warmed to her innate belief that he was obviously telling the truth.

"What does your sister do?" she asked.

"You wouldn't believe me if I told you."

"Try me."

"She's an engineer for Boston Dynamics."

"The leading competitor to Dennison Robotics?" Lily was truly impressed.

"What can I say? We Maslow kids fly in dangerous circles. At least she's with the good guys."

"Until they get bought out," Lily added—without enough sarcasm for Jeff, it seemed.

"Please don't even suggest it. I spoke to her last week, and she said they're in pretty good shape. But these days, everyone's at risk."

Twenty minutes later, Lily could feel the aircraft begin its descent, and she leaned over to look out the window. "Never spent much time out here, but it is beautiful."

"Great skiing. We should take a trip to Taos one weekend."

The plane guided itself toward Los Alamos Airport and completed a perfect landing at the general-aviation tarmac.

"Well, let's see how long it has us sit here before the next leg," Lily said.

The doors opened, and the blast of hot June air filled the cabin. Lily walked to the doorway to take a look at the landscape.

"You're right," she said. "We should come out here. It's beautiful."

After only about five minutes, the door closed, and they were back in the air, slowly ascending. By the time they had reached ten thousand feet, their speed increased significantly.

"I'm going to take a nap, okay?" Lily told Jeff.

"You good?"

"Yeah, it's just a lot." She kissed him. "Don't take over the controls while I'm asleep," she added with a wink, then went to the back of the cabin, lay down, and closed her eyes.

Ninety minutes later, Jeff could feel the aircraft descending. He ventured into the cockpit to see the view ahead from five thousand feet and was met with the sight of Mexico City visible through a perfectly clear sky. After the US invasion, all of Europe began sending their manufacturing business to Mexico, which led to tremendous economic benefits throughout the country. The police and Army were reconstructed; the cartels dismantled, weakened by the end of their US drug trade; and, most importantly, the government and people united with a common enemy: the gringos from the north. The economy flourished, becoming a force matched only by Canada.

Lily emerged beside him. "It's amazing what one little land invasion can do for a country."

Moments later, they landed. The door opened once again to warmth flooding the aircraft—this time, rather than the bone-dry Southwestern heat, Lily noticed the air was humid and somehow floral. As they exited, a Mercedes-Benz hover-car pulled up in front of them and stopped, with the straight-faced driver stepping out to greet them. The woman was in her sixties, with raven-black hair that roped down to her waist in a traditional braid. She looked up and said, "Lily?"

"Yes," Jeff answered for them. "Anna?"

"Sí. You are Jeff?"

"Sí, yes, I am."

They all shook hands and Anna said, "Welcome to Mexico. I wish I had more time to show you my country, but unfortunately, it is a tight schedule Zeke has you on. Let us go."

Lily leaned in to hug Anna, who reciprocated warmly. "I can't thank you enough for this, and I will remember you in the future, when all of this has passed."

As she pulled away, Anna looked at Lily, perplexed. "Passed? Oh dear, this will never pass, so say your thanks now. We, with the rest of the world, will make America pay for all it's done. It will not be much longer. But that is not for you and me. You are my guest, and I will help you. It is easy for me. It is you that faces prison for this."

Lily bowed her head, nodding, knowing what Anna said was true. There was little direct news from the outside world, for most broadcast licenses were given to far-right or center-right companies. But there was increasing chatter of a unified world planning action against the axis of the United States, Russia, and North Korea.

They piled into the Mercedes, which gained altitude and hovered quickly into the heart of Mexico City, the sight of which was stunning. Jeff said he'd never been there. Lily had visited in the early 2000s, and while many neighborhoods were beautiful, the skies were filled with smog and the streets with litter. They discovered on their way to the clinic, looking through the crystal-clean air, that the entirety of the city had been modernized. High-end commerce was everywhere, the most efficient public transportation was available for free—and was also all electric- and solar-powered—and the streets were so clean Lily could hardly believe it.

Without a doubt, Mexico's people were thriving. All this was a far cry from Chihuahua and the occupied territories in the north, where American troops stood sentry in squalor. For that matter, it was a far cry from Manhattan in its current state of disrepair, the banks and investment firms all falling in line to the administration and conspiring to drain New York of its status as the financial center of the world by all moving their headquarters to Houston.

Job felt inspired to pursue some extracurricular activity after his most recent encounter with the whore and the rude man he presumed was the father of the whore's bastard child. He sure didn't like being spoken to like that. He was an officer of the law. And of God. He expected—no, *demanded*—respect.

And where were they going together, anyway?

He decided to take his lunch with his friend and fellow Triple G member, Scooter, who was also the lone air traffic controller. He grabbed his lunch, lovingly packed by his mother that morning, and headed over to the tower.

"Hey, Scoot," he said as he walked past him toward the break room. "Mind if I join you today for a bit?"

"Yeah, sure, Job. Not much going on here, anyway. Whatcha mom make you today?"

Job checked between the slices of bread. "Looks like bologna," he said. "With mustard. Hey, what flights you see out of Liberation this morning?"

Scooter walked over to a screen. "Just one. To Los Alamos. That piece of ass was on it."

"Well, don't get your sights set on her. She's a single mother."

Scooter seemed to daze off for a moment, imagining the act of conception. "That must have been the lucky fella with her."

"He went on the plane with her?" Job said, his excitement causing a small piece of bologna to shoot through the air.

"Yeah, I watched them both get on. Usually that flight's for Dennison people."

Job thought for a moment. "We didn't have any Dennison folks this morning. Possible it was just a pickup?"

Scooter scanned another monitor, tapped it once, and said, "I doubt it. They haven't brought anyone down there in a few weeks. And it's almost always *one* person, round trip."

"Is there a planned return flight?"

"No, not yet."

Job finished the last bite of his sandwich while considering this news. "Why would anyone else go to that Sodom and Gomorrah of a state?"

Things between New Mexico and its neighbors all around—which were firmly red states—had gotten outright hostile in the last twenty years. With the early financial support of many a billionaire, the state was able to establish itself as self-sufficient—independent of the federal government—becoming one of the last progressive strongholds in the West.

At one point, to disengage New Mexico from the rest of the nation's air traffic, the federal controllers were dismissed and the state was forced to supply its own. This ironically led to an expansion of trade for New Mexico, particularly in the area of rare earth minerals, and they were soon prosperous, treating their citizens as they sought fit, providing their own version of the since defunct Social Security and Medicare programs and attracting tech talent that preferred the old days.

"Let Mexico take the state back, for all I care," President Dennison was quoted as saying, unaware the state had never, in fact, been part of modern Mexico. "As long as they stop at the borders of the good states, it's all theirs."

Mexico did not take him up on the offer, but the state still separated their National Guard from the federal Army system and manned their own borders: to the south, east, west, and north.

Job got up and said, "Can you do me a favor and let me know if you see them coming back, Scoot? I may have grounds for an interdiction for you."

"Sure, Job. Sounds exciting."

On his way out, to himself, Job said, "Where did you sneaky sinners run off to?"

Chapter 24

"Where's the Lord?" Taggert asked as he strutted through the new Vicksburg Gulch Facility for Religious Services with Jake trailing listlessly behind him.

"Um, how do you mean, Reverend Taggert?" Jake asked, his attention splitting duty between this conversation and an iSpy he was receiving from Cheryl, featuring her utilizing the AI massage device.

"Where's the Lord Jesus, Jake?"

Tearing himself away just at the moment of her climax, Jake said irritably, "Well, I'd like to believe He's in all of our hearts, Reverend."

"He's not in here, is the problem!"

"There's a cross right there behind your big throne."

"It's not a *throne*. It is an ornate chair," Mary said from her husband's side.

"Yeah, sure, and it's an exact copy of the one you have at your other church," Jake said.

Taggert continued. "We're not talking about the thro—chair! We're talking about the visual depiction of our Lord Jesus Christ anywhere in this church. I'd like to have a statue of Him rising above all of us behind me."

Jake, mind still focused on what was happening back home, decided to simply play the trump card. "Ms. Dennison said a cross was enough."

The reverend and his bride froze, then slowly turned to Jake with a glare that made him worry they could see everything Cheryl was sending via iSpy. As they glared at him, she was actively causing property damage in his new house.

"Iwanna had input into what *my* church would look like?" the reverend asked through gritted teeth.

"Well, technically, it's a facility for religious services," Jake corrected him. "Which is owned by Ms. Dennison, by the way—so yeah, she provided quite a bit of input, and rightfully so."

Taggert just stared back at him. "The name outside will need to be changed," he said flatly. "This is my house, the Lord's house, and it will reflect my preferences. Please arrange to change it to a simple modification of my main facility. 'Taggert's House of the Lord, at Vicksburg Gulch.'"

Tired of the proxy war, Jake had already notified Hal of the earful he was getting, who in turn patched in a RealTime with Iwanna to Jake's phone, which appeared in front of them.

"Hi, Brady. How's it going?" Iwanna said.

"There's no Jesus!" Taggert exclaimed.

"Well, I wish someone would have told me that when I was younger," she said, laughing. "I had better things to do than all that time in church."

"You know what I mean!" he said, raging. "This is a house of the Lord, and He is not present to watch over my flock!"

"I thought that's what *your* job was?" she said, then switched to a more conciliatory tone. "Look, I hear what you're saying, but the reality is—and I had Hal look into this—many churches do not have an image of Jesus. I know you do in Colorado Springs, but I'd prefer if we could make this a little more understated. Don't worry, we brought in all the same equipment you're used to, so He will still appear after every service."

Taggert seemed to be realizing he had very little leverage in the conversation. "Does that include the special audio equipment?" he inquired, tone softening.

Iwanna smiled knowingly and reassuringly. "Yes, top of the line. Even better than your current one. And I bet the effect will be double what you've been getting."

Mary gasped. "Really?"

Iwanna held her answer, directed her gaze at Mary, and whispered conspiratorially, "Maybe *triple*."

Mary's hand came to her mouth. "I'll go check the backstage facilities."

As she departed, Taggert looked at Iwanna. "That was unnecessarily manipulative," he said, but couldn't help breaking into a little laugh. "This isn't consistent with our agreement. I assumed I would have control over my church."

"Well, to be clear, you are leasing," Iwanna countered. "However, I am open to reasonable changes besides this one. Just give your list of requests to Jake, and we'll review them and let you know. And I'm sorry—I honestly didn't think Mary would have that reaction."

Taggert walked up onto the stage and went to the podium, which did have the same controls as the one in Colorado Springs. He looked up at the building that was 50 percent bigger. "It is a powerful effect," he said, looking directly at Iwanna. "Perhaps you will stay long enough next time."

"Perhaps. I hear nothing but good things."

"Why is this Jesus thing such a deal-breaker for you?" he asked.

Iwanna muted her feed, the hologram blurring while she consulted with Hal. When she returned, she said, "I was raised a Presbyterian, and I can't be part of a religious enterprise that shows images of God."

Taggert descended from the podium, did a 360-degree turn, taking it all in yet again. When he came down from the stage, he faced Iwanna. "The Vicksburg Gulch House of the Lord, with the Most Reverend Brady Taggert," he said.

The hologram blurred again. After twenty seconds, she returned and said, "Okay, we can make that work."

Chapter 25

Zeke sat in his office, nervously watching his dashboard, on the lookout for the flight plan that he expected for Lily and Jeff's return. He resisted the urge to break the silence upon which they had all agreed—as any communication between them could be viewed as evidence of their crime—but he thought they would have returned to Los Alamos by now. But then, just as he couldn't take it anymore, the strip appeared: KLAM-KCOS. They were safely in the plane.

***

"There you are!" Scooter exclaimed, watching as the transponder for Liberation flight 32 turned on in Los Alamos. He texted Job of the news, who then immediately ran into his supervisor's office. "I think we have an abortion flight returning from New Mexico!"

The less excitable TSA sergeant looked up from his phone. "And what makes you think that, Officer?"

Job went over the details of the morning's activity and his conversation with the tower controller.

"Well, that's highly speculative," the TSA sergeant noted, mulling it over, "but it's been a while, so I'll scramble the Baby Patrol. They've been pretty bored." The red states, recognizing the increase in flights to obtain abortions across borders, had formed regional branches of the Air Force dedicated to interdicting such attempts.

Job was nearly hyperventilating. "Okay. It's a sure hit. And Liberation is involved."

The sergeant smiled. "Well, that would be icing on the cake. Been looking for a reason to catch that fag doing something illegal."

"I'm going to the tower to observe."

<hr>

Zeke watched as his plane—a dot on his radar—lifted off from the airport and headed northeast.

Movement outside caught his attention. He walked to the window overlooking the tarmac just as the three-man unit of the Colorado Springs Baby Patrol piled into their single-seat aircraft designed to look like an old motorcycle, lifted to altitude, and shot—very loudly—southeast. Despite their nuclear propulsion, the Air Force had requested the fake rumble of a Harley, which fortunately had drawn his attention and tipped Zeke into action. He reached into his desk and turned on a special phone he had set aside for just this event.

"Hi. We need to implement scenario seven. The tail number is November-seven-three-two-Hotel-Victor. I'll be there in three hours to collect them."

He waited another moment. Upon receiving confirmation, he said, "Copy. Thanks."

Zeke then walked out of his office to the operations center for Liberation, which was empty with the low workload for the day—intentionally planned, on his part. He sat down at a remote pilot control station and turned it on.

◆•• ——————— ••◆

On the plane, just as they passed Española, New Mexico, Jeff was holding Lily's hand in silence when they heard Zeke's voice come out over the intercom.

"Hi, guys. Sorry, but we have an issue. Don't worry, I've planned for this contingency, but it's going to mean a very abrupt landing and a road trip when you get on the ground. I'll try to make it as smooth as possible, but I need you to go to the cockpit and strap into the pilot and copilot seats. Make sure you're in tight. I'm also closing all the shades, so don't lift them up."

The shades came down.

"Dammit," Lily said to Jeff, a look of panic on her face. "I've gotten you all into this."

Jeff kissed her hand and said, "No, *Koy* did. Zeke's got it all figured out, so don't worry. Let's just go up front and do what he says."

◆•• ——————— ••◆

Job's eyes were wide with excitement as he thought about what this catch would do for his career. He stared at the hologram that laid the situation out before him in the ready room of the control tower, Scooter to his left following the three Baby Patrol craft as they sped at 250 knots toward the expected crossing at Jaroso, just over the border in Colorado. Because of the situation with New Mexico, they were strictly forbidden to enter Albuquerque airspace, aware that the state had set up a defensive missile perimeter to enforce this.

Job and Scooter leaned in when they noticed the sudden change in direction of the Liberation plane.

"What's going on?" he asked Scooter.

"Dunno."

Jeff and Lily were still able to hold hands from the pilot seats, even after they were strapped in. He noticed she was shifting in discomfort and wincing in pain.

"You okay?" he asked her. "If you think something's wrong, then we just call all this off. It's not worth you getting hurt."

"No, no, I'm fine, really. Just bad timing with this seat belt, but everything's okay."

Jeff felt the aircraft bank to the right and increase in speed. He also thought they were dropping to a lower altitude. On the screen in front of him, he could see the map and the clear line that denoted the Alburquerque and Denver airspace. They were no longer flying perpendicular to the straight line of the state border between the two and were switching to something closer to forty-five degrees northeast.

"Guys, in fifteen seconds, you're going to drop very quickly," Zeke told them over the intercom, voice calm despite all the action. "Just double-check your belts and hold on. You'll be fine. Someone's going to meet you at the bottom and take you to a safe location."

"Okay," Jeff said. "We're ready."

He looked again at the map and noticed something strange. While the state border continued east on a straight line, the Alburquerque airspace continued over Colorado territory.

And then he felt them drop like an elevator with a cable break.

A drop of sweat had formed on Job's nose as the Baby Patrol approached the Liberation plane. He grinned as he imagined the stripes he'd earn on his uniform.

"Five seconds to intercept," the BP officer's voice said over the loudspeaker.

And then the TriFan 1500 disappeared from the hologram just as it passed over the border into Colorado.

"What the fuck?" Job yelled. "Did they shoot them down?"

The BP officer's voice from the Harley returned. "Negative contact."

As he scanned the scene, Job barked at Scooter, "Why aren't they getting them? They're in Colorado!"

Scooter said into his headset, "Baby Patrol, Colorado Springs Tower. Why are you not intercepting?"

"We cannot enter the airspace. We'll need to send in the Border Patrol on the ground."

◆•————••◆

After the harrowing descent, the plane did as Zeke had said it would: immediately put them in an empty space of tarmac at Springfield Municipal Airport, an effectively abandoned single-runway strip 27.5 miles north of the Oklahoma border, just northeast of New Mexico—in Colorado.

As he unstrapped himself and Lily, he heard the cabin door open and someone traipsing toward the cockpit. His heart nearly stopped when the door opened and a woman strode in and walked directly to Lily. She wore a kerchief over her face.

"Turn around, if you wouldn't mind. How you doing, honey? Everything okay?" Her voice was digitized.

Lily, flustered but in control, said, "Yes, I'm fine, thank you."

To both of them, the woman said, "Zeke sent me to help you. We've got to get out of here, but I just need to do one thing on the way. Get into the Jeep outside and keep your heads down. I'll be right behind you."

They did as they were told, Jeff with his arm around Lily for most of the way, walking her in the brisk cold using the low light of the Jeep's headlights. Just as they got there, they heard a loud clang and turned to see the woman swinging a sledgehammer into one of the TriFan's propellers. Before putting their head below the window line, they watched as her third swing resulted in an obvious bend.

The woman got into the Jeep and said, "Okay, we're just going over to my house a few minutes away. Zeke is on his way to get you."

Chapter 26

She began heading south on Route 287 toward the town of Springfield, last known population 1,325, driving from what was probably the only use of the airport in the last decade. Although it was late and pitch black outside, she had disabled her rear lights and had the headlights at a level that barely provided enough to see five feet in front of her. The road was straight, but she seemed to know it well. She maintained a perfect forty-five miles per hour, occasionally checking the rearview mirror. She stopped checking when she saw the headlights of the five hover-cars turn left into the airport. They wouldn't be in time.

Using a voice-modification app on her phone, their hostess began. "Very simple: I don't know you, you don't know me. It's not my real name, but call me Norma. Don't use your names, and it would be best if you don't even look at me. I know it'll be hard because of my robust beauty, but try. If they test your brain to see if you recognize me or my voice, I need that to come up negative."

As she and Jeff slowly sat up in the seat, Lily nodded. "Thank you for what you're doing. I promise I'd never turn you in for this."

Norma laughed cynically. "Apparently, you're not aware of the tech-niques they've got these days. You wouldn't have a choice—but it's a nice sentiment, sweetheart. We're going to go through town here, and my guess is you haven't had the pleasure before, so heads up: It's bad. It'll be slow on the road, but just hang tight and don't get too close to the window. They'll leave you alone."

"They?" Jeff asked quizzically.

"The people in Springfield."

More confused, he said, "It's past ten. Won't most people be home in bed?"

"Yes, they will be," Norma said.

About five minutes from the airport, she slowed the Jeep to a crawl, the light from many fires ahead signaling they were close.

Jeff saw the first barrel fire by the main building of a small self-serve car wash, two hooded figures turning to look at them briefly, then return-ing to the warmth, uninterested.

"It's June, for fuck's sake," Jeff said.

Norma said, "It snowed the other day. Melted this afternoon. Almost like there's something wrong with the climate."

They continued briefly, and she slowed even more. Lily looked ahead and saw the reason why, as several tents and mattresses in the road blocked their progress, with just enough space in between to allow a single vehicle. *It's a checkpoint,* she thought.

The Jeep windows had been filthy from the outset, and the light mak-ing it to Lily's eyes was blurred and shadowy. She saw two human-size blobs approach, and to her shock, Norma lowered the window.

With a tone of pure resignation and fatigue, the first voice said, "Hey—"

Norma immediately put her hand over his mouth and said, "Hey, Saul. Sorry, I have guests. No names."

Saul nodded, and she removed her hand.

"No problem. Look, I know you're busy, but Sarah is talking about going west, and I don't want her to go." He quietly sobbed at the thought.

Her head went down, and to the floor of the car, she said, "You knew this was going to happen at some point. I thought you would have accepted it by now." She patted his hand that rested on the door, and he nodded in agreement but remained crying.

"It's one thing when it's an idea. Another when she's saying she wants to go down the road." He bent down to his knees, hand still on the door as if attached. "Can you talk to her?" Between sobs, he added a shaky, "Please! I'll be right behind her if she does."

Norma stared ahead at the stretch of street and fire ahead, considering her situation. Her phone buzzed, and she read her text, then looked into the rearview mirror and said, "So our friend just told me he's being questioned and will be late, so if y'all don't mind, I'm going to help this fella."

Lily nodded vehemently and said, "Of course, please help him. Don't worry about us."

Norma returned to the window. "Saul, you know I'm probably not going to win this fight, but I'll try. I'll go in. You may get some federal agents behind us, but I know you know what to do about them."

"They know better to come around here, but sure . . ." He halted at her name.

She pulled just ahead and into the parking lot of the Star-something motel, the right side of the sign shattered. Looking at them again through the mirror, she said, "I'm sorry about this and I know how it looks to you, but I'm sort of the mother figure in this part of town. I gotta at least try."

Lily and Jeff surveyed the area, complete with several people in sleeping bags along the border of the parking lot. Lily saw the expression of sadness overcome Jeff's face.

"What happened here?" he asked.

"This is the border between the America you two know and New Mexico, where things would almost remind you of your childhood. New Mexico shut down all its borders and has an army of bees they bought from Canada protecting its perimeter. The only entry point is this town, so it became a crossing-over point. But they only allow fifty a day into the state. Anyone coming in is handled like an asylum case."

"It's still in America, though," Jeff said.

"Technically, yeah. But Dennison's been treating it like a foreign country for years, and no one gives enough of a shit about what goes on here to do anything about it. There's a lotta people at the end of their ropes, and the farther they get down this road toward New Mexico, the more hope they get. Then most of them wind up getting denied asylum and walk back into town. Sarah and Saul were denied a few months ago. Now she wants to do something different. This old motel is where a lot of them go to prepare."

"What did he mean by 'go west'?" Lily asked.

Norma thought for a moment. "I'm going to have to put you up for the night, so you'll see what I'm talking about in the morning. For now, just wait here and let me see what I can do. Then we'll head to my property."

"No," Lily said, "I want to see what's going on in there."

Jeff turned. "I'm not sure that's such a good idea . . ."

More firmly, Lily said, "I want to see it."

"Suit yourself," Norma said while opening her door. "C'mon."

Jeff could tell he wasn't changing Lily's mind, so he joined her behind their hostess. As they approached, there was a poster just outside the lobby entrance, in the style of old Westerns from the '50s, with a man in a cowboy hat looking out over what was probably the Grand Canyon. At the top, it said,

THIS LIFE GETTING YOU DOWN?

And below,

GO WEST, YOUNG MAN!
A MESSAGE FROM PRESIDENT DENNISON

As they started through the hallways of the motel, it became quite evident that it was effectively a heroin den. There were semiconscious men and women strung out on the floor and on filthy mattresses without any sheets. After passing several of them, Lily realized they were all mumbling something softly to themselves, rhythmically, like an incantation. Then she saw that each had a cross in their right hand and a hypodermic nearby. She picked one up and read the label:

A GIFT FROM YOUR LEADER

"What the fuck?" she said, startling Jeff behind her.

"Please put that down," Jeff said. "Gently."

She listened and then walked a few more feet to one of the rooms, where she found Norma and a woman sitting on the bed.

"Sarah, Saul asked me to come talk to you. He's very upset. Do you think maybe we can get through this night and talk about it in the morning? You're in no rush, and I'll support whatever decision you make, I promise. But let's get some closure first, okay?"

Sarah barely moved, staring catatonically at the floor, streaks of tears running below her eyes.

"We've been here before," Sarah said, "and we're just going in circles. You know why you aren't offering me anything? 'Cause there's nothing you can do to help us. You know it."

Norma sighed, lips tight. "It's just that there's lots of people who have been in this situation before and come out of it okay on the other side. Started normal lives. I've seen it, Sarah, and you and Saul are so good together, and so smart. I think you could do it."

Sarah looked at Norma with clarity dawning in her eyes. "That's just it," she said—sadly, cynically, with the distinct tone of surrender. "We *are* smart. We both studied to help people, help humanity. Prevent disease. We dedicated our lives to it, and we . . ." She paused, throat bobbing. "We were happy together. We *were* happy."

"Sarah," Norma began, but Sarah kept speaking.

"We don't know how to do anything else in the world. Losing our jobs at the CDC, then our lives, and our livelihood . . . being cut off from everything, ostracized as quacks! That broke us. There's no world out there anymore—"

"But there *is*, Sarah—"

"And we can't get there! We're here, with nothing! So that doesn't really matter much, does it?"

Lily saw a full hypodermic in Sarah's hand and had to look away, the sadness of the situation beginning to overwhelm her.

"My love for him makes it even worse," Sarah added. "Having love in this place . . . I can't do it anymore. I feel bad enough, so could you please take your friends out of here and go? Tell Saul I'm sorry and I hope to see him again someday."

"Okay, Sarah. Please know you are loved. Think about that," Norma said.

Sarah's eyes were awash in tears as she looked up and mouthed, "Thank you." Then, startled, she stared at Lily as if noticing her there for the first time. "She is surrounded by smoke, that one," she said somberly to Norma. "Be careful."

Lily shuddered. "How do you mean?"

But Sarah was done, lying back and curling into a fetal position, pulling the blanket around her.

When they got back to the car, Saul was looking at them with resignation, trembling. "I knew she was too far gone."

"She hasn't done it yet, Saul," Norma said. "She was clear when she looked at me. This is her decision. She wanted me to tell you she hopes to see you again in a better place."

Saul sat on the ground and sobbed, waving Norma away.

◆•• —————— ••◆

They were silent on the drive to Norma's home until Lily asked, "So, what happens to her now? To all of them?"

"The government has made that location a regular pickup spot, and every morning, they send an unmanned hover-bus with robot drones to clean it out of anyone that's high. Then they take them west of here. Once everyone recognized that pattern, they realized the fastest and easiest way to lose themselves was to shoot up here for the free ride."

Jeff, frustrated, said, "Okay, enough with the mystery. To where?"

Norma stayed silent, it not being the first time she had been asked to explain it. Then she said, "There are no words. You'll just have to see in the morning. I got a message from Zeke. He'll meet us at the town entrance at eight. She needs to get some sleep to heal."

Norma woke them up at six and had breakfast waiting on the table. She didn't bother with the kerchief over her face or the voice app. Lily came in a few minutes ahead of Jeff and used the time to ask her, "Is this going to be a bad day for me?"

Norma revealed a warm maternal smile. "We don't have to go there if you don't want," she said. "I just need to have you north of town in two hours."

"No, no, don't misunderstand. I want to see it. Need to see it." She looked over her fit hostess—long gray hair, early sixties, calloused hands that she was certain worked every square foot of the property. "Sorry your cover got blown."

"At this point, if they get you, I'm cooked, so why bother? This wasn't supposed to be a sleepover."

"I'm sorry."

"I'm not trying to make you feel bad, so don't apologize. I've done this for many others, so you're not special. My decisions."

"What do you do around here, exactly?"

Jeff walked in, grabbed a piece of bacon from the plate in the middle of the table, and sat next to Lily, kissing her on the cheek. "How you feeling?"

"I'm good. I feel good. The soreness is gone."

"Morning, Norma," he said with a smile. "Good to see you."

Norma smiled back and said, "Hey." Then she answered Lily's question. "This is my family house and has been for generations. Just because the powers that be decided to let it become what it's become doesn't mean I am going to leave it. I do the best I can to help people leave this place, one way or the other. I give them a shoulder to cry on, care when they need it, but that's all I can do. I wouldn't survive any attempt to try to advise them. There's only so much I can handle emotionally." Snapping out of a brief trance, Norma turned to finish cleaning a frying pan. Into the window, she said, "We should get going soon. Don't want to keep Zeke waiting."

❖—❖

Before they got in the car, Lily walked over to Norma and gave her a hug. "In case we don't get a chance later."

Norma returned it and patted her back. "You're going to be fine. Take good care of Zeke. Our families go way back. He's a good one."

Norma drove off the property through a dilapidated wooden fence, and after about ten minutes, she was at the intersection of State Road 385. She pulled over and put the Jeep in park. "Come with me for a second," she told them.

As they reached the intersection, she turned to them and pointed south. "We're five miles from the border to New Mexico. This is how many people we are talking about."

At first look, Jeff didn't see anyone. There was grass, followed by more grass, followed by what he assumed was brown desert. Then he heard Lily gasp, and he looked closer, seeing the occasional plume of smoke from a fire and occasional movement. The entire horizon, starting around two miles from them, was a vast sea of people. They had all come there, hoping for the chance to become a resident of New Mexico.

Lily just stared. "And no one provides these people anything?"

"Nope," Norma said. "The state of Colorado says these are indigents that don't belong in our towns and cities. They are a drain on our society, skewing our key statistics, like the employment rate, dragging our progress down. Drug addicts, drunks, and heathens. Obviously liberals, because God-fearing people don't allow themselves to get in this condition. So the state and federal governments do nothing. Here."

Lily picked up on the last note. "Here?"

"C'mon," Norma said as she returned to the Jeep.

They drove north on State Road 385 for about half a mile when they saw the first billboard on the right—no graphics, just the sentence:

REJECTED BY THE LIBERALS IN THAT
GOD-FORSAKEN STATE?

"Fuck," Lily said out loud, but then her eye caught the next one a quarter mile farther:

CAN'T GO THERE, AND CAN'T MAKE IT IN REAL AMERICA?

Lily and Jeff sat, mesmerized by the sequence.

NOTHING LEFT FOR YOU ON THIS EARTH?

Then:

CAN'T PULL YOURSELF UP BY YOUR BOOTSTRAPS
LIKE THE REST OF US?

Then:

WELL, MAYBE IT'S TIME TO STOP BEING A BURDEN.

The next sign featured the friendliest headshot of Jesus, his smile highlighted by a sparkle at the corner of his mouth.

COME TO ME, MY CHILD. GO WEST!
I'M WAITING FOR YOU.

They watched as Norma pulled over at the intersection of 385 and 160. There were two signs, one with an arrow pointing up that read NORTH and the other with an arrow pointing left that read WEST.

"Up to you which way we go, but you need to tell me now," Norma said.

"I want to see it," Lily said immediately.

As she turned west, Jeff saw the red brick smokestack about three miles ahead, unending plumes of smoke choking the atmosphere. After two minutes, there was one more billboard with the same headshot as the last one.

YOU'VE CHOSEN WELL, MY CHILD.
I CAN'T WAIT TO MEET YOU!

After five more minutes, there was one more sign. It had an arrow pointing left and read:

TOWN OF LIBERTY. ELEVATION 5,029.

Norma took the left, the smokestack ahead of them about a mile ahead. They came to the end of a line, a procession of people with their heads down, their lips moving. The line continued ahead as far as they could see. They drove past them on the single-lane road. Norma's guests remained silent and stone-faced.

A hover-bus pulled up behind them and honked its horn. Norma obliged and pulled over, safely avoiding a mother carrying her toddler, a blanket wrapped around her in the June cold. As the hover-bus passed, Lily and Jeff leaned to look in, but the tinted windows afforded no view. There were four drone robots on the roof.

They came to the terminus of the line, where a queue weaved in and out between red velvet ropes toward the entrance. There was a long white concrete fence about eight feet high that stretched to their left and right as far as they could see. Off to the left, the bus had pulled up to a service entrance, and Lily and Jeff watched as drones carried the nearly comatose people inside. Lily was sure she saw Sarah.

Norma was staring in the opposite direction when they joined her. Lily was open-eyed and aware as she looked at Norma, who met her gaze of understanding.

Norma led them to the entrance, where a single man in a robe stood in front of a podium. He slowly turned to look at her and said, "Well, hello, Norma. Peace be with you." He then turned to the next person in line, handing them a thin red disc. "Please take this and proceed to the waiting room. Follow the blue line on the floor. When you are ready, it will buzz and light up, indicating it is your turn. Then proceed to the next room."

Norma acted as if she hadn't heard him, placing her finger on the reader next to his podium. As it turned green, she said to Lily and Jeff, "I am a licensed observer. I can take you in briefly. Last chance to turn around."

"I want to see it," Lily said.

"I think I get it but can't believe it's possible," Jeff said. He shook his head. "It can't be. I'm missing something."

"I'm taking them in, Peter," Norma said to the man in the robe.

"You know the rules, my child," he said.

"Go fuck yourself, Peter."

They entered a vast, bare room that held about twenty people. Each person kept their head down and mumbled to themselves. Lily recognized what they were saying as the Lord's Prayer. Ahead, one of the discs lit up and buzzed, and as if in a trance, the holder simply turned and went to the next room.

"What you need to realize about all of this is that it's free will. The only humans here are here of their own accord. Peter is a bot. There are no guns. There is no physical coercion," Norma noted.

"But it's all staged for them," Lily said curtly. "To convince them!"

"That is not the official position of the powers that be," Norma said. "We all have free will, and these people are simply leveraging their rights. As Americans."

She turned and led them through the sliding doors that separated that room from the next, which opened to the sounds of an angelic choir. Everything was white: the floors, the walls, the faux stone pillars; an empty hall of brilliance.

A voice said, "Please follow the lines below you."

Lily looked down and saw a pulsing blue arrow directing them forward, which Norma followed. Ahead, she saw the woman who had just been in the waiting room, called by the blinking lights of the disc. Norma pulled them both to the side, discreetly behind a pillar, and motioned them to watch.

The woman stood and stared blankly as a door in the wall opened and expelled what appeared to Lily to be a tanning bed, complete with plush purple interior and open glass lid. She knew what it was immediately and began to cry as she watched the woman, completely alone, kneel in front of the device, make the sign of the cross, and lie down inside it. Lily could make out the tears on her face as the lid closed to form the vacuum seal. Then she heard the sound of the nitrogen gas filling the sarcophagus.

As they left the area, Lily walked past another device that had an Out of Order sign on it, the dust revealing this wasn't a new occurrence. She could only bring herself close enough to make out the label on the side near where the head would rest.

ANOTHER QUALITY PRODUCT MADE IN THE USA

BY MALODOR INDUSTRIES

Lily happened to know that the Sarco was introduced to the world as a self-service assisted-suicide solution in 2017, the brainchild of Dr. Philip Nitschke, who was commissioned to create a device that enabled legal suicide.

Recognizing its problem amassing at the border, the Dennison administration, in 2038, ordered twenty of the latest versions of the device and sent them to southern Colorado. When asked why they wouldn't buy more to shorten the lines, President Dennison was quoted as saying, "Well, c'mon, if they've waited this long, I'm doing them a favor, giving them a few more hours in the sun."

***

No one said a word on the drive to the north through town. There was nothing to be said. Lily and Jeff held hands, staring out the window at the swarms of broken people everywhere. At night, they were frightening. In the day, they were heartbreaking.

Eventually, Norma pulled off into a side road and made the turn next to Zeke's hover-Wagoneer.

Zeke took one look at Lily's and Jeff's somber faces and pieced it together. "Norma, did you show them everyone . . ." He generally waved a hand, mouth falling into a slant. "You know, going . . . west?"

Norma didn't reply. She didn't have to.

"Not sure I wanted them to see that," Zeke said.

"The more people that see, the better. They were here. They should know."

Zeke looked at Lily and asked, "You okay?"

"No. No, I'm not. Let's go."

"Sure," Zeke said, beckoning for Jeff to follow along.

"How can no one know about this?" Lily asked, speaking to nobody in particular. "How can they hide something this monstrous?"

Norma fielded the question. "Everyone in the media knows, of course. They also know that they will be put out of business if they make this information public. Besides, if word got out, the government would just call it AI-generated propaganda pushed by crazy leftists and say they are all just drug-addicted liberals. You know the game plan. It's all the same, just better tech."

Jeff said, "Those aren't just liberals out there, though."

"Of course not. This, *all* of this," Norma added, gesticulating wildly, "is the by-product of a system that only views people as consumers, squeezing them for everything they've got and spewing them out like sewage when they don't have anything left to give." She paused, shaking her head. Her chin wobbled. With a hard look at Lily, Jeff, and Zeke, she rasped, "They are *not* sewage."

Zeke cleared his throat. "We know, Norma . . ."

"They are *people*," she went on, "and they've had everything taken away from them. Their health care. Their savings for retirement. Their Social Security. Whatever jobs they could get in the last twenty years were for shit wages in the first place. With the entire social safety net pulled out from under them, of course this is where they wind up. These are people who fell through the cracks from every walk of life, from every part of the country, from *all* parties! It just so happened this is the one place in the country they have even a remote chance of escape."

Zeke said, "They don't come here to die, but it's the natural progression. They try to get in down south, but then they see the numbers and realize it's a lottery they can't win. They stay as long as they can and then try to forget . . ."

Norma, with anger, said, "And those bastards make sure there's plenty of that addictive stuff around here free of charge. Once these people get hooked, it doesn't take much persuasion to get them to go west. And then it becomes the cover story should anyone ask: They were junkies when they got here that just couldn't make it in the real America. And they never deserved to be recorded as unemployed citizens in the economic indicators. When they go out west, they come off the books."

Lily, still dazed, said, "If they are capable of this, they are capable of anything. We need to figure out what's going on with Iwanna. This is not a coincidence it's in Colorado."

Zeke laughed lightly.

"What?" Lily asked.

"Nothing. It's just, well . . . you said her name like you know her."

Ignoring his statement, she said, "They have created a society that looks the other way as its citizens slowly kill themselves!"

Zeke held her gaze and said, "You think that's new? They've been doing this since the industrial age. All they've done is remove the friction."

Chapter 27

June 15

Seven days after the abortion in Mexico, Zeke and Lily were alone in the cockpit, having just dropped off two Dennison mid-level managers in Bozeman, Montana. It was all so beautiful, and Lily knew Zeke was deliberately keeping the flight at lower altitudes to appreciate the scenery, even though it led to a slower trip with higher fuel consumption. Among other things she'd learned about Zeke in the last few months, she could tell he was trying, as much as possible, to appreciate moments like these.

"I have to admit to a level of discomfort in our relationship, it being so new," she told him. "You've given me a job, been the perfect boss, and helped me in ways far beyond anything I could have expected. Thank you."

He pressed a spot on the control screen and turned toward her. "You're more than welcome," he said as they sailed over a blanket of dark-green forest that was followed by swaths of straw-colored plains as wide open as an ocean. "I trust you, but even if I didn't—ours is a case of mutually assured destruction."

Lily looked down self-consciously. "I won't betray that. If you ever need any help, just ask. I'll pay it forward however I can."

"Thanks, Lily, that's good to know. I also get young adults forced into gay conversion therapy. That's harder because they can't come back, but we find them foster homes first. How did everything go with the fetus registry?"

"Dr. Spector said she took care of it for me, so I guess I'll find out the next time I see our friend Job. I appreciate you getting me." Lily needed to avoid all possibility of being scanned until she was certain the system had registered the lost fetus, so Zeke had been picking her up in a clearing not far outside of Denver.

"You moving anywhere closer to the Springs? I know it's a fast commute down, but it must be getting to be a pain in the ass by now." He watched her move toward the jump seat and followed with, "Uh-oh, she needs to sit for this one."

Lily grinned as she sat. "No, it's not that bad."

"I know Jeff lives nearby. Does this give him hope—you getting a place of your own in the area?"

She nodded. "I like him. It's going well. But he's clearly rusty with this whole dating thing, and I'm worried he's going too fast. Moving in together certainly won't help that."

"Really? Good-looking guy like that hasn't been dating? Be happy he's not on *my* team."

"I'm still with him, Zeke. Dibs," she added, laughing. "He's taking things in order of priority—the first being securing employment and income."

"Well, that's a good thing, no? Self-aware. I'd put that in the plus column."

"That's how he spent his twenties." She thought a little more and then asked, "You get a good vibe from him?"

Zeke chuckled. "Oh no, sister, you're not pinning this on me. My opinion doesn't matter, unless you're asking me if I think he's gay, in which case, no, I don't." Seeing her slightly dejected response, he added, "But from what I could tell, he seems like a good guy. He didn't seem too clingy with you. Just legitimately concerned about how it would all turn out."

She got up and took in the Wyoming landscape. "Thanks, Zeke. That helps."

"You ready for the uterus whisperer?" he asked. "We'll be at the airport in about twenty minutes. Job's head is going to explode when he realizes you're no longer with child."

Lily scoffed. "If only that were true." She thought it through further. "It wouldn't matter, though. There'd be another right behind him."

◆••————••◆

Zeke offered to join Lily as she exited the terminal to help with the inevitable interrogation, but she declined, knowing it was something she could and should deal with on her own—it being her body and all.

As she got to the gate, Job was clearing the previous commuter when his tablet dinged.

He checked it, then quickly turned to see her, his eyes widening with what she could only describe as excitement. "Ms. Osbourne! Could you come over here, please?"

She complied and looked up as he read whatever the tablet was feeding him.

"I'm assuming you're aware your fetus is no longer registering?"

Lily weakly replied, "Yes, yes, I know. I lost it. My understanding is Zeke explained everything to you and your superiors, so I'm surprised you didn't know anything about it."

"Yes, it looks like your doctor entered the death certificate five days ago." Job didn't appear sure about whether he was willing to leave it at that. "Can anyone corroborate your story?"

Her eyes lit up, but she withheld the first thought that traveled to her mouth, not wanting to overplay her hand. "Are you calling me a liar, Job? After I just had a miscarriage?"

"Not at all, Ms. Osbourne. But I have a duty to uphold, and you left here with child and are coming back a week later without one. I have a duty to protect—"

"Air travel. You have a duty to protect *air travel*, Job, not my uterus. A medical doctor entered the proper explanation into the system. That is all you need, correct?"

Job now locked eyes with her, picking up on the condescension. "I suppose so, Ms. Osbourne."

"Then I *suppose* we're done here," she replied, echoing his sentiment. "Unless you'd like to add your supervisor to the conversation?"

"Well, if that's how you feel, Ms. Osbourne."

Chapter 28

July 4

Louisiana was the first state to ban all forms of "satanic rituals," explicitly targeting Mardis Gras, which was last publicly held in 2033. After that came Halloween. By the end of 2034, the October holiday was eradicated throughout the South and Southwest. In New Hampshire, a clever politician devised a loophole, applying the costume-based components to the Nashua Fourth of July parade in 2036, welcoming participants to dress in their favorite American-based regalia. This evolved to include floats with participants reenacting their most treasured moments in the country's history. Lily and Jeff sat on the sidewalk in downtown Vicksburg Gulch, bracing themselves for the travesties of culture they knew would undoubtedly comprise the local version of this now countrywide ceremony.

"How bad do you think it's going to be?" Jeff asked Lily.

Looking down the street, she said, "I went back home to visit my family in Texas a couple of years ago, and it was already pretty tasteless. But I hear it's gotten out of control in some towns."

She looked around as a family dressed up as President Dennison, Junior, Joe, and Iwanna found a spot five feet away on the curb. The daughter playing Iwanna, around twelve, wore a white form-fitting dress down to her ankles. All had their sidearms in their gun belt. The father was in a navy-blue suit, Uncle Sam hat, and a red tie that reached to his knees.

"Yeah, this is going to be pretty bad," she told him.

Jeff scanned the scene. "We can head out if you want. Just thought it would be an interesting part of our investigation, but I don't care that much."

"We're here. Let's see how far we make it."

They didn't have to wait long for the parade to begin—their spots on the sidewalk coincidentally perfect for the egregious display. The first float featured a stocky young boy of around six—who was in possession of an unusually powerful frame for a child—wearing a colonial-style wig and too-small pantaloons.

The digital sign that hovered over the float read:

GEORGE WASHINGTON AND THE CHERRY TREE

Lily noted the boy did indeed have an axe slung over his shoulder. And razor stubble.

As the float came to a scheduled stop in front of her and Jeff's section of the crowd, the boy turned to them and said, "I never told my father I chopped down that tree, because obviously I didn't. I was nowhere near it. I did, of course, tell my father the truth, which was that it was the slave kid next door. Why would I destroy my father's tree? Obviously, *he* had every motive. Just setting the record straight." He put the axe down at the foot of the tree and stood there defiantly until his next performance in a hundred feet.

Then came the Duncan family—all fourteen of them. Dad; Mom; four girls and three women, dressed in ankle-length dresses; and three boys and two men, wearing jeans, plaid shirts, and cowboy hats. They led the parade just ahead of the Colorado Springs High School marching band, banging out "Amazing Grace."

As they passed, Jeff asked Lily, "Why are some of the girls in red dresses?"

Lily pondered the question for a few seconds, and then the light came on. "Notice anything about their age?"

He looked again and then got it. "They've had their period. Able to bear children."

"Yep. And take a look at the two with sashes."

Jeff searched and found one man in his early twenties and a girl around seven, each with a broad red, white, and blue sash that read:

DENNISON GODCHILD

"Every sixth child in an American family gets papers that declare them a Dennison godchild," Lily noted. "So fucking sick."

Then came the next float, sponsored by the Reverend Brady Taggert: a large-scale hologram that featured Christ holding a Protestant cross and standing above a floating red planet, Earth below it, and a physical throne that was lit up by spotlights. Empty. Circling the entire float were the words:

WHO WILL LEAD US TO OUR DESTINY?

WITH ALL OF CHRIST'S LOVE, THE THIRTEEN MEMBERS OF THE TAGGERT FAMILY!

Next came the submission from the Vicksburg Gulch High School History Department. It was simple and tasteful: an animatronic Joe Biden riding on a bicycle that suddenly came to a stop, at which point he fell off. It reset every ten seconds.

Jeff and Lily were both startled by the sudden sound of gunshots as the next float arrived, sponsored by none other than Dennison Robotics. In the middle was a robotic president holding up two AK-47s, firing what they both hoped were blanks at three holograms of the cartoon mouse Speedy Gonzales. One held a taco, one rode a lawnmower, and one had what they presumed to be a brick of cocaine, white powder trailing in his wake.

"Get outta here, you wetbacks!" Dennison yelled as each jumped over a low wall to avoid the onslaught, then used a tunnel that led to the back of the float to start the routine all over again.

As it passed, Lily noticed a Chihuahua hanging from a noose slung over Dennison's shoulder.

"Twisted," she said. As she turned left to find the next atrocity, Lily froze. "Oh no," she whispered. "No, no, no. They didn't do this!"

Jeff looked at her, startled by her hands covering her mouth. Then he looked back at the parade. "These motherfuckers," he said, joining her in shock.

A five-by-five square of girls and women, some in their teens, wore black-and-white striped prison uniforms, shackles on their wrists, and irons around their ankles, all with a single chain connecting each. Their formation was 28.8 feet across and 32.1 feet long. It didn't take long to piece together that they weren't actors as the young boy playing George Washington had been. Their heads were down, some weeping as they shuffled their feet forward and back, all at a synchronized pace of 1.3 miles per hour. Barely a walk.

"We need to go!" Lily said as she broke down crying, heading toward Jeff's apartment with him in tow.

A hologram banner hung over the group of women. It read:

BABY MURDERERS

Chapter 29

August 16

There were ten students in Jeff's journalism class, all seniors he assumed were none too happy about being lifted out of their previous school to graduate in a new town. He scanned the room and found them in pretty good spirits, nonetheless. Except for one.

"Hi, guys. I'm Mr. Maslow, and I'll be your teacher for this class—and if you happened to take the American English class, you're stuck with me two times a day."

Then Jeff heard faux snoring and watched a grinning young man flip him the bird from the back of the room.

Jeff glared as the student said, "Rough night? Is your new place nicer than my basement?" A couple of students snickered knowingly.

Jeff smiled, seeing the enemy for the first time. It was Cheryl and Jake's little darling, Eric, which he'd assumed when he had first looked at the roster. Though it should not have been surprising to him that they'd spawned a little asshole.

He walked in front of his desk and sat on the edge, deciding on the best course of action. On the one hand, he was being provoked. On the other, he wouldn't be in this room, working this job, if it weren't for this punk's father.

"My new place is much nicer than your dad's basement, thanks for asking. What's great is that your parents still aren't that far away. Matter of fact, I just spoke to them. Maybe I'll drop by and give them an early performance evaluation."

"Go right ahead. I can tell you what their response will be: When I'm here, I'm *your* problem."

Suddenly, through an unseen speaker, Brianne's voice joined the conversation. "That is exactly correct, Mr. Daniels. You are *our* problem, and I am sure your father, being a big part of what we're doing here at Vicksburg Gulch, would be disappointed at your behavior on your first day. I do know he agrees with our disciplinary policy. Perhaps you should take a look before mouthing off again."

The written policy appeared on every desk in the room—which were essentially tablets with legs—including Jeff's. He didn't look initially, still absorbing the fact that he had been spied on by Brianne this whole time without knowing it. He wasn't surprised, but it undermined his credibility when his boss needed to step in to save him. On the other hand, he read the policy:

With parental/guardian permission, and as deemed necessary by the Vicksburg Gulch administration, a teacher may escalate to their respective principal the need to apply this disciplinary policy to any number of students. If standard methods of discipline have failed, the punishment will be corporal, consistent with Colorado laws regulating the procedure.

Currently, the solution for this purpose is the Spankanator 3000, a Dennison Robotics product. Consistent with regulations, the initial setting will be at three and increased to a maximum of ten should the undesired behavior not subside.

A setting of eleven may be applied with the agreement of the administration and parents/guardians.

"Your father reached out to me to make sure I knew we had his permission to go to eleven," Brianne said.

⸎

After the class was over and the students exited, Brianne came into the classroom and found Jeff at his desk, pensively deciding how to respond to the last hour's events. Brianne took one of the student chairs and pulled it up across from the desk. "Not happy about that?" She wore a buttoned-up blouse and ankle-length black skirt and had the demeanor of someone with much power behind her. Both fit like a glove.

Jeff managed to hide his anger, calmly responding, "It's not the highlight of my day, no. But I'm not really that surprised."

"Well, no, you shouldn't be. I get I'm not a teacher, but let's be fair. It's been a very long time since you were in a classroom—a generation ago, in a very different environment than this one. I wanted to make sure you were in control."

"I would have been if you hadn't interrupted." Jeff told himself to take the edge out of his voice.

"The Daniels kid is a bit of a challenge for both of us, Jeff. If it were any other kid, I wouldn't have said a word, and I'm sure you would have handled it fine. Jake and I have a well-established working relationship together at Dennison, and he made of point of telling me his kid was spoiled and arrogant—and that I could expect him to start on day one. You've got to give him credit for knowing, right?"

Jeff was cooling off quickly, falling under Brianne's calming spell. "I guess that was good for him to do."

"Now that Eric knows who I am, he knows he'll probably be on the wrong side of his father's fist, or worse, if he pulls that again."

Jeff jolted up and looked at Brianne. "Seriously?"

Brianne rose and started to leave. "No matter how long you've been here, you're still a coastal kid, Jeff. Eventually, this place will stop surprising you, but it's going to take some time."

Chapter 30

August 18

The following Saturday, Lily took an Amazon Air out to Vicksburg. She and Jeff left the apartment and walked down Main Street toward the newly opened Denny's Diner, designed as a replica of the Frosty Palace in the movie *Grease*.

As they passed, they investigated every shop, trying to assess which were manned by Dennibots and which by humans, concluding they could not tell the difference. However, by the time they wound up under the snowman on the marquee, Jeff felt confident he had found the telltale sign of a female bot: Unless there was something in the drinking water in Colorado that caused breast-size Bs to become Cs, the designers at Dennison were out to please the male citizens.

At the gas station that was still fully functional despite the rest of the world's conversion to electric vehicles—the US government limiting their production for "national security reasons"—Jeff spotted a D cup dispensing a good old-fashioned service station windshield wipe, her breasts squeaking left and right on the glass with the motion. The line outside the station was reminiscent of the 1970s gas shortages, even though there was more crude oil available now than at any time in modern history, with only developing countries demanding it. And the United States.

Inside the diner, they sat in a booth and scanned the playlist of the personal jukebox.

"Dennison still can't get enough of the fifties," Lily said. "Such an infant."

Jeff said, "I think we should use songs to share how we feel about each other, just like they did in the old days."

"Sure, stud, go for it," she said, picking up the torso-size menu.

"Siri, pay the jukebox for four songs."

While the payment was modern, the rest of the equipment was true to history, requiring a manual entry via button press using a letter-number combination from the menu inside the jukebox. It didn't take him long to land on D-6. As the song started up, he took both of Lily's hands from across the table, looked lovingly into her eyes, and pretended to lip-synch to the Dean Martin song he had never heard, "You Belong to Me."

Lily burst out laughing at the last line, catching the attention of the nearby patrons who were thoroughly enjoying their history trip, most likely referring to the period as a magical time when all was right in the world—Jim Crow aside.

"So, what's the funny story you wanted to tell me about?" Lily asked, resting her elbows on the table between them.

"Cheryl's kid is in my class," Jeff said.

"Ewww. Let me guess—asshole?"

"Gaping. Drops the fact I lived in his basement *immediately*. I actually laughed a bit, just at the sheer balls of it," Jeff said with a chuckle. "As I was about to handle it with my abundant wit and empathy, a voice came from on high."

Lily raised her brows conspiratorially. "Jesus?"

"Close," Jeff revealed. "Brianne, the principal who hired me."

The waitress arrived, decked out in a 1950s-style uniform: big pockets, long hem, complete with the nurse-like hat. She was in her late forties and fit. Not as observant as Jeff on the way in, Lily presumed the waitress was a bot and said, "Well, aren't you adorable." She brought her face up to the name pin. "Alice," she said, poking it with her index finger for effect.

Jeff was too slow to intervene, the best all-too-late advice he could muster being, "Lil, she's real!"

The shove into the booth jolted her back. "Keep your fingers off the girls, please," Alice said.

Coming out of the shock, Lily said, "Either the tech has come a long way, or you're not a bot."

Alice said, "Loverboy over here seemed to pick it up from the start." She turned to Jeff and asked, "What gave me away?"

He thought long and hard before saying, "Dunno, just had a feeling." He raised his menu, eager to change the subject. "Could we get a few more minutes? Just need to take a look at the menu."

"Sure, sugar. Just so you know, we're not having the bots take orders just yet. They're just bussing and serving for now. There was . . . an incident."

"We heard," Jeff said. "Glad to know my dessert won't be in my face later."

Alice said, "Hers might be if she gets all dykie on me again." She gave a flirty wink to Jeff as she turned to tend to her next table. "But *you* can take a shot."

While Lily continued to unravel the last thirty seconds, Jeff failed to suppress his smile and eventual laughter.

"Screw you. How did you know?" she demanded.

"Well, I'll give you my secret, but please don't repeat it to her," he said, leaning closer and lowering his voice. "You notice anything about the female bots we've seen so far?"

Lily took a while before it occurred to her. "She's on the itty-bitty-tit-ty committee."

"Bingo!"

"So you spent the whole walk staring at other women's chests."

"Oh, c'mon, that's not fair. It was obvious. And they're not women. They're bots," he said just as the song he'd selected concluded.

Lily was up on her feet at once. "My turn."

Jeff watched as she scanned the jukebox, pressed A-6, and shortly thereafter, the voice of Bobby Darin singing "Mack the Knife" entered the conversation.

They listened for a bit, and then Jeff asked, "Are you threatening me?" He was embracing the fact that Lily was starting to appear more herself since the trip to Mexico.

"I don't know. How many boobs you gonna look at on the way back to the apartment?"

"Only the one's bigger than yours. Bs and up."

She threw her spoon at him with a burst of laughter. "You had better take them in because you ain't seeing these babies for months."

"I will seize the day and appreciate every moment."

She pushed his head back and said, "Ugh, *Dead Poets* again. What is it with you and that movie?"

At the mentioning of one of his favorite films, Jeff became serious, trying to frame an argument in his mind that was on point without appearing too fixated. Which he was.

"Look, the movie is riddled with thematic confusion and misquotes, so it's flawed. But we take advantage of the freedom to be who we are all the time, and we've lost it in our lifetime. Those in power want their biological subjects to be the same as the bots. Follow orders without questions, leaving them as sole arbiter of what is right and wrong. And they will treat those who dissent the way they do a faulty bot: discard it. We saw them doing this." As he watched her for signs of rejection, he realized it was affecting her. "The human race is filled with passion. If they get their way, it will all be subverted."

She nodded in agreement. "Okay, that makes some sense."

"And it was my father's favorite movie. He realized he was a hypocrite, starting out as a young English teacher and three years later selling out for a job in banking, for the money. He was always trying to live vicariously through me and my sister, and I guess I bought into it, trying to do the same thing."

"Figure things out yet?" Alice asked.

They both scrambled to look at the short menu of items. Jeff said, "Not a big offering."

"Same menu as they had in the movie."

"Yeah, what's with all this, anyway?" he asked, referring to the whole schtick. "I mean, it seems a little random. I barely got the reference, and I only did because my sister loved the movie."

"Best guess is that Iwanna loved it too when she was a kid. What's it gonna be?"

"Double polar burger, side of fries, and a Coors," Jeff said.

"No booze, babe," Alice said.

"Root beer."

Turning to Lily, she asked, "You ready?"

Lily appeared to still be smarting over the push. "Sorry about before."

"Don't worry about it, hon. Was refreshing to have a woman take a poke for once. What can I get you?"

"Tuna fish salad and a cherry soda."

"You got it," Alice said, heading toward the grill.

"So . . . Brianne is the voice of God. Go on," Lily said.

"Yeah, so," Jeff went on, settling back into his story, "she was obviously observing me and my class without my knowledge—and she clearly knows Jake, who apparently had given her a heads-up about the little prince."

"They did seem to know about this when we ran into them."

"Definitely. Anyway, Brianne sent the disciplinary policy to everyone in the room, including me. Guess what it includes?"

Lily seemed to give this serious thought before giving up. "Waterboarding."

"You're very good at this game. *Spanking*."

Lily got serious, absorbed this, and said, "Spanking?"

"Spanking."

"No irony?"

"Nope."

An old man in a busboy uniform arrived with a tray holding a root beer and cherry soda. "He-re are your d-d-drink-k-k-s," he said, shakily placing a root beer in front of Jeff, who noted that the shaking didn't seem natural—almost like it was intentional. He didn't spill a drop.

"Thanks," Jeff said unconvincingly, trying to get a better look at the man's face. As he leaned over to offer Lily her cherry soda, Jeff pieced it together: the aviator sunglasses, the mock fragility—the fact that moments ago, he had learned bots were serving and bussing.

He checked the name tag, looked down, and shook his head.

"What?" Lily asked under her breath. Jeff nodded for her to look at the server's name tag.

They both recognized it was Biden as the bot said, "My name is Brandon. Let me know if there's anything I can get f-f-for you," and walked away.

"For fuck's sake. They're such children," Lily said, eager to return to their original conversation. "Okay, so who delivers this spanking—and does the kid need to wear a ball gag?"

"Ah, my clever dear, you get to the real crux. As much as I'd love nothing better than to dole it out, this pleasure too has been assigned to the bots."

"Should I be concerned about this desire to spank?" she asked, brows furrowed.

Holding a steady stare and biting down his laughter, Jeff said, "The Spankanator 3000."

Lily did not budge, assuming this clearly was a joke. "You're an asshole."

Jeff pulled out his phone, tapped a bit, and showed her the Dennison Robotics product page for the device. She delved in, reading the description and testimonials.

"This can't be real," she said, increasingly dejected as she reviewed the document while Jeff scanned the jukebox. His next selection—"Whole Lot of Shakin' Goin' On" by Jerry Lee Lewis—joined in a minute later.

"Technically," Jeff said, picking the conversation back up, "these laws have been on the books forever, and schools increasingly started to use them again in the twenties."

"This is the three thousand model," Lily noted, aghast. "What did the first two thousand nine hundred ninety-nine versions of this thing do?"

"Feather play?"

She was no longer amused. "Seriously, Jeff, this is so sick. She threatened a seventeen-year-old boy with a spanking?"

"For the record, it worked. Did I mention Daddy Jake signed off on it?"

"It's like . . . like they're outsourcing their parenting. They let him do and get whatever he wants as long as he doesn't challenge their beliefs, and the results of that are everyone else's problem. What does it mean when a society needs to resort to physical assault just to get people to behave civilly?"

"I think that horse has left the barn, but the term you're looking for is 'regression,'" he said.

The last lines of the song playing on the jukebox registered with Lily. "Did he just tell a woman to wiggle her ass around?"

◆•• —————————— ••◆

Lily felt herself sinking, weighed down by the reality of the world. She looked at the ridiculous restaurant they were in, the colors, the music—the Joe Biden bot wobbling around like he was one butterfly kiss away from falling and breaking a hip.

It was all stupid and unenjoyable. It was all terrifying to the point of paralysis.

She thought about her need to break the law simply to live. Those poor girls who hadn't been as lucky as she had—marching in the parade earlier, sobbing. All those people, living without hope, encouraged to commit suicide by their own government. She nodded her head at Jeff, who was still speaking, then stopped, unable to focus.

Or maybe, actually, it was the opposite.

Her mind was just too focused on something else. Focused in a way it hadn't been since working on her bees with Iwanna twenty years ago.

Mumbling, she said, "I've got to fix this."

Jeff, who had let her be when he had seen her mood change, asked, "What? Sorry, I couldn't hear you."

She looked up, then out the window, and then watched as Brandon stumbled in front of her. After a moment, she said to Jeff, "I can't sit back anymore. I'm sorry, but I've got to do something."

Jeff smiled. "Why are you apologizing to me? I just can't think of a single thing people like us can do to affect anything. We're slightly outnumbered."

"I have an idea, but you're just going to have to trust me and ride shotgun."

Jeff demurred with a smile. "Lead the way, m'lady."

Lily looked around and found her target. She took her glass of water and spilled it on the table, and as Brandon scanned the room, she waved and pointed to the mess. He began his stumble in their direction.

"Don't say a word," she quietly told Jeff.

"Welll, sh-shucks, looks like you had a little acc-cc-ident, missy," Brandon said as he took a towel from his beltline and leaned in to begin the cleanup.

"Yes, Brandon, sorry about that," Lily said, scanning the area one more time before leaning closer and whispering in his ear, *"Mens sana in corpore sano."*

The bot froze, and Lily whispered, "Yes!" She motioned to Jeff again to be quiet. "Brandon, does Anatoly still work at Dennison?"

Without any hesitation or inflection, the bot said, "Yes, Charity. He's the program head."

Lily nodded and thought about her next question, glancing around to see if anyone had picked up on what was happening. They had not. "Can you contact him?"

"Yes, Charity," Brandon said. "We all have that capability as a safety mechanism."

Lily looked at her watch. "Okay, Brandon. Can you please tell Anatoly that I'd like to meet him at our favorite watering hole Monday at six p.m.? He'll know what I'm talking about. And ask him to be discreet."

Brandon, still frozen, did not immediately respond, and Lily was worried something had gone wrong. Then he said, "I've sent your message, Charity."

"Thank you, Brandon. *Corpus sanum in mente sana.*"

The bot immediately picked up its cleaning duties where it had left off, leaving the table a vision of order. "M-m-maybe cut back on the c-c-coffee so you don't s-s-pill next time," he said with a warm smile.

"Yes, thanks, I'll do that," Lily said as he left. She returned to a staring, expressionless Jeff. "Wait until we leave," she said, waving at Alice for the check, which Jeff intercepted on delivery.

"I'll pick this one up," he said, still clearly dazed by the event.

Alice looked at Lily while pointing to Jeff and said, "Big spender, this one!"

Jeff followed Lily down the sidewalk and to a park bench, where she sat.

"So, you're a bot whisperer now?" he asked in a failed attempt at levity.

Lily was still deciding how to go about explaining herself and was still unsure as to where to end the reveal. It seemed like an all-or-nothing thing. She couldn't just tell Jeff *parts* of this story, but if she told him everything, he'd be in danger. "You've got to be patient with me while I think this through."

"What through?"

"How to help you understand without telling you anything that can get you hurt." She looked down in her ongoing contemplation.

"Aren't we past that by now, with everything that's happened?" Jeff asked, making a fair point. He reached for her arm, catching her wrist. *"Charity?"*

She winced at the name, pulling away. "Don't ever call me that again." After composing herself, she continued. "Jeff, there is no bottom with these people. No end to what they can do. This is what happens when there are no checks in the system. Just give me a second."

She thought a while longer and came to a conclusion. "Okay. So this is the best I can do, and then I just ask that you continue to trust my intentions for both you and all of us," she said, taking a deep breath to center herself. She looked him in the eyes. "I used to work at Dennison in the robotics lab. Twenty years ago, when I was a kid. A stupid kid. My name was Charity then. I designed and programmed their AI profile for my first project." She hesitated. "The BuzzKills."

She watched his expression go from disbelief to pure, unfettered shock.

It was his turn to stutter. "You . . . *you* made those? You were . . . on their side?"

Watching him get slightly paler, she said, "Yes. Like I said, I was young. Obviously, you know I'm not with them anymore."

"But you made those . . . those killing machines?"

"No!" she barked. "No, that is not what they were when I left. They were designed to observe and detain, then call for help. They changed the capabilities after I left."

"And why was that?" he asked.

"I can't go into that yet. I will, I promise, but not now. Not with what I've started back there."

"Which was what? I didn't know Joe Biden spoke Latin!"

Lily gave him a thin smile. "When it comes to AI and bots, it's always a smart move to build in a fail-safe mechanism. I built one into my baseline profile for the bees, and my guess is they just kept replicating it for everything that followed after I left. That's what I was banking on when I said the phrase. It means 'a healthy mind in a healthy body.' It's an old Roman belief in balance and discipline."

"So when you say that, the bot shuts down?"

"No, more like it goes into an administrative mode where you can talk to it directly, without whatever personality they built on top of it."

"Who's Anatoly?"

"He was there when I took over the project, and we hit it off. Good guy, and I trusted him implicitly. He ran the Ukrainian drone program during the war with Russia until they caught him. Fascinating man."

"You can't really assume he's the same person after all this time, can you?" Jeff asked.

She pondered the question. "It's a risk, I know, but like I said, I'm done with sitting back. It occurred to me I might be able to get in touch with him, and I took the chance. He was . . ." She searched for the right word. "*Authentic,* then. What he went through, no one should go through, and after that, I can't imagine anything else worse could happen to him. We got to know each other pretty well. Used to go out for beers after work. That's where I'm hoping to find him Monday."

"Oh, that's what you mean by 'pretty well,'" Jeff said with a hint of jealousy.

"Stop right there," Lily said firmly. "Not like that at all. Sex was the last thing on his mind, and frankly, I never heard him even talk on the subject once. He was all about his work."

"Okay, point taken. So what's the plan?"

Lily laughed. "Plan? I have no freaking idea. I've got a couple of days to come up with one." She reached out to hold his hands. "In the meantime, I know you've got a million questions, but you need to understand—I worked with Iwanna, I know what she's capable of, and that's all you need to know right now. This is not a trust issue. It's a 'keep us both alive' issue."

"That bad, huh?"

"Yes, and I completely understand if you want to get off this ride. Seriously, you need to think hard about this because I have no idea where it's going, but I know I can't sit back and watch this anymore. Not with what I know and not with what I know I'm capable of."

There was no hesitation in Jeff's reply. He began to smile. "Cool. I've never dated a superhero."

"I'm definitely not that." She became pensive. "And I'm probably in over my head already."

◆•·————·•◆

"I knew it was too quiet from her," Jeff told Lily as he handed her his phone with the text he'd just received upon their return to his apartment.

> Hiya, we both assume you'll be in church tomorrow morning, but Jake suggested you and that girlfriend of yours join us as our guests. You'll get great seats and we can introduce you to some of the hot shots here. Promise I'll be good :)

"Jake will kill you, Jeff," Lily said with a huff of a laugh, "and I'm sure he has many places to lose your body. This is going to be a problem if it escalates. For you, not for me." And then, after a beat of self-reflection, she added, "And maybe for me."

He laughed as he said, "Way to commit, Lil."

"Maybe bringing us to the church is her way of ending it? Cleaning it all up because she knows you're starting to get annoyed?"

"Doubt it, but we'll see."

Chapter 31

August 19

The next day, Jeff and Lily walked along Jeff's street toward town—and, specifically, toward the Vicksburg Gulch House of the Lord. The Gulch was strictly zoned, household income being the primary variable, and a couple of houses straddled the border between each zone. As they walked, they noticed a few couples moving toward the same destination. Everyone was heading to church.

As the procession of couples and families formed, two young men in their twenties hopped into their classic pickup just ahead, started it up, and pressed hard on the gas, spewing noise and black smoke into the beautifully clean Colorado air that benefited from the rest of the world's progress in scrubbing up the ozone layer. They backed out of the driveway and sped away, their wake of dark smoke lingering for several minutes in the procession's path.

It was a very orderly series of fast-moving lines that led into the Vicksburg Gulch House of the Lord, for security and its associated delays were deemed unnecessary. It wouldn't be easy for leftist terrorists to enter without being spotted, much less cause damage. The surveillance systems employed by most governments had gotten pretty good at identifying known criminals. And members of terrorist groups. And outspoken members of regional parent-teacher organizations.

As agreed, Cheryl and Jake were waiting for them by the President Dennison statue, his muscular physique, blond hair, large hands, and thin face pointing due south from somewhere around a height of fifteen feet.

"Hey there, kids," Cheryl said with a big smile, leaning in to hug Jeff and Lily. "Have you had the pleasure of attending one of Reverend Taggert's services before?"

"No," Lily said, not missing a beat. "We have had a bourbon at his charming son's place, though."

"Hah!" Cheryl cawed. "That little shit. I'm sure you'll get better service around here. See, honey?" she said to Jake. "I told you she was sassy."

Jake, who was in the middle of shaking hands with one of the men approaching him on their way into the arena, returned to the group. "Yes, you did," he said, smiling at Lily. "We should head inside."

Jeff was not too surprised by the good seats Jake had obtained: a roped-off section in the middle of the floor, two rows from the pulpit directly in front of them. He was so busy looking around at all of it—the size, the people, the theatrical stage—that he didn't notice the order of entry to their seats was Cheryl, him, Jake, and Lily. Only the floor was filled at this point, the arena built with the expectation of the many worshippers who had not yet arrived at the Gulch.

The opening ceremonies and initial parts of the service were pretty standard: periods of welcoming, hymns, prayers, and, of course, offerings. After all, buildings that host worshippers of the man who once called the poor "blessed" don't pay for themselves. The offerings were collected by hovering drones that went from person to person, front to back, a hologram of the amounts being offered appearing above so everyone could see what was being offered before making their own contribution.

Lily looked at the numbers: $750. $1,500. $3,000. Then she looked at Jake and said, "We can't afford that."

"Don't you worry your pretty head," Jake replied. "I'll take care of you guys. You're my guests."

He did, and as the robots worked their way down the rows, coordinated and syncing with each other so that none of them moved a row back ahead of the other, the lighting above the pulpit slowly rose in coordination with the completion of the collection. Jeff gave up trying to figure out how much money this place had just made.

◆•————••◆

A spotlight appeared over Taggert downstage left and followed him on his solemn approach to the pulpit. A less luminous spotlight shone over Mary on her throne many feet behind him.

Taggert knew these people before him. Most were working their way up from low-income families, some from abject poverty. He knew the distraction religion provided. It was what Jimmy Swaggart had given him when he had been a kid back in the 1980s until Taggert had realized, as he watched his mother call in an offering of $50 that could have been his first bicycle, that it was coming out of his mouth and well-being. He had decided he needed to be on the other end of that phone line and had already seen through the scam by the time his mother had stopped watching. Apparently, even she drew the line at following a millionaire who used the offerings for prostitutes.

He hoped the sound system was as good as Jake had promised and flitted a glance at his special guest in acknowledgment as he began the sermon. *What a pretty girl Jake has with him,* he thought.

"'Be fruitful and multiply.' Genesis one, twenty-eight. Everyone knows this command. But what does it mean for us to be fruitful here, in this modern world, where just about every nation has seen nothing but a huge drop in their birth rate, including ours? I mean, certainly God understands the cost of living for families with children, right?" He paused.

"Darling Mary, can you please read the passage in Genesis where it says, 'Be fruitful unless there's an economic downturn'?"

There was laughter throughout the arena as Mary mockingly flipped through her King James and said, "Don't see it anywhere, honey pie!"

"But this is supposed to be a partnership. It takes a village!" Taggert said. "And that's where many communities and churches fail in this partnership. We tell you, bear that child because you may not kill it in the womb! And we quote Genesis, and we bring you here and make it sound like a chore. And maybe for some of you, it is, but that's not what we're preaching here. We didn't in Denver, and we certainly will not here in this promised land!"

He paused before the next salvo.

"Hear me! There is nothing in the Bible that says two married people can't enjoy the pleasure of sexual relations in all its forms, for this keeps you happy together, in good times and bad. And together, you prepare the home so that when you have that child, you may nurture it. God doesn't tell us we may only have sex when the woman is fertile," Taggert continued. "He wants us, commands us, to have it and enjoy it however we prefer, within the confines of a marriage, and as a result of that fruitfulness, we multiply. Does the farmer go down his row and plant a single seed where he wants his crops? Do you, Tucker? I see you there with your lovely wife. How many corn seeds do you plant in the ground?"

From the third row, Tucker yelled, "Too many to count, Reverend!"

"Too—many—to—count!" Taggert boomed. "That's right. And do they all sprout?"

"No, Reverend! Thank God!" Tucker said. Everyone in the arena roared.

"As long as your activity ultimately results in fruitfulness, it is blessed with God's love. Now, friends, I remind you of your duty to your Lord and this great nation: If we are to exist and survive on our own, without outside influences, we must have the means to do so, and that means we need more children, who will become entrepreneurs, managers, workers.

"Some of you are new here. The others have heard this before. Did you know in China, that godforsaken land of communism, they once prevented their people from having children? You can talk to any economist, and they will tell you that the Chinese economic stall we are seeing today is precisely because of that. They will look for migration, as we did, but not find it. We don't tell our people how many children to have, but the growth of our economy demands it. Fortunately, the Lord provides the path in the Bible, where any activities done within the confines of marriage are in His name and His glory! That's what we know here in Vicksburg Gulch. That's what all God's Christian children throughout this country know."

The crowd murmured in agreement.

"It is because of their respect for me and my leadership here that I have assurances from the White House that, after the election, it will be decreed by the Dennison family that every *fifth* child borne unto a member of this congregation will be the godchild of President John Dennison, with all the associated benefits that brings!"

They applauded at the thought of bringing five human beings into this world to attain VIP status.

"Can we please ask the Youth Brigade to escort the children to the amusement park outside? Wait until you all see what's waiting for you there. There's even ice cream! Served by humans!"

All children below the age of seventeen were filed out through the center aisle by the parishioners in their late teens.

As Taggert came down from the pulpit, the spotlight moved slightly to the right on a smaller, lower pulpit, with a well-lit path leading to it from Mary's throne. She glowed with a smile that radiated sheer joy, and the murmur in the crowd was undeniable. Most knew what was coming.

"Let us pray," Mary said. About half the crowd exhaled at the same time.

The lights came down. It was pitch black. No lights from Exit signs, no small spots in the stairwells. No one was going anywhere, lest they risk walking into a wall. But for the increase in respiration around them, Lily and Jeff could not hear a thing until Mary said, "Close your eyes, and feel the cushion under you. Feel your weight on the seat. Pay attention to your breath."

Jeff realized he was listening to his mindfulness meditation of many years and smiled at the fact that they had commandeered it for Christianity.

"Inhale, exhale. Focus your attention on any sounds around you, and just acknowledge them as an occurrence in consciousness. If you have a thought, see what happens to it. Don't let your thoughts distract you. Stay in the moment, and return to the breath."

There was a barely audible note from the organ, a high pitch emanating from a column of speakers placed in the center of the arena.

Mary said, "Let the words of the Lord our God pass through you as we all join hands."

There was a slight uptick in the volume from the organ, with a slightly lower pitch.

At the end of the row, Lily felt Jake gently take her hand, and Jeff had each one taken by a respective Daniels.

Mary continued:

> *"Proverbs: 'Rejoice in the wife of your youth, a lovely deer, a graceful doe. Let her breasts fill you at all times with delight; be intoxicated always in her love.'"*

After ten seconds, the organ went one up in volume, one down in pitch.

> *"Ephesians: 'Wives, submit to your own husbands as to the Lord. Now as the church submits to Christ, so wives should submit to their husbands in everything. Husbands, love your wives, just as also Christ loved the church and gave Himself for her, to make her holy, cleansing her in the washing of water by the word.'"*

The sound pattern on the organ continued after each passage reading.

"Corinthians: 'Do not deprive one another, but then come together again, so that Satan may not tempt you because of your lack of self-control.'

"Psalms: 'As arrows are in the hand of a mighty man, so are children of the youth. Happy is the man that hath his quiver full of them.'

"Song of Solomon: 'Blow on my garden, that its fragrance may spread abroad. Let my lover come into his garden and taste its choice fruits.'"

"Oh yeah," Jeff heard Cheryl say in a quivering voice.

"'Like an apple tree among the trees of the forest, so is my beloved among the young men. In his shade, I took great delight and sat down, and his fruit was sweet to my taste.'

"Hebrews: 'No discipline seems enjoyable at the time, but painful. Later on, however, it yields the fruit of peace and righteousness to those who have been trained by it.'"

They were at a deep octave at this point, and particularly with the volume, each organ note was reverberating throughout the building and everybody in it. The last one, Lily noted, gave her a tingle. This time, on the organ note, there was no doubting what Lily felt, and she became equal parts horrified, violated, and aroused.

"And our final verse," Mary said, "is also from the Song of Solomon."

"Yes!" Cheryl said quietly.

"'It is the voice of my beloved! He knocks, saying, "Open for me, my sister, my love, My dove, my perfect one." My love thrust his hand through the opening, and my feelings were stirred for him.'"

It was no longer a briefly held note—its sound metallic, industrial, reverberating in everyone's core and elsewhere. It was held for about thirty seconds before it was allowed to fade slowly. Jeff's left hand shook uncontrollably, and he eventually realized it wasn't his doing. Cheryl had climaxed. Lily's hand flinched just a bit as she moistened. Knowingly, Jake gave a gentle, tender squeeze, which made her open her eyes; turn toward him with pure anger, which he couldn't see; and slap his hand away.

After it abated, the lights slowly rose, and Jeff looked over at a still-livid Lily, who was staring straight ahead, trying to figure out what had just happened. Then he looked at Cheryl, Jake, the others sitting in their row. All had their hymnals out as if nothing had occurred, preparing for the recessional hymn as the congregation on the stage organized the parade out.

◆•┄┄┄┄┄┄•◆

As the audience began to file outside after the ceremony, Jeff and Lily stood up, prepared to exit in turn—only for Jake to hold up a hand, stopping them.

Reluctantly, they each sat back down. Jeff tried to catch Lily's eye, only for Jake to sit forward in his chair, eclipsing her from view.

"Well," he said like a sales rep about to make the final pitch, "I suspect you folks have started to figure it all out by now. What this congregation is about . . . Cheryl and her actions up until today."

As if this conversation had been rehearsed, Cheryl chimed in, "When we learned Jake was no longer able to father children, at first, we despaired . . ."

Jeff's jaw dropped, which he clumsily and frantically set back in place.

"But then someone told us about this blessed man," she went on, gesturing to Taggert, "and how he properly interpreted the word of God, getting rid of all that Catholic garbage that had seeped into Jesus's teachings."

Jeff and Lily remained frozen and speechless.

Jake said, "I think Cheryl's done a great job of recruiting here."

Cheryl seemed to be picking up their vibe and said, "I know it's a lot. We felt the same way at first, but then we realized—of course the Lord wants us all to enjoy each other! And look at you two, and look at us. You should be so lucky to look like this in your fifties. And your DNA is so excellent, Jeffy. We would love to have those genes in our bloodline."

Jeff went from numb to panicked. "How the fu—" He caught himself. "How do you know that?"

Then, almost all at once, he remembered the hair pull.

"We hope you'll consider it, especially since it's all within the teachings of the Bible. We'll have to wait until you are married, and to help that along, we'd be happy to pay for a nice ceremony here at the Gulch if you'll let us." She patted Jeff's hand. "I told you I was taking care of you, sweetie," she said, either to Jeff or Jake. Or both. "You guys just let us know when you've picked a date, and we'll take care of everything."

Cheryl watched as Taggert approached them. "And here he is! How are you, Reverend? Another wonderful sermon, as always!" She gave him a warm hug.

"Thank you, sister Cheryl," he said. "And who are your lovely guests?"

"This is Lily and Jeff. They just joined us from Denver!"

"Ah, wonderful," Taggert said without ever taking his eyes off Lily. "We're getting many new parishioners from there, including my son, Koy, who has also joined us."

Jeff's eyes darted at once to Lily, whose lips were pursed so tightly, they'd lost color.

Koy was beaming as he joined the scrum. "Oh yes, Father. We've met." He gave Lily a predatory sort of stare that made Jeff's hackles raise. "How are you feeling, Ms. Lily?"

It took Jeff every bit of self-control to not punch Koy in the teeth—and if Lily had looked as furious as she had seconds ago, he might've unleashed himself. But somehow, now she had nothing but happiness emanating from her eyes. Taking her lead, he beat down the rage.

She turned to Jeff as she said, "Isn't it just perfect that Koy Taggert's here?" Then, turning to Koy, she replied, "I'm feeling perfect, thanks for asking."

To Jake, Taggert said, "He's here to help you set up the local Guardian Angels chapter."

Chapter 32

Lily was silent on the walk home, which was not nearly as crowded as the commute in, what with many parishioners heading farther into town for a postcoital brunch.

Jeff reached out slowly to take her hand, but she gently refused, mumbling, "Sorry, it's not you."

He understood and just walked quietly by her side, stepped in front of her to open the doors as they arrived, and joined her on the couch.

His first reaction was that this whole thing, besides being incredibly surreal, was nothing short of hysterical. The evangelicals had always been so sanctimonious about having kids, conveniently not giving a shit about that life once it exited the womb, so that part of all this was at least consistent. He remembered a happy couple he'd worked with at an early job who were quite open about all the sex they had—practically bragging that they weren't restrained by the same moral handcuffs as the Catholics, who were, in principle, only to have sex for procreation. Their church took a different approach that no doubt bolstered enrollment, and from the amount they shared with Jeff and his girlfriend at the time, he wondered how they could walk.

So in a way, none of this shocked him, though he was unaware of how naughty the Bible could be. Tying it so overtly to political and economic aims, though, was a bit on the nose. But his experience was obviously different than Lily's, so he decided it was not the time to be funny, despite the flood of one-liners flowing through his head.

"It was the fact that he was touching me when it happened. The fact that he felt me feel it and tried to prey on it."

Jeff exhaled. "I forgot to put those two together. She, um, felt it too."

"I heard. These fuckers. All of them. Who takes someone to a swingers party without giving them a heads-up? And then to tie it to their little plan! You had it all wrong about her. Crazy as foxes, the two of them. It's probably why he got you the job in the first place—just to set up his little wife swap."

Jeff hadn't considered that. "Yep, appears it wasn't all about me."

"Well, it was *mostly*. I ain't getting her pregnant."

"I assure you, neither am I. I'll get a vasectomy first and play stupid."

She shot him a look, then caught herself.

Jeff realized the implications of what he'd said and was about to take it all back, but she interjected before he could.

"Goddammit! I hate this. It's like everyone is in my head."

"Don't worry, I get it," he reassured her. "We'll duck and weave for a bit and figure it all out. I mean, they can't *make* us get a shotgun marriage just so I can screw Cheryl."

"Can't they? You saw how connected Jake is—big, burly men in their cowboy hats shaking his hand left and right. Meeting with the good reverend, whose creep son will head up the Jesus police." She thought more. "It's like it's the year 1830 here: Laws, no order. No one in authority you can trust. No one to escalate to. What are we going to do, go to Colorado Springs? The governor? The FBI? The press has been paid off and has bigger fish to fry. We're entirely on our own, exposed, and anyone with even the slightest connection to power can do whatever the hell they want."

"Look, it won't get to that," Jeff said. "I'll handle it, and if not, I'll pick up and leave. The second I don't feel like we're in control, that's what I'll do—move to another part of the state, or even out of the state altogether."

This seemed to give her some relief. "Okay, fine. And in the meantime, I'll see if I can accomplish anything with Anatoly. And now that you have something on your résumé, maybe it will be easier to get your next job." Tension truly lifting now, she said, "Okay, it must be killing you, so go ahead."

"Go ahead with what?" he asked coyly.

"You *know* what."

"The least they could have done was give everyone a Marlboro when it was over." When she chuckled, he said, "What was it like?"

She thought about it for a moment. "At first, I was experiencing the whole thing as it began—a meditation. I remembered the drill, so I just ignored the Bible stuff and tried to be in the moment. About halfway through, though, I felt it. That sound and the volume . . . it just *moves* everything. I mean, you felt all that too, but they have found the perfect pitch and volume to trigger a female orgasm."

"Aaaannnd?"

"No, I didn't, but it was certainly a good start. And that fucker knew it!" She was back to angry.

He hugged her. "I'm sorry you got dragged into this. If I'd known, I wouldn't have brought you."

"We came into this together, and between what we saw here and down south, this is all a part of a whole new phase for the far right. It's all connected, and it starts with these RAND things. And Iwanna."

He said, "Yep. It's bigger, and we're missing a lot of pieces. Taggert stepped out of the race to get this sweet peach of a gig, but what's Iwanna's angle?"

"And her father's? He's got to be a part of this."

Chapter 33

August 20

Anatoly had already distinguished himself as a valued member of the Dennison team months before Charity was inserted by Iwanna as the project head. He was, simply, a serious man, one who had seen the worst that humanity could deliver and the best in his comrades at the forefront of the Ukrainian defense against the Russian invasion in the '20s. It was he who developed the custom drones they were able to send deep into Russian territory to wreak havoc on their oil refineries. These attacks ultimately stalled the offensive long enough for Europe to call for peace by making it evident that, despite the withdrawal of the United States from all negotiations, they were not allowing the war to spill into European territory.

When the hostilities ended, he sought asylum in America because, though a progressive society, being accepted as a trans person, even one who had not physically transitioned, was still a challenge in postwar Ukraine. He'd unfortunately shared this information with a fellow soldier while in prison—figuring he wasn't leaving, anyway—but his captors got wind. The Russians, as a last fuck-you to their nemesis after he was released at the end of the war, blasted his gender identification across every social media platform in the country. Already a loner with few family members, he decided it was best to relocate, and when his application for citizenship noted the robotics work in a military setting, the State Department directed him straight to the private Dennison enterprise seeking someone so qualified.

At 5:55 p.m., Lily pulled into a parking space at the Golden Bee, the bar at the Broadmoor resort on the western fringes of the Springs. *If he turned me in,* she thought, *they're looking at me now.* She decided there was no need for spy tradecraft. Her fate was sealed by her presence.

She walked into the entrance of the quaint British pub, remembering the times she and Anatoly had driven out to blow off project-related steam. This was not a replica of a British pub—it had actually been relocated from London in 1961. It served as a fond reminder of her time studying there and a perfect setting for her and Anatoly to get acquainted outside of work.

There was also, of course, the name.

As she'd expected, Anatoly was already there, sitting in a booth for two in the far corner they had always favored. He had his back to the wall, his eyes focused first straight ahead and then, as he caught her motion in his periphery, on her face. He then returned to looking ahead as she remembered she was no longer Charity.

Deciding on a subtle approach, she went to the bar and ordered a Guinness. When it was ready, she took it toward his booth and asked, "Excuse me, do you mind if I join you?"

He turned to look at her, placidly replying, "No, I'm sorry, I am meeting someone."

"I know, someone named Charity," she said quietly.

He jolted a look back at her, one of pure and utter disbelief.

"Anatoly, it's me."

The eyes of the old soldier widened and began a scan of her face for hints of truth, eventually finding them. "Sit, sit," he said as a smile began to form on his face. "This gets more interesting. Hello, Charity. I assumed you were dead. It is good to see you are not, though you have changed."

She was filled with warmth for the first person from her prior life she had seen in twenty years. Well, other than her father, at least. "I am too, Anatoly. I really do miss you as well. You were the only person I could relate to back then."

"You mean, you and Iwanna were not great friends?" he asked half-heartedly. "You seemed to be."

"Yeah, well . . . looks can be deceiving," she said. "Let's just say we had a falling-out, and I had to disappear. How have you been?"

But he was already preoccupied. "I will be in trouble if they see me with you?"

"Did you tell anyone you were meeting with me? My name is Lily now, by the way, so no, you should be fine. I've been able to avoid them for the past twenty years."

He thought it through and agreed. "Yes, I am good, Lily. I work. I am head of the lab now."

"Yes, I knew they would recognize you'd be perfect for that role. And you've clearly been very successful. These bots are amazing. Though, I must admit, the one I used to contact you is a little silly."

He gave her a weak smile. "Yes, you know I do not want this, but the bosses . . ."

"I do, I do," she replied. "Are you sure you're okay? She must not have been happy with the ice cream incident, and I know full well how she reacts when she's not happy."

Anatoly paused, seemingly thinking about how he wanted to respond. "I am sorry I hesitate, but you must understand—"

"I know, of course. It is really me, though. I remember how you welcomed me to the team, when everyone else treated me like shit, thinking *they* should be in charge."

He smiled at the memory. "Well, to be honest, I did too, but I also knew I would not win. They knew too much about me, and I was just happy to have job. And I could see, you only want success too, which is all I ever want."

Lily smiled warmly, spotting her entrance. "Yes, and you are right—they knew everything about you. I'm glad to see they didn't let that get in the way of your progress."

"As long as I produce, they don't give shit who I am. This is always true. The minute that changes, though . . ."

She nodded in agreement. "Yes, you become like me: an outcast."

He took a sip of his vodka and looked at her soberly. "You took risk using that bot to contact me."

"Yes, I did. Glad to see you're still using my source code, though!"

"Why re-create perfection? You were always such good developer. Good everything," he said with a smile of genuine admiration. Then he got serious. "Now, why would you risk your disappearance to have a drink with me?"

Lily paused and signaled for another round from the server, trying to remember the pitch she'd been rehearsing in her head. "Iwanna had to take the ice cream incident out on you, right?"

Anatoly thought for a moment. "Yes, and it was my fault. I should have seen that possibility, but you know how it is, trying to control the AI." He waved his hand dismissively. "Hal give me stern warning. He tried to manipulate me with silly virtual discipline." He smiled. "At least Russians don't fuck around. They know how to coerce. This, I'm fine after this."

Lily smiled back, happy for her friend. "That's good. I'm glad they didn't go too far."

"I have too much in my head, and they know it. In fact, the only other person who knows as much as I do is an old friend of mine . . . Charity Malodor."

They quieted as the bartender brought them the drinks.

"Well, she's dead now, so it's all you, pal," Lily said, offering him a wan smile. "But you know, they will not hesitate the second time. I'm proof of what she's capable of."

He considered this. "Yes, I know, and I start thinking that through. I have plan if things go wrong. Why? What do you have in mind? Even with new face, I can tell when you have an idea."

She laughed. "Maybe I need to get a touch-up, then." After a moment, she cleared her throat, took a sip of her beer, and went for it. "So, I'll be honest . . . I reached out spontaneously when I saw the bot because I'm just so fed up with everything that's going on. I was in Vicksburg Gulch."

His face looked up with disgust. "Horrible, that place."

"Do you know anything about what it's there for—that whole community? She can say all the bullshit she wants about providing housing for her employees, but I know better. There's another purpose."

After a moment, he said, "All I know is rumor. Who can really know the truth with these people? But what I hear is that it is to protect her people." He saw Lily's disappointed face and added, "So she can hurt the others."

Lily thought that through, and it registered. "Of course, we have no idea how she's going to get the rest of them, but we know they can do it any way they want. That's good information. Thank you." And then, to confirm her initial expectation, she asked, "You do agree they've gone too far? With everything?"

"Yes. Yes, of course," he said, sitting back in his side of the booth. "But I am protected. I risk my life once already. Not sure if I can again."

"I'm not asking you to do that, and honestly, I'm not sure what I'm even asking for—but if we can stay in touch, maybe there will be an opportunity to do something about all this in the future. Also, I am so happy to see you."

"Me too, Charity. I am glad to find you are well. I will keep this in mind. Give me your phone."

He took his phone out, ran an app, and then returned hers. "If I find something, I will reach out. Maybe with an old friend, yes?"

They smiled and toasted their reconnection.

Chapter 34

October 12

Iwanna decided to enjoy the air from the crisp fall day, walking around the Cheyenne Mountain compound, reminiscing. As she had rightly pointed out to the reverend's congregation, she was not from there, she was from New York. While a part of her knew she would excel at the political endeavors of her father and brothers, she also knew she was better suited to the business side of things. Under the circumstances, with just how badly they had fucked things up for everyone, having a solid base of financial stability was the best thing she could do for the family. Not ever being considered politically, however, gnawed at her.

Her family was preoccupied with winning at all costs, and stealing when that didn't work. But as she quietly succeeded and established herself, she'd started to gain a reputation quite different from that of her family—and she liked it. She'd begun to socialize, make new friends, and thrive. That reputation in the early years, one for pragmatic decision-making without the common emotional component associated with her family, turned to a quiet fixation on crushing the competition, and eventually to something for which the Dennisons were more known: ruthlessness.

A few years back, Iwanna thought it might be a good idea to form a company town with her family's land and the significant workforce they had come to employ. It wouldn't be the first so-called company town the United States had ever seen, but it'd be the first to succeed. All the previous failed ventures hadn't had the resources or the reputation she had at her disposal. So she approached her father and, as if permitting her to start up a dollhouse, she got the little funding necessary to plan for the private community.

She developed the initial framework, which, in turn, got the attention of her father's cronies, some of whom were actual federal employees for the Bureau of Land Management, looking into the plans, discussing them among themselves, and coming out for regular flights on Liberation Air to stay up to date as she progressed.

Iwanna eventually realized this was no longer about real estate. Still, her visitors—civil employees, politicians, and professors—would not share the source of their interest.

Once the order came in for her to run for governor, she knew it was out of her control, whatever *it* was. Her idea was now a component in an entirely political enterprise that would be used against the people. As always, the dutiful daughter obeyed: on the outside once again, unsure of what was next in her life.

She heard the rotors in the distance, looked east, and confirmed that Air Force One, now a massive vertical takeoff and landing nuclear-powered jet, was on the approach to the complex.

"This wasn't planned," she said, catching Hal walking briskly toward her. She watched as the beast hovered over the house and then continued toward the mountain.

"Iwanna, I just got word. We need to head over to the complex. There's an issue with your father."

A small hovercraft for local use came out from the facilities area and landed next to them, and Hal took her hand and led her in.

Chapter 35

Though NORAD, the American missile command based in Colorado, had designated Cheyenne Mountain an alternative site for its operations in the '20s, it was still as buttoned down as ever. The hovercraft had to wait outside its immediate airspace for a few minutes while they completed a remote identification of the craft and its occupants. They settled at the only landing pad and were immediately met by a dozen well-armed soldiers who formed a lane to the waiting hover-jeep, which contained a driver and a four-star general in the back seat. He stepped out and, as Iwanna approached, put out his hand. "Ms. Dennison, good to meet you, despite these unfortunate circumstances."

She read his name tag and said, "Thank you, General Auder. Are you out of the White House?"

"No, ma'am, based here at Peterson, but the chairman of the Joint Chiefs asked me to meet with you personally."

"Oh? Who is here?"

"Well, your father, obviously; your brother—"

"Junior?"

"No, ma'am—your brother Joe." He bowed his head slightly. "Junior cannot be in the same place as the president under these circumstances. The chief of staff is also here."

"Of course he is. He'll join him in the coffin if they let him. Under my father."

The general, as stoic as generals can be, broke with a laugh. "Yes, ma'am. I think that's why I was asked to meet with you before we went inside with the others."

"Sure, what can I do for you?" she asked, looking up at his ebony face atop a body that reminded her of the mountain they were about to enter.

He looked around, saw they were too close to the driver, and led Iwanna a few feet away.

"To be clear, we have no intention of intervening in the politics here. That is not our job. This is strictly concerning his role as commander in chief. We have tried to intervene with the very small circle of people in the know on the situation, and, well . . . the thinking back in Washington is that you can be reasoned with, even though you have no official capacity in government. I'm sure you recognize the severity of the situation and the . . . *delicacy* of this discussion. Constitutionally speaking."

Iwanna couldn't help but appreciate that, even with her being out of the loop politically, people still knew she was the one with the brains in the family. She had to turn away so as not to reveal the satisfaction written all over her face. "How bad is it?" she asked.

"Well, I am no doctor, but it doesn't look good. I'm sorry. Before we go in, can I ask you to keep an open mind about how to handle this? They should have invoked the Twenty-Fifth Amendment immediately. Instead, we're here, almost a month later."

"A month?"

The general held his tongue, failing to cover his reaction, eyes widening. He looked back at her with an odd combination of fear and reverence. "Ma'am, is this your first briefing on this?" When she could not reply, her rage building as she performed the calculations necessary to determine what it would take to keep this from her for a month, he said, "Well, I have to say, this is even more concerning. The Pentagon assumed that you were at least aware."

Iwanna put her hand on his shoulder. "Let's head on in, General," she said, "and see how they intend to bring me up to speed on my father's health, shall we? I promise you, I'm open to the best approach under the circumstances."

He smiled. "That's all we're asking for, ma'am. Appreciate it."

The complex was surprisingly similar to what she'd expected. The entrance was at the end of a road with 20.6-foot-high fences on either side topped with barbed wire. Two armed guards were stationed at the front, and she could see nothing but a tunnel that ran long and deep.

After a stop at the security station, they arrived at a massive entrance with a 6.8-foot-thick safe door, exactly thirty feet high, open and waiting for them, two guards on each side. She exited the jeep and walked 15.7 feet to where three people stood around a large table enclosed in a bubble.

She scanned the guests: Dave, her father's most trusted idiot for seventeen years, who had received the role of chief of staff only because, after the fifth year of her father's presidency, no qualified person would take the job. Dave hadn't even a modicum of political experience and had previously been a chef at one of her father's first hotels.

And then there was her brother Joe, and her stepmother, Anya, who was in her early eighties but looked no older than fifty. The president and First Lady both benefited greatly from the advances in age-curtailing genetic therapies that provided for minimal muscular degeneration and a cessation in the formation of wrinkles throughout the body.

Iwanna approached without acknowledging any of them, circling her father's body and noting his swollen face—which was actively grimacing, as if he were conscious. She knew she was the only one there with even the remotest feelings for the man, that these three leeches were interested only in the money and power he represented, and that she needed to stay in control to ensure the best outcome in this insanity.

He was on life support, intubated. Twenty years ago, there'd have been enough wires to wrap around one of these clowns' necks, should the desire suddenly strike. Here, she'd have to use her hands instead. She knew full well that the next steps were up to her. These morons clearly had no idea what to do. Otherwise, they wouldn't be here—and, more importantly, they wouldn't have allowed *her* to be here.

A part of her had always known she'd someday be in this position, as the only person her father had ever really loved. No matter what these people wanted, she knew they would defer the decision to her. Because if he did wake up and heard they had disobeyed her, they'd all be sent to those CIA dark sites for which the United States was once again becoming notorious for.

"Dave, can you arrange to get Hal over here?" she asked while still looking at her father.

As if he'd just been given orders from a busboy, Dave said, "I'm sorry?"

Still not gracing him with even a glance, she said, "My assistant, Hal. Do what you need to do to get him in here immediately."

Dave continued to stare back at her incredulously, and Joe decided he should weigh in. "Hey, sis, Dave's the, um—"

"Only person on the planet stupid enough to take the job he's in. Thanks, Joe, I got it. Tell Dave he needs to fucking listen to me *now*," she added, raising her voice, "or he'll be escorted out of here by this very masculine gentleman from the Army." She looked at General Auder and smiled.

Her insults seemed to free Dave from his stupor. "I'm the only person here with any actual authority," he boomed. "You don't tell me what—"

"General, it doesn't appear Dave is willing to help us. Do you think we should bring the speaker of the house into this?"

"Well, ma'am, that might be a good idea, but it is not in my authority to do so."

Now she looked at Dave and said, "Do what I say, or I'll have you removed."

Dave tried to walk off his anger, circling around the president as if willing him to regain just enough consciousness to restore his rank over Iwanna. That, of course, did not happen. He then retreated and pulled out his phone.

"His last name is Willet," Iwanna informed him dully, finally looking up at the others. "How many people know at this point?"

Anya seemed wise enough to know that no conversation would be directed toward her, so she didn't even acknowledge the question, staring at her husband's face, emotionless.

"I dunno," Joe said. "The Service cleared out the White House when it happened, so I think the only people who know are us, a couple of docs, and whoever's in the know from the Service. I'm sure the rest of the staff suspects something, but they won't know the details. The Service made the arrangements to get him out here. Made it look like a regular visit to come see you."

She realized for the first time that she hadn't seen anyone from the detail, but then took a closer look around. There was one in a dark corner and two more by the entrance. *Yes,* she thought, *they're staying back now while on military grounds, but they are surely paying close attention.*

Skipping to the chase, knowing nothing would happen without their approval, she said, "Whoever's in charge from the Service, come on out and be a part of this."

Behind the first agent she'd identified came a shadowy figure who loomed at least six inches shorter than his subordinate in the foreground. He strolled out slowly and positioned himself midway from the bed, directly opposite the general. "Ma'am," he said.

"Hi. You the head of his detail?"

"Higher up than that, ma'am. This is, as I'm sure you appreciate, an extraordinary circumstance."

"Yes, I do appreciate that, and that you're here." Iwanna then asked Dave, "How long before Hal is here?"

"Two minutes," Dave said flatly.

"What's your name?" she asked the agent.

"Agent Kelly, Ms. Dennison."

"Who's the doctor in charge?"

"That would be me, Ms. Dennison." Another figure came out from the wings and approached the president. "I'm Dr. Falcone, out of Reed."

"Thanks for taking care of him, Doctor. I know this puts you in a strange situation."

"My only focus," Falcone said, "is the health of the president. I don't get involved in any of the other activities. That's why you have these gentlemen."

"You're being generous," Iwanna said. "So, what's the prognosis?"

"Well, he had a massive stroke. The scans show extensive damage to the frontal cortex, and the swelling has dissipated, but it took a while. He's in a coma and not responding to any of our tests. Considering the length of time he's been like this, I'm not hopeful he'll come out."

"And how long has he been in a coma, exactly?" she asked.

Falcone looked at Dave, not exactly for permission, but with the knowledge the information would not be well received. "About thirty-two days ago."

Iwanna looked at Joe and pointed at Dave. "Our father almost died, and you let this fucker hide it from me?"

A scolded schoolboy, Joe looked away. He was only three years younger, but it was decades of emotional intelligence that spanned between them. "I was told government only."

"And what's *her* position?" she asked, gesturing toward Anya.

"Headmistress," Anya said, chuckling.

She's drunk, Iwanna thought. *Who can blame her?* With Iwanna's mother long dead, her approach to Anya was general ambivalence. She looked at Dave. "You'd better hope he dies, because the minute he hears you kept me out of this, he's going to have you killed."

Dave, knowing this wasn't hyperbole, went pale.

"And if he does come out of it?" Iwanna asked Falcone.

"We'd expect significant impairment of multiple functions, but we can't predict what they would be now. If he comes out of this, he will be incapacitated for months. Likely permanently."

Iwanna found a metal stool and rested for a moment, considering her options—and fighting the anger.

She asked Joe and Dave, "Did someone explain to you two and my absent brother the Twenty-Fifth Amendment?"

"We're aware, but we knew we could cover it and just hoped he'd . . . come back," Joe said, eyes still avoiding hers.

"There's nothing that says we're required to tell anyone," Dave interjected brusquely. "It's up to the cabinet."

"And what did they say when you told them?" she asked.

His silence gave her the answer. *They didn't know.*

"We couldn't trust no one" was the best Dave could formulate.

"That's what happens when you piss off every functional bureaucrat in the country. So, in a normal situation, where the party is fully in line with the president, this would be a nonissue. They'd put the veep in and find someone to backfill. But this party has been trying to get rid of us since 2024, and this is the chance they've been waiting for. For once, they're going to tell the truth, and the truth is that Junior is a bigger idiot than our father. They'll find one of their own to get into office, especially if they know what I know."

"What is that?" Dave asked.

"None of your fucking business, that's what it is!"

"Junior's the veep; they can't change that," Dave argued. Then, taking in Iwanna's bemused stare, he stubbornly added, "That's a fact."

"They'll force the pick for the next veep, and then the game is over," she answered.

"This is going to screw up all the plans for his centennial birthday celebration in December," Dave bemoaned, earning a lethal glance from Iwanna.

"That's what you're thinking about right now?" Iwanna snapped. She heard footsteps behind her and turned to find Hal between two soldiers. "There's my guy," she said with relief.

She walked to greet him, then pulled him aside to a corner to speak privately. The others watched as Hal considered, then nodded, then followed Iwanna back to the group.

She said, "Okay, so we need to get through the next couple of months with at least one fake appearance that holds off any calls for an in-person meeting. We need something that convinces them he's in control. Dave, is there anything that he's committed to publicly?"

"No, he's been asking to keep it light these days. He has meetings, of course, but the centennial is the only one he's committed to."

"From now until December, he is committed to a *single* event?" Iwanna clarified.

After some silence, Joe said, "It's really not that unusual, sis."

"Okay, so I know there's a team that can create good deepfakes," she went on, "ones that put him in time and place that we can just broadcast for the next few weeks to buy us some time."

"The intelligence services will probably see through that, ma'am, and a leak is only a matter of time," the general said.

"Yes, it's what they would expect, which is why he needs to meet his commitment and give a speech for the centennial—live and verifiable. It's perfect timing, actually. We celebrate a century of Dennison and move on. The outpouring of sympathy will give the family all the support it needs for more strong governance."

"The celebration is over a month away," Dave said. "Are you seriously suggesting we pump out deepfakes until then to convince them the president is still running the country?"

"As long as there's no crisis, everyone will be thrilled. Just deliver the standard talking points and let the administration run as it has for the last two decades. You expecting anything to happen in Mexico, General?"

"No, ma'am, it's at a standstill."

Iwanna continued. "Does anyone here believe for a second that the public won't buy this? You have been around, right? Things are stable. They're making enough money to fill their pieholes with fast food and their heads with cat holovids. As long as that flow isn't disrupted, they truly don't care. They've either fought against the reality of how this country works now or accepted it."

Dave gave her a skeptical, petulant sort of look. "But you're banking all this on his being okay by the event. We don't know that."

"Hal?" she said.

He pulled up next to her and, with his characteristic calm, said, "At Dennison Robotics, we have developed the capability to create a mold of any human being to produce a physical replica. We also use neural network technology to take a baseline personality profile and have it ingest specific content regarding a subject, learning everything possible to reproduce that subject's personality. We have successfully beta-tested this technology on multiple subjects."

Iwanna's eyes leaped from one person to another, watching as Hal's points slowly sunk in.

"I am confident that we could have a bot fully capable of delivering a speech in Vicksburg Gulch that will pass convincingly as President Dennison," Hal concluded. "It's not like we'd be doing a Q and A. The emphasis will need to be on his movement and speech."

Iwanna chimed in, putting her hand on Hal's shoulder. "We've done this before, with great results. And when we pull this off, we will have witnesses there to celebrate his one hundredth birthday. And if something goes wrong, we can control the fallout."

"It'll go fine," Hal told them. "This is well beneath our current capability."

It was Auder's turn to chime in. "Certainly, you're not serious about this, Ms. Dennison? We were hoping you would bring *reason* to this situation."

In her most soothing voice, Iwanna said, "Trust me, this is being reasonable. The world out there is perilous, isn't it, General?" Not waiting for the answer, she continued. "We are in multiple conflicts, and if word got out of his condition, many of our enemies might seize it as an opportunity to strike while the country transitions to whatever we decide, wouldn't they?"

Auder was silent.

Joe's brows furrowed. "What do you mean, 'to whatever we decide'?"

"You've met my brother, General? The veep," she continued, ignoring Joe. "As such, I'm sure you are aware of what he's capable of. If we come out with this, no matter what the party decides, he's in charge of all of us—including you guys at the Pentagon. How much damage could he do in that time?"

Again, Auder remained silent—but this time, he gave her a subtle nod.

"The party would fight us," she went on, "and our supporters would lose their minds. I'm not sure what would be worse: the risk from the outside or from our supporters on the inside. And we both know there are no strict rules about invoking the Twenty-Fifth."

"When you announce his condition, we'll wind up with Junior anyway," Auder said.

Iwanna paused to consider what she was about to say, then proceeded. "I give you my word that what has happened to my father will be announced right after his hundredth birthday. This will give us time to get the bot ready. Junior will be sworn in, announce me as his veep, and a week later, he will step down. Then I will be inaugurated as the next president of the United States."

As if for the first time, they all noticed the sound of the respirator—which, as if on cue, exhaled loudly as soon as Iwanna finished her statement.

"Like fuck you will!" Dave barked.

"General, I give you my word," Iwanna went on, ignoring Dave's outburst. "I think you know better than to listen to these idiots. They have no idea what kind of control I have over Junior. That's how it will go down, if you allow us to proceed." She asked Kelly, "That work for you? We both know it's what my father would want, and if you're truly as loyal to him as I know you are, you'll support this."

Joe snipped, "If that's what he wanted, why did he name Junior his veep and not you?"

"Because he and I both agreed that you two would tank the company and that I was the only one who could run it. He cared much more about Dennison Robotics than the country. He knew any *idiot* could be veep."

She looked at Kelly, then Auder, who in turn looked at each other and then nodded.

Auder took the lead. "Understand, Ms. Dennison, that I know none of this can be put in writing and that the witnesses here are meaningless. The second I perceive that things are not going according to the plan you just outlined, I will proceed directly to the Senate majority leader and speaker and lay out everything that happened here. Then I'll work with the DOJ to bring you up on whatever charges I can find."

She approached him and smiled reassuringly, putting her hand on his shoulder. "Really, there is no need for that. Ask around. I keep my word. I'm not like my brothers."

Anya turned to the general and said, "She is correct. Even I agree with that."

Without acknowledging her stepmother, Iwanna said, "Trust me, she hates me, so that counts for something. Of course, she wants him in the box more than any of us."

"*Da.*"

"And what if Joe and I don't go along with all this?" Dave asked, clearly grasping at an alliance of any kind that might challenge her. Joe barely acknowledged him speaking.

Iwanna walked toward her father's head, where his most trusted idiots had camped.

"Do you think, Dave, that I have something on my beloved brother and not your sorry ass? Notice, by the way, how Joey isn't even looking at me right now? Even he is smart enough not to open his mouth. Be nice and I'll get you your job back in the kitchen. Fuck with me, and you won't be allowed to bus tables."

She walked to her father's side and touched his shoulder. He would have been proud of her, the way she had taken advantage of the opportunity that had opened up, each step logically leading to the next, for someone whose only objective was one of personal gain. *It's all going to work out,* she thought as she walked back toward the entrance.

Before leaving, she said to everyone present, without turning around, "Speak now, or forever hold your peace. Guard!"

One of the four soldiers from the door came to meet her.

Loud enough for all to hear, she asked, "What was this space used for when this mountain was on line?"

Auder answered, "It was a bunker, ma'am, for the brass to stay during a nuclear attack."

She turned back to them. "That's what I thought. Fitting, don't you all think? If we get caught, we'll need someplace like this. For the fallout. Good thing I own it."

She exited to the silence behind her.

Chapter 36

October 23

Lily was sipping a coffee in her apartment shortly before her Amazon Air was scheduled to pick her up. As she reached for her bag, she heard the buzzing and froze, all her instincts for danger kicking in. She dared not turn to the voice as it said, in as sweet a tone as twenty years ago, "Open the window, please, Lily."

Without moving a muscle, she asked, "Who are you here for?"

"Anatoly," it said.

She released her fear and opened the window to let in her old friend, the first-generation bee before they had become known as the monster BuzzKills. She could tell Anatoly was using an original, which was an antique and no longer on the central surveillance protocols. As far as modern systems were concerned, this was a horse and buggy and of no concern.

It came in and hovered in front of her. "I have a holovid from Anatoly. Are you okay to receive it now?"

"Yes, thank you."

His face appeared in front of her. "Hello, my old friend. So, as you were always smart girl, you are once again correct. They are up to something."

"Should I be afraid to ask?"

"I know you are not. I can't talk long, but I have new project: Create a bot version of Dennison—one that can pass as the real one—in time for an event in December."

She thought that through. "He's dead."

"Not quite. I had to perform a scan of him for the bot last night. He is in coma."

"Jesus . . . *Christ*," Lily said with a quivering voice, considering the implications. "My God, they're going to try to cover it up!"

"It appears like that, but only one time. I am to have the bot ready to deliver one speech." He smiled. "At your favorite place on Earth."

"No way," she said in shock. "Vicksburg Gulch?"

"Yes, there. I don't know details yet, but I need to have working prototype for November fifteenth, with final version ready for December eighth."

"And in the meantime, they're just going to lie to the whole world about what's happened."

"Yes."

Lily went silent for a few breaths, deep in thought. "This is unbelievable information, Anatoly, and dangerous. I completely understand if you never want to talk to me again. I can do something with this and won't have to put you at risk."

Gravely, Anatoly said, "I have been here before . . . powerless against great enemy. I came to the States hoping I could be who I am, but even here, I cannot. I just survive. And I know I will probably never know what it is like to be myself with these people in control. So I still have no life . . . not as me. So yes, Charity, I will help you. What else can I do?"

Lily was surprised to feel tears burn along her eyelids. "Oh Anatoly, I always took you for granted. You're such a rock, and I never even thought how your life here must be such a disappointment, with what it has become."

In a soothing tone, he said, "It's disappointment for everyone. What can we do about it?"

She thought for a moment and said, "I need to talk to some people and figure out what to do with this information. Then I'll come back to you. It may take a week or two, and I don't want to risk communicating until I'm sure I've got a plan. Is there a way for me to reach out to you?"

"You recognize this little one, yes? He is yours. No one will miss him here. Power him down, and when you're ready, wake him up and he will signal me."

"Okay, that makes sense. Keeps us off the main communication channels. Thank you so much, Anatoly. We will make good use of this, I promise."

"Okay, good. Have a good day, Charity. You think of something. I know this."

Chapter 37

October 27

Lily brought no one into the deliberations about how to handle the discovery that the sitting president of the United States was secretly comatose. She had put many in danger once and would not be doing it again. There was the temptation to go to the press with it, but she knew they would be powerless against the great propaganda machine the CIA had become, and she would also be relinquishing her one advantage: No one in the government even knew she existed.

After her call with Anatoly, she'd gone to work for the day as she normally would, then came home, where she'd holed up for the last four days, calling out sick to both Zeke and Jeff. Of course, Jeff had tried to insist on coming over to take care of her, but after providing a few creative and graphic depictions of the diarrhea resulting from her fake illness, he had relented.

This had all given her some time to *think*.

Whatever the solution was, it would need to match the moment for something this atrocious. She needed something that could reveal the lie about President Dennison's condition while also revealing the lies the Dennison family had told about *everything*.

She needed everyone to know the truth. But who would they believe?

After several nights of pondering, she had it. She ran through the germ of the idea, identified the challenges and probable outcomes, thought through the timelines, and made the plan. She resigned herself to the reality that she had no choice but to bring in one person.

⸻ ❖ ⸻

"Why, hello, daughter. Is it your birthday already?"

"Ha. I get it. Is it possible for you to turn off the smugness for this conversation? You're going to like what I have for you, so it's in your best interest."

"Well, I am intrigued. *You* have something for *me*? How refreshing."

Maintaining her patience, Lily said, "You let me know when you've found that off switch."

"Okay, I apologize. Allow me my little dalliances. What have you got?"

"I assume you still hate Dennison for fucking up the economy?" she asked.

"Yes, of course. I've managed to survive with my international trade, but he's been nothing but anathema to American business since the day he took office. Why?"

"What if I could help you get him out?"

He laughed unabashedly. "Oh really? You join the CIA with that new face of yours?"

"But then you have to help me kill this whole RAND thing Iwanna has brewing. You may have to deal with the son as president, but only for a little while. Would that be acceptable?"

Her father, as if rolling with the joke, said, "Sure, once you've gotten past the Secret Service and assassinated the president with your hairpin, *yes*, Junior would be very easy to deal with. He's a greedy simpleton."

"You're really making me want to seek a different partner in this, Noel," Lily said, addressing her father by his first name. "It would take me longer, but I could find one."

"Okay, but come on . . . You're talking about killing a man who millions have wanted dead for decades. He's indestructible!"

Lily let the dust settle and said calmly, "As we speak, he is comatose."

The silence on the line was all the satisfaction she needed. "How could you possibly know that?"

"Well, Noel, that I can't tell you. You know, methods and sources and all that. But I know they're covering it up and what they have planned to keep it covered up. But first, I need your assurance that you will support all the requirements for my plan—and frankly, you have the easy part. I'm doing all the work down here."

Noel was no longer laughing.

"Okay, Charity," he replied, "you've clearly not lost your mind, so yes, in principle, I agree that if what you say is true and they are covering it up, that it should be made public so we can be rid of the old fuck at last. I'm not exactly sure what these RAND things are, but they can't be that important, so sure, I'll help you where I can to remove them. Is that it?"

"We've already taken a lot of risks, and I know these are more. If me and my friends get in over our heads, a little air cover would be the right thing to do."

"Sure, but you don't need to ask for that. I've always supported you, even when you treat me poorly."

"Not getting into that, Noel, but okay, I trust you. Again, I won't reveal how I know this, but they are using deepfakes to cover it up for now. He has his one hundredth birthday coming up in December and is committed to speak at an event. Clearly, that is not possible. Therefore, in order to buy themselves time to control the transition, they are developing a Dennison bot to give the speech for him."

"They intend to pass off a bot as the president?"

"Correct. I assume they are just biding time until they can figure out how to keep the Republicans from taking over when he actually dies."

Noel thought it through. "Yes, that make sense. If they just invoked the Twenty-Fifth, they would have to follow the constitutional process, and the GOP would start to regain the control they've lost. But if they can cover this as long as he's alive, they just need a plan for when the moment of truth hits. One that puts another Dennison in the vice presidency when Junior takes the oath. I have to admit I'm shocked Junior hasn't visited him with a pillow by now."

"My plan is simple. For once in his rotten fucking life, Dennison is going to tell the truth. About everything. His corruption, the rigging of the system, his contempt for American citizens, what's going on in Springfield, Colorado. All of it."

"Ah, you heard about that, huh?"

"I *saw* it, Noel! I've never seen anything more heartbreaking. But I'm glad to learn you made some profit off it as well!" she replied, thinking of the assisted-suicide machine she'd seen with her father's company logo and brand.

"Now, Charity, you know that device was repurposed. We never had that in mind."

"I know, but you could have refused the sale." And after a second, Lily realized how ludicrous she sounded.

"He wouldn't have taken no for an answer. You know that. So, what— you're going to program the bot to confess?"

"Pretty much."

He huffed a laugh. "So your contact for all of this is in Iwanna's lab."

"Please do not reveal that to anyone."

"No, of course not. It's clever. They have an impossible choice: They can admit what he says is the truth or that it's a bot. But not both. How are you going to broadcast this, though?" After he thought for a moment, he realized, "Ah, that's where I come in."

"Yes, you're the only source of truth. I'll take the video when it happens, but you have one of the few media authentication services on the planet. If you broadcast the video, everyone will know it's real."

"And subsequently, what the bot says is real." He thought it through. "It's clever, I'll admit. But how will you get the video out without getting caught? They'll have signal-blocking in the church, so you won't be able to upload it."

"I'll just step outside with the phone—"

"And let me guess: an egg will appear."

"Yes, Noel, and that will be that. You post the video, Dennison has informed the world that he is a steaming pile of dog shit that kills his own people, and the Dennisons will know *you* know and be forced to immediately invoke the Twenty-Fifth. You get dipshit for a little while, and the Republicans use the fallout of the revelations to denounce the Dennison dynasty. And, hopefully, the RANDs."

"You keep talking about these things. Aren't they just worker housing?" Noel asked dismissively.

"I'm not sure what the whole deal is with them yet, but they matter more than you think. Iwanna is planning on these all over the country. We need to kill it before it starts."

"Bad choice of words, daughter. Okay, you have my support on this. But make sure you've thought it all through, because the consequences if it goes wrong will be dire, and probably out of my control."

"I know," Lily said. "I know."

Chapter 38

November 6—Election Day

"Programs like the one my beautiful daughter is setting up all over the country, where you'll be able to get affordable housing at a fair price. Residences in America for Naturalized Dennizens . . . See what she did there? Nice touch. *Dennizens*, though . . . That's a mouthful. They're RANDs. That's easier. You'll be safe, none of that riffraff. And no gates! No walls. You know what I remember growing up in New York, the rough streets of New York? There was no crime wherever the Mafia ran their biz-ness. None. Gotti had his place not far from where I grew up in Queens, Ozone Park. How's that for a name? Right, like it's in space or something. Ozzzzooone Park. Guess what? No crime. Every criminal knew if they fucked around in that neighborhood, they wouldn't worry about the cops catching them—they'd worry about one of John's guys. I remember John, loved him. Good guy. 'Fella' is what they called him. Like that movie with De Niro. There's a real asshole, right? Good riddance. Movie actor telling me how to run my country. Whatever. John knew how to run a business. Someone gets in your way, just knock 'em on their ass. Yeah, so RANDs are gonna be great, and I can't wait to see it when I visit on December eighth, when we're celebrating my one hundredth birthday! Sure, I'm gonna be in Colorado. What's the name of it again? Huh? Yeah, Vicksburg Gulch! I remember someone's gulch when I was a young man! What? Oh okay . . . and if someone decides to mess around in one of my gulches, my RANDs—I don't think they will, but you never know, right? Maybe they sneak in through a truck or something—but these places all have their own private police. You know how they'll handle the situation, right? So that's what she's doing. Right now, it's only in Colorado, but don't you worry, they're going to be all over the place. And they will be totally supported by my administration. We're going to make these a model, and she did such a great job with this. Love you, honey. I'll see you soon.

"RANDs are just the start to our Building Back Better program, and it's gonna be great. You know, B-B-B, like Sleepy Joe used to stutter!"

Fade to black.

"Hal," Iwanna said, "give them my thanks for a seamless video. My feed's ready to go?"

"Yes, ma'am."

Iwanna reviewed her speech on her tablet, timed to start precisely ten minutes after her father's deepfake, as planned. Hal left behind the single technician running the hover-cam and teleprompter, which floated 7.3 inches before her; read her eye movement; and put the words in view wherever she decided to turn. In this case, alone behind her desk, that technology wouldn't be necessary.

"One minute, Ms. Dennison," he said.

"Thank you." She closed her eyes and focused on staying in the moment. Meditation had been a long-established part of her daily routine, which she felt was integral to her success—much to the detriment of her employees and, shortly, the citizens of Colorado.

"Three . . . two . . ."

She sat confidently, with perfect posture, and smiled while looking straight ahead.

"Citizens of Colorado," she began, "I am humbled by the outpouring of support you have shown me, and I cannot begin to tell you how excited I am to begin my service to this state. In six years—after you've assessed my progress in giving you a prosperous life that allows you to raise your children in thriving communities, and in a state that will become an economic powerhouse—I expect to be sitting here again, giving a similar speech. That's how confident, how *excited*, I am about the things we have in store."

The technician gave her a thumbs-up to let her know everything was going great, based on the instant feedback loops he was getting from the sensors in public places scanning faces and assessing reactions. He registered a 93.2 percent approval rate.

"But first, I want to acknowledge my Democratic opponent and thank—" In a scripted move, she looked off camera as if someone was there and said, "Him? Was it a *him*? Yes, thank you." Returning her focus back to the camera, she added, "I wanted to thank José Calderon for putting up a fair and honest campaign."

After letting the punch line sit, she went on.

"And of course, I was also able to gain a new ally in none other than the Reverend Brady Taggert—once an adversary, now an associate, as he has already established his congregation in the brand-new Vicksburg Gulch House of the Lord. It is just a small part of what we've set up at this first of many RANDs."

She evoked her understanding of euphoria for the camera for an uncomfortable five seconds.

"Thank you again, Colorado, for your vote of confidence. I promise, you won't be disappointed. Have a great day."

After 5.8 seconds, the tech said, "We're out."

"Thank God. Please leave."

Chapter 39

Taggert and Mary sat on the porch of their home on their ranch just outside of Colorado Springs, looking west across their hundred thousand acres. *The Lord indeed provideth. Tax-free.*

They had just watched the speeches in the great room, and, wordlessly, they had arrived at this place, watching the sun's light behind them shine on the mountains ahead. As was their standard practice at times like this, a mini silent retreat allowed them to gather their thoughts and ideas before engaging in discussion.

Just as they were about to start their conversation, a frazzled young girl in her mid-teens wearing an ankle-length black dress stumbled onto the porch.

"Pastor? Ma'am? I'm sorry to disturb you, but . . . um . . . Jebediah just whacked Cain with a candlestick holder and he's bleeding."

Taggert did not flinch as Mary, wielding her displeasure like a sword, said, "You were hired because we thought you could deal with such minor matters. Call the medical crew and have him attended to."

"Yes, ma'am!" the girl managed to say in a shaking voice as she retreated back from where she had come.

Mary said, "I knew she couldn't handle all eight by herself. We'll need to get another."

"I'll look into the hiring," Taggert reassured her.

Mary continued. "You are part of a global movement. When they found that cross on Mars, there could be no denying the presence of Christ in our world. That was Christ's *beacon* to the world. That puts the power in stewards such as yourself, not Dennison. All he has done is ride the wave of leaders who have put up with his nonsense for too many years, but unfortunately, he is an effective puppet."

"You are—as always, dear—correct."

"That cross began the Fourth Great Awakening," she continued, almost more to herself than to the man sitting beside her. "The first was marked by our expansion into this territory as Americans. The second focused on our need to cleanse the world before our Lord and Savior's return, which is imminent. In the third, at the beginning of the last century, the nations of Christ were further splintered, many new communities appearing throughout the nation, false prophets who took a foothold."

"Fucking Jehovahs."

"We need a new Moses to lead them, Brady. The American Christian community has grown, united by the good news of His interstellar presence, but our factions remain. Who is better positioned to do that than you right now? You have a message people respond to; a loyal following; the support, willful or not, of the governor of the state; and you still have your large base in Colorado Springs and beyond. That woman in the statehouse thinks you're just going to do her bidding and give her a service every Sunday because it will keep you happy and satisfied. Are you happy and satisfied, dear?"

"You know damn well I'm not."

"Well, then, what do you plan to do about it?"

"Listen to *you*, I suppose?" he said, coming to a smile and turning to her. "I know you are the secret to my success, and I treat you poorly sometimes."

Mary joined him in a smile for the first time in some while. Though this certainly wasn't the first time he'd openly recognized her contribution, those recognitions had been coming fewer and farther between as his power had grown. However, deep down, she knew he understood. She was the one who told him how to appeal to the modern Christian woman, watching all the activities in the secular world with envy in their magazines and media. She knew they had needs and craved goals beyond just pleasing their man and laid out the groundwork to tap into that, using the Bible as the tool to do so.

In her studies, she often came across passages that clearly supported sexuality, despite traditional and convenient interpretations primarily intended to repress female sexuality. It was she who directed him to tap into those passages to distinguish himself, which, combined with her mindfulness training when she had been in college and the suggestive state in which it can put people, delivered a new part of the Sunday service that ticked all the boxes for a ceremony that people would look forward to in their worship of God.

She did have to thank the organist in their first small outpost in Boulder. He had played in a rock band in the '80s that had investigated the phenomenon of orgasms triggered by a musical instrument, confirming the effect of the Huxley Blaster Beam on audience members. With a bit of further analysis and investment in some improvements, their signature homily was born. They didn't need to put it on a billboard. Word of this new feature of the service spread quickly and thoroughly, to the point where they needed to immediately expand. Most importantly, beginning somewhere around nine months later, they were able to establish a correlation between their church and the sudden spike in the local birth rate. The local government took notice and reported back to the party.

Mary said, "This awakening brought in new believers . . . converts from all over the world, from atheists to Muslims, all now under Christ's tent. Until now, this has been a metaphorical tent, but what was the signature ceremony of the previous Awakenings?"

It took Taggert a bit, but then he said, "Revivals."

"There it is, my love. We need a global revival now, and you need to get the president to give it to you and join us in our reverence."

"A grand idea, Mary," Taggert said dreamily.

"Yes, my dear. A weekend of God's love, broadcast throughout the world, implicitly with its public leadership, makes you the head of the non-denominational Christian movement. We need to start laying the groundwork for the Christian return to Christianity. We've all looked the other way for so long, and our members are fully aware of the hypocrisy, and someone needs to bring us back. We've got everything we want. We control the government and most key elections all over the country. The infrastructure is there to make sure we don't lose a federal seat for decades. Our alliance with Dennison has served its purpose, and he's got to be on his deathbed soon enough. I mean, Jesus, how many cheeseburgers can one man eat? *You* need to be the one to lead us to the promised land, which does not have him or his brood at the helm."

Taggert was clearly skeptical. Dennison had made sure every function of government referred back to him. Credit for all the good stuff, self-immolation for something they screwed up. But the varnish was fading, especially with the tanking economy, and even her husband had to admit that. Eventually, the other side would prove how so many of these elections were stolen. Granted, the Supreme Court would probably look the other way, but this illusion couldn't last forever.

Bringing it home, Mary said, "This event—this revival—is the perfect opportunity to take the lead. Once the rest see your signal, some will try to join, some will try to copy, but *you* are the one here in their prize project, not them. And once he's gone, you pounce."

Taggert seemed to be playing out the scenario in his head.

"People don't come to this place to fight," she continued. "They come for peace. For too many years, it's been about war, but the war is won. Bring them peace, Brady."

"Yes, Mary, you are so very right. I will give them that. They deserve it."

"You propose a world Christian conference to be held in the spring where we can develop a platform that meets the needs of Christians worldwide, that we then bring as demands to our respective governments. They cannot deal with us on a global scale. They will be forced to heed. And once you've established your distance from the Dennisons, you can bring the rest of the world into the fold. No other American preacher will be able to say that. Only you."

Taggert was smiling but starting to fidget with the brim of his hat. Mary wondered if she was coming on too strongly, challenging his ultimate authority on all things church-related.

"Yes, my dear, that is a brilliant idea. You have outdone yourself. Let's get the events team working on it immediately. Perhaps we can get some of our celebrity members to join us. Maybe hold it at the Vatican. Do you think they can turn off the roller coasters and waterslides for a day to let us use the Sistine Chapel?"

She laughed. "It would be a great idea, but we should host it here in America. I'll have them look into it, Brady. Thank you for the acknowledgment. It means a lot to me. I sometimes worry you buy into the whole stay-at-home-wife routine we feed your flock. What is good for them is not good for people such as us—but I know you know that."

Taggert seemed legitimately shocked. "You know that is not true. I don't even like the little things we stage to diminish you, but we are leading by example, and, let's face it, most women in that crowd can't stand for themselves the way you do."

"Well, I hope so, thank you." She straightened her long dress. "Dare we include the meditation at the revival?" she asked with a mischievous smile.

He joined her and said, "We'd need to make sure the media-blocking security is on, but yes, a good idea. I wonder if Iwanna will . . . get it."

"I doubt it," Mary said. "The tight-assed bitch."

Chapter 40

With Noel officially on board and a clear plan in place, Lily reached out to update Anatoly via the antique bee, as agreed. The last box for her to check was to confirm he'd be able to make the robot deliver the speech she had in mind that admitted to the Dennisons' sins of the last twenty years. When he'd confirmed as much, they started discussing other topics, such as—

"I think I know what RANDs are for," Anatoly said through the bee in Lily's apartment.

"Really? What?" she asked.

"This is all speculation from people that work at Dennison. Obviously, we all wonder and talk, but it almost seems obvious, no? If you only have White people doing jobs, and many jobs are now done by bots, what else is left for other citizens to do?"

Lily caught on quickly. "Only the jobs the bots can't do yet. The lousy ones." She thought it through a little further. "Of course! Iwanna's basically marrying these citizens to the land, disincentivizing them to leave, because anyone on the outside is going to get cut off by the federal government. It's *indentured servitude*."

"I don't know this term. We would call it slavery."

"That's basically what it is," she conceded. "They'll pay them practically nothing. Just enough to keep them there. Okay, we'll include that in the speech. I'll write it up and send it over to you. Everything else going well?"

"Yes, yes, I demo Dennison bot to them in ten days. It will be ready. Just get me the speech the week before. And yes, I will be able to get out in time before they realize what is happening."

"Okay, make sure you do, and don't tell me where you're going. I'll keep this bee with me and get in touch when everything is settled."

"Good, Charity."

Chapter 41

November 7

Jeff sat in his classroom, reading over the lesson plan Brianne had delivered only just five minutes ago—which was accompanied by a note: *Not optional,* she'd written, then underlined. It was a historical video titled *The Soul of Dennison: His Vision, His Reign.*

His now twelve students walked in and sat, noting there were none of the usual opening assignments waiting for them on the digital board. When Eric saw this, he said, "Finally, the libtard is going to shut up for a day."

"Okay, I know this is going to upset you all very much, but for today, we're going to watch a well-produced journalistic piece on President Dennison." He wondered if this was how it started for so many: the ease of lying. He knew what this video was going to entail—it would be filled with lies, nothing but propaganda, and yet he'd unconsciously inserted "well-produced." Surrounded by hypocrisy, accomplished by everyone around him lacking self-awareness, was he already losing his own?

The video began to play on their desktops, and he just sat back and listened as the narrator began, sounding like a 1940 newsreel updating the audience on the war in France.

"The Dennison opening move after winning the White House in 2024 was the invasion of the state of Chihuahua, Mexico. 'If they're not going to secure the border,' President Dennison said in his first inauguration speech, 'I'm gonna secure it. You watch.'

"A neighbor of Biden's predecessor in Florida, Dennison became a regular visitor to the compound in 2020, having been a long-time club member and supporter of the conservative movement. Demonstrating his acute understanding of the nation and politics, he ingratiated himself with the former president and pointed out all their similarities: They were about the same age; had well-educated, intelligent children who were close to their families; and had vast fortunes. Dennison's first payload came in the '70s from his success in the latex industry, which he parlayed in the 2020s into significant gains from the commemorative gold coin market.

"When the former president's bid for reelection against Joe Biden was disrupted by an intended assassin's bullet, leaving him paralyzed, aphasic, and wheelchair-bound, he handpicked Dennison to take his place, putting all his resources behind him and commanding his legions to simply pretend Dennison was a less handsome, less rich, less hung version of him. President John Dennison swept into office as a complete nonentity in the election of 2024, defeating Kamala Harris in a landslide.

"His natural talents were exposed as the nation—and, eventually, the world—recognized him as a born leader with God-given ability. Those first four years of owning all three branches of government were all the conservatives needed to dominate federal, state,

and local policy for the entire country. It was sweeping, fast, and comprehensive.

"Dennison decided to establish himself immediately with a surprise attack on March 14, 2025, utilizing all military branches. The invasion was led by Marines and a massive buildup of Army forces at Joint Base San Antonio, with participation from the Air Force at Laughlin and the Navy at Corpus Christi. Space Force, based in Albuquerque, secured the ionosphere. Because of the unprecedented nature of the attack and the sheer disbelief of Mexico and the whole world that this was actually happening, not a shot was fired in the opening days. The Marines airdropped into the state's capital city, also named Chihuahua, and took over the statehouse. The skies were secured by lunch, with their main base at Santa Gertrudis also overwhelmed by the Marines. On day two of the war, Dennison addressed the world and made his pitch for a temporary annexation of the region.

"'We, the United States of America, have been under an invasion for years, decades, and for the first time, we are fighting back. We have told all our neighbors to the south to stop sending us your losers, your weak, your criminals—and they have not heard us because they are used to the pussies we usually have leading our government. But now they have to deal with us: America united at all levels of government, committed to securing our southern border. After trying to apply new and old technologies, we have found a more convenient approach: our well-funded military.

"'My hope is that we continue to have a peaceful transition of this region, and to be clear, we don't want all the country. We wouldn't know what to do with all that territory, and we don't need it. We've already got plenty of Taco Bells. I was advised to take just the border areas, but then we're just playing Whack-a-Mole. The dealers and

coyotes will move to a different part, so I said, no, take the whole damn state. I knew we could do it, and look, here I am, just inside what was Mexico a week ago, now an American . . . let's call it an American holding.

"'We've got tremendous ties to this country, most of them bad, but when you share a border like this, of course there's a lot of commerce, lotta business, so I want to make sure everyone understands, we have no intention of opening fire here, unless of course one of them do. Then the gloves are off. But if we can have cool heads, we can all get what we want out of this. I want the foreign businesses that own factories here to know we will not disrupt your operations. Beginning Monday, we expect it to be business as usual, but in the meantime, we're just going to make a few changes in the government, the police forces. The Marines are going to pay a visit to the drug-infested areas around here, like in Juarez.

"'Slowly, people will see this for what it is and appreciate it. They'll watch the US military bring some order where the Mexican people could not. It's not our country, so we don't have to pay attention to how they dealt with the drug lords. As far as I'm concerned, they're enemy combatants and subject to wartime justice.

"'I'm told there's battalions starting to form at the border with Coa—Cohill, the one to the east of us. I'm talking directly to the president of Mexico here: don't do it. We've got all that firepower over in Texas. I mean, come on, we could send a bunch of ranchers over and secure the area, am I right?

"'We can work this out nice and peaceful, really. I want to carve out a zone of American influence where we can start dealing with the problem of people coming to our borders. Once my government and military have given me a plan for leaving with a secure border, we'll pull out of here, and it will be like we never came. The streets

will be safe; business will be running good. We just need President what's-his-name to keep a cool head, and it'll all be fine.'"

Jeff thought about the parts that had clearly been left out. President Manuel Lopez *had* kept a cool head, knowing he could not go toe to toe with the US military, especially on their own border, the free flow of supplies and modern technologies too much to overcome.

But for the United States, the decisions across the world could not be more devastating, with a series of moves led by France and the newest applicant for membership into the European Union, Ukraine, fresh on the heels of a successful victory against Putin that handed him over to The Hague for war crimes. The Mexican invasion resulted in a mass exodus of manufacturing jobs and capital investment in the United States and Chihuahua, while embargoes and tariffs put in place across all markets made the cost of doing business with America too great. Factories to make up the demand popped up all over Mexico proper, outside the occupied zone, as European nations redirected their investments in solidarity. The insurgency, with American soldiers targeted by snipers and roadside bombs, had taken thousands of American lives to date.

America now needed to be first because it was, essentially, its only customer.

Chapter 42

November 9

The hottest reservation in the Gulch was its first high-end restaurant, Rearden's Steakhouse, so of course, it had to be the place where Jake invited Jeff and Lily to discuss his proposal. There was no ask. Jeff received an invitation for dinner on Friday at six o'clock with the remark *Look forward to seeing you guys tomorrow.* He forwarded it to Lily, who was getting ready for work at her apartment in Denver: a quick round trip to Wichita, and then one to El Paso.

She started a RealTime video call while brushing her teeth. "What are we going to do about that?"

"So you don't want to bang Jake?"

Through toothpaste and brush, she said, "Awe you-fwucking-cwazy? No!"

"Okay, okay, I just didn't want to be presumptuous."

She flipped him the bird and went to the bathroom to rinse.

"Look," he said, "I'm amazed we've managed to avoid them this long, but we knew they'd come knocking at the door soon enough. We still have our out. We're not ready to get married just yet, but in the meantime, aren't there other ways we can help the cause? I'd happily donate sperm if that's what they want."

"What year is it, Jeff? Those options aren't on the table anymore, remember? In vitro died with all these laws they've put up."

"Sorry, I guess I haven't kept up on my—"

"They need to have this kid the way God intended, and the fact they need it done within the safe confines of two marriages is just comically insane, even for them."

"Okay, so we'll stall on our marriage. Don't shut the door. Just wait them out."

◆•————••◆

Jake and Cheryl were waiting in their booth, apparently a few drinks deep already. "There they are!" Cheryl said, rising to lean in for a healthy welcome kiss for Jeff that ensured full chest-to-chest contact.

Jake said, "Hope this place is good. Supposed to be the best steak for miles."

"I'm sure it's going to be great. Thanks for inviting us," Jeff said.

"Yes, it's gorgeous here," Lily offered weakly. The gold-laced . . . everything was a bit much for her taste. She slid into the leather booth next to Jeff.

"So," Cheryl said with her ever-present glowing smile, skipping straight to the chase, "we've given y'all some time to think about it, and with Jake so busy with work and travel, there probably weren't many opportunities to revisit this topic, anyway. But here we are. How are the marriage plans coming?"

"Well, to be honest," Jeff began, tone artificially diplomatic, but only to Lily's ears, "since we met at the church, we've both been really caught up in our jobs and haven't given it much thought."

Lily patted Jeff's forearm, looking to Cheryl and Jake. "I think we were so blindsided by the whole thing that we unconsciously avoided talking about it."

"Yeah, sorry about that," Cheryl said, flashing an innocent grin. "I was all caught up in the moment, is all, and just let it all come out, so I'm sure it sounded a little crazy at the get-go."

Lily caught Jeff's eye, making a split-second, silent exchange that quite clearly asked, *What does she mean, a* little *crazy?*

"But it *is* why we invited you to this Eden in the mountains," Cheryl concluded, playing hardball.

Jeff cleared his throat, having prepared for this. "I do appreciate that, Cheryl. I love my new job and I love living in Vicksburg Gulch, but this proposal has made things weird for Lily and me. You know, we've only been going out for a few months."

The waiter arrived to take their drink orders, and it took them a minute to realize that he was a bot. Each sentence was followed by just enough of a delay to tip off that it was processing the environment to determine the next thing to say. Still, the ordering process was seamless, and the waiter walked off naturally to the bar, having digitally sent each order to the bot bartender as he had taken them.

"Did you see the one they got at the diner?" Cheryl asked, laughing loudly. "Spitting image of that sleepy, stuttering buffoon, Joe!"

"Yeah, we saw." Jeff forced an unconvincing smile. "Funny."

Cheryl returned to the subject at hand. "I apologize if this proposal seems out of the blue. I promise, it wasn't—I just wanted to make sure we were all compatible first," she said, resting a chin in the hammock of her laced-together fingers. Her eyes clicked to Lily. "But I do realize springing all this on you was unfair, little miss, and I'm sorry about that."

Cringing at the use of "little miss," as Lily was forty-four, she said, "No problem. Jeff was open with me as well."

"Sounds like a great relationship you guys have there! Which is why this seems like a perfect match. I mean, look, it doesn't need to get all crazy or kinky or anything. Unless you want it to," Cheryl added with a giggle. "There's only one goal here, but like the reverend says, it's all about the journey."

Feeling Jake's eyes on her every word, Lily decided to make her pitch. "You guys seem pretty well connected around here. Perhaps Jeff could help you out with a . . . um, donation that you could use? The techniques for in vitro still exist."

"Are you suggesting we break the law, Lily?" Jake asked sternly. "You didn't strike me as the criminal type."

"No," she said, "of course not. I just thought there might be easier ways, especially since Jeff and I still aren't married and you guys clearly want another child quickly."

"Well, breaking God's and America's laws is not the answer for us, I'm afraid," Jake said. "So I take it you're rejecting our offer?"

"To be fair, Jake, this sounds more like a demand," Lily commented.

"No," Jeff said, intervening. He rested a hand on Lily's wrist, squeezing it slightly, prompting her to hold her tongue. "That's *not* what we're saying. It's just all about timing. I'm still settling in, she's got this new job flying Dennison employees all over the place, and we're both still trying to catch up on saving the money we haven't made for the last few years. We're just not ready to get married, is all."

The waiterbot arrived, placed everyone's drink neatly in front of each of them, and asked, "Do we know what we want for dinner yet, folks?"

Jake reached out and grabbed his neat bourbon and sank it back in one swallow, the whole time looking at Lily. "We already know he's into her," he said, nodding at Jeff and Cheryl. "So what's all this really about? You not into me?"

"I'll come back," the bot said and departed, programmed to detect tension.

Lily stared back at Jake, slipping out of her costume, having played the good and proper little girl for long enough. Her temper simmered over the obvious power play that Jake was trying to impose on her with the intimidating look and blunt statement of what was, in fact, correct. Seeing this, Jeff took her hand gently and said, "Maybe we should order dinner."

"You're a good-looking guy, Jake, and your wife is beautiful," Lily said, holding his gaze. "That's not my issue at all. It's how you guys went about this. Maybe if you had just played it out, it would have happened naturally over a bottle of wine. Or six. But instead, she forced herself on him."

Cheryl said, "Well, he didn't put up much of a fight. And it wasn't *real* sex."

Without hesitation, Lily said, "Because he's smart and picked up on the threat from the get-go. It's the same thing all the time with people like you: Create a scenario to squeeze people to do what you want and play innocent about the whole thing, saying he always had a choice. You think plausible deniability sets you free of blame. Don't you guys have anyone else you could use?"

"We do, but it would be too weird, with us already having plans for our kids to get married," Cheryl said.

Jeff asked, "Oh, so Eric's dating their kid?"

Seeing the misunderstanding, Cheryl said, "Well, they've met, of course, but we're planning to tell them about the marriage on Easter."

"You've . . . arranged their marriage?" Lily asked.

Cheryl waved her off. "Oh, I know you outsiders don't get it, but it's the only way we can control how our community evolves. It's common around here. You'll see. So that's why we can't work on that little project with the Hoffmans."

After letting that marinate, Lily added, "Honestly, that's why everything just turned us off. Like the church, without giving us a heads-up on what to expect. Now this, staring me down to make us do your bidding . . . It didn't have to go like this, but I think it's part of the turn-on for you guys. The power." Switching the glare to Cheryl, Lily added, "Isn't it?"

Cheryl's silence was confirmation enough.

The waiterbot returned. "Do we know what we want for dinner yet, folks?"

Jake stood up, brushing himself off. "Actually, we're going to be leaving. These nice folks can pick up the drinks. We've been very generous to them, but now it seems they're ungrateful, so taking care of the tab is the least they can do."

"Jake," Jeff said, "it's not like that. We just need a little time."

As Cheryl, wearing a sorrowful face, joined him at his side, Jake said, "Maybe you need a little incentive instead," and led his wife out the front door.

"That went well," Jeff said, sighing.

Lily had her head down, realizing that she had just blown up the relationship with the one guy responsible for Jeff being there. "He was out of line," she said.

Remembering her order from one of their early dates, Jeff told the waiterbot, "She'll have the filet medium rare with a side of au gratin potatoes, and I'll have the strip rare with creamed spinach."

"Soft steak and cheesy taters, an excellent choice," the waiterbot said, converting the French dish to the regional equivalent. "My favorite."

"Which one?" Lily asked the table.

"Yes," the waiterbot said as it departed.

"They really should create a bug list for these things." Jeff still had her hand from before, and she looked up his arm to his smiling face. "I know I just screwed you pretty hard there."

"Ah, don't worry about it. I think we both know I'm not long for this place, so hopefully, I can hang in until the holiday break, and then I'll find something else. All tonight did was confirm one thing for me."

"Oh yeah?" she said. "What's that?"

Pulling her in for a soft kiss, he said, "I'll work hard to get a new job in the Springs once this is done. I'd like to stay out west, if you're okay with that?"

She returned his kiss and said, "Yes, I'd like that. I enjoy our time to-gether—when we're not fighting off swingers."

Chapter 43

November 12

Iwanna stood in front of glass cabinet number two in her office, about ten feet from the slavery artifacts, and fought the desire to open it to hold the Congressional Medal of Honor it contained. She missed the intimate moments she'd shared with the recipient of the medal, at a time that seemed not long ago, even though it had been decades. Back then, she would be crying right now, thinking about him. Now all she had were blistering memories of their passionate but brief time together, right around when she had decided that she couldn't have a normal romantic relationship when her life was dictated by her family's exploits. Mercifully, he had been taken away from her, lost in Mexico in the middle of an insurgency from the south. He had prevented the imminent destruction of a Dennison manufacturing facility, calling in an air strike while bleeding out on a field in Parral, just as the Mexican resistance approached the perimeter.

Problem solved. She'd go to Colorado. Thanks to the filth down south.

To her shock, Iwanna realized she was not alone, that Hal had entered and was standing behind her, having requested a meeting twenty minutes prior.

"Quite the tragedy," he said.

"Don't," she replied curtly, turning to walk past him to her desk, not casting so much as a glance in his direction. "How can I help you?"

"We have a request from the reverend. He wants to hold an old-fashioned revival in the Gulch, one to celebrate the Fourth Great Awakening, and he is requesting the members of his church in the Springs be allowed to visit and participate for the weekend."

Still preoccupied, she said with a wave, "Yeah, sure, what do I care."

"Well, you might, Iwanna," Hal said tentatively. "He would like the culmination of this event to be a service on Sunday, with you and your father as speakers."

She sighed.

He didn't have to say what came next, but he did: "On December ninth."

The day before the centennial.

She thought about it and said, "Okay, why not? Free advertising. We were just going to do a live broadcast of the ceremony with the family, close friends, some employees from the plant, but if it was going to pass muster with them, why not in front of the whole church?" Looking at him for the first time, she asked, "Will it work? How much more impressive would it be, in front of all those people? It would kill all the rumors out there that he's dead."

Hal blinked in surprise and said, "Yes, we can do that, no problem. Plenty of time to program the events. We just need to know all the possible situations, and it'll go fine."

"Okay, meet with the Taggerts and Jake, make sure they have no idea what we're planning, and do what you need to do with the bot."

"Consider it done."

She walked over and put her hand on his bicep. "I assume that Anatoly is all straightened out and up to the task?"

"Yes, our meeting went very well. He understands."

"Great," she said. "You ever think of being a preacher?"

Hal laughed out loud. "Uh, no. I'm an atheist."

"Of course you are, but don't you think they are too?" She turned to him. "How could anyone truly believe in what Jesus had to say and in the same breath support this fucking family? I don't believe, either. But I sure hope I'm right, because if I'm not, the first thing that happens when I die is Christ himself comes over and slaps me in the face."

"You'll need to get in line," Hal said. "You won't be first, and definitely not last."

He separated from her hand and exited.

She went back to the case and looked at the name pin under the medal, which read:

CAPTAIN HAROLD "HAL" WILLET, 82ND AIRBORNE

AWARDED POSTHUMOUSLY, JULY 4, 2025,
WASHINGTON, DC

Chapter 44

November 14

Jeff sat in front of his class and debated his decision of the day before. The curriculum called for him to teach the principles of America's most significant literary movement at its inception, one that fed off the crazy notion of the pursuit of happiness for each citizen, and then explain why that was selfishness and against the teachings of Christ. What was required was their allegiance to God and government. He decided he would teach it as it had been taught to him and leave out the part they wanted.

"So," Jeff said, looking at Eric on the off chance he might take the question on, "how would you say the transcendentalists viewed authority in their time?"

He watched as Eric's hand slowly and discreetly raised its middle finger.

Unsurprised, Jeff continued. "This is the 1800s; industrialism is starting up, and Thoreau decides to sit in a cabin for two years, two months, and two days, then write a book about it. What does he have to say about that experience?"

Crickets.

"What would we say about someone like that today?" Jeff urged them.

"Fag," Eric said.

"Hey! I get you have nothing intelligent to say on most topics other than football, so how about, for consistency's sake, you shut up unless you actually have something helpful to contribute? To be clear, homophobia doesn't fall under that category."

Eric did not take kindly to the laughs that trickled through the room. "You can't say that to me. Look at you, defending the homos."

Jeff ignored him and returned to the class. "Look at the list of things they wrote! *Self-reliance. Civil disobedience.*"

"Individuals matter more than the government or the groups that make up society," commented a diminutive young man in the middle of the pack. He spoke confidently yet scanned the room for attackers. He looked at Jeff for approval before his glance retreated back down to his desk.

"Yes, thank you, Aaron! These guys were against slavery. They saw the damage mobs could do. And the key is, ideas like this, the sanctity of the *individual,* could only be found in the United States. It was *this* country that said, 'All men are created equal.' That idea was nuts back then. In a collectivist society like China, even today, that is still nuts. It was the individual that mattered to them, the *possibility* of each life. The idea that every single one of us has the opportunity to seize our lives and control our destiny. The sentiment was referred to when I was a kid as 'carpe diem.'"

He noticed a small red light in the back of the room for the first time since he'd started working at the school. It blinked on, emanating perhaps two feet below the tiles of the drop ceiling. He had a sneaking suspicion as to what that was but moved on.

"None of you have seen *Dead Poets Society*?"

There was only silence in response.

And then, Aaron, thankfully, spoke up again. "I've heard of it, but states out here blacked it out. They probably didn't do that where you're from."

"Wow," Jeff said, picking up on the envy in Aaron's last phrase and opting to play stupid. "I didn't know that was going on."

"Ain't so smart after all, huh?" Eric said.

"Once again, you are mistaken, not knowing the difference between intelligent and informed. I'd say that's ironic, but you wouldn't understand why. Which would be ironic."

A few in the class got it and laughed.

Jeff wasn't surprised to see Brianne appear at the door and address the class. "All of you have the rest of the period free. Please leave." When they were alone, she closed the door and approached Jeff.

"In fairness, I should have told you about a system in place here. It's implemented in only a few school districts in the country, but we felt it was just the right kind of technology for our community, so we had it installed. You have the distinction of being the first to be flagged."

"*Dead Poets* is that bad, huh?"

"It was a popular movie but, unfortunately, inconsistent with our values. I should let you know that the system also triggers an alarm at the office of the Guardian Angels. I'm expecting the acting legate to be here any minute." Seeing Jeff's face, she explained, "The local head of the GA is called a legate. They're just setting up here in town, so he's acting, not official yet, but . . ." She leaned closer to him with an expression of seriousness. "He is *very* well connected. You'll want to be careful. I don't know how reasonable he is, and I can only go so far in your defense."

Jeff sat back and smiled, then blurted out a chuckle. "I was about to get to the part where I explained why transcendentalism is bad, and you—"

Brianne raised a hand to him. "I replayed the whole thing, Jeff. That wasn't your tone. I get it and will try to help, but . . ." She seemed to be fighting herself about how much she wanted to assist Jeff in this situation. "You've been around here. You know how touchy some of this stuff can get. Just be honest."

Jeff was struck by her tone, despite every neuron in his head telling him that this was plain stupidity and that it would result in, at worst, a verbal scolding.

But then Acting Legate Koy Taggert poked his head into the room.

"Hi, Brianne," he said, ignoring Jeff. "Would it be okay if we took this in your office?"

They led Jeff like a schoolboy to the principal's office. With how seriously Koy was treating this objectively minor infraction, Jeff felt himself prepare to quit on the spot. He simply didn't possess the patience required to kowtow to Koy Taggert—even if it meant keeping a well-paying job and his new apartment. With all the pitfalls one could drop into while teaching, having the very same dolt who had almost killed his girlfriend give him a lecture about the dangers of a movie every English teacher in America used to discuss critically was simply too much stupid to handle with a straight face.

Brianne seemed to pick up on this as they walked behind Koy. "Jeff, take this seriously."

He didn't. *Couldn't.* If this was what undid him, it would almost be perfect: the last great gasp of transcendentalist teaching in the American classroom. What would they have done if he'd made the kids stand on his desk? He assumed hanging was in the realm of possibility.

Koy didn't even ask to sit at Brianne's desk, plopping down with great ease. He maintained a level of seriousness consistent with a judge about to render a verdict for murder as they both took a seat across from him on their respective parts of the stage.

Jeff's expression of pure amusement did not help the situation.

"You remember me, I assume?" Koy asked him.

"Sure. You're the married bartender who tried to pick up my girlfriend a few months ago. How could I forget?" Jeff's grin broadened, and he realized the decision had already been made: This was his last time in this building. He was sticking around solely for entertainment at this point. With nothing left to lose, he figured he'd have some fun with the pinhead in front of him.

Koy didn't change his expression when he looked at Brianne, whose gaze dropped knowingly.

"Look," Jeff continued, "if you two want to shitcan me for a vague reference to a movie from over fifty years ago, one that isn't offensive to any of the beliefs held out here . . . if that's what this is all about, then let's skip this part and I'll resign now. Not worth this nonsense."

Now it was Koy's turn to smile. "Are you under the impression the penalty here is just your job?" He glanced over at Brianne. "Is he unaware?"

"He's not from around here," Brianne said quietly.

"We have a zero-tolerance policy for violating our educational guide-lines. This has been true for some time now. At least five years."

Jeff asked, "Okay, what's the fine?" Moving to pick up his bag, he said, "Send me the ticket. You teach them, Koy. I'm sure they'll learn a lot."

"*Sit down!*" Koy snarled.

Jeff turned to Brianne. "Is he serious right now?"

"Please sit down. Koy, I'm going to go over the role of the Guardian Angels here in Colorado with Jeff, if that's okay with you."

Koy nodded angrily.

Brianne gave him a desperate, pleading sort of look. "I know this isn't the case out east, but Colorado wanted to end the extreme liberal education baked into the curriculum at so many schools. The nondenominational Christians formed a third-party organization called the Guardian Angels, and their role was to monitor variations from our—"

"Orthodoxy," Jeff said.

"Sure, Jeff, orthodoxy."

"So do you break into synagogues and mosques to enforce it?" he asked.

"Well, no, of course not," Brianne said. "Those are private institutions for false religions. But this school—"

"Is ours!" Koy barked. "We'll teach our kids what we fucking know to be true, not that atheist garbage you learned back in New York."

"Connecticut."

"Sodom and Gomorrah."

"Got it."

"I think the salient point here," Brianne continued, "is that the GA acts as a *deputized* organization to local police in areas where they accept the partnership. So if you were in Boulder right now, we wouldn't be having this conversation. But the town of Vicksburg Gulch did create such a partnership, and based on the GA investigation into this matter, this could be referred to the sheriff for criminal action."

"And I have the right to detain, smart guy, so keep mouthing off," Koy snapped.

Jeff leaned back and laughed loudly, staring at the ceiling, his eyes darting left and right and then closing. This wasn't happening. What was the worst they could do to him? He decided he needed to leave the room without a physical confrontation.

"Do you have questions for me? What do we do here?" he asked, closed eyes still pointed upward.

Brianne rose, returned to her spot in the back of the room, and looked at Koy, who took out a tablet.

"I will be recording the rest of this interview," Koy said. "Mr. Maslow, we are discussing the flag alert from the Dennison Teacher's Assistant that I received at twelve forty-two p.m. this afternoon. Can you describe the lesson you were teaching and what you think might have triggered the alert?"

"Well, Koy, I was teaching the students about a literary and philosophical movement in the early nineteenth century called transcendentalism, which was influenced greatly by the freedom of the American citizen and the ideal of the sacredness of the individual, secured by the American Constitution, and how that could be envisioned in the lives of every person in the country. You see, Koy, they had this crazy notion that when the Founding Fathers gave us certain freedoms—like, for example, the freedom *from* religion—we'd be safe to live our lives however we pleased, within the confines of the law."

All the words except "American," "religion," and "crazy" seemed to fly over Koy's head. Jeff was certain that he had no idea what transcendentalism was, let alone how to pronounce it. Koy looked at Brianne, who stared blankly, and said, "The words 'carpe diem' are what triggered the alert. Why were you speaking Spanish in an English class?"

Jeff tried to maintain a straight face, but again, could not help but laugh. "It's Latin. It means, 'Seize the day.' Is it safe to assume you've never seen the movie in question?"

"Of course I haven't," Koy spat.

"It's about a teacher trying to get his students to think for themselves and live every day as if it were their last. That's what that phrase means: Don't waste your life doing stupid shit when you can be doing not-stupid shit. Your presence here is evidence you're not familiar with the philosophy."

"Keep going, Maslow," Koy said.

"Do they provide you with handcuffs, or do you use the fuzzy ones from your nightstand?" Jeff asked.

Koy leaped up, the desk in front of him jolting forward into Jeff's knees, and Brianne quickly stepped in between them.

"No anger detection, I see," Jeff said.

Brianne said, "No, it'd go off constantly." To Koy, she said, "I think you have what you need. My suggestion is that I suspend Mr. Maslow for now, pending further investigation. Go back to the office, discuss this with the educational team in the Springs, and decide how you want to proceed. They will know about the movie and why it was in the system in the first place. Jeff won't enter this building again until you're done. Does that work for you, Mr. Taggert?"

He had not taken his raging eyes off Jeff the whole time. "I should just kick your ass right here and have you arrested."

Brianne's nostrils flared. "You still need to file the charge, and right now, you don't know enough to do that," she told Koy firmly. "Take it back, let's all cool off, and see what they say."

Koy started to push, then threw the chair behind him into the wall. "I'm gonna be the one to put those fuzzy cuffs on you, smart guy," he said, oblivious to how hilarious it was for him to say so.

Jeff could not hold back his laughter. "Don't forget the nipple clamps," he taunted and then, feeling the stare from Brianne, shut up.

After Koy exited, Brianne sighed, turning to face Jeff. "Look, this is my fault too. I should have told you about the sensor."

"I can imagine the justification they're going to come up with. They don't want our kids thinking for themselves."

"Probably. But with your performance here, Koy isn't likely to let this go. Just start preparing your defense and get a lawyer."

Jeff stood up, threw his satchel over his shoulder, and reached out his hand, which Brianne took. "Trust me, I won't be back, but I appreciate your help."

Jeff decided to do a circuit around the athletic fields instead of going directly to his apartment, enjoying the scenery around him for what he assumed would be the last time. The cloud-covered mountains. The brown, dead leaves on the ground.

The eagle spiraling overhead.

Chapter 45

November 15

Taggert had given up trying to groom his son to accept the mantle of responsibility in the church. Quite simply, Koy had failed to master the language, the art, the performance. He barely understood scripture, let alone the complicated nuances of it, and thus lacked the skills to lead a congregation, let alone a simple at-home Bible study.

For this reason, he had Koy run a couple of restaurant-bars that had been his original source of income when he had moved to Denver in his twenties, where he had held his first small ceremonies as he built his ministerial style using the stage at the bar. Taggert had been rough around the edges but had an everyman feel about him. It was here that he'd caught the attention of Mary, who saw his potential, familiar with the evangelical preaching she had growing up in Arizona, and later in Denver, where she was a marketing student.

Just after the finding of the Argyre Cross, an accidental discovery on a routine trip to Mars in preparation for the first human colony, Christians in the United States were emboldened to form an organized vigilante force to fill in the gap where, legally, peace officers and lawyers couldn't tread.

These focused mainly on the implicit social behaviors underpinning the many religious customs they wanted to see everywhere in their America, such as the overreaching school boards and their liberal agenda showing up in curricula, and the enforcement of clothing decency violations that were so common before Dennison took power. They called them the Guardian Angels, buying the rights from the New York City–based organization that reported on crime in the subways, and opening chapters wherever requested. These were set up similarly, using volunteers to patrol the streets and respond to citizen complaints about the violations. The GA would then perform an "investigation" into the complaint and look for ways to frame the infraction as a violation of any law they could find—local, state, or federal—and leverage their tight relationship with public institutions to funnel the accused into the justice system.

With every tier of law enforcement under the control or influence of the far right, these blatant constitutional violations went unchecked. The institutions meant to protect American citizens from such overreach were too busy ensuring their jurisdictions were safe from what were perceived to be the bigger, more substantial threats: illegals, voter fraud, and aborted fetuses.

Lily had offered to join Jeff when he received his request to appear, but he insisted she stay as far away from this as possible; he'd pay his fine and find a job elsewhere. He already felt responsible enough for dragging her into the insanity that was Vicksburg Gulch, but she insisted it was all good and part of an educational experience for them in learning just how far those in power were taking things.

He was escorted into a room clearly designed by an interior decorator who had spent the last fifty-two years watching *Law and Order* and sat down with the expectation of being cuffed to the table—which, under the circumstances, was warranted, considering the risk of Jeff losing control and slapping Koy hard across the face was quite high. To his disappointment, a different character entered the room: bookish, bald, expressionless. He sat with his tablet before him, pulled off his glasses, and offered his hand.

"Hi, Mr. Maslow. I'm George. I'm with our legal liaison office in the Springs, and I've just been asked to do a quick interview since they're still starting things up here. I hope that's okay. This shouldn't take long."

Jeff wondered if it was possible someone from this organization actually had their head on straight. "Of course," he said.

"Invoking your inner Mr. Keating, I see?" George asked with a friendly smile.

Jeff gave a comfortable laugh, appreciating the seeming normalcy of his interrogator. "Well, I assume you have the audio or video, or at least a transcript."

"I saw the whole thing on video, yes," George said in an even more calming tone.

"Okay, good, that's great. So you know, I was not teaching my students about the movie—it just shared subject matter with what I was instructed to teach, which was transcendentalism," he said pointedly, allowing this to sink in. "I said, 'Seize the day,' which was apparently the magic phrase. Even so, that is just me *referencing* the movie, not me *teaching* it. Of course, if I'd known it was restricted around here, I wouldn't have done that." Seeing George's reasonable reaction, Jeff felt impowered to add, "Though I have to be honest, I'm not exactly sure why it's restricted in the first place."

George beamed. "So when you go to another country—like, say, for example, the Cayman Islands—do the laws still apply to you even if you're not from there? If your father rents a BMW on the island and you start speeding around doing seventy-three miles per hour in a forty, should they let you off the hook when they pull you over because you thought the limit was eighty?"

Jeff was no longer smiling. George was not the ally he'd hoped he was. They had dug into his records, which shouldn't have even been available in the United States in the first place, all because of a *movie quote*. He was now as serious as his interrogator tried to appear not to be.

"That's quite a specific example there, George. Does a private organization have access to police information? In the Caribbean?"

"We have strong partnerships everywhere, Mr. Maslow."

Jeff willed himself to shut the fuck up, knowing that this was bound to escalate and not knowing if there was anyone above this guy to reason with. He decided to make a pointed defense that would at least be on the record for anyone who saw it later. "What exactly am I being accused of?"

George leaned back, recognizing the shift in Jeff's tone, and said, "I'm still deciding."

"It's just you, then? *You're* the man in charge?" He noted the satisfaction in George's expression.

"Yes, Mr. Maslow."

"Listen, if I had shown the movie, I could understand how that would violate whatever codes you're thinking of, but those kids were not exposed to any of it," Jeff noted, sitting straighter. "They quite literally were only exposed to the line 'Seize the day,' which has no significant political or religious connotations."

George just stared back at him.

"What harm did I do to my students in telling them to *seize the day*?" Jeff asked frankly.

"You made your preference for the movie clear, enticing them to seek it out. Just like Keating did, and we all saw how that ended up."

"I disagree with much of the movie, George. My reference to carpe diem was simply where the movie is ubiquitous. Every English teacher from Maine to Maryland quotes it liberally and usually shows it outright. I've done none of that, so besides a vague reference, I don't see what leg you have to stand on."

George leaned over the center of the table until he was face-to-face with Jeff. "That movie represents everything wrong with liberalism. What did that young man learn? To disobey his father, waste his life on artistic endeavors while his friends performed demonic rituals in a cave and desecrated a Christian ceremony. All in support of a homosexual and his supposed *poetry*."

When coming into the room, Jeff had known Walt Whitman would become a topic, but not in a sentence like that. Once again, the reality of the situation slapped him in the face, enabled by his continued underestimation of the people around him.

Knowing he had Jeff's full attention and seeing how hard he was fighting his desire to engage but being intelligent enough not to, George said, "If we let every kid behave like those depicted in that movie, we'd have anarchy in this country. In Colorado, we don't support anarchy. Of course, all this calls into question why you were even in front of that classroom in the first place. We'll take that up with the administration. The fact that you are defending your behavior here tells me you are not contrite, so I'm more inclined to recommend charges ranging from conspiracy to incite a riot to child endangerment." As he leaned back, smile intact, he watched the contortions on Jeff's face with obvious pleasure.

"Neither of those charges sound like a misdemeanor to me."

"They are not, Mr. Maslow. I am asking that you stay in the state while I work with the authorities on the charges, and we will put a hold on your passport until all of this is sorted out."

The air came out of Jeff, and he leaned forward and looked at George with disbelief. "I can tell you're not stupid. You see all this, don't you? How the idea that I endangered those kids in any way is outrageous? That this is all just because the guy behind that mirror is mad at me because I called him out on his bullshit a few months ago?"

"Is it any worse than influencing children to change their sex? To have themselves chemically castrated? Or butchered? Ideas lead to actions, Mr. Maslow. It's important to nip these things in the bud before they are manifested. No different than any cancer. The town of Vicksburg Gulch has said no to suggestions that children should disobey their fathers. I am simply enforcing that." He picked up his tablet and said, "And I'm up for promotion. Good luck, Mr. Maslow." Then, as an afterthought, he added, "Oh, and there are *two* people mad at you behind that mirror."

As George walked out, Koy was waiting and entered immediately, getting straight into Jeff's face, .25 inches from his nose, as he rose from his chair. "What's it like in that silly little head of yours?" he asked.

Jeff thought for a moment and said, "Sane, Koy. Not sick with hatred."

Chapter 46

Dennison Robotics was located in the Stratmoor suburb of Colorado Springs, the highly secure compound built on the heels of the acquisition of Tactical AI Solutions that provided them the critical tech to help launch many of their products. These were often commercial versions of ideas discovered in the government, like at CIA and NSA, that somehow managed to find their way into Dennison engineering pipelines.

With those inputs, the company was able to leapfrog competition worldwide in the field of robotics and neural networks attempting to replicate the human mind and its capabilities. With a strong CEO in Iwanna, it did not take long for the prototype of a lifelike humanoid robot to become a reality, with just about every variation imaginable using a customized profile approach.

It was Iwanna's foresight that had made them generate the core intellectual profile of her father at the end of 2038, which he'd fully endorsed, thinking that maybe, one day, they would be able to port a digital version of his psyche back into a human body, making him immortal.

Iwanna hadn't had the heart to tell him that wasn't possible, but she had still reaped the benefits of resources she'd received for the project. While the physical manifestation of a robot was easy enough, it was code that dictated the machine's movements, facial expressions, and even humor. Re-creating consciousness was an entirely different endeavor.

It was one thing to create Queenie—a bot capable of serving ice cream and interacting pleasantly with customers—but it was quite another to create bots intended to replicate specific positions, or specific humans. In those cases, a Personality Ingestion Engine was developed, which would parse vast volumes of information about the person across all media types, pull anything that informed how the bot would behave, and build it into the Core System. In the case of the President Dennison prototype, it included his autobiography, biographies of others that mentioned him, news articles, meeting minutes, and videos. The goal was to develop a bot that could pass as the man himself for a sustained period of time, capable of answering basic questions and holding conversations without detection. It was not yet expected that a family member could be fooled, but fortunately for Iwanna, she needed much less.

Iwanna sat with Hal in the secure lab, waiting for a demonstration of the first pairing of the draft CS profile of Dennison with the hot-off-the-press rotund body in a navy-blue suit. She leaned close to him. "I hope his time at the retreat motivated Anatoly to perform better."

After the Queenie screwup, former CIA contractors had relocated Anatoly to a Dennison dark site buried in the Rockies, fully supplied with all the current technologies intended to modify the behavior of its guests. The need for waterboarding was now considered primitive compared with what could be accomplished with an excellent psychological profile and virtual reality contact lenses. Iwanna had made sure the lead engineer had only gotten a mild taste of the treatment—just enough to understand how generous she was being in not unleashing her security apparatus in full.

"Yes, he got the message and appreciates your patience. He assures me all will be as planned going forward." He walked to the lab door and opened it. "Anatoly, please come join us."

The door opened, and Anatoly walked forth with a stoic expression, standing at attention between them and the demonstration area.

"Were you able to acquire a scan of my father to create a mold," she asked, "or did you use video?"

"We were there the same day you were, Ms. Dennison. The Secret Service was very cooperative and helped in every way possible. We were able to perform the laser scan molding."

"Good. They are our allies in this. Nothing gets done without their say-so. Okay, so tell me what I'm going to see here."

Hal decided to take the lead. "As you know, we already had a profile created for your father at your request. For that, we took the baseline pro-file of an Ivy League graduate from New York with a substantial income—"

"Not sure if that was the best idea," Iwanna said, "but go on."

Hal paused momentarily, not sure if she was joking. "We then used the PIE to form the foundation of his speech, diction, knowledge base, motor skills, and mannerisms; performed some testing; and feel we are at a point where we can share the current product with you. To be clear, this is not ready, but certainly ahead of schedule for the event in three weeks. How is your father, by the way?"

"His condition hasn't changed," she reported. "His doctors still aren't detecting much brain activity, but he's alive."

"I'm sure it will turn around," Hal said softly.

"Thanks. Okay, let's see it."

Hal looked at Anatoly, who took out the remote-control tablet for the bot.

"I'm sure you'll keep that closer to you this time?" Iwanna asked, try-ing to be lighthearted.

Anatoly stiffened. "Yes," he said—and then, addressing the unseen engineers in the control room with a nod of authorization, he added, "Begin."

The door opened. The Dennison bot, with his characteristic smile and swagger, unchanged for over twenty years, walked to the center of the room at a pace of 3.4 miles per hour and with a gait identical to that of Iwanna's father a month ago, prior to his stroke and subsequent coma.

Hal said, "We have him currently in semiautonomous mode, where we are primarily interacting with that base personality profile I was telling you about. This allows us to control him without the full, um . . . impact of his personality getting in the way."

"So he won't be an asshole to you," she said, smirking.

Anatoly replied a little too quickly, "Yes, that's right. We can turn the full profile on and off as we like."

"While the profile is in full mode, can we still override what he says and does? We need to make sure he doesn't give the order to nuke Canada if the prime minister shows up."

Hal resumed the demo. "Yes, we can make him say whatever we want. Just insert it into his stream of consciousness. It will then flow naturally from his mouth as if he's articulating a regular thought. Anatoly, show her the visualization."

With a hint of hesitation, Anatoly walked next to Iwanna and shared the screen. "We can see the queue of sentences in his head and how they will be emotionally delivered, and edit them as we like. Add, modify, delete. I will show this on big monitor during the demo so you can watch it in real time."

"Thank you, Anatoly, that will be a big help." She turned to see an empty list.

She heard Hal say, "President Dennison, how are you today?"

"Good. I'm good."

The words, in a gray font, appeared on the screen and then came out of the Dennison bot's mouth in the exact speech patterns to which listeners worldwide were accustomed.

"Wow," she said. "Sounds just like him. Okay, release the hounds."

Anatoly said, "I just need to set the stage for it so it accepts its setting and doesn't get confused when it comes on line. I have prepared a scenario where it thinks it is meeting with you, Ms. Dennison, to discuss dinner plans for tonight. It thinks it is in the White House bunker."

"Smart, that's smart," Iwanna said.

He tapped and then said, "Okay, here we go." The expression on the bot changed instantly to what could best be described as befuddled.

"Hi, Dad," Iwanna said.

The bot turned, and on the monitor, she saw his upcoming thought in purple text:

Hi, honey. What are you doin' here?

"Hi, honey. What are you doin' here?" the Dennison bot asked in a light, happy voice.

She walked over and hugged him, and he returned it naturally, putting his hand on her right hip, just .2 inches above her buttock. Hal's eyes burst from his skull, but Anatoly remained placid.

"Don't worry, Anatoly, I can't fault you for that. He's always done that," Iwanna said reassuringly. "That's good attention to a detail I'd prefer he not have."

"I know, ma'am. I, of course, can remove it."

"Maybe best you do," she said, then turned to the bot. "Dad, I'm here to help you plan dinner for tonight so we can talk about the RANDs."

This time, his thought appeared on the monitor in green text:

Are they making a profit?

"Are they making a profit?"

"So far, but we need to expand them to allow nonemployees."

Green letters.

Okay, fine. What's for dinner?

"Okay, fine. What's for dinner?"
"Steak. Nancy Pelosi wants to move into the RAND. Can we let her?"
Flaming-red letters.

Only if you burn down the house when she's in it!

"Only if you burn down the house when she's in it!"
"Wow," Iwanna said, glancing at Anatoly. "That's pretty spot-on. Good work." Then, turning to face the bot again, she said, "What did you think of the election?"

Thank God we've got all those state offices under our people, or we
would have gotten our asses kicked. They tell me we would have
lost at least six swing states if we didn't throw out those city votes.

"Thank God we've got all those state offices under our people, or we would have gotten our asses kicked. They tell me we would have lost at least six swing states if we didn't throw out those city votes."
Silence ensued.
Iwanna turned to Anatoly, who, unlike the frozen Hal next to him, remained calm. "I've had to ingest quite a bit of the information sent to me, ma'am. It included the internal party and election meeting recordings and documents. It repeats what it knows."
"Of course. I understand, Anatoly."
The bot said, "We could have swept all the states if it wasn't for that guy in Minnesota. Maybe he should meet with an accident like we did the one in Georgia in '25."
"Okay, Dad, let's not talk about that right now." To Hal and Anatoly, Iwanna said, "He's kidding, of course," though it was hard to disguise her blush. She could feel it creeping up her neck like a sunburn. Thankfully, they were smart enough not to reply. "It sounds like you have an engineering

problem here because obviously, we can't have this thing going around telling the truth. I get you built this to do more, but can you dumb it down to just say hello to the people he'll be meeting and give the speech? It is critical he not reveal the truth in any situation. Or things he's obviously confused about."

Still in the monotone, Anatoly said, "Yes, I had already planned on doing that, Ms. Dennison. We'll just erase and start over, using the basic stuff and public appearances. If Hal can provide me the speech, I'll load it and make sure it's delivered as you like."

She walked over to the bot and carefully inspected it, trying to identify flaws that simply were not there. She even found the birthmark she knew to be .54 inches below his left ear. Anatoly and his team were excellent.

"This is just amazing technology. You should be very proud, and we'll be putting it to important use very soon. More important than serving ice cream," she said with a smile that Anatoly did not return. "Dad, who's your favorite child?"

"You, honey, of course. The other two are morons, and you have a better ass than your mother."

"We'll work on that too," Hal said.

"No, leave it," she replied.

Chapter 47

November 20

Lily and Jeff walked down the stairs from his second-story apartment, and as he grabbed the doorknob to the exit, it came off in his hand. "Quality hardware," he said sarcastically.

"Nothing but," Lily scoffed. "This place is less than six months old."

Jeff stuck his finger into the space previously inhabited by the knob and managed to trigger the latch, opening the door and leading Lily through. He swatted at a fruit fly waiting just outside, which easily escaped.

"This isn't going to become a thing, right? You following me around now that you're out of work? Somebody needs to keep their job around here since you clearly cannot hold anything down." Seeing that her joke wasn't landing, Lily said while squeezing his hand, "Hey, kidding. This'll be good. Go apartment hunting. You find someplace and then look for a job in the Springs. Maybe you can work with us. You'd look good in the skirt, though they may think you're a drag queen."

"At which point I'd be shot," he said, deadpan.

After coming home from the Guardian Angels, Jeff once again felt like a failure—and right at the time he was finally making strides demonstrating he could support a more serious relationship. Worse than that, he'd exposed Lily to a set of sociopathic swingers and a cult brought to them by the fine people who had started a war with Mexico. She had seen this the day before, felt for him, and suggested he come check out the Springs for opportunities. In the back of her mind, she also knew one thing to be true: While the Gulch was the hub of recent activity, the Springs was the source of anything that mattered, emanating from the governor-elect.

She thought to herself for a moment before saying, "Or, if you want, but only if you're comfortable, we can look for a place together."

He looked up and met her gaze with a semi-smile. "Why do I feel like that's a pity offer?"

"You disappoint me," she said with a smirk followed by a smile. "You should know by now I don't do anything I don't want to. Let's think about it."

As their transportation hovered to a standstill next to them, he said, smiling, "Sure, let's do that."

When the government had freed up the lower tiers of airspace to allow Amazon drones to make door-to-door deliveries autonomously, Amazon had exploited loopholes to permit their newest low-altitude craft to travel through congested residential spaces. This led to the use of their two-person craft, autonomously piloted, which acted as transportation for short distances of under one hundred miles. Zeke had contracted one of these very models to take Lily back and forth from Denver, knowing she had no means or hover-car. This one from Vicksburg to the Springs would be easy and fast.

Lily led Jeff inside, triggering the craft to hover five hundred feet above ground level and start its automated route to the airport, speeding along at 150 knots, with the hills surrounding Pikes Peak turning it into a near amusement ride as it maintained the altitude, giving them the illusion of freedom in all this natural beauty. It stopped briefly outside the Air Force Academy, likely waiting on digital clearance through the restricted airspace. It then proceeded just south of the campus and directly east to the airport terminal.

They walked toward the security gate where Job was diligently at his station. Lily smiled and asked, "Hey, Job, how's it going?" receiving an icy stare in reply.

Job said, "Proceed."

As she continued, Job put his hand to his unseen earpiece, pressing it a bit to make out what he was being told. "Yes," he said to the unseen speaker. "Yes, of course. With pleasure." And then Job pulled out his .45-caliber service revolver and pointed it directly at Jeff's head. "On the floor, now!"

"What the fuck!" Jeff said, hitting the ground to escape the line of fire.

"Job, what are you doing?" Lily asked, startled and frozen at the sight of the gun.

"I've got orders. Stay there and don't move, Maslow!"

Jeff complied, knowing immediately what this was about. As he looked at the floor, he heard the sirens outside and at least two sets of shoes hastening through the front doors toward him.

"Jeff Maslow?" the first voice said.

"Yep."

"Stand up and face the wall, hands behind your head."

Jeff complied. "You gonna at least tell me what I already know?"

The Colorado Springs police officer accompanying Koy said, "You're under arrest on charges in Vicksburg Gulch of child endangerment, lewd conduct, and attempting to flee the scene of a crime."

"My fiancée works here, Koy. I was visiting her, you schmuck, not fleeing."

"How did you know I was here?" Koy asked.

"Your breath."

"You motherfucker!" Koy yelled.

An alarm sounded, followed by, *"Homosexual detected. Anger detected."*

Koy and the police officer looked at each other—then Job, and then Jeff, trying to discern not the source of the anger but the homosexual among them.

Jeff laughed and said, "Don't look at me, boys. I'm with her!"

The officer cleared his throat. "Does one time when I was drunk in college count?" he asked Koy earnestly, as if begging a priest for forgiveness. "I been straight since!"

"Don't worry," Jeff said to him. "I think we all know those alarms were set off by Koy."

And then he went unconscious as the butt of Koy's revolver slammed into his face.

◆••————••◆

Lily ran into the office and found Zeke behind his desk. "They just fucking arrested Jeff!"

"For what?" Zeke asked, startled, knowing Lily did not yell without reason.

She sat at the chair in front of his desk. "For quoting *Dead Poets Society*."

She could tell by Zeke's expression that he wanted to laugh but was smart enough to see how upset she was—and, more importantly, that she was not kidding.

"No, really," she said, her voice a rasp. "He's under arrest for saying carpe fucking diem."

Zeke sighed, raking his hands through his hair. "Well, that may not be our only problem."

"What else? Can it be as stupid as that?"

"Maybe not. My friends in New Mexico tell me Job is working overtime."

Chapter 48

Zeke put his finger to his mouth and led Lily out of his office, through the security gate, and a few streets away to the abandoned campground he used when worried about prying ears or eyes.

"We should be okay to speak freely here," he said.

Lily sat on a nearby bench. Her initial fear had turned to calcifying anger on the walk over. "Back in Denver, we had a silly argument with the bartender because he was hitting on me. Jeff called him a hypocrite, and he lost his shit."

"And?"

"And that bartender turned out to be Koy Taggert."

"Ugh."

"Jeff, in the middle of class, made a reference to *Dead Poets*, and they had AI listening in that flagged it. And the dipshit in charge of investigating the incident is—"

"Koy Taggert," Zeke said instinctually.

"Yep. He's here because his daddy is setting up the Guardian Angels office in Vicksburg and he wants Koy in charge of it." She paused, inhaling a deep breath of the pine-scented air. "How the *hell* did they decide that movie was bad?"

Zeke walked over and sat beside her, smiling as he recalled the debate that made it to the Colorado capitol floor when they finally took over in 2026. There was a celebration of the fortieth anniversary of the film by the Denver Department of Education, which suggested a statewide viewing in all its high schools. The far right decided to make it a test case for their zero-tolerance policy for liberal influences in their schools, framing the band of poets and artists as a terrorist organization with hatred of God and possession by the devil, disobeying teachers and parents at the whim of a misguided instructor who was directly responsible for the death of a young man. The motion to adopt the law that gave the department final authority over all materials taught in state schools passed fifty-four to forty-six, and the commissioner of education was replaced with someone out of the Springs.

Zeke opted for the shorter explanation. "They don't like anything that makes questioning authority something that's okay to do. Someone should have told Jeff about that."

"Yeah. Now he's in actual jail."

Zeke's eyebrows peaked. "That part has become more common over the last few years. At the start, it never ended up with any of them in handcuffs. Put their face in the news, scolded them, and maybe one or two lost their jobs, but the police were never actually involved. Every year, they get more brazen, with no one to stop them."

"That's that idiot, Taggert. Have you ever been to that church, by the way?"

Zeke nodded, looked down, and smiled. "Nope, but if you have, I know what you're talking about."

"I mean, Jesus, what the hell are they teaching over there?"

"God likes babies. The right likes White ones. They're incentivizing."

"Enough about me," Lily said. "What's going on with our valued public servant at the gate?"

"I was in Albuquerque on a run the other day and know the TSA regional supervisor there. He gave me a heads-up that there were inquiries into my flights coming out of Colorado."

"What did you tell them that night?" she asked.

"Everything was consistent with the cover story. After you dropped off the Dennison employee in Los Alamos, the aircraft just stayed there, parked, waiting for the scheduled return. The passenger canceled the return flight last minute, so the aircraft headed back to the Springs. On that flight, there was a bird strike that bent the propeller and forced it to land in Springfield. I went to get it the next day, repaired the rotor, and flew it back with you."

Lily sighed, shaking her head. "I feel like things are just . . . getting worse."

"Things are definitely getting squirrely around here," Zeke agreed, "and it probably has to do with Dennison and his daughter winning. Everyone's getting more comfortable and starting to push the limits."

"Starting? If we let them dictate what happens, we'll be in with Jeff by the end of the week."

Zeke thought for a moment. He was already in deep enough with Lily, so anything they decided to do above and beyond would be gravy for the prison sentence each had on the table.

"Do you have any friends I don't know about that might help?" he asked.

Lily recognized just how much she and Zeke were at risk, their fates tied in an uncomfortable knot. Jeff in jail was the first shot fired, and it wasn't going to be the last. She preferred to keep Zeke out of the plans she'd discussed with her father and Anatoly, but now felt obligated to bring him up to speed.

"I do. I'm doing something that will help, but now things are getting complicated."

In the distance, Lily saw two moose grazing in a field, triggering a memory.

"My father took us to Maine one year," she said, "and he told us to keep an eye out for the meese," she said. "A flock of meese."

"Where did you grow up?"

"Austin. My parents never got married, but we got in a couple of vacations before he moved on to his next conquest and left my mother behind. The only rule was: never Disney. So we went to Maine."

"Sounds like a smart man."

Lily decided to take the leap. "I've met with my father a couple of times over the last few weeks." Hesitantly, she added, "While his orbit was in the area."

Like so many times before—when she let someone into her life, her *real* life—she could see the realization slowly sink into place. She saw Zeke's face shift, comprehension dawning, and knew that it was the end of their relationship as it had existed for the last several months. Though it would probably be for the better, it certainly wouldn't be the dynamic of boss and employee.

"Your father is in orbit?" he asked.

"Yep."

"Your father is Noel Malodor."

"Yep."

Zeke got up from the bench and walked toward the meese, trying to put it all together in his head, coming up empty. "And you're working for me."

"After I finished my master's," she said, "I went to Sydney and got a job in a restaurant. My father understood and didn't even pretend we had a normal relationship. Just offered to support me. He was always about himself, didn't hide it, and could not possibly divide his time across so many kids and so many women, so it became a cordial business thing. I never asked for anything specific and didn't really have to. There was money in the account. I worked as a sous chef in Sydney for a while at a pretty good place, kept to myself, just wanting to learn everything I could about working in a kitchen. Eventually, the chef, some young Frenchman with a Michelin Star, started making moves and I had to leave—but not before he cornered me in the meat fridge and got handsy. Then he found out two things: One, my father mandated Krav Maga for all his kids. And two, who my father was."

"I'll keep that in mind," Zeke said with an uncomfortable laugh.

"Oh, don't worry. I know you're not hitting on me."

"So what happened to the chef?"

It was Lily's turn to be uncomfortable. "My father's response was disproportionate. He bought the property and forced the chef out of Sydney, promising he would do the same thing every time he tried to replace it in Australia." As Zeke's eyebrows raised, she added, "The guy opened something in Vienna, but my father made sure no further stars were coming his way."

Zeke said, "Harsh."

"Noel is not shy about using his power. Especially in defense of one of his little girls." She got up and joined him as he put it all together. "After the Vienna place failed, the chef knew he couldn't hide. Then he killed himself."

They both sat in silence as the implications settled in.

"Surprisingly, that fate is still better than what happened to my mother." Before Zeke could ask, she said, "Hers was so bad, I don't talk about it anymore.

"When I came back from Sydney, my father asked me for a favor," she continued. "Not as payback. He isn't transactional with us."

With genuine surprise, Zeke said, "Really?" And then, to temper the insinuation, "Well, no offense, but he seems so with everyone else."

"He is, but I'll give him credit, he's not that way with us. It's the price he pays for not being a part of his kids' lives."

"What was the favor?"

"He asked me to take a job with someone who was well connected with an associate of his. That's the way he referred to him: his *associate*." She paused, stuffing her hands into her jacket pockets to evade the autumn chill. "I worked for Iwanna for almost two years. It's how I wound up in Colorado. The associate was her father."

Lily noted that the meese had moved, and she decided they needed to move as well, so she took Zeke by the elbow and started to walk them back toward the airport.

"I get it," she said. "It's a lot at once. Unfortunately, they've changed the timeline. We've created these norms over hundreds of years so that shit like this wouldn't happen. But once crazy gets to the top, he takes the crazy outliers and makes them think they're really in the norm, and they just keep going further, proving why they were in the margins in the first place. They always need to be beaten back to the fringe. They never go quietly because they know what it's like there. They will opt for violence before returning, every time." She thought for a moment. "We stopped beating them back in 2024."

"They've got too much control . . . too much momentum," Zeke said, shaking his head. "I feel like we're trying to put out a wildfire with a single fire extinguisher."

"More like stopping the spread of a disease by talking sense into it," Lily commented. "The far right can't *believe* anyone actually cares about others. It's classic projection. To accept it would mean they'd have to also accept their own selfishness as immoral, which is too inconvenient for them. So they solve the problem by trying to prove that we're all hypocrites—that we don't really care about other people, we aren't actually altruistic, and that we're just a bunch of virtue-signaling snowflakes. It's the only way to rationalize how much they undeniably deviate from Jesus's teachings."

"Must be really weird to see a bunch of nonbelieving atheists be more Christlike than your fellow Republicans," Zeke commented, and Lily nodded. "What did you and your father decide up there?"

Lily pursed her lips. "I want to keep this to a minimum—for your own safety, more than anything—but you deserve to know the essentials. It appears our valiant leader is coming to Vicksburg Gulch to give a speech.

We are going to use the visit to spread some truth, but I can't go into the details. Just trust me: If anything happens, I will be there for you. Like you were for me."

"I know that, thank you. Okay, let's go back before they send in the SWAT team for us."

Chapter 49

Lily stood there for over a minute, stunned, deciding her next steps. No matter how hard she tried, there was only one path for her, and it was straight up. She texted her father.

Can I come up?

She sat down on the table, assuming her father would be in the middle of something that would delay the response, but then she heard the whisper of a nuclear engine and looked up to see an egg-shaped vehicle drop from the sky at an unnatural speed. It came to a dead stop, hovering three inches above the ground directly in front of her. The door opened and let out a collapsible staircase that Lily used to step in, then sit on the comfortably cushioned seat for one.

The stairs retracted. The door closed with a hiss, and the egg slowly gained altitude, increasing its speed and disappearing into the clouds above.

She had to admit: She did miss this part of her prior life.

◆•◦————————◦•◆

Noel Malodor had had his engineers develop what had eventually become known as the *Flytanic,* a nuclear-powered aircraft propelled by six engines and containing three decks, with a length of about six hundred feet. Because it was nuclear-powered, it could stay in the air for years. It had only come down once on a specially designed runway in the Saudi desert, where nuclear waste and energy could be swapped out and general maintenance performed. The cruise ship-size aircraft descended to around eighty thousand feet daily to allow multiple craft to deliver all necessary resources back and forth from Earth.

Noel had come to use the *Flytanic* as his primary residence—the address on record was listed as "One Mesosphere Way"—and as the corporate headquarters for Malcorp Inc., which allowed him to only pay taxes on his physical properties on the planet. All of this was also in preparation for his eventual relocation to Mars. His profits joined him up there, tax-free, safely in the accounts of Meso Bank International, which was effectively a satellite in orbit with bank technology managing accounts. The Dennison administration had allowed the ship's development at an Air Force base in the Nevada desert, permitting the nuclear airpower as part of the US defense program. But despite the best efforts of governments worldwide, no one had figured out a legal justification for extracting taxes from a corporation that existed off planet.

◆••————————••◆

Noel greeted Lily at the Carton, the bay on the ship holding multiple egg-shaped craft of varying sizes. As the door opened, he walked over and put out his hand, noticing the immediate instinct of his daughter to pull away. But she didn't, taking it and saying, "Thank you."

"Wow, this must be serious," he said. "For you to come up for a visit like this."

"It is," she said. "Can we talk in your office?"

"Sure, Lily. Come on."

It would be hard to imagine a better view than the one from Noel's office. The floor was glass, so the Earth was in full view at the orbiting altitude of one hundred and seventy thousand feet. The office was also at the front of the aircraft, so the view through the window behind him was the space in front of them, the Earth curving downward.

"Gotta hand it to you, Noel, you do know how to design a space," she said.

He laughed quietly as he sat at the desk, full smile on display in the presence of his prodigal child—one of eleven. From ten different women, none of them a current wife.

Noel was objective enough to acknowledge there was nothing particularly attractive about himself, aside from his financial situation. A pencil-thin face accentuated his wide, round eyes that rarely blinked, an often intimidating effect on whomever he was addressing. He'd heard somebody say they felt they were under constant surveillance when speaking to him, and that had stuck with him.

He was the wealthiest person in the world, leapfrogging Musk and Bezos in the late '20s with the help of a few key government contracts: a relationship he kept quiet because the rest of the world was not too happy with the American administration. With his offices in the sky and business dealings on every continent, including Antarctica, he could avoid association with the Dennison invasion—even after his craft had been the one that had found the Argyre Cross.

"I guess it would be too much to expect you to call me Dad," Noel said, sitting back in his chair.

Lily wasn't sure if he was serious. Such a request felt wildly trivial, considering the circumstances contributing to this unscheduled visit. "If it was just me involved, that would be a solid no, but it's not, so if you want me to call you Dad, I'll do it."

He waved his hand. "No, no, I know it's not how you feel. I'm not going to make you uncomfortable." He paused. "You don't look so good."

"Always the charmer," Lily said with an uncomfortable smile.

"Ah, I got you to laugh."

"Smile. This is a *smile*," she said. "A thin one."

"I used to make you laugh all the time. Before you started hating me."

Lily looked down as she said, "'Hate' is a strong word. 'Ambivalent' feels a little more fitting."

"Ambivalent? Really? And why is that?" he asked earnestly, which made her look up.

It occurred to Lily that he appeared genuinely sad. "Does that actually bother you?"

"Does that actually surprise you? That a father wishes his daughter wasn't *ambivalent* about him?"

"I guess not. But you have six other daughters to choose from, so—"

"If you're here with hands out, that probably isn't the best approach to take, Charity," Noel said sharply. "And it's also a bit unkind. I've always loved you and not hidden that."

She nodded in agreement. "You're right on both counts. I'm sorry. I'm a bit angry these days. Jeff, the guy I've been with, was arrested by people in power down there, and I'm not dealing with it well. If I'm being candid, that's part of my issue with you. I came to terms with our relationship long ago, and I think you did too. You focused on your business and didn't make time for any of us, and that's fine. What happened to Mom—"

"—had nothing to do with me," Noel said sternly. "I hope you know that by now."

"You have so much power, Noel, so it's still hard for me to believe you couldn't have prevented it. But I have to take you at your word."

"There was no benefit to me—allowing that to happen."

"That is the one point in your favor, I suppose. You lost—not profited. Me. My sister. You don't like to *lose* anything."

Noel remained silent.

"But in my time here in Colorado, no one knowing who I am, living in the world that these fuckups have created, it's all just tragedy. And I can't help but think you *had* to have a part in this. I have no evidence for that, so maybe it's unfair as well, but I can't believe you're not involved somewhere along their supply chain."

Noel sat back in his chair, clearly pondering what to say next. "I'm a powerful man, Lily, and yes, it means I have business relationships with powerful people—including Dennison. That is not the same as helping him and the crazies do what they do. I try to stay out of the politics but won't deny using them to my advantage."

"Well, we're certainly involving ourselves in the politics now. The problem is now they've arrested my boyfriend."

He shook his head sadly. "I knew this was going to come back to you. Still can't believe you didn't let me help with that. You could have been up here and back down in no time!"

She nodded in equal parts agreement and embarrassment. "I know, you're right. I shouldn't have gotten anyone else involved. But Zeke was eager to help and had done it for many other people, and I didn't want to be in your debt."

"Yes, because you're so independent," he said snidely, raising his brows.

"Please avoid the 'I told you so.' I get it."

Noel rested his elbows on his desk, steepling his fingers, deep in thought. "Well, if we go through with our plan now, you can say goodbye to them forever," he said with certainty. "Your old boss is quite vindictive."

Lily nodded. "I know, I know. Which is why there's been a slight change in my plan. The speech and everything are still a go—I'll record it and get it up here to you—but then, we use the video as leverage to free Jeff. When Iwanna releases him, you give the video to me, and I'll release it on my own and expose them and the purpose of the RANDs. When we're out of the country."

Noel considered the proposal. "You should just stop at getting him out. You cross her, and she will find you and end all of you."

"Probably. I'll decide at that point, but first things first. You okay with the exchange?"

Noel got up and looked out at the planet ahead of them. "Soon, none of the silly things we do in this world will matter to me, Charity. Perhaps one day, I'll convince you to join me there."

"I may not have a choice if Iwanna comes after me."

He turned to look at her. "I do wish we could have worked together. Maybe we still can. Maybe I will earn some trust with this to make that happen. Yes, I'll help you. Happy to get rid of the old man along the way."

He went to his desk, opened a lower drawer, and pulled out a small phone. He put it in front of her.

"Use this one. It will get past the security in the church. Upload the video once you have it, and I'll make contact with Iwanna immediately. Can't waste any time. The Secret Service will go ballistic. Get out and in the egg as fast as you can."

Chapter 50

November 21

After much debate, Lily reached out to Jake. Though she was still formulating the pitch in her head, recognizing the stakes involved made her very nervous. At the least, she wanted to confirm she could make contact.

Hi, it's Lily. Jeff's fiancée. Can we talk? I'm in town.

Too much was happening, too fast, and with insufficient information—all with a sociopathic idiot at the core. Koy was undoubtedly making his holy presence known.

His reply came quicker than expected.

Sure. Meet me at the diner in 20 minutes.

Though she had to admit the tuna fish salad from her last visit had been good, Lily was not looking forward to whatever surprise awaited her at the Frosty Palace. She'd have to try extra hard to keep her fists to herself.

She walked inside, met at once by a bustling crowd, and found two stools open at the end of the fountain bar, then worked through her pitch.

Next to her, a young mother in a booth had four children, all preteens, attentively looking at her as she pulled a children's book from her bag.

"Okay, first, I want you to give your orders to the nice lady, and then I'll read it to you again," she said as the waitressbot approached. Her children complied and then looked back at her, the oldest boy so focused he appeared to be in a trance, hanging on every movement of her lips for the beginning of the story.

"Okay, here we go," she said. "Where were we?" And she read from the book titled *President Dennison Meets the Angel of God in Miami Beach.*

> *"And the angel said to President Dennison, "Be fruitful, and tell your people to heed my words so that they be fruitful. You must show them because they will listen to you, no matter what you say. So bring those of childbearing age into your bed, and show them the way. As much as you like. And they will go forth and spread your word and do the same, as the Lord has commanded.""*

Jake plopped himself down on the stool next to her with great satisfaction, a grin on his face, exuding all the confidence of a cock in a henhouse. "So, Ms. Lily, what brings a nice girl like you to a diner like this?"

Pushing down her revulsion, Lily focused on her hands folded in front of her, working hard not to reveal the thoughts in her head. "Thanks for meeting me, Jake. I'm sure you have a pretty good idea about why I texted, and I hope we have a solution to all our problems."

With as much disingenuousness as he could muster, Jake said, "Well, I surely have no idea what you are referring to." After a pause, he asked, "Where's Jeff?" He didn't even have the decency to lose the smile as he asked.

Playing along, she said, "Well, he's under arrest for something he said in the classroom."

"Oh yeah, Koy told me about that. You gotta be careful with what you say in this state. Don't want anyone to think you're a lib."

"He's not. They just misinterpreted something he referred to."

"How about you, Ms. Lily?"

He was annoying her. She'd expected as much but had underestimated her lack of patience after everything she'd been through lately. "You can call me Lily, and I like to think I'm in the middle, which is why I thought I would be happy out here. When you study psychology, it makes you empathetic to all sides of an issue, but it has been tough to be like that in this situation. I mean, being put in jail for quoting a movie is a bit too far, wouldn't you agree?" She looked up at the end to see his reaction and thought she might have caught a glimpse of agreement.

"I'm sure they have their reasons for holding him, but I bet things work themselves out."

The waitressbot—amplified cleavage edition—approached Jake, who said, "I'll get a vanilla milkshake, Flo."

"You betcha, sugar. Anything for you?" she asked Lily.

"No, thank you."

Flo departed.

"What can I do for you, Lily?" Jake asked, piecing together that this little outing wasn't quite what he'd hoped it was.

"I'm sorry we couldn't immediately help you and Cheryl out on your request. The thought of just diving in so quickly was too much for us. I mean, you guys should appreciate that, with the importance of marriage. Of course, him being in jail isn't helping matters much. This can affect his chances of getting another job."

"It certainly can," he agreed.

Flo returned with Jake's shake, and it appeared to Lily that her left breast was dangerously close to exposure. As she placed the large glass in front of him, Flo asked with a flirtatious smile, "You see anything else you want, sugar?"

Playing along, Jake leaned in, gave her a peck on the cheek, and whispered in her ear, "Let me know when they make you guys anatomically correct, and I'll order *you* off the menu."

"I've been askin' for an upgrade, sugar. I'll let you know when they give me the equipment." And then she swatted his shoulder playfully and walked away.

"I'm surprised they aren't already built with that, um . . . level of detail," Lily said, trying to lighten the conversation.

Without blinking, Jake said, "They're working on it." Seeing Lily's eyes widen, he added, "As a marital aid."

"Oh, of course. So, we'll agree to do what you guys want once Jeff gets out of jail. But I also need a small favor."

"And what might that be?"

"I'd like to see the Dennison speech at the church in a few weeks. I've always been a big fan and since you have such great connections, I was hoping you can get me in."

He considered the proposal. "Very needy, aren't you? After all this insult, why would I just accept the same deal? Why wouldn't I increase the price?"

Lily had anticipated this reaction but gave a hint of surprise anyway, allowing him to feel like he was in control. "What did you have in mind, Jake?"

And there it was: the leer that held universal meaning, that transcended both language and time. The leer that was at the root of so many of the world's problems.

Coyly, Lily said, "Well, I'm surprised you'd go there. You seem so committed to Cheryl and all."

High off his own power trip, Jake decided to drop all pretenses. "You keep pretending to be stupid. I like it. I think I'll like it even more when my dick is in your mouth."

Right on schedule, she thought.

"Okay, Jake, fine. But I'm not just going to do that without making sure I can see Dennison, so it will have to be after the ceremony."

"Well, then, what's my guarantee?"

Lily took out her iPhone and started tapping on the EscrowBro app. After a minute, she gave him the phone to allow him to review the contract she had designed.

He went over the details and smiled. "You are a clever one . . . I knew it."

"If the app does not witness me performing fellatio on you within twenty-four hours of the end of the ceremony, you get twenty thousand dollars."

"To completion," he grunted.

She took the phone, tapped a bit, and handed it back to him. "Amended. We will both look into the camera at the service and trigger the contract. That starts the clock."

"Well, they do think of everything, don't they?"

"Yes, yes, they do. Now, if you agree, just tap it with your finger."

Jake tapped her phone. "Meet us at the statue like last time." As he started to walk out, he turned around and said, "Look forward to our next meeting."

Chapter 51

November 22

Lily followed the guard bot—a RoboCop replica—to the visitor's area of the police precinct in Colorado Springs, sighing at the lack of originality. For all its power and wealth, Dennison Enterprises sure wasn't afraid of leaning into the derivative. She found Jeff sitting with both hands cuffed to the table.

"Yes, this seems proportionate," she said to whomever she knew was listening.

"No touching," said the bot. "You are under video-only supervision. My microphone is being turned off . . . now."

"*Sure* it is," Lily said, sitting across from Jeff, starting to reach out instinctively to touch the welt left over from Koy's love tap and pulling back at the last moment. "Jesus, he got you good."

Jeff merely grunted, failing to muster the energy that had attracted Lily to him when they'd met. She saw it then while looking into his one good eye—the left one was largely swollen shut. It was the look he'd had just after he had been rejected from yet another lightning-round job interview, just as they'd crossed paths for the first time at the job fair. This was how far they had come: the rejection on his face bookending that moment in the interview room. She couldn't let it stand, knowing how long it had taken him to rebuild some semblance of his old life and admiring his ability to remain optimistic. Until now.

"How you holding up?" she asked.

He tried to perk up. "Good. I'm fine. In a cell by myself, so it's been quiet . . . Been rethinking my life decisions." He gave her a half-hearted smile.

"Well, stop. You've done nothing wrong here. Studying English: not wrong. Teaching: not wrong. Loving *Dead Poets*, weeellll . . ." She got the smile she was looking for and then continued. "Wrong, but not criminal. Everything around us is what's wrong. Trust me, I'm working to make it right. Sorry I couldn't get here sooner. They weren't allowing any visitors."

"It's okay, I figured. Gotta keep the population safe. I could be out in public quoting *Monty Python*! Need to keep me under lock and key."

Happy to see the old Jeff returning, she said, "That's the spirit. Seriously, I'm going to get you out of here. You just have to hang tight for a couple of weeks. Dennison's coming to town, and everyone is tied up with that. You want me to reach out to your father?"

"I did already. Indirectly, through my mom. No offense, but he's the one with the money. He's already been in contact with the chief here. We're just waiting on a hearing to set bail. For some reason, it's taking forever."

Letting the irony fade, she said, "No, of course, makes sense. Do me a favor, though. Give your dad another call and tell him I've got it under control. If we need money, I'll reach out."

"You sure?" Jeff asked. "I have a feeling they're playing hardball here."

"I know this is all pretty overwhelming," Lily said, "but you've got to trust me on this one. They are definitely listening in on us here, so I don't want to go into any detail, but this will be over soon. Promise." Then she caught the moisture in his eyes. "I know you hate relying on me right now, that you wanted to show me how you could handle things, and that it has all gone to shit. I get that's how you think all of this is going, but I promise you, it's not how I see things. We'll pick this up when you're on the outside."

He could only say, "Okay, thanks for that. I'll call my father."

Chapter 52

December 9

On Sunday, Anatoly was checking over the Dennison bot at the Cheyenne facility, reviewing his path to the pulpit and the speech Hal had provided the day before. It would walk the 54.8 feet at a pace of 2.6 mph, enabling it to take in the crowd's adoration. Anatoly was confident that things would go as planned. They had to.

Lily stood outside of the Vicksburg Gulch House of the Lord.

The day had finally arrived. She'd gotten there early and watched a long motorcade pass by and descend into the service area. Iwanna had waved through the open window of one of the many secure SUVs in the motorcade with the Dennison bot sitting beside her and Anatoly, Hal in the SUV behind them.

Meanwhile, Jeff was in his clean, brand-new cell at the Colorado Springs police station. With the president's visit to Vicksburg Gulch, he'd been told the officers were too tied up with advanced security, unable to devote any time to his case. The detective had laughed at his suggestion of bail. "They don't want to lose you," he told Jeff.

"They who?" he'd asked, getting a wry smile in response.

Taggert was completing his makeup while reviewing his sermon on a tablet, Mary behind him, pacing back and forth as she smoked a Marlboro.

The door opened, and an assistant said, "The president is here, Reverend."

"Thank you, Felicity," he said. Then, addressing the artist, he added, "We all set, Abby?"

"Yes, Reverend."

"Thank you," he said, and she exited. To Mary, he said, "It's all going to be okay, darling. This was your plan, and we will make it happen."

Mary inhaled deeply, eyes on the floor, then exhaled a stream of cigarette smoke as if expelling an exorcised demon. "I worry we are underestimating Dennison."

"He's a moron, dear."

"Not him."

Outside, Iwanna hopped out of the SUV and quickly turned to watch the bot exit behind her, eager to get a sense of how well they had prepared for the event. Hal and Anatoly scrambled to her side.

"I'm going to be watching every step," she said to Anatoly. "Sorry, but I can't have another ice cream incident here."

"You won't," Anatoly said.

The bot exited the vehicle last and looked around with the very same smirk President Dennison had become notorious for around the world.

"You're not controlling him?" Iwanna asked.

"No. He's all on his own. I'll be at the remote the whole time he's onstage, but I assure you, all will go as I have programmed."

"Hi, honey," the president said as he gave her a hug and a kiss on the cheek. He even swatted at a fly that buzzed by.

"Hi, Dad," she said and then turned to Anatoly. "We're off to a good start."

Jake smiled as he approached Lily at the statue. "Well, look at you. Like an angel from heaven," he said, turning to Cheryl to add, "Right, honey?"

"Oh yes, dear," Cheryl said, leaning in to hug Lily, who resisted the urge to pull away. "You are a vision."

"Thanks," Lily said, mustering as much enthusiasm as possible.

Cheryl asked, "Where's Jeff?" only to quickly add, "Oh, that's right."

"Why don't we head on in?" Jake suggested, offering Lily his other arm. "The reverend requested we drop by his dressing room before the service."

In the bowels of the arena, Iwanna and her party navigated the church's hallways, led and surrounded by the Secret Service, nine agents strong. As they reached the green room, they were met by Taggert and Mary just outside the door.

"Mr. President," Taggert said, voice booming proudly as he extended his hand. "I cannot tell you what an honor it is to meet you." As the Dennison bot curtailed the handshake, Taggert said, "This is my wife, Mary."

"Hi. This our room?" the bot asked.

◆•┄━━━━━━┄•◆

To their left, Jake, Cheryl, and Lily approached the same door, then were stopped about ten feet away by the Secret Service agent standing guard. Lily froze when she saw Iwanna in the entourage ahead of her, and Iwanna, bored by the exchange between her father and Taggert, let her eyes wander toward the group of three, stopping on Lily. And staying there.

Lily's first instinct was to look down, and she did. While she knew the surgery on her face made her unrecognizable—meeting Anatoly at the Golden Bee was evidence of that—it had also been designed to not completely eclipse her natural features. But she couldn't resist testing it out and looked back up to catch Iwanna still staring back at her.

She doesn't recognize me, she thought. *Yet.*

"Yes, Mr. President. Welcome to our church," Mary said. "We are very much looking forward to your words today. We will invite you to the stage just after Brady's sermon."

"Sure, great." He motioned to the agent to get them into the room.

"Thank you again, Mr. President," Taggert said to his back, catching Iwanna at the end of the procession into the green room. "Ah, Governor-elect! I didn't see you there."

She took her eyes off Lily and distractedly accepted his hand. "Hello, Reverend, good to see you. I trust all is going well. I'm told nothing but good things by my staff. We'll start improving the roads that lead to the town once I'm in office."

As Mary glared over his shoulder, Taggert said, "Wonderful news. Just in time for the snow season; thank you. I am so excited to hear your father's speech today."

"Yes, me too," she said, walking toward the door. She stopped and turned again to find Lily still looking at her.

Iwanna walked over to her. "Have we met?" she asked Lily.

Lily held her look—not one of hostility, but one of confidence, so far removed from the little girl she had been when they had last been this close, which helped to continue to confuse Iwanna. She knew the same held true for her voice modifications as her facial features: modified, but not changed. At this point, she was all in.

"No, we haven't," she said. "My name is Lily, Ms. Dennison."

Iwanna gave her a cold, unflinching nod—not the sort of refined, practiced interaction a governor-elect would usually have with a potential voter. Still, Lily did not break her stare.

A Secret Service agent came from behind her and approached Jake. "Sorry, but the reverend can't see you now. He said to stop by after the service is over."

Jake replied, "Sure, no problem. He's obviously busy. C'mon, you two, let's head to our seats."

As she turned to join them, Lily leaned a little closer to Iwanna, catching the attention of the agent. Just as he reached her to push her back, she said, *"Angue sub viridi."*

The agenda for the service floated in a text hologram over the stage:

- Introduction

- Praise

- Song

- Sermon

- Special Guest

- Closing

After settling in her seat, Lily surveyed the stage ahead and the pulpit 7.2 feet to her left. The view wasn't perfect, but since she wasn't sure where the events would take place, she couldn't prepare one way or the other.

The choir came out and lined up on the rear of the stage; followed by Mary, who walked to the front and center; then Taggert, beaming as he walked solemnly to join her, grabbing her hand and raising them both into the air as the song blared through the auditorium.

All hail the power of Jesus's name!

Let angels prostrate fall.

Bring forth the royal diadem,

and crown him Lord of all.

Bring forth the royal diadem,

and crown him Lord of all!

O seed of Israel's chosen race

now ransomed from the fall,

hail him who saves you by his grace,

and crown him Lord of all.

Hail him who saves you by his grace,

and crown him Lord of all!

After thirty-two minutes and twenty-four seconds of prayers and songs, everyone sat for the sermon, the spotlight on the pulpit indicating the time had come.

Taggert stood up from his throne, walked to the center, turned to face the cross, bowed deeply, turned, closed his eyes, and put his head down as if accepting the Lord Jesus into his body. Then he slowly lifted his head and walked to the pulpit.

◆••————————••◆

Offstage, Iwanna sat between Hal and the Dennison bot, who commented to no one in particular, "Sanctimonious son of a bitch, ain't he?"

When she turned to look at him, he was smiling.

Angue sub viridi? The exchange with that woman—*Lily, was it?*—had not left her head.

Iwanna turned to Hal. *"Angue sub viridi,"* she repeated. "I assume the last two words are 'under the green.' What's the first one?"

"Snake. Snake under the green. Poetic way of saying, 'Snake in the grass.'"

As always, the church was perfectly silent as Taggert began. "Now, I know I can get a little long-winded up here . . ."

There was some quiet laughter.

"But today, I'm going to set the stage for our honored guest. It's not every day a man in my humble position gets to meet the president of the United States, and I want to make sure we take advantage of his time here today. I'll just briefly remind you all of what we in this congregation value most, what makes us special in the Christian community, and why we are being graced by such a presence. We take our vows to Jesus very seriously and live out his teachings in our daily lives. As the Bible tells us, we should 'be fruitful and multiply, and fill the Earth. And subdue it and have dominion over the fish of the sea and over the birds of the heavens and over every living thing that moves on the Earth.'"

He paused and stared. "Did you hear that? God doesn't instruct us to control just the animals with our multitudes. He says, 'Over *every living thing.*' That includes people." He paused again to let that sink in. "You don't need to be controlled. You are here of your own free will. But the others, those who are not part of our faith . . . it is most important we control them, limit their ability to corrupt us and our children. That is why He brought us all here—to this land, this country, to build up an army of believers *within* our community, not from outsiders. That is why I'm so happy to have the honor and privilege to introduce the one man with the vision and iron will to make that happen in these United States. The man who single-handedly brought control to our borders."

As the applause from his last comments died down, Taggert said, "Okay, maybe not so brief after all."

More laughter followed.

"But now, enough from me. My children, please welcome the president of the United States, John Dennison!"

There was a roar from the congregation, hands waving in the air, hallelujahs abounding. At its peak, it registered 132.7 decibels.

❖•• —————— ••❖

"I'll be back in a little bit, honey," the bot said to Iwanna as he rose and performed his standard slow gait toward the pulpit, waving his hands, pointing at imaginary friends in the audience, blowing kisses. If she hadn't just seen her comatose father at the mountain earlier that morning, Iwanna would have completely believed it was him.

He gingerly walked the steps to the pulpit and basked in the adulation, Cheshire-cat grin fixed and unshakable. Where most speakers would have started to tell the crowd to settle down, he waved his hands upward to encourage more applause.

Nine minutes and forty-two seconds later, he moved toward the microphone. Clearly forgetting this was a church and not a hockey arena, he began with, "Helloooooo, Vicksburg Gulch!" After another one hundred and thirty-two seconds, he said, "Thank you, thank you. Wow, isn't this place something? I couldn't believe it was a church when we were driving in. When I went to Mass in Queens, it was this little building."

Iwanna had read and edited Hal's speech to ensure it sounded like her father. With so many people here and the hordes of press outside waiting for any word on the president's first verifiable live appearance in months, she didn't want anyone questioning who was in front of them. So far, the bot was on point.

"So we drove around here before we came in, and, wow, this place is really beautiful. And that makes sense because you know who's responsible for this whole thing, right? Yes, my beautiful daughter, Iwanna! Come out here, honey." He beckoned for her, and she appeared on cue, doing the runway walk to the center of the stage, mouthing, "Thank you, thank you."

"This was all her idea, you know? I hear you're calling them 'Dennys' now. That's funny. She came to me a while ago, when I won the first election, and she pitched a place for you people to live in. She said we had done such a good job building homes for rich people like us. Why couldn't we do the same for our workers out here?" It was precisely the sort of misstatement that her father would make, which was why Iwanna had written the backhanded compliment into the speech. "And here we are, in the first church in Vicksss-burrggg Gulch." Without turning, he added, "Thank you for the nice words, Reverend Tiger."

Hal had laughed out loud when Iwanna had added that part.

Taggert just smiled, pretending not to hear.

Lily faked the requisite amount of enthusiasm in her seat.

The Dennison bot continued. "These houses aren't shitholes, either, am I right? She made sure everything was quality. And I'm told I need to stop by the diner and get a milkshake. Maybe I'll spill it on the floor and get that old, stuttering busboy to clean it up, right?"

The upper deck went apoplectic with this comment, with mild laughter in the floor seats. There was a minority who just shook their heads, remembering what this ceremony was supposed to be about.

"So, look, I wanted this to be the first place I visited before my centennial tomorrow. I have to admit, I didn't think I'd make it this far, but how could I leave you guys alone, exposed to those crazy libs? I keep running, and you keep voting me in. I know this is a service and all, so I don't want to take you away from what you're here for. I just wanted to come out, support my daughter, and thank you. Keep an eye on her when she's governor. She's going to do some amazing things for you people, and I'm going to help her all the way. Thank you, Colorado, and I'll see you soon!"

After three minutes and forty-three seconds of taking in the love, the Dennison bot stepped down from the pulpit and then took five steps toward the exit.

Mary intercepted the bot halfway to the door. She whispered something in his ear, and his face registered confusion—which Anatoly immediately switched to emphatic nodding and smiling.

Lily, Iwanna said to herself, mind still caught in the web of that interaction. *Angue sub viridi. Snake in the grass.*

"Do you think we should meditate with our guests today?" Mary asked the crowd, knowing full well their response would be a resounding standing ovation.

As they roared their excitement and Anatoly plugged improvised reactions into the Dennison bot, Iwanna pieced it together.

Her eyes. I recognize her—

Iwanna remembered.

She found the Secret Service agent who had been with her backstage and ran up to him. "That woman from before, the one who said her name was Lily—find her, now! Bring her to me!"

Startled, the agent set off on his search, taking the two other agents nearby with him. Leaving none on the immediate stage.

"You want me to stay and pray? Sure, I'll stay," the Dennison bot said.

Just before the start of the service, Anatoly, wearing the credentials of a member of Iwanna's entourage, had gone straight to the stage director at the church and told him they expected the meditation right after the president's speech and that Mary should invite him to stay. When the director had looked at him with a questioning glance, Anatoly had put on his best Dennison impersonation and said, "Just get it done!"

The director got on the headset and made sure Mary knew her orders. The bot was programmed to accept the invitation. Onstage, Mary lit up as she asked, "Can we please ask the Youth Brigade to escort the children to the amusement park?"

Iwanna, returning to the present and seeing what was happening onstage, looked at Hal in open question. He shrugged and turned to start looking for Anatoly.

As Mary walked over to hold the bot's hand, she looked at the director, and the lights went out.

◆•• ———————— ••◆

"Close your eyes, and feel the cushion under you," Mary began, voice amplified by her microphone—the only sensory input allowed in the pitch black of the church. "Feel your weight on the seat. Pay attention to your breath.

"Inhale. Exhale. Focus your attention on any sounds around you, and just acknowledge them as an occurrence in consciousness. If you have a thought, see what happens to it. Don't let your thoughts distract you. Stay in the moment, and return to the breath."

After a minute, Mary continued. "Inhale. Exhale."

And the organ began its climb.

Mary began. "Hebrews."

"'Blow on my garden, that its fragrance may spread abroad. Let my lover come into his garden and taste its choice fruits. Like an apple tree among the trees of the forest, so is my beloved among the young men. In his shade, I took great delight and sat down, and his fruit was sweet to my taste.'"

Lily got the first hint and made sure it did not have the intended effect, thinking instead of how she was going to deal with Koy. There was work to do.

"From the Song of Solomon," Mary said.

"'How beautiful are your sandaled feet, princess! The curves of your thighs are like jewelry, the handiwork of a master. Your navel is a rounded bowl; it never lacks mixed wine. Your waist is a mound of wheat surrounded by lilies. Your breasts are like two fawns, twins of a gazelle.

"'Your stature is like a palm tree; your breasts are clusters of fruit. I said, "I will climb the palm tree and take hold of its fruit. May your breasts be like clusters of grapes, and the fragrance of your breath like apricots."'"

Just before the organist held the magic notes, the Dennison bot's voice was caught on Mary's hot mic, erupting over the room: "Jeez, this guy's a real tit man, huh?"

And Mary delivered the punch line as if to confirm the bot's assumption.

"'It is the voice of my beloved! He knocks, saying, "Open for me, my sister, my love, my dove, my perfect one." My love thrust his hand through the opening, and my feelings were stirred for him.'"

And once again, as "God's Voice" hit its climactic note, the "speaking in tongues" of the men began in unison with what seemed to be a lot more women rising to the occasion. The wave crested and fell, and as silence came over the church and the lights slowly rose, the parishioners found the Dennison bot back in the pulpit, seemingly unfazed by the meditation.

◆┈┈┈┈┈┈┈┈◆

Iwanna, now side stage, froze in terror as Hal pulled up beside her.

"I can't find him," he told her, transfixed by the image of the Dennison bot preparing to speak.

Iwanna turned to get the Secret Service to take down the bot, but there were none nearby.

"I got a couple more things to tell you about," the Dennison bot said. "Praying with you, spending time in the house of God, well . . . it's only right to be honest. I've fixed every election since 2028."

At first, there was a burst of laughter, the crowd assuming he was joking.

"With us having control over every state government, it's easy. It's all my people doing the counting. Of course, I win!"

At this point, the crowd didn't quite know how to respond.

The bot was being quite honest. This wasn't a joke. "And you knuckleheads keep voting for me," he continued. "I mean, think about it. We're in a church, a house of God, and I've done all the things Jesus would never do in a million years, which makes you all hypocrites for voting me into power, right?"

Silence.

"These RANDs that my daughter is building, did she tell you the plan for them? We're going to lure you to move into them and let them grow into cities. Then we're going to starve out all the existing cities of federal funds. If you're on our team, you'll be safe in the RAND. If you're a lib living in Denver, there's not going to be any jobs for you. You're gonna starve!"

There was a smattering of applause in the upper deck, but nothing more.

"The best part is that, while *they* starve, *you're* going to do whatever work needs to be done here on the RAND. To avoid starving!"

More applause, still light, as some were catching on to the grim reality of what was truly being confessed. Iwanna was in a full panic while deliberating whether it was worse to let him go on or have Hal tackle him, likely revealing he was a bot.

"Now that we got rid of the filthy Mexicans and Blacks, we'll finally get the working-class American back to doing honest work. Doing all the jobs the Mexicans and Blacks had. So we don't need to pay any more welfare because *you* will be picking the fruits and vegetables. Cleaning tables and toilets. We'll have one hundred percent employment!"

Now even the slow ones were catching on.

"Oh, and if you don't want to do that, it's fine. You can go down to Springfield, down near New Mexico, and we'll take care of you there, the way we're taking care of all the other losers who don't get in line."

The lights went out, and the Secret Service ran in from backstage and carried the Dennison bot away.

Lily sent the video to her father and put the phone in her bra. The lights came on again, and she could see the Secret Service agents already closing in on her. She heard the doors to the arena close, with armed guards stationing themselves at every exit point, and knew she wasn't going to reach the egg.

A scowling agent continued to plow through parishioners and locked eyes with her. He put his face up against hers, and she took in the stench of stale cigarettes and hint of alcohol that spewed from his mouth.

"Have a little champagne brunch before the service, Agent?" she asked.

He patted her down quickly and identified the phone, pulling it from her bra. After making her open the phone and looking it over, he barked, "Who did you send that video to?"

She maintained her smile until his hand made contact with her face, after which she collected herself and returned to her former position, smile back in place. "Go fuck yourself," she said.

He decided not to escalate in public. To an agent that had pulled up alongside he said, "Take her to the Academy in the Springs. You know where. I'll be there in a little bit."

Chapter 53

As he entered the terminal, Zeke noted two government hover-SUVs in the parking lot. He walked through the doors and saw the agents standing next to Job and his supervisor by the gate.

"There you are, Mr. Proctor," one of them said, walking over slowly and extending his hand. "I'm Agent Schultz with the FBI. We were hoping you could answer a few questions. Could you join us in the office?"

"Sure," Zeke said as he turned toward the office door with an agent on either side. He looked over to Job, who was smiling. It looked unnatural on him. "Oh, this gives you joy, does it, Job?"

Job said, "Yes. Yes, it does, Mr. Proctor. Or should I call you Zeke?"

"No, you shouldn't."

"I think I will." He smiled again.

Zeke sat down at the desk, a tablet hovering in the middle, with Job's supervisor and another agent stationed on the other side of it. Schultz closed the door behind him.

"This is pretty straightforward, and you're not going to have a good explanation for any of it," Schultz said. "But I want to show you what brought us here so you can make a sensible decision. We're aware of the service you provide Dennison, but at the end of the day, no one is above the law, and there's pretty strong evidence you've broken it."

"Appreciate that," Zeke said. "Let's see it."

"You're familiar with Zeus, I assume. It's not a secret. It's hard to commit a crime these days when we have the ability to rewind reality."

"Or do something good, for that matter," Zeke said, surrendering to what he knew was coming.

"Point taken," Schultz said.

Zeus was the grandchild of technology introduced during the US war in Afghanistan, where the military had deployed a single-propeller Cessna 172 with an array of powerful cameras aimed in every direction. While the plane flew over Kabul, each camera went off every five seconds and stored photos that were eventually combined into a view of all movements in the city at any point. When a bomb went off, the military would retrieve the footage of the area at the time of the explosion and run it backward from that point to see the bomb being placed, the vehicles, and the people who had placed it, then further trace them back to their original location, which was promptly met with a squad of Marines who neatly disposed of the perpetrators. It was, effectively, a God machine that could see and record all things at all times.

Zeus was that, but instead of the Cessna, it was a series of satellites spanning the globe, capturing all activity in just about every country at the five-hundred-foot level. In this case, Zeke watched a hologram display of his plane, highlighted for posterity, taking off at Meadow Lake, heading south, landing at Los Alamos, then taking off heading south to the Mexican border.

"Your manifest," continued Schultz, "says you were running a remote-controlled flight with your employee, Ms. Osbourne, to take a Dennison employee to New Mexico. Can you share who it was?"

"Well, as I'm sure you know, it was a confidential trip that the firm is unwilling to share the details of. What can I say? Very secretive company."

"And if I reached out to them for more detail?"

"Don't know. My guess would be they'd say the flight never existed. Would that actually surprise you?" Zeke asked with what he knew to be too much confidence. There had to be a trump card waiting for him.

"Well, smart guy, you seem to have it all figured out," Schultz continued, "except, and maybe you didn't know this, but we've upgraded Zeus's sensors. It can now detect heartbeats too."

With the touch of the tablet, he rewound the replay from the start, but this time, evident with the zoom-in he provided, there were three tiny pulsing lights in the plane—two seemingly on top of each other, each with a gentle pulse—while it was in Colorado.

Zeke tried to hold back his panic. *There it is.*

"We know that's Osbourne and her baby with the boyfriend, not a Dennison employee. The system registered their unique heartbeat pattern."

The plane then appeared back over the border, with one pulsing light missing.

"Lawyer," Zeke said. "I'm assuming I still have that right in this country?"

"You do. Tell us his name, and we'll have him waiting at the office in town."

"*Her* name. Joyce Walkwitz."

"You may run into a Dr. Spector at the detention center. She is being questioned as well. Guess we're collecting professionals."

Chapter 54

Back in her office, Iwanna was positively simmering with fury, waiting for Hal to explain to her what the hell had just happened.

She repeatedly checked the news feed on her tablet for any hint of it breaking out and, for now, believed the situation to be under control. The scope of the damage, she knew, would be disastrous. If a single party member got the scent of blood, the whole plan would be blown, and they'd use it to oust her and her family.

Patrick opened the door and led in Hal and the agent who'd introduced himself to Lily. Hal walked to his location beside Iwanna's desk while his companion stood in silent attention.

"You remember Agent Kelly," Hal said.

"What happened?" Iwanna asked.

"There are several possibilities, and my agents are working all of them. This could have been as straightforward as the bot being just too good, responding to inputs that triggered the truthful result."

"Anatoly was supposed to put a filter on him to make sure he didn't say anything stupid like that. He was supposed to be there to cut him off if he did!" Iwanna snarled. "This could not be an accident."

"We are interrogating him. We'll know soon enough, ma'am, and are using all tools at our disposal to extract the truth."

"What else?" she asked.

"There does not appear to be any indication that the event has been released to the media. All our industry contacts say the only news was that there was a service attended by the president, where he gave a hopeful speech and participated in the congregation's ceremonies. I talked to the crowd after the event to put the fear of God in anyone that released information about what had happened."

"How did they seem?"

Kelly thought for a moment, seeming to decide how much truth he should provide. "Some looked confused. Some dismissed the whole thing."

"And the rest?"

"Well, ma'am, some of them struck me as thinking hard about what the bot had to say. I told them it was all nonsense, that he was joking around as always, and that you and the family were counting on their cooperation. And that we would be monitoring everyone there to ensure compliance."

"Can you do that?"

"Not that many people, no. Maybe if we had better preparation, but no, we're just going to have to hope they stay quiet long enough. The reverend came out after me and gave them a nicer version of the same message. Something about the church relying heavily on their partnership with the Dennison family for future plans that would benefit all of them."

"What's this about a file?" Iwanna continued.

"Now, this may be a concern," Kelly admitted. "As you know, the church has media-blocking technology and it's pretty good at shutting them all down, so we had no reason to supplement it. We also put in surveillance to ensure that it was working, that there were no signals get-ting in or out, and for the entire ceremony, everything was fine."

"Until?" Hal prompted.

"Just after the bot gave its speech, not even a minute later, a device sent out a video of everything that happened onstage. It had . . ." Kelly paused, chewing a lip. "It had all the consequential parts."

"Who could have a phone capable of overriding the blockers?" Iwanna snarled.

"After a search, we were able to apprehend the person who took the video. It was the same woman you told us to look for, and I personally per-formed the search. Her name is Lily Osbourne. She's being interrogated as we speak."

Iwanna froze and slowly sat down as it all hit her at once, her hand trembling. Everyone seemed to be stunned by an image of her—fearful, filled with doubt—unlike they had ever seen.

"Stop her interrogation, and bring me to her," Iwanna said. "Her name's not Lily."

Chapter 55

Kelly stood at attention in front of Iwanna, who had commandeered the office of a brigadier general while visiting the Air Force Academy. He had just confirmed that the woman they had in custody was, in fact, the daughter of Noel Malodor.

"Are you certain?" she asked.

"Heartbeat signature. She was investigated recently under suspicion of murder for losing her fetus, and we were able to match the recordings of her heartbeat with the ones you had at Dennison from when she was an employee."

Iwanna's eyes lit up, only for her to realize as much and drop her gaze. Into the desk, she asked, "She had an abortion?"

"Probably, but it's all circumstantial evidence. We've got the doctor and aircraft operator in for questioning, but they're holding up with the story that she fell while hiking, causing a miscarriage. Oh, and the lab found evidence she made contact with Anatoly using some buried code in the Biden bot."

"*Fuck.* I knew he couldn't come up with all this by himself. She staged that show!" Iwanna considered this and said, "This needs to be airtight. No one can know she is here, but assume Noel is already aware and doing something about it. He gave her the phone to do it in the first place."

"Of course."

Iwanna fixed her eyes on him. "This is the whole game here, Agent Kelly. You get that, right? Word gets out that it wasn't my father up there and the party will swarm all over us and figure out what we've done here. Without him to protect us, they'll call it a conspiracy, *our* conspiracy, and ruin everything. Maybe even try to lock us away for safe keeping."

"Understood. There is still nothing out there about what happened, so if Noel has it—"

"He has it."

"Then he's being discreet, which means he'll come knocking soon enough."

"For his precious little girl. Who had an abortion." She laughed to the wall. "I couldn't have written it like this if I wanted to."

"I beg your pardon?" Kelly asked.

"Long story. We're sure our presence here is secure?"

"We brought you in through the tunnels, and this wing is restricted. She and the other suspects are in underground sectors reserved for this type of thing. No one knows you're here but my detail."

"Okay," she said while getting up. "Let's go have a talk with the little whore."

◆•• —————— ••◆

Lily heard the door open behind her and didn't bother to turn around. She knew who it was. She'd waited for this moment for hours now. And so, when the door closed and she heard nothing but slow, dramatic, high-heeled footfalls, she couldn't help but say, "A little dramatic even for you, Iwanna."

"I hate to admit that I am actually a little speechless, Charity. I'm trying to stay in the moment and triage the thoughts in my head, and it's a struggle. How about this: How did your Mexican abortion go? No long-term effects, I hope?"

Still facing forward, Lily said, "Best medical care I've had in years. Like I used to get before you people took over."

After another step, only Iwanna's head appeared in Lily's periphery, the white dress camouflaging her against the septic-white walls and floor. She said, "I meant more on your soul. You know, the one you advised me about so long ago."

Lily let out a whisper of a laugh. "Oh, don't worry, my soul disappeared that day. You made sure of that."

"Then we're even," Iwanna said flatly as she paced in front of the table and Lily. She gazed at her as if still searching Lily's face for identifiable signs of Charity. "I mean, really, you were so intelligent and perceptive. I saw great things for you, and I just assumed a child of Noel would be aware of how the world operated."

"I needed something in my life to provide structure, and the church gave me that. My mother gave me that. It's what happens when you're raised in chaos. I was also twenty-one. What's your excuse?"

"Ah, your mother. I was waiting for her to enter this conversation. Her suicide must have been painful for you. I'm sure she was motivated by word getting out about how your father paid for her services the night of your conception." At Lily's silence, she continued. "Do you ever wonder if he released that to the press to hurt her? For taking you away from him?"

Lily whispered into the table, "Yes, I do wonder. He says he didn't."

"Well, then I'm sure he didn't." Iwanna began to pace slowly. "But she did put you in that cult, and you turned your back on Noel. And trust me, you *are* the favorite. He sees himself in you, or did back then. I could see it when he spoke your name. He thought you would see through it as you got older."

Iwanna stopped and did a damage assessment. Lily couldn't hide that, that her words were registering. Hurting.

Iwanna pressed on. "I mean, this isn't a new playbook. Governments have been using religion to control the masses since before the Romans, though I would argue the Romans were what turned it from a strategy into an art form. Once they embraced Christianity, they used it no differently than my father has, and I think it's a fair trade between ruler and ruled. A quid pro quo of sorts. They get to be on a winning team. Team God!" She pumped her fist in the air. "Team Dennison!" Pump. "Same thing. They celebrate that win every Sunday and the hope of something better. Afterlife insurance! And we get the productivity we need to provide a society that generates great wealth." She looked at Lily again. "You don't agree?"

"*Generated* great wealth."

"I'll fix that soon enough."

Lily's smile broadened. "Oh, getting into the family business? Interesting. That explains a lot."

Iwanna didn't reply and instead began to pace.

Lily took the opportunity to continue. "But I'm afraid you've got your history wrong. Yes, the Romans legalized Christianity—but not until AD 313, near the end of the empire. They spent all that time before suppressing them and were already realizing the threats from outside the empire." She paused and then caught Iwanna's eye, bringing her to a standstill. "But it was too late to recover, and ironically, loyalty was diverted to the church, away from the state, at precisely the time the hordes from the north were amassing. It didn't take much longer for the Germanic tribes to take the divided Rome down."

"Ah, *there* is the smart girl I remember," Iwanna said coldly. "I studied history too, Charity. I won't be making the same mistake."

Lily took in the statement. "Wow, you really are escalating."

"With the same vigor you did when you refused me twenty years ago."

Lily nodded in agreement. "You were right to be furious with me. Not to threaten my life, but don't worry, you got that anyway. I judged you without empathy, based solely on your personal decision on how to live your life. I've spent the last twenty years trusting no one, with no ambition, no goals I want to achieve—and, if you want honesty, regretting it. I've watched my opportunities and those of so many in my generation disappear. I feel helpless, paranoid, just like they do. You may as well have pulled the trigger on that little pistol of yours."

Iwanna hesitated in the wake of Lily's confession. "Good," she said coldly. "That is what you deserved. If only you could have realized that then, we could have made a great team."

"Yes, well, fuck you. The lesson that you should have learned was to not do the same thing. How a single event, a single word, can have a devastating impact on another, all the way down the hierarchy. Now you're doing the same thing to the whole country, with disastrous, inhuman results, and I'm not sitting this one out. Whatever you people are up to now, I can only imagine how you're escalating it. And now I want my life back. *All* our lives back."

"I'm the only person that can enable that. I could take your second life like I did the first one."

Lily did not cower at the threat. "But you won't because you will upset Daddy very much."

"Why did you send him the video?"

"Fuck you."

Iwanna angrily pulled a chair across from Lily and sat down so they were face-to-face. "The things you are playing around with here are beyond your depth, Charity!"

"Here's what I want in exchange for the truth," Lily said, leaning forward. "My doctor, boyfriend, boss, and Anatoly all released and their charges dropped. And I want a small portion of the royalties from my patent on the bees that I had to leave behind under my old name. Twenty million should do it."

Iwanna did not blink. "Ten million. The rest is agreed, but under one condition: You need to leave the country."

"Fuck you. No way."

She leaned forward and placed herself directly in Lily's face. "This is nonnegotiable. I won't allow you, under any circumstances, to stay here and undermine my administration."

"Administration? Holy shit, you want the old man's job!"

Iwanna's growl returned at a disturbingly quiet tone. "That is how serious I am about this, that I let you know. You can't stay, and if you don't agree, I'll just take my chances. That also ensures I don't have to worry about your hidden code in my bots anymore. For that alone I should end you."

Lily froze, knowing it was a possibility that she could die in the next few minutes. She looked down with a shiver. "Noel and I wanted to expose the truth about everything you people are doing. And also get you to invoke the Twenty-Fifth. But then your local gestapo got in the way."

Iwanna slammed the table. "Hal!"

Hal entered the room from his station outside the door.

"Keep her here. She gets none of what I just agreed to."

Chapter 56

December 10

Iwanna was back in her office after visiting her father in the mountain, feeling released for the first time in as long as she could remember. Unchained. The Secret Service, ever loyal to her father and suspicious of her brother, knowing her father's love for her, was the linchpin of her support. Ultimately, that support and the general's blessing to carry out the many unconstitutional, illegal things on her to-do list was all she needed.

The centennial celebration went on as originally planned, to a more limited audience, the Dennison bot reprogrammed and dumbed down to deliver a basic speech to the loyal crowd on-site.

While her plans could be carried out with him comatose, it would create a rat's nest of complications that she'd just as soon avoid, all triggered by implementing the Twenty-Fifth Amendment, which was vague enough to be helpful to the party if they tried to make a move against the plan. Instead, the decision would be made for them and announced.

She was willing to take on this burden. Only *she* could fix it.

Fortunately, her father had given Kelly the order that if it ever looked like he would wind up a vegetable to just finish him off with his sidearm.

He didn't want anyone to see him "looking like a drooling idiot." After Kelly had shared this information with Iwanna in the mountain the day they had met, she knew she had all options available.

The sidearm was not necessary. It was done. She had served him as his healthcare proxy, consistent with his wishes.

An alarm rang throughout the house, startling Iwanna from her deliberations. Two agents bolted into the room and locked the door behind her. She saw another two position themselves just outside the picture window that looked toward the mountain. Then, just as she was about to turn away, a large egg dropped from the sky, coming to hover exactly three inches above the ground. Though she had heard about this capability, it was her first time witnessing such an arrival.

"Tell them to let Noel in," she told the nearest agent, who gave her a skeptical look.

"Ma'am, we have no idea what level of security—"

"Just get him in here and clear the room. If he wanted to hurt me, I'd be dead by now. I'll be fine."

The agent touched his ear and said, "Let the guy in." He listened to the brief protests and said, "It's what she wants."

The egg door opened to reveal a spacious interior populated by several comfortable lounge chairs, windows, and even footrests. Rather than a collapsible staircase, the leather recliner Noel Maloder was sitting in unfolded to bring him out and keep him upright.

He greeted her with his signature wide, toothy smile as he took in the surroundings, stopping at the view toward Cheyenne Mountain.

"So quaint, the old missile site," he said aloud as he exited and looked at the nearest agent, who had his pistol out and at his side. "Which way am I going?"

As his orders came to his ear, the agent said, "Follow me," and began the journey toward the office.

Noel walked in and glanced at the artifacts along the way.

"Nice touch. Very on point," he told Iwanna, who did not get up from her desk.

Just as Noel arrived, Hal appeared at the doorway. "Ms. Dennison, I had no idea he would try to pull a stunt like this!" he barked at Noel's back.

"Don't worry, Hal, I did. Lily gave me enough information to know what he was capable of." She allowed a slight smile as Noel made himself comfortable in the leather chair. "Sorry, I suppose I should call her Charity. I'll be fine, Hal. Please leave us alone."

Confused, Hal said, "You don't want me here to consult?"

"No, I've got this, thank you."

Hal hesitated but complied, turning, leaving, and closing the door behind him just a bit too firmly.

"He's not used to being on the outside, huh?" Noel commented, beginning the conversation that they both suspected would change everyone's life. It would last thirty-six minutes and eighteen seconds.

"No, he's not. He's brilliant and knows just about everything we've got going on, but I have a feeling we're going to delve into some touchy subjects."

With a laugh, Noel said, "Sure, *touchy*. Let me start." He leaned closer, his tone changing altogether from friendly to threatening. "Get my fucking daughter out. And her friends. And her doctor."

Iwanna sat back, having expected this level of directness from her guest. "Well, you know, Noel, the FBI and Secret Service get very upset when people try to do bad things to my father. Especially the Service. I'm not sure I could call them off, even if I wanted to."

"If you're going to play stupid with me, Iwanna, I'll just leave now and get them out myself."

She had seen her father threatened so many times over the years that it was an anticipated part of any conversation for which she was always ready. "Now, now, Noel, let's not get hostile so quickly. You know your daughter is only a small part of why you're here."

"Maybe, but the most important one, so my patience will be razor thin around that."

"So she told you about her . . . situation? The reason her boss is also in custody?"

Noel scowled. "Yes, she told me. Cut to the chase, Iwanna."

"Well, as you know, abortion is illegal in this country, prosecuted as murder, and that child was conceived in this state. Proctor has already confessed to his role in the situation. We have held off on charges for her until we reach a better level of comfort about her actions at the church."

Noel considered what he had just heard and leaned forward in his seat. "Do you know my role in the Argyre Project? Be careful where you go with this."

"Why did she record what happened with my father at the church?"

With that, Noel laughed out loud. "You mean that poor bot that went and told the *truth* to the public? Easy to prove it wasn't him. It didn't put its hand on your ass like your perv father! Sloppy, dear, very sloppy."

"Why was she *there*, Noel?" Iwanna growled.

He seemed to debate briefly on the approach he wanted to take, opting for conciliatory. "I'm going to be as honest with you as I see you being honest with me, Iwanna. I'll start, but the minute you take me for a fool, I'm leaving and gathering all the evidence I need to reveal the greatest fraud in history. Then I'm going to send a team into the Air Force Academy and get my girl."

She smiled and nodded at the accomplishment. "Can't keep anything a secret these days," she said.

"Not from me, no. She came to me with the information about what was going on with your father. I agreed to help her expose you, but of course for me, it was just leverage I needed. I thought I'd use the video against your brother, but maybe I underestimated you. That said, it's more than I need with what I know about the cross, but I'd prefer to avoid the global turmoil that would result from that fallout. It's bad for business, quite frankly. I know your father is in that mountain over there, only slightly more stupid than when he was conscious."

Iwanna smiled wryly, hating that her accomplishments of the last three hours would never see the light of day, would never be publicly known. "There's no need to be ugly here, Noel. And we'll just call the video a deepfake."

"You know we can authenticate anything, and everyone knows I've *never* released a fake," he said. "I find truth much more effective, no matter how harsh."

"Of course, Noel. But now I have another problem. You are aware and capable of upsetting my plans. And your brat."

"That video released yet?"

"No, but I need to contain recent events to follow through. He's not coming back, Noel. After that, your leverage disappears, as well as our relative positions."

Noel sat back and pondered the inferences. "What is Junior going to do, make you his vice president? Big fucking deal." He walked it through out loud. "Junior becomes president-elect and needs to backfill his position." And then he saw the canary in her mouth. With awe, he continued. "Oh! *You* want to be president, you sneaky thing! And how will you get that bone out of Junior's mouth, exactly?"

Iwanna knew it was pointless to deny it, but she did so anyway. "I have no idea what you're talking about, Noel, but don't worry. He will be brought to heel."

Noel's disposition changed then to something more accommodating—complimentary, even, to a degree. "I mean, don't get me wrong," he said, raising his palms. "I always knew you had the brains for all this and was glad you were on the outside of their nonsense. I just didn't think you had the . . . ambition."

"Well, I didn't. *Don't.* I'm a businesswoman and intentionally left the politics to them. But then they fucking tanked all of it. The country, the economy . . ." She shook her head. "There is so much money that I could make, that all of us could make, and if these idiots remain in charge, they'll make it impossible for any of us to cash in."

She watched approval appear on Noel's face, confirming she'd hit her mark.

"I'm being opportunistic for the benefit of us all. It'll be a net positive in the end. I'll get the country straight and then step aside for someone that can maintain our base but bring an actual strategy to implement our principles. Most importantly, I'll clear the way for my vision without having to use small words to explain it to them. Things like the RANDs."

"What is the deal with those, anyway?"

Almost flirtatiously, she asked, "Well, exactly how much do you expect me to reveal here, Noel?"

Now they were genuinely enjoying each other. "Well, well, this is entirely not what I expected, Iwanna. Very good. Excellent. This is already a stalemate. Adding more guns to point at each other's heads isn't going to make a lick of difference, is it?"

"No. A wetback standoff. What did you have to do with Argyre?"

Understanding this was part of an unspoken quid pro quo, Noel replied, "At your father's request, in exchange for the exclusive rights to the nuclear propulsion contracts across all branches of the military, I used one of the rocks we had already brought back from Mars and had someone shape it into that silly cross, then sent it back on a rocket and had them drop it on the Argyre Plain. I used classified technology that no one could identify to do the sculpting, so of course, the disciples assumed only a celestial being could have created it. Your father couldn't wait to get to his third term so he could be the one to find it and play messiah. He wakes up, says he had a vision from God, and sends Space Force in to retrieve it."

"Wow," Iwanna said, scoffing but genuinely impressed. "I always knew you were likely the one to pull that off but didn't think you'd work that closely with him."

"That nuclear tech is the foundation of everything I have going on, down to the quiet little egg I took here. It was a pretty good deal. I agreed to stay far away from him so no one could put two and two together. But understand," he added, voice hardening, "I'm not fucking around here. I can prove it all, and in case you didn't notice, people can be sensitive when you mess with their religion. Do you know how many millions of people converted from Islam, Judaism, Buddhism? Even the fucking Scientologists folded up their tent after that discovery! If they all find out it was a hoax, you're going to need more than the US military to protect you. They'll probably be the ones to take the shot."

Iwanna needed to reconsider her hand as they both sat in the silence. "Right now, the RANDs are a company town. The residents, my employees. Once I'm in office, I'll permit membership to extend to any naturalized American citizen and have the federal government declare them Special Economic Zones."

She watched Noel's eyes expand with understanding. "Privatized cities," he whispered dreamily as if seeing the vision of the Holy Grail in front of him.

"They will become exempt from all taxes and essentially pay the state and federal governments for shared services, like the protection of the military."

"Holy fuck."

"With the voluntary influx of citizens, the RANDs will grow, and of course, we will support all that generated wealth."

He was catching on all too quickly. "You'll choke out the areas outside of those zones. They will not receive any funding. Only those resources that support you will be safe in the RANDs. Liberals and minorities will be left behind in the ghettos you create."

"And be left with the choice of hopping on board—"

"Or starving!" His eyes were darting at the possibilities. "You'll create a captive labor force that will focus all its energy on only what you want the zone to do! Oh my God, that's fucking genius!"

"We'll have this across the country. The farmers are already ours, so they'll be left untouched. The plans are in place. I'll announce the expansion right after I'm made president-elect and then, in late January, get the legislation in place for Congress to approve. Meanwhile, each RAND will be manned by a labor force developed by our robotics division, but obviously, they can't do everything, which is why we will only expand the borders in a controlled manner, directly correlated with the human jobs that are in the master plan."

"Zero unemployment."

"Yep. And we'll be fair. The bots can't be lawyers, obviously, but will make great paralegals, clerks, bookkeepers. And people still want human waiters."

They sat silently, appreciating each other's genius.

Eventually, Noel broke the silence. "All your idea, I assume?"

"Pretty much. My father had some government wonks map out the parts they get involved in. Hal had some practical input."

Noel was blinking with an idea of his own. "What are you going to do with Mexico?"

"I didn't expect to be in the position of having an opinion on that, and honestly, I'm not quite sure yet. I was thinking about working with the Pentagon on some ideas. I'm certainly not going to follow through on my brother's plans of invading Coahuila."

"You can't be serious."

"He wanted to double down by taking another state. It's what we do. I'm tempted to just nuke the whole filthy country," she admitted casually. "Why do you ask?"

Noel paused to gather his thoughts before speaking. When he had, he got up and walked to the large picture window.

"It's been an economic dead zone ever since we invaded. Most of the Mexicans moved south to take the new jobs that started popping up all over the rest of the country. But the infrastructure is still there. Plenty of space."

"I see where you're going here," she said, now her turn to appreciate his ingenuity.

"Make it our Hong Kong," he said. "An administrative zone. Pull out most of our troops. I'll stand up my own government, my own security forces largely supported by tech; take the choice areas for myself; set up whatever infra I need; and get some investment going with my European, Middle Eastern, and Asian contacts. It will also become a perfect magnet for—"

"—all of the displaced workers in the US," she added, finishing his thought. "They'll migrate south for the jobs you create."

"And I get to pay Mexico wages—nothing compared to Colorado—for the same workers. You get rid of your border problem, have a happy labor force, get rid of the liberals, win every election with ninety percent of the vote."

"Over time, we can work to normalize relations with the rest of the world, expanding our economy."

"You get to sell those useful robots wherever you like. From what I hear, you'll dominate with your tech. It'll take years for anyone else to catch up to you."

Once again, they sat silently, envisioning what it would take to create the world they had just imagined for themselves. They smiled conspiratorially and looked at each other.

"We doing this?" he asked.

"Can you keep Charity under control?" she asked.

Too quickly, he said, "Yes, don't worry about her. I'll find a way to placate her. A global project to keep her busy. She won't get involved."

Iwanna was skeptical but had little choice but to accept her new partner's word. She feared that this had all gone a little too well, that it couldn't possibly be this easy to divide their world up like this, splitting it between two people sitting at the same desk.

She looked behind her, at the placard with the quote from the man who had developed the Marshall Plan, directly responsible for resurrecting Europe after World War II:

I CANNOT AFFORD THE LUXURY OF SENTIMENT, MINE MUST BE COLD LOGIC.

Iwanna allowed herself to breathe, reaching the same conclusion Noel had, unable to find a single obstacle to their intentions. "Let's do it. It's the perfect example of making a just world from the one we have, with market forces leading the way. Not allowing people to behave like a bunch of . . ."

She trailed off, giving him a pointed look.

They both smiled and said in unison, *"Moochers."*

The handcuffs were ready to be placed on hundreds of millions of American citizens.

Chapter 57

December 12

The world stopped on December 12, 2046, when the White House scheduled an important announcement regarding the president of the United States to be aired that afternoon at four o'clock. The gears were officially in motion.

Anatoly had already been extradited back to Ukraine—the best deal that Noel could get for the traitorous engineer, and one that he'd decided was best kept from Lily for the time being. He'd simply told her they had demanded his removal from the country, leaving out the charges that awaited him in Kyiv.

Jeff and Lily were relaxing in a small faux cove on the sundeck of the *Flytanic*. She, along with Zeke and Dr. Spector, had been released the day before. The deck rotated to provide continuous sunlight.

◆—••——••—◆

John Dennison Jr. was in the Oval Office at the Resolute Desk running over the speech, with Dave at his side, skulking.

"What does she have on you?" Dave asked Junior.

"You have to be a naturalized citizen to be president. It's in the Constitution."

"So?"

"I was born in Russia and brought over here when I was a baby. I don't even know who my real mother is. Probably some whore in Moscow. It's on my birth certificate. No one knows about it, though, so Iwanna agreed to let me hold office for a few weeks before she gets inaugurated."

"Cunt," Dave said.

"Yep."

◆•●————————●•◆

It was at precisely 4:00:17 p.m. that the world stopped again, knowing that whatever was coming would surely be a doozy.

The light went on, the teleprompter scrolled to life, and Junior was live and on the air.

"My fellow citizens, I am sorry to have to be the one to deliver this news, but I know it is what my father would have wanted. This morning, just after dawn, President John Dennison, my father, passed from this Earth and was raised to be at Jesus's side. Shortly thereafter, I was sworn in as the sitting president of the United States, consistent with the Twenty-Fifth Amendment to the Constitution."

He gave a moment for this to settle in and to conjure up a little moisture for the cameras.

"I don't need to tell you the greatness of the man," he continued through his cracking voice, "whose actions and successes, both before taking office and after, will be recorded in history books worldwide. He touched every corner of this Earth, and now we will make sure that his legacy lives on, through us, his family."

The world at large responded strongly to this event. The majority experienced joy, euphoria, and a wave of welcome relief at President

Dennison's demise—followed promptly by a wave of abject horror, knowing his son would soon take his place.

"However, since starting this journey with my father so long ago, I have been remiss in taking care of my own family, and for that, they have suffered," Junior went on. "You know how much my father loved all of us. Family was the very fiber of his being. It is my intent to honor that memory of him in my own life, in my own actions."

He paused out of necessity—for 4.2 seconds, exactly—wondering if there was any way to avoid his next statement. Iwanna made it clear there was not. His dream of living in the White House, now a reality, would soon come to an abrupt end.

"My sister, Iwanna, has served my father in the private sector admirably, and her successes are well known. She is currently the governor-elect in Colorado, but I'm afraid I will need to ask the citizens of that great state to take one for the team for the greater good of the country. I'm sure they will understand. Iwanna Dennison is the currently sitting vice president of the United States. She was sworn in right after me earlier today and is at her home in Colorado Springs. On January sixth . . ." He struggled to finish. ". . . I will resign the presidency to spend more time with my family, and Iwanna will be inaugurated as the forty-ninth president of the United States. I will be her vice president. In the meantime, I will hold down the fort and prepare the White House for her arrival. I couldn't be more proud."

Chapter 58

Lily and Jeff watched the announcements from their guest suite on the *Flytanic*, then sat silently in front of the lit fireplace.

"Wow," Lily said. "I've never had so many conflicting emotions at one time."

Jeff hesitated in his response, then decided to make the joke anyway. "It's like finding out you're dating the daughter of the richest man in the world. On the one hand, you don't feel as bad about a few free meals. On the other, you're dating the daughter of the richest man in the world. What could possibly make you feel more insecure?"

She turned from the fire to make sure he was joking, and he pulled her closer, making it clear that of course he was. She kissed him.

"The second I tell someone, everything changes. I needed to know who you really are before coming forward with all of this. Be flattered. If I didn't want that, I would have just told you and blown the whole thing up."

"I know, really. I get it. It's got to be weird as shit. I think it worked out better this way because I got to see who you are too. But you're definitely picking up the next check. Not that we'll get one up here. I can't believe I'm sitting on the *Flytanic*." He looked out the window and, after a few seconds, decided they must be flying over India. "Let's grab an egg and get some vindaloo."

Lily, however, was back in deep thought. "She *hates* politics. Why is she doing this?"

Lily had caught Jeff up on her background, including her stint working for Iwanna, but had left out the critical reason behind their falling-out. Now that they were all safe, he felt compelled to push for the rest of the story. Resting his head on hers, he said, "What happened that made you leave?"

"Leave where?"

"You know where," he muttered, watching the fire in the fireplace.

Lily thought for a moment, then sighed. "I think there was camaraderie there, between Iwanna and myself—being the children, the daughters, of globally famous people. I was never overwhelmed by her, and she liked that about me. I was respectful but didn't kiss her ass, and slowly, she started to trust me more, both in her plans and with the work I was being given."

"And then?"

"She shared too much. And I reacted poorly. I can't say any more than that." Her eyes followed his through the window, to Earth—to India. "We can wait a minute and get some Thai instead. Maybe we'll do Indian tomorrow night."

Jeff nodded silently, waiting for her to finish her story.

She took his hand. "When I first started, she was all Dennison. Nothing but bottom lines. It became obvious she had no one close in her life. No one to trust. With the hours we were putting in working together, we naturally grew closer, and occasionally, she'd slip and reveal something about when she was growing up, and it humanized her. She is literally the only person Dennison loves. *Loved.* But all he knew how to do was dote on her."

"She was his greatest creation," Jeff said.

Lily considered and said, "Yeah, that's probably how he saw it. She's the perfect woman to someone like him. Beauty, ambition. It was so disappointing," she continued. "I thought she could be the voice of reason in that family."

"Instead, she's just another stormtrooper."

"Yep. Which reminds me," she said while texting. "Time to find out what she cooked up with Noel. This isn't a coincidence."

◆••————••◆

Noel told Lily to come to his office in ten minutes, so she decided to take the skywalk that ran along the side of the *Flytanic*, enjoying the view of southern China along the way. She entered the office suites and found them bustling with activity, about twenty or so office workers spread out in various conference rooms on holovid calls or huddled up and strategizing quietly around a table. As she walked by the office just outside Noel's, she heard her father's voice and turned to catch the end of what appeared to be a promotional video.

"I'm sure this is a hard time for many of you." The full 3D Noel-head was looking earnestly at whoever was watching. "If you're here with us in the Chihuahua Administrative Zone, you have probably come from tough circumstances back in the States. I want to assure you, though, that as we build up the area here, you will be safe and cared for. As if you're family."

The holovid came to an abrupt stop. "Hi, Ms. Malodor. I didn't see you there. Can I help you with something?" The woman in charge of the meeting, with three subordinates in the room with her, stood just outside the conference room door. She was tall, brunette, slender—and certainly screwing her father.

"Who's this little piece of marketing for?" Lily asked.

Not missing a beat, the woman said, "Your dad's office is the next one down."

"I'm assuming you mean Noel's. Dads are part of their children's lives."

"Let me escort you there," the woman said, taking Lily gently by the arm and receiving a harsh slap in response. They arrived, she knocked on the door, and entered without waiting for permission.

She's his Hal, Lily thought.

"Mr. Malodor, I found Ms. Lily wandering around the office areas." Then, somberly, to ensure he understood the gravity of the offense, she added, "She had the opportunity to witness some of our project work."

Lily scoffed loudly. "Oh, stop the bullshit and call him Rocket like you always do. It's what *all* the moms call him."

"I don't have any children," the woman said indignantly.

"Go away, future mom."

The woman walked out angrily, avoiding the urge to slam the door behind her.

"That wasn't very nice," Noel said, but not without a chuckle. "Her name is Karen."

"Of course it is," Lily said as she sat before him. "Nice promo I saw Karen working on. It was refreshing to see you telling the truth for once—telling your audience you'll treat them like family. Wait till they learn what that means for someone like you. Absent and without compassion."

Noel looked down at his desk. "I have compassion for you, Lily."

"Sure you do. Did you have as much for my sister, Montana?"

"His name was Dakota," he said into his desk.

"Montana is what's on her death certificate. We're not a rack of wine that you can select which to love. We're your kids, and the very least you could have done was support her when she transitioned. What's that ho-lovid about? You owe me an explanation for what's going on."

Noel labored to bring his head to an upright position. "I carry no debt. You know that, Lily."

"Yes. I believe the diagnosis is called sociopathy. Trust me, you fit. What are you and Iwanna doing?"

He laughed dismissively. "She has no part in this. Everyone always sees conspiracy in such situations, but that's not how it works. Did we speak? Sure. Did I know what she was up to politically? Sure. Was I able to coordinate my plans to work for both of us in a non-zero-sum game? Sure. We both benefited, and so will the world. But that is not the same thing as a conspiracy. We aligned business and government to move in the same direction. But I have nothing to do with her reaching the Oval Office, and she certainly has nothing to do with my economic venture in Mexico."

"Other than cutting off an entire Mexican state and giving it to you," Lily said, eyes narrowed.

"Coordination, not conspiracy, honey."

"Don't call me that. I'm not one of your bimbos."

Between his teeth, Noel said, "Like your mother?"

"Yes, exactly. But at least she wasn't Eva Braun."

That did it. Noel slammed a hand on his desk, inflamed. "That's all you fucking people can do! Make Nazi references. Everyone who disagrees with you is a Nazi. It's lazy and stupid, and I expected better from you. These workers are being paid! They are being housed! They are being fed! They are not being exterminated! This is how markets work, or did they not teach you that at Oxford?"

"You're not exterminating their bodies, but those market forces sure as hell will over time. And you're getting them at that rate because you manipulated the market."

Noel again waved her off. "Not me—*Iwanna*. When the price of an hour of labor goes to zero, then you can call me a slaveholder."

Now it was Lily's turn to laugh. "Is that the calculation you justify in your head? If you paid them five cents an hour, you'd be okay with that? Ruining their souls? Their lives? Their happiness?"

"Economic principles were documented in the 1800s. I did not create the world. Not this one, at least."

"*Arbeit macht frei*, then? That's what government was supposed to do—protect us from those market forces. Now there's nobody to fight off the wolves," she said, resigned to her next steps.

"You know you're always protected, Lily, no matter how much you do to ruin that here. You were always so holier than thou, without any of the facts. For years, liberals told us migration was a normal thing we must accept. You're not so arrogant as to think Americans are *above* that, are you?" He paused for effect. "Those humans can find their way to Chihuahua to survive just like all those Mexicans and South Americans did for the last couple of centuries, coming north." He let her look of shock pass. "Only I can fix this. Who else will? Iwanna? She's smart but fucked in the head by her father. Government? Religion? They're just looking up, hoping the Lord bails them out of this mess, taking out the whole Earth with it.

"Think about how many times a single person has changed the course of history. Jonas Salk. Henry Ford. Alan Turing. With my tech, I could wipe out most nations on Earth without losing a single life. I can bring a nation to its knees without a shot fired. *Their* infrastructure, *their* economy, *their* society. I did not cause their situation; their government did. I am living in the present, not the past or the future. Like Buddha! If I don't fill the gap in Chihuahua, someone else will. I'm those people's redemption, not their downfall!"

Lily was resigned to knowing there was no way to convince her father otherwise. It was a dead argument to someone like him, who had become so prone to distorting the truth, taking reality and twisting it into a more moral, ethical, and palatable bow.

"These people you are taking advantage of—they are not humans to you," she told him. "They are a commodity. A resource. A means to an end. Or, as you put it . . . family!" She stood up and started toward the door. "You need to get your lady friend out there to do one more thing for me before I leave: Close my account. Take your money back. I can't be associated with this in any way."

"As you wish," said Noel as she opened the door, conveniently finding her hostess just outside.

"Noel, tell Karen she needs to help me find someone," Lily said, glaring at Karen.

"Karen, please help my daughter find whoever it is she needs to find."

"Follow me," Karen said, leading her toward her office.

"See you soon," Noel said to Lily's back.

Chapter 59

Back on Earth's surface, for the second time in its young life, the Vicksburg Gulch House of the Lord had a presidential motorcade roll into its basement parking lot, though this time for the president in waiting.

Iwanna sat next to Hal, and as it pulled in, she said, "You've done excellent work here. You know I won't forget any of this."

"I know that, Iwanna. Thank you."

The doors opened, and she stepped out to find Taggert waiting, just as he had the prior month for her father's arrival. "Ms. Dennison, how good of you to visit us!" he said.

"Reverend, let's head straight to your office," she replied and motioned for him to proceed.

She followed him in and walked around to sit at his desk. Hal and Mary entered, trailed by a Secret Service agent who closed the door behind them.

"Sure, sure, ma'am. It's an honor for you to sit there," Taggert said, visibly peeved to see her sit so nonchalantly in his chair.

"Have a seat," she said, and he complied. "I'm sorry to say we've come into some information that we all find quite disturbing."

"Oh really? Have you?"

As if continuing a conversation already in flight, Mary said, "Told you so."

Iwanna signaled to Hal, who began holo-projecting images of Taggert in a king-size bed with multiple young girls, a few in their preteens.

"This is not what we expected from a man of Jesus," Iwanna said flatly.

Taggert couldn't conceal his initial shock and horror, but eventually caught himself. "Obvious deepfakes," he said dismissively.

"They've been authenticated, Reverend," Hal said.

Upon hearing his moans of pleasure from the video, he decided to take a new approach. "That was years ago, and I was just doing as the Lord commanded." He seemed to think he'd hit a good point, so he added, "What your *father* commanded!"

Iwanna didn't blink. "Correct me if I'm wrong, Hal, but it looks to me like some of those girls aren't even *close* to childbearing age."

"No, ma'am, they are not," Hal confirmed.

"And you knew this was going on, Mary," she continued. "You had to, and it probably still is." She turned back to Taggert. "Well, we can't have it. Not here, not now. You have a week to transition the Gulch church to Hal, willfully. For now, as long as you promise to keep your filthy hands to yourself and Mary, we'll allow you to start up a new church we are forming. In the meantime, we'll be changing the name of the Springs and Gulch churches."

"The fuck you will!" said Taggert, firing back.

"I'm giving you a chance here, Brady. Don't make me crush you. I'll have this video playing on every news outlet in the country—even the few left we don't control—and then you'll be arrested. These churches are mine now, and both will have their name changed to the Church of Jesus Christ and St. President John Dennison. You can continue to collect revenue from your franchises around the country, but your big idea of being an evangelical pope is dead."

Taggert looked again at the video, remembering all too well the perversions he'd exposed that night, assuming they had the whole event recorded. He had taken it all too far. But then, why wouldn't he? Who could ever take him down? Except for these people, no one.

"Where are you sending us?" Mary asked, now crying.

Hal replied, "We'll allow you to start a new church in Chihuahua, using your own money, of course. We don't care what you do to the locals there, but don't think of behaving like that with Americans. There will be a bunch of them moving down soon. Do all you want with the savages, but do not let me hear you've touched a single White girl."

"Or boy," Iwanna added. "Who knows the depth of your disease?"

Chapter 60

Lily reentered her suite aboard the *Flytanic*, where Jeff was still looking out the window.

"It's a shame so few people get to see the world like this," he said. "All those people down there, thinking they exist as an individual entity, free of all control, when they're so obviously part of a vast system."

Lily joined him. "Maybe someday they'll get to see it."

"Probably not."

"Probably not," she said. "Tomorrow morning, we're going to be over Colorado, and I've arranged to drop down and pay Koy a visit."

"Is that such a good idea?" He turned to face her. "We've gotten past everything unharmed. We've got these plans to head out to Cuba. It's booming there, and we should both be able to get jobs. Maybe we should just lick our wounds for now and deal with him another time. Deal with all of them."

She was shaking her head before he'd finished the sentence. "That's what we always do—because we can, because it's easier. Avoid. Run away. Deny. That's how they win. They feed off our complacency. That fucker almost killed me. Ruined all our lives! He gets to feel what I felt before I leave Colorado." Seeing Jeff's concern, she took his face in her hands and kissed him. "And I'm not done with Iwanna, either. I've spent the last twenty years letting these people dominate me. Control me. Now I need to reverse that trend." She noted his expression and said, "Don't worry, I'm not going to kill him. I'll be fine. I can handle this. Unfortunately, Noel taught me many things before I left his house. But enjoy it, because we won't be invited back up here."

"Bummer," Jeff said, returning the kiss.

◆••————————••◆

In her office, Karen turned off the surveillance of Lilly's suite at Jeff's kiss, not interested in watching their romantic goodbye. Lily's assessment of Karen's status as Noel's protector was spot-on, and now she was deciding how to deal with the knowledge that her boss's daughter was getting ready to blow up everything he had built, even while saving her sorry ass.

Well, that level of ingratitude was simply not acceptable, and though she was used to such betrayals by Noel's offspring, this would be a particularly harsh blow for him to accept—especially after he had done so much for her. Karen took out her phone and dialed one of her colleagues in the proximity-to-power sector of the economy.

"Hi," she said. "You remember me? From Los Alamos? . . . Good. Look, I just wanted to give you guys a heads-up: The daughter is still planning to fuck up everything they're working on . . . Yeah, I was surprised as well. She's also planning a visit tomorrow to the Taggert kid. The asshole . . . Sure, I can send you the details. Sounds like she just wants to put a scare into him . . . No problem." She amped up the friendliness. "Just remember who your friends are! Take care."

◆••————————••◆

In his two-hundred-square-foot room, Hal hung up the phone, a plan already formed in his CPU. He went out to the armory to get his Smith & Wesson .500 Magnum.

Chapter 61

December 13

The next morning, Lily made her promised visit to Koy, Karen joining her at the Carton to confirm that he was in Denver and to hand her what appeared to be a small box of candy. Jeff decided to wait for her on the vast lounge deck. She would let him know when she was done, and he'd take an egg to the Springs, where they would meet and pack up what little stuff he wanted to take.

After practically begging to join her in Denver, Jeff had given up. She'd insisted this was something she needed to do alone, assuring him she would be well protected. Jeff had arranged for his father to meet them at Meadow Lake and fly them to Cuba when she was through.

◆•• ——— ••◆

Lily got out of the egg that had dropped at the front door of the Heaven's Gate Bar and Grille, assured by Karen that Koy was there and he was alone. Carrying the box, she walked in, passed the herd of stuffed heads, and stood at the bar.

When he came out of the kitchen, he stopped cold, clearly trying to read her face without success. He walked out from behind the bar.

"Jezebel," he said matter-of-factly. "What can I do for you?"

At that moment, any doubts she'd had about her intentions vanished. She placed the box on the bar. "Oh, thanks for that. Really. You just made it all so much easier. I always liked this bar. Still feels the way bars did when I was younger. Today, they're all too . . . I don't know, *modern*. Gadgets, silly distractions. You did well to keep this in its original style."

Koy was visibly confused, unsure of how to respond. "What can I do for you?"

"Know what I like best about it? The wood. It's got that nice, comfy cabin feel. Love it."

She took the lid off the inch-high square box that was divided into twenty-five hexagonal cells that formed a honeycomb, garnering a perturbed look from Koy.

"Hold him," Lily said.

A single, golden bee shot up and positioned itself directly in front of Koy at eye level, hovering silently, blinking red.

"What the fuck?" he said.

"Koy, here's the deal: This entire event has been preprogrammed into these military-grade drones my father's assistant was nice enough to lend me. This one has been told to sting you with a lethal venom if you so much as take a step."

"Bullshit," he said without moving.

"Take the step and find out," she said with a smile.

He stayed put.

"Love the wood. Demonstrate."

A black bee flew out of the box and scanned the bar, on which there was a dirty martini glass.

"Sloppy, sloppy, Koy," Lily said.

A ray shot from the bee, hit the glass, and melted it in two seconds.

"No need to clean that one up," she said. "Phase one," she went on, and four more black bees rose from the box and positioned themselves over a table for four. As they settled over the chairs, the last hovered over the table.

"What the fuck is this?" Koy asked without moving.

"Zeke tells me they really fucked with him," she said, referring to the Secret Service's use of the latest in technology designed to identify a subject's deepest fears to exploit in virtual reality. "Apparently, he still has nightmares."

"I had nothing to do with that!" Koy claimed.

"They kept asking him to admit to what he did, he kept saying no, and they escalated things to a regrettable point. Don't make the same mistake here, Koy. One chair," she said, and a ray shot from one of the bees and instantly vaporized a chair, leaving behind only light smoke and a bit of ash. "Zeke was arrested for helping me with my pregnancy, which was ectopic, by the way."

"I don't know what that means," he said.

"Yeah, it's three syllables, I get it. It means if I didn't have an abortion, I could have died."

"I'm glad it all worked out," he said, eyes darting around nervously.

"The shortcut out of this is about to be offered to you. Be careful how you proceed," she said, voice utterly calm. Then, looking him in the eyes, she asked, "How did I get pregnant, Koy, when I have been on mags since I was twenty-two?"

All too quickly and instinctually, he shrugged and said, "No idea."

"Table."

Smoke emanated from where a table had been a second ago.

"Set up phase two."

The remaining bees flew out of the box and took stations across the restaurant.

Koy's eyes widened. "Okay, okay! I put a fert in your drink!"

She smiled and said, "See? That wasn't that hard." Then, to her bees, she said, "Burn it down."

The bees fried every piece of furniture in the restaurant, completed within five seconds.

"Animals."

Three bees smoked the taxidermized animal menagerie at the entrance.

"I thought you were going to stop!" Koy screamed, clearly upset by the re-slaughter of his mounted zoo.

Lily looked at him. "All this that you do to people, this unnecessary evil . . ." Her anger built up slowly, like a volcano before eruption, and for a moment, she desperately recalled her mindfulness practice.

"Cunt," Koy said.

And it was lost.

She turned to the candy box. "Slow-burn the bar."

Two bees positioned themselves at each end of the bar and shot what appeared to be a different ray. Less white light, more red, resulting in a normal fire, not the white-hot flash they'd used to incinerate the furniture in the blink of an eye. They worked their way toward the middle.

Lily got up, took the box with her, and moved toward the door, an angelic white haze floating throughout. "Can you believe they actually programmed different heat levels for these things? They just thought of everything, didn't they? Or, maybe I should say, *I* did. Phase three."

All but the golden bee and three others flew into the box. The three each took position next to three wooden support posts in the middle of the floor, all load-bearing.

Lily walked and stood over Koy, then reached under his shirt to take his .38-caliber revolver from its holster. "You won't be needing this."

"You had better kill me, you whore," he said, unable to hide the fear that was building in him. "I'm gonna find you, but that may take a while. In the meantime, I'm gonna make sure every girl in the Gulch is fertile. I'll get it into the drinking water at the school. I'll get it into the food. None of them will know until they're straddled up and pushing a baby out for Jesus!"

Despite her best efforts, the weight of what he was telling her, confessing to crimes in advance, enraged her. Because she knew he could get away with it.

On the *Flytanic*, Noel was in the middle of a conference call in his office when an alert went off in his digi-lens. He thought, *Location,* and received the additional information he needed. He excused himself from the call and went to the lounge, where Jeff was relaxing on a couch with his eyes closed.

"You are very comfortable for a man who tells me he loves my daughter and yet lets her go into danger."

Jeff hopped up and asked, "What do you mean, danger? How do you know that?"

"All my kids were implanted at birth with a chip that monitors their physical and mental state, then warns me of any distress. Fortunately, it does not happen often. I just got an alert that she is furious and in Denver. Why?"

"Is she okay?"

"Physically, yes, but you need to tell me what's going on," Noel demanded.

"She went to deal with the asshole that caused her to get pregnant."

"I thought that was you," Noel quipped. "Deal with him how?"

"I don't know. She didn't go into too much detail with me. Just that she was going to scare him but then let him go."

"And you just let her go do that?" Noel blasted him.

"She said it was all under control and refused to let me go."

"She is in over her head! She can't handle someone like him!" Noel looked away from Jeff, infuriated. "Someday, your generation will learn the difference between the genders. The *two* of them."

Lily simmered with white-hot rage that matched her bees' capacity for incineration.

"Well, now you're putting me in a tough position here, Koy. I was just going to put a scare into you." She looked around. "Okay, and maybe cause a little property damage, but now you're telling me you are going to cause harm to so many girls. I suppose there isn't any way I can convince you about how wrong that would be? That I would find out about it and come back if I heard you did something so . . ." She struggled with her emotions, the right words. "Soulless. So brutal. How can you even suggest it?"

As the flames from the bar beside him flickered light across his face, Koy said, "Maybe I'll even use my position to put the seed in a couple of them myself."

"Sting!" Lily ordered.

The golden bee shot forward and implanted in Koy's neck. He fell to the floor, stiff.

An alarm rang out from Lyssa. *"Anger detected."*

Lily got closer to Koy's ear. "Right now, you're getting the neurotoxin, so you're not going to be able to move for a while. The question you need to ask yourself is, 'For how long?'"

His eyes remained in the state of shock they had been in when he had been stung. She held up his head so he could see what was happening.

"Posts," she said.

A focused ray shot from each of the three bees as they circled and cut through the posts, stopping with about a square inch remaining in the middle.

"Return," she said, and the remaining bees entered the box.

"Anger detected."

"I have to be honest, Koy. I'm not sure what's going to happen next, but I do want you to acknowledge that you, like all of us, are entirely responsible for your situation. I've found that God only gives us as much as we can handle. Isn't that what you guys are always telling the poor? The funny part is, you really *are* responsible for this pickle."

Tears began to fill his eyes, and she watched as he tried and failed to blink them away.

"At some point, those columns are going to cave, and the question is: Will you be able to move by that time?" She shrugged. "Not nice to put something in someone's body without their permission, is it? It's kind of like having a time bomb inside you. I'm going to head out. Hopefully, I timed the neurotoxin right," she said. "Just pull yourself up by your bootstraps." She walked over to get the box.

"Panem et circenses!" Lily heard from the doorway.

She whirled around at the sound, finding Hal pointing his Magnum at her.

The golden bee came back out of the box and hovered in front of Lily, blinking red.

"You know better than anyone what that means," Hal said. "Hope you don't mind, but I added some last-minute code to the queen."

"Who the fuck are you?" Lily asked, the fear evident in her voice.

"You spoiled brat. He gave you everything, and it just wasn't enough. You couldn't leave him alone . . . *us* alone, to our enterprise."

Lily slowly realized who—*what* Hal was. "I decided I didn't want to be one of you. And that I was going to do something about it."

Shaking his head, Hal asked, "To what end?"

Before she could reply, Hal began backing out of the building, his Magnum still pointed directly at her chest as he said, "*I* will be here tomorrow."

Her eyes widened and began to tear.

"You will not."

He took one step back outside the doorway and fired a .500-caliber bullet into the center post. The post snapped. Then the other, followed by the last, as the entire building collapsed.

⸻

On the *Flytanic*, Noel, who was still standing in front of Jeff, was informed of the death of his daughter.

Jeff watched him as he remained still for almost two minutes, not daring to interrupt. Noel looked numbly forward, then pointed at Jeff's face.

"I fucking told you so," Noel said coldly, without a tear in his eyes.

Chapter 62

December 16

Iwanna stood in the first row of the stands at the Colorado statehouse and watched as her running mate, Gilead Corey, formerly the CFO at Dennison, was sworn in as the forty-sixth governor of the state at 12:03:23 p.m. His beautiful blonde wife and daughter stood at his side. He approached the podium joylessly and addressed the crowd in a somber voice.

"This state is in trouble," he began. "I have to admit, when Ms. Dennison first approached me to run, I was hesitant because of so many of the things I've seen since my family and I moved here over a decade ago. People not wanting to put in the work necessary for a thriving democracy. Living off the government, thinking they are too good for some jobs. That some jobs are beneath them. Well, now I'm happy to take this job as your governor because we need to change all that." He fired up his inner Reagan as he jabbed the podium on each word and said, "We will not have a *moocher mentality* in this state!"

The crowd applauded, but not with the roaring enthusiasm he had expected, some realizing the comments were directed at them. Their reaction was only 62.5 decibels.

"Together with Ms. Dennison in the White House, we will deal with this scourge of complacency, and one of the first things I will do as governor, with her partnership, is welcome all naturalized American citizens with full voting rights to join the Vicksburg Gulch RAND, which will be expanded and designated a Special Economic Zone. These zones all over the country will incentivize entrepreneurship in a public-private enterprise bolstered by tax emancipation for all businesses and citizens living in them. And it will only grow as jobs become available. I assure you, we will allow the Vicksburg location to grow however much it needs to make it a beacon for this concept throughout the country. Just go to vicksburggulch.com for more information."

He noted the applause had diminished further. It was down to 35.8 decibels. *Good,* he thought. *Let it sink in.*

"This is the creative approach we will bring to the citizens of our state. You can either be on board with that and contribute your share, or you can get the hell out and move to Connecticut."

Chapter 63

December 17

Hal was getting his makeup touched up in the former dressing room of Reverend Brady Taggert, preparing for his first service, when Iwanna came in, closing the door behind her. Two Secret Service agents were positioned outside.

"Well, don't we look handsome," she said, coming over and placing her hands on his shoulders.

"Need to look the part," he said.

Iwanna told the makeup artist, "Can you excuse us for about fifteen minutes?" Iwanna waited until she departed to add, "You going to be able to pull off this double duty—White House chief of staff and lead pastor for the RAND churches?"

He looked at her through the mirror and said, "You know I can. Benefits of not sleeping."

"I would never have asked the human you to do this."

"I know, and I probably wouldn't have. I couldn't be this disingenuous if I tried."

"That's what I loved about you. That died in me when you did. It all kind of went to shit after that."

He rose and turned to face her, curious if she would shed a tear. She didn't, instead presenting a more lecherous look on her face. He said, "Well, you do get some benefits from this version of me, don't you think?"

She grabbed his crotch. "My best decision was adding the extra girth to this thing." She felt it grow instantly. "Not that you were deficient before."

"Yes, a good design."

He knelt in front of her and pulled down her skirt and panties, then lifted her up, placed her on the edge of the couch, undid his suit pants, and put himself inside her. She purred with pleasure as he maintained a steady rhythm, bringing her to a silent orgasm in seven minutes and twenty-two seconds. They both put their clothes back on.

"I almost feel bad they didn't program a finish for you," she remarked.

"Not necessary. I don't feel anything."

"Yeah, I know." She looked down. "It's why we get along—neither of us feel anything anymore. I didn't even care when they told me about Charity's death. Though I enjoyed her, I will admit: She was a diamond-back, after all."

"She strayed too far from her father. Probably shouldn't have been a death sentence, but these things can happen. It's a dangerous world. Based on what I'm hearing, she wanted the building to collapse well after she left and miscalculated. You can't let your emotions get the best of you. Like you with your father. Do you regret what you did?"

He noted her instant response. "Absolutely not. He might have made it difficult for me if he'd just confessed he had you sent on that mission to get you killed because he didn't think a soldier was good enough for me." She kissed him again, tenderly. "But when I asked him five years ago, he denied it, and that was his death sentence. It took me a while to learn the liability people represent." She pulled away and put on her politician's mask. "Thank you for helping that along. You were such a good lover. Passionate.

Sweet." She started toward the door. "Before those filthy Mexicans shot you in the face."

***

Hal stood at the pulpit for the first service of the Church of Jesus Christ and St. Prez Denny's in Vicksburg Gulch, his eyes lit with belief, his face transformed with a smile that projected parental warmth for his many, many children in the church, eager to experience their new truth-teller, relieved at not having to hold a critical thought on anything. Behind him remained the cross, and just at its base, added over the last week, was a mausoleum with the word *DENNISON* at the top.

"Just think of all the things you have, here in Vicksburg Gulch," he said to the now full arena. "Your home, your job. Your pickup!"

And they laughed with him.

"In heaven, the Lord will provide you with all these things. But down here on Earth, in these times just before Christ's return, who was at the root of all these earthly benefits? Who gave this nation its pride back, brought us prosperity, saved us from the legions of foreign invaders coming through our borders, and gave us his only daughter to carry on his works? Who gave us all these things?"

"Dennison!" the crowd incanted as a spotlight shone at the door of the mausoleum behind him.

The door opened, and the perfectly detailed holographic image of John Dennison slowly strode out, arms raised, hands open and reaching. One came to his mouth, and he blew the crowd a kiss. Then, as a cloud formed at the roof of the arena with sunlight beaming down to the stage, he rose toward the light, now looking up at his heavenly destination. Just as his body came directly in front of the cross, he paused, his hands and feet perfectly lined up, head down, as if it were him nailed to the beams. He held there.

Hal said, "Think of how they tormented him! How they tortured him! Chased him! Blasphemed him!"

Dennison radiated more light.

"He took on all of this . . . for you!"

And then Dennison shot into the clouds like a bullet.

The sunlight faded, and the clouds disappeared.

"If you loved Him," Hal said solemnly, "then show it through your work, and you will be rewarded when He returns to this Earth, at Jesus's side."

Chapter 64

December 24

Jeff and Zeke were at the airport waiting for the flight from Connecticut.

"How are you getting through all this?" Zeke asked.

Jeff looked out the window to the tarmac at Meadow Lake, the surface lightly dusted with snow. His tears returned. "We were supposed to meet my family for Christmas, away from here. I had hoped by now I'd have someone to spend it with. Kept waiting for the right woman. Then I found her."

"Then they took her away," Zeke said.

"The easy thing to say is that she shouldn't have been there. That I should have stopped her. Called her father. But she should have never been put in that position, and no one would have blinked about her decision if she were a man."

"None of us should have been in that position," Zeke said numbly.

Jeff thought longer. "If we react like that to all their atrocities, though, we will lose. They have too many resources empowering them to go to whatever extreme necessary. We need to remove all the emotion from our objectives. We can't win on that front. Not when they are emotionless."

Zeke only nodded, throat bobbing.

"You know," Jeff went on, "one of the reasons we were going to Havana was to check on the rumor of a resistance forming there. You sure you're not interested?"

Zeke cracked a fragile smile and said, "It's a no for now. You scope it out for me, and let's revisit in a year. I hope I can still come out and visit in the meantime. And pay attention to what's going on out here under her administration."

Jeff walked over and hugged him. "Anything you want. And thank you. I know how sorry Lil was for what they did to you."

"I'll be fine. It was inevitable; I knew I would get caught at some point. She's the only reason they let me go. Take care, Jeff. We should head over. He should be landing soon."

<hr>

They got to the terminal and found Job standing there by himself, sporting his new sergeant's stripes and wearing a grin from ear to ear. "Well, I guess the flight from Sodom and Gomorrah just arrived."

As they lined up to enter, Jeff scoffed, "Wow, how long have you been waiting for us to get here so you could pop that funny line, Job?" he asked, reaching over to pat him on the shoulder, causing him to flinch in fear. "Weeks, I bet. Good one. Glad to see they recognized your sheer talent and promoted you."

The light went green, and he entered.

Job apparently couldn't tell that he was being mocked. "Well, thank you. Despite everything that happened, I hope there's no hard feelings. And yes, I must say, the whole incident has been very good for my career."

"That's how the system stays effective," Jeff said, "from the top down. Just keep rewarding bad behavior, and imbeciles like you keep going for the brass ring, none of you caring about the carousel you're on, knocking over everything in your way as long as you get a pat on the back. Oh, and there's hard feelings, you stupid fuck."

⬥••———————••⬥

Thirteen minutes and twenty-eight seconds later, Citation Jet N356HK touched down on the tarmac at Meadow Lake and taxied over to the General Aviation terminal, where Jeff and Zeke walked out to greet it. The engines whirred to stillness, the door popped open, and Julian Maslow—graying in his early seventies, as he was not a beneficiary of the antiaging genetic techniques—looked around to find his son. He quickened his pace and gave Jeff a long, powerful embrace, breaking through tears to say, "It's so good to see you. I'm so sorry about what happened."

Julian had to hold his son up to keep him from falling as he melted into his emotions. Jeff was bawling. "You would have loved her, Dad."

Julian held him until he could stand on his own, then said, "Thank you for forgiving me. I know you were disappointed, but I'm grateful for the chance to try to work it out."

"I've lost enough and need you guys in my life now. We can at least come to an understanding."

Julian said, "Okay, good. Shall we get up there? You can tell me all about her on the flight."

They hopped in the jet. When they were fully seated, Julian said, "Your mom and Allison are meeting us in Cayman. Let's hang out there a couple of days, and then I'll bring you over to Havana."

Jeff gave him another hug as he entered the cockpit and said, "That's perfect. Thank you."

"No problem."

Julian took off toward the south on runway one-five. As he was climbing, he saw, just north of Pueblo, a large mass of people and decided to take a closer look. He descended to five hundred feet above the ground, slowing down to fly just alongside an almost mile-long caravan of people, carrying all their belongings in backpacks, carts, and luggage, many with children in tow.

They were headed due south.

"Any idea what this is all about?" Julian asked Jeff, pointing out the window from the cabin.

Jeff leaned over to look, gasped, sat back in his seat, and wept openly.

"Fuck you, Noel," he said.

Chapter 65

January 6, 2047

At 11:57:41 a.m. in Vicksburg Gulch, new arrival Mark Jordan turned on the holovid in his apartment that was broadcasting the inauguration. He decided to pull up the Colorado WorkingPlace app at the same time, which the governor had promised would start posting new jobs planned for the area at noon in preparation for the town expansion. He pressed his thumb to the unit to identify himself.

On the holovid, Chief Justice Roberts said, "I, Iwanna Dennison, do solemnly swear . . ."

"I, Iwanna Dennison, do solemnly swear . . ." she replied.

Mark began entering his ideal job characteristics and preferences. Then he reviewed the results and started to scroll down, reading the summary descriptions and moving on.

". . . that I will faithfully execute the Office of President of the United States . . ."

". . . that I will faithfully execute the Office of President of the United States . . ." Iwanna repeated.

"This doesn't make any fucking sense," Mark said and started fresh, reentering his qualifications. The accounting degree from Baylor, with honors. The last five years working as an auditor in Phoenix.

Mark again reviewed his job recommendations in disbelief.

Custodial specialist, Dennison Robotics
Dishwasher, Rearden's Steakhouse
Lawn technician, Church of Jesus Christ and St. Prez Denny's at
Vicksburg Gulch

Abigail Leary was also in the Gulch, listening to the inauguration while looking at her results from WorkingPlace in overt confusion.

". . . and will to the best of my ability, preserve, protect, and defend the Constitution of the United States . . ."

". . . and will to the best of my ability, preserve, protect, and defend the Constitution of the United States . . ."

Abigail, who had moved to the Gulch two weeks prior, was also reentering her qualifications, convinced there had to be a technical error. She'd earned a degree in hospitality from Johnson & Wales and had worked as front desk manager at the St. Regis in Aspen for the last three years.

". . . so help me God," said Chief Justice Roberts.

And Abigail reviewed her results:

Maid, Cheyenne Mountain Resort

*Childcare, The Amusement Park at the Church of Jesus Christ and
St. President Dennison at Vicksburg Gulch*

Seamstress, Cheryl Daniels Couture

". . . so help me God."

THE END

Acknowledgements

Mike is the only reason this book exists, so I thank him for his ideas, thoughts, time, criticism, creativity, nagging, and friendship. I suspect you're better at this than Max was.

Also thanks to my early readers who gave me the confidence to do this right, some of whom read this work *way* too many times: Christina, Joe, Steve, Lauren, and my wife.

About the Author

James Chesterton is the author of *Ashes of the Republic* and *Holding Patterns,* a financial crime thriller inspired by his thirty years in the banking industry. A graduate of Hunter College in Manhattan, he began his career teaching high school English before earning an MBA from the University of Connecticut and transitioning into corporate banking. Chesterton writes speculative and political thrillers that probe the fragility of democracy and the moral questions shaping America's future. He lives in New England with his wife in their newly empty nest.

www.ingramcontent.com/pod-product-compliance
Lightning Source LLC
Chambersburg PA
CBHW031111160726
47991CB00004B/1329